Spectrum Award Finalist 1999
Inaugural Competition for
first title to be inducted into the
Gaylactic Science Fiction Hall of Fame
www.spectrumawards.org

Lambda Literary Award
Science Fiction/Fantasy
Winner 1990
www.lambdalit.org

READERS LOVE THIS BOOK

Toby Johnson's awarding-winning *Secret Matter* was a
Lambda Rising #1 bestseller when it appeared in 1990.
It received rave reviews.

Now it's back, revised, expanded and updated
for a new generation of readers.

WHAT ARE YOU LOOKING FOR IN A GAY SCIENCE FICTION NOVEL?
A science fiction novel creates a new reality by making technological,
futuristic, mystical and mythical extrapolations from everyday reality.

A gay novel describes everyday reality as it is experienced by gay and
lesbian people.

A better science fiction novel incorporates the technological, futuristic,
mystical, and mythical extrapolations into the story, so that the new reality
of the novel is not simply a backdrop for an adventure but is an intrinsic
part of the development and resolution of the plot. An even better science
fiction novel uses those extrapolations to reveal new and surprising insights
about present, everyday reality.

A better gay novel incorporates the characters' sexual orientation into
the story so that it is not simply a backdrop for a standard adventure but is
an intrinsic part of the development of the plot. An even better gay novel
uses those issues of sexual orientation to demonstrate how certain traits and
virtues peculiar to the characters because they are gay or lesbian help to
resolve the conflicts of the plot.

A gay science fiction novel, then, could simply have gay characters
dealing with a standard science fiction adventure.

But the best gay science fiction novel would have to tell an interesting,
engrossing, and entertaining tale that incorporates the characters' sexual
orientation into the extrapolated reality in a way that reveals new and
surprising, even life-changing, insights about traits and virtues that
characterize gay and lesbian people in our present, everyday reality.
Secret Matter is such a novel.

PRAISE FOR THE ORIGINAL EDITION OF SECRET MATTER

"Don't begin the book in the evening unless you are willing to stay up all night. YOU WILL NOT PUT IT DOWN! I began in the morning and left absolutely everything unattended until some five hours later. It will unquestionably draw you into its own reality and you will be captured there —and love every minute of it! Don't miss this one."
Ralph Walker, The Loving Brotherhood

"...fly blend of sweet romance, social commentary and entertaining science fiction—the sort of easy-going read rarely found in gay fiction, and very welcome."
Richard Labonte

"The creation myth of the Visitors, based roughly on a Biblical theme with a surprising twist, is an eye-opener and very beautiful—worth reading the book for alone. Bravo."
Hyperion, *RFD*

"...beautifully developed and quite moving ...a cosmic coming out story full of metaphysical truths about the rainbow. I loved the whole ride. The love affair gave me a golden glow, and I redden self-consciously when I think about the provincialism of earthlings Johnson so effectively lays bare."
Toby Marotta, *Sons of Harvard*

"Toby Johnson's beautifully told utopian fantasy keeps hope and promise alive. Sweet, sexy and suspenseful, *Secret Matter* affirms a transcendental vision of being gay. Johnson's 'secret' is really about the abundance of joy that all those living a truly gay life can share. But because human beings can lie, for too many such a vision withers before it can bloom. By refreshing the dream, Johnson disarms old lies."
Mark Thompson, *Gay Spirit: Myth and Meaning*

"It's fantastic! I ...really, really liked it and will give it as gifts to friends."
Daniel Helminiak, *What the Bible Really Says About Homosexuality*

"...funny and clever, emotionally complex and socially astute."
Michael Bronski, *The Guide Magazine*

"...even if one has little sympathy for the utopian vision inherent in Johnson's conceptualization of theVisitors and the idealized romance of Kevin and 'Bel, the narrative thrust of *Secret Matter* is sufficiently powerful and the writing so passionate and thoughtful that Johnson's philosophical conceit is hard to resist."
Bob Satuloff, *New York Native*

"When Toby Johnson turned his hand to the coming out novel, you just knew it'd have to have a twist—and what a twist! ...a writer with a positive vision and a wonderful attitude."
Rich Grzesiak, *Philadelphia Gay News*

SECRET MATTER

Also by Edwin Clark (Toby) Johnson

The Myth of the Great Secret: A Search for Spiritual Meaning in the Face of Emptiness

In Search of God in the Sexual Underworld: A Mystical Journey

Plague: A Novel About Healing

Getting Life in Perspective: A Spiritual Romance

The Myth of the Great Secret (Revised Edition): An Appreciation of Joseph Campbell

Gay Spirituality: The Role of Gay Identity in the Transformation of Human Consciousness 🔱 winner

Gay Perspective: Things Our Homosexuality Tells Us About the Nature of God and the Universe 🔱 nominee

Web Page:

The Queer Gay Spirituality of Toby Johnson
Meet Toby Johnson & Kip Dollar
http://tobyjohnson.com

SECRET MATTER

Toby Johnson

with an Afterword
by Mark Jordan
for this revised, expanded,
and updated edition

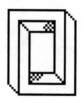

Copyright © 1990, 2005 by Toby Johnson. All rights reserved. No part of this book may be reproduced in any form, except for brief review, without the written permission of the publisher. For information write: Lethe Press, 102 Heritage Avenue, Maple Shade, NJ 08052

Printed in the United States of America by Lightning Source, Inc.
Cover art copyright © 2005 by Sou MacMillan

Published as a trade paperback original
by Lethe Press, 102 Heritage Avenue, Maple Shade, NJ 08052
lethepress@aol.com
LethePress.com

First U.S. edition: Lavender Press, July, 1990
Re-released: Peregrine Ventures, 1995

Revised, updated edition: Lethe Press, November, 2005

ISBN 1-590210-17-4

Preface to the Updated Edition

Secret Matter was first published in 1990. It was set in "the near future." Fifteen years later, the little soft sci-fi romance has become a genre classic, but the near future it was set in has come and gone. And so for this rerelease by Lethe Press a little updating was in order.

With a few changes to the plot and some tweaking of politics and high-tech devices, I think I've made the story accessible to contemporary readers. I've introduced a new explanation of the Visitors' reality (based on—and extrapolated and fictionalized from—the mind-transforming concepts in the remarkable book *The Dimensional Structure of Consciousness* by Samuel Avery). And I've honed the message and, I think, made the revised and updated *Secret Matter* a better novel.

As a frontispiece and *in memoriam* for the first edition, I'd used a calligraphy exercise done back in the late '70s by my first lover Guy Mannheimer (1943-1989). It was a quote from the novelist E.M. Forster, friend of proto gay spiritual philosopher Edward Carpenter and best known in gay culture for the novel *Maurice*. Guy's sampler used the provocative word "queer" in the most charming way. It seemed perfectly to capture the innocent message of *Secret Matter* and the meeting with the Visitors.

An aristocracy of the
sensitive, the considerate,
and the plucky . . .
Are to be found in all
nations and classes, and
through all the ages,
and there is a secret
understanding between
them when they meet.
They represent the true
human tradition, the one
queer victory of our race
over cruelty and chaos

E.M. FORSTER

I've used the wonderful words "queer victory" in many things I've written. I loved how the adjective "queer," with its meaning of strange yet also slightly alluring, implied homosexuality without appealing to the word as the mean-spirited epithet. This quotation exemplifies just the right use of this contentious word of self-identification. So now for this updated edition of *Secret Matter*, I went searching for its source.

E.M. Forster's words come from an essay "What I Believe" in a book called *Two Cheers For Democracy*. But they turn out to be slightly different from the words Guy used in his calligraphy sampler.

Forster actually wrote: "They represent the one permanent victory of our queer race over cruelty and chaos." Not as neat, and not as gay-specific. It now seems to be about the contrariness of human nature, not about the "aristocracy of the sensitive, considerate and plucky." Too bad!

Did Guy Mannheimer change the wording? Was it to give special meaning? Or was it simply to fit space constraints? And then where did he get the quote from? Guy had been in attendance at the First Radical Faerie Gathering in Arizona in 1979 only shortly before. Did he learn the quote there? Maybe from Harry Hay, titular Father of Gay Liberation? Did Harry change the words? (Hay's first exposure to what—in great part thanks to him—would later become "gay consciousness" was a book about the spiritual nature of "homogenic love" by Forster's friend and influence Edward Carpenter which Harry discovered in a public library when he was 11.) He'd have certainly preferred the gay-specific implication.

That I've used these words in so many essays about our queer gay consciousness—and then discovered the words were different from those I knew—has made me question whether the past might change around behind us. What an audacious idea!

Time is a quirky thing.

Well, "the near future" has certainly changed from what we thought it was going to be in 1990. The queer lives of lesbians and gay men have been vilified and devalued—because of AIDS, because of the priest pedophile scandal and the fight over same-sex marriage, because of the cultural coup of Fundamentalism worldwide, and subtly because of the usage of "gay" to mean "stupid and ineffectual"—even while we achieved amazing, but maybe self-defeating, visibility in TV, movies, and the news media. Could the new version of negative spin on what it means to be gay and queer have changed the Forster quote out from behind me?

That's certainly a topic for a science fiction novel! That's not what *Secret Matter* is about, but this novel *is* about a different way to understand the nature of gay consciousness.

Maybe what determines what we experience in life is our focus and expectation and intention, more than "hard reality." If not able to change the past, how gayness gets spun and how we think about ourselves certainly changes the future. So maybe holding in mind *Secret Matter*'s innocent and hopeful little myth of what gay consciousness is really about is one of the ways we can change how time is changing around us.

It would be a wonderful near future if we can actually achieve that queer victory over cruelty and chaos.

The author is grateful to gay cultural commetator and theologian Mark Jordan for contributing an Afterword for this updated edition explicating just how science fiction becomes a new kind of mythology for post-modern, post-religious culture. I'm glad to think *Secret Matter* and the romantic adventures of naive and conflicted Kevin and sweet Visitor 'Bel could perhaps help change the future for us all.

Toby Johnson

Prologue

*B*illy McMasterson felt a tremor shake the building. He had no idea what was really happening.

Sitting at his web-talk broadcast console, looking out at the expansive view of the San Francisco Bay from his aerie atop the mega-church he was now pastoring, he interpreted the vibration as a truck rolling noisily along the Golden Gate Bridge entrance ramp below or perhaps something "scientific" going on even further down the hillside in the Rumsfeld Research Park. The high-tech industrial park had been developed on the grounds of Crissy Field in the old Presidio Army Base. McMasterson craned his neck and noticed that there were blue and white lights strobing brilliantly out of one of the recently renovated former military buildings below.

The Reverend McMasterson was feeling proud of himself. This was only the end of the second week of his broadcasting from his newly built, 10,000 seat church. He knew the broadcasts were successful; last Sunday the main service was practically filled. He was hoping for an overflow crowd this coming week. Suddenly, it seemed, he'd created the largest and most successful congregation in the Bay Area. He knew this success was, in part, because of good advice he'd been given about using the most up-to-date technology to spread his ancient, but timeless (or at least he thought so) message of Biblical authority, in part, because of the three bands he'd employed to play at his services, making them the hottest musical events in the City, and, in part, he had to admit humbly, because of his movie star good looks.

Billy McMasterson looked like a composite of all the dark and handsome actors who'd played James Bond down through the decades. The most recent Bond, an Australian, Rob Grant, World Magazine's "Sexiest Man on Earth" for last year, had recently proved an embarrassment to McMasterson. But, in general, Billy never minded being told he looked like James Bond. "007 for Jesus," he'd always rejoin with a warm and winning smile and just a twinkle of honest humility in his eye.

Peering out through the dark tinted windows of the booth, he noticed the microwave dish antenna that transmitted his words, along with a series of auto-mutating high res images of his smile, directly across the Bay to a repeater station in downtown Tiburon, then to a substratospheric solar-powered web-streamer broadcast platform circling high overhead, and thence, through podphone, dime devices, satcom terminals, laptop computers, and satellite radio, to the whole western half of the United States. The dish looked like it was quivering. *Could vibration from the highway down there cause that much resonance up here?* he wondered. He'd get his technician to look into that tomorrow. *You never know about new construction*, he thought. *You can't trust anybody to do anything right anymore. Who can you believe?*

Five years ago, in an effort to get some control over California's exploding budget deficit, the State Legislature had voted to privatize many of the state's parks. Too much money was being wasted on keeping valuable landscapes in government's hands, the New Conservative Party politicians had argued. One of the first pieces of property to be privatized was the area of Golden Gate National Recreation Area on the northeast corner of the San Francisco peninsula that had previously been the site of the Presidio Military Reservation. The Army had closed the base back in the 1990s, and ceded it for a park and nature preserve. *But now the land was being put to good use*, Billy thought, *for the people, not just the possums and seagulls.*

The freeway leading to the Golden Gate Bridge that shimmered in the distance, only slightly obscured by light rainfall, cut right through the Presidio. To the east, below the freeway, were the airplane hangars and warehouse buildings of the old Crissy Field. These had been bought up by a consortium of high-tech firms and converted to research labs; Homeland Security research had been given first priority. The most cutting-edge science in the country was going on right down there, Billy knew. It made him feel proud that his church was associated with such efforts to save the world from tyranny, spread democracy, and ensure that Christian values would triumph on Earth.

The land uphill from the freeway, mostly wooded hillside that had included the residential areas of the old Fort Winfield Scott, had been put up for sale to real estate developers. One of the developers of the neighborhood that had come to be called, San Francisco-style, Seacliff Heights, was a member of Billy McMasterson's congregation; he'd suggested to the handsome young preacher that a big, nondenominational Charismatic Christian church was exactly what was needed to anchor the upscale neighborhood as family-friendly residential property. The developer helped Billy and his Board of Elders prepare a bid that would guarantee them a prime location. And prime it was, perched high above the entrance to the City from the north. Every driver coming south over the Golden Gate Bridge beheld Reverend Billy McMasterson's black glass and marble Tabernacle of Jesus' Love standing stately and high above them as they entered the City, the icon for the new San Francisco.

Billy MacMasterson grinned at his reflection in the glass of the broadcast booth. He was indeed proud of himself. He was literally changing the San Francisco skyline—*for Jesus*, he told himself.

"*F*or Jesus," he repeated the words outloud into the microphone. He'd been sparring the last few minutes with a caller who'd objected to the anti-gay stance of McMasterson's teachings on the Bible. "That's why a believer would be willing to give up his unnatural desires."

Billy had given up a lot of his own desires to get where he was now—changing the San Francisco skyline for Jesus. Not that his own desires were homosexual. He'd never believed that notion that people who opposed the homosexual agenda were all latent homosexuals. Billy was disgusted by the thought of homosexuality. He clearly felt in his own body that women were what was sexually attractive—the natural thing. And he'd indulged in that natural thing, though after his first marriage to his high school sweetheart failed because she was too eager to settle down and start having kids, he decided to put off another attempt at marriage and family till his ministry was successful. He'd certainly given up some of those perfectly *natural* desires.

But what Billy McMasterson had really given up for his work for Jesus was precisely his longing for God and spiritual delights. As a boy he'd wanted to receive a message direct from God; he'd wanted to see angels. He thought one time that he had. In a beam of sunlight coming through the treetops one day, he was sure he'd seen a face. She smiled at him, and the light had turned golden and dazzled his eyes. The angel was gone in an instant, but the vision had called to Billy his whole life.

The longing for that vision had motivated his interest in church. It had called him to study religion and go to Bible College. But as he had become more and more successful as a preacher and then a pastor, he'd had to realize working for Jesus was more about business than it was about visions. It was about being influential, in order to influence how other people acted. That's what Jesus wanted. That's what saves the world.

The angel never came back. And Billy'd had to give up those longings for angels, discarding them as things of youth, as St. Paul said. If he could give up his things of youth, then the homosexuals could too. Grown up men don't behave like that, he told himself—and listeners throughout the western half of the United States—for Jesus.

The caller, who'd identified himself as a gay psychotherapist from San Antonio, Texas, had just demanded to know how a constitutionally-oriented homosexual, created that way by God, was supposed to deal honestly with sexual and romantic feelings.

"For Jesus," McMasterson repeated. Thinking of himself as a progressive Christian, concerned more with proclaiming the prosperity of the Gospel promises than with making people wrong, Billy quickly added, "I'm certainly sympathetic to the plight of the poor homosexual. It must be difficult to renounce those urges. But they're the urges of children, not adults. That's why sinners need a church like the Tabernacle of Jesus' Love. The homosexuals are welcome in our congregation. We'll give them the support they need to obey God's Law. *And* that is God's Law. The Bible clearly says 'Thou shalt not lie with a man as with a woman.'"

"Look," the caller said with frustration in his voice, "the primary doctrine of the Protestant Reformation was private interpretation of Scripture. That means that the Bible means to me what I understand it to mean when *I* read it, not what the Pope or preachers like you get on the radio or TV or the Internet to proclaim what you think it means.

"When I read that verse about a man not having sex with another man the way a man would have sex with a woman, I hear that to mean he should treat his partner as an equal with respect and affection, not as a piece of property the way the ancient Hebrews treated their women." He said this with a tone of confidence, as though the socio-theological argument were so convincing the radio preacher was going to have to back down.

"Well, Tex, *you* look," McMasterson answered (he was proud to think his voice was reaching as far as Texas, and pleased with himself for finding such a homespun way to dis the caller). "You may be right about the Protestant Reformation. But, hey, I'm not a Protestant, I'm a lover of Jesus and his natural plan for the human race. And sex between man and man is just unnatural. It doesn't take interpreting the Bible to tell you that.

"You think God cares how you interpret His Holy Word? What you think doesn't matter. We *all* know the Bible condemns homosexuals to death. And we all know that's true no matter how you 'interpret' the words of Scripture." The quotation marks on the word "interpret" were clear to every listener.

"That awful disease that ravaged you people is all the proof any of us needs. God was putting the homosexuals to death."

"AIDS was not a gay disease," the caller from Texas shouted back. "And medicine has given us the cure. It was a medical issue, not a moral one, all perfectly natural, no divine intervention. Science developed the RNAi nanozyme that deactivates the virus. There haven't been any AIDS deaths in this country in nearly two years."

"AIDS was a result of unnatural behavior," McMasterson answered.

"Then how come it affected other people? Most of the victims over all these years have been straight people."

"All the more reason why we have to stop the homosexuals' unnatural acts, defiling holy matrimony and sinning before God. Beware, America," Billy waxed prophetic. (*This is what they are paying you for*, he thought.) "If we allow these sinners to live in our midst, they will take us all down with them.

"God works through nature. And nature is indiscriminate. Innocent people get hurt in the collateral damage.

"The Bible says this is an evil that will make the land itself spew the people out. Yea, Lord. Spew the people out—Listeners, doesn't that sound like an earthquake? And doesn't the rain of fire on Sodom and Gomorrah sound like a meteor fall? It should be no surprise God's punishment comes through natural disasters.

"AIDS was God's first attempt to show his will. Now that the doctors have foiled that will with this nanozyme treatment the caller mentioned just means God is going to have to take more aggressive measures to get his Holy Law obeyed. Will we here in San Francisco suffer the punishment of an earthquake or meteor collision because of the immorality and perversion around us?"

It was just as the Reverend Billy McMasterson was saying those words that the vibration that he thought might have come from a truck passing on the freeway rocked the broadcast booth and that he noticed the lights flashing out in the Rumsfeld Research Park.

A moment later the vibration started again. The brilliantly strobing lights went out down below. But the vibration kept getting stronger.

The microwave dish on the wall outside the broadcast booth trembled and shook and then suddenly broke off and fell the five storeys to the parking lot below. *This isn't coming from a truck on the freeway*, McMasterson thought as the building continued to shake. He was aware now a loud roaring seemed to fill the room.

With a crash a section of the ceiling outside the broadcast booth fell to the floor. And then the whole floor slumped forward with a jolt.

Billy felt his chair start to roll as the console broke loose and slid toward the tinted windows. Outside, he could see the lights on the Golden Gate Bridge were dancing. Then everything went dark as the power failed.

Chapter One

$\mathcal{K}$evin Anderson fell asleep worrying about the new job he'd be starting soon after graduation next week in San Francisco the width of the country away.

Kevin was proud of himself for getting this lucrative appointment, but worried his ivory tower schooling in Virtual Architecture wasn't going to have prepared him for the real world work of the reconstruction of the City after last year's devastating earthquake.

He had been working at his computer now for hours, and was a little groggy. He was finishing the final revisions on his senior thesis, "Generating Autosolidifying Plane and Solid Surfaces in Parameter-free Virtual Space with 3-D Force Replication: A Computer-Assisted Energetic Design Model." *What's that got to do with the real world*, he fretted.

As he prepared for bed, he was also fretting about his roommate's absence. Not that it was unusual for Tim to spend weekends in New York. The City was so close and, after all, Tim had the money to enjoy its cosmopolitan delights. But, in spite of—or perhaps because of—their friendship, Kevin disapproved of what he suspected Tim was doing down there.

Even though unconsciousness came hard for Kevin, once he fell asleep, he slept soundly, drifting in and out of dreams of an idyllic vacation with his family in the backwoods of Maine where his dad had sometimes taken the family when the kids were young. Kevin slept so soundly, in fact, that he was not aroused by all the noise in the yard outside his Harvard University dorm a little after 1 a.m.

For weeks afterwards Kevin was going to regret sleeping through that event.

$\mathcal{T}$imothy Lewiston combed his hair, still wet from the shower. He glanced over at the clock to see it was after 1:30 a.m. *Social hour in New York City*, he thought to himself. He'd told a friend he'd meet him between 2 and 2:30 at Zoncko's in the West Village. *The cab'll take about twenty minutes,* he figured. *I've still got about fifteen before I need to leave.* He turned back to the mirror.

Tim Lewiston was an attractive young man. He was small but solid. Except for his height he looked all the part of a rangy redheaded Texas cowboy with tight wiry musculature, a brush of reddish hair across his chest and down the centerline of his torso, blue green eyes, and a smile as beguiling as a country cowpoke. His Texas cowboy appearance was a little deceiving. It correctly identified his Dallas roots, but belied the fact that his grandfather had made a fortune in the oil business and had had the incredibly good luck to sell his holdings just before the Texas oil slump in the 1980s. His father, in turn, had the same good fortune to get out of the market at the end of the '90s just before the dot com collapse. Tim's mother and dad had retired to the California gold country about the time Tim started college in Cambridge. They had a ranch in Nevada City and a condo south of San Francisco in Hillsborough. And the family still maintained this bachelor apartment on the Upper East Side, though Tim was now almost the only one to use it during occasional jaunts to New York.

And the fact was, Tim did make those jaunts fairly often and without his parents' knowledge. He wasn't quite ready to tell them yet that he was "experimenting" with his lifestyle, hanging out at the bars along the newly renovated and hyper-chic Christopher Street. *A young queer has to learn to hide things,* he told himself. Indeed, he'd learned at Harvard he'd survive only if he kept on top of his feelings. Sometimes that had meant being practically merciless and occasionally quite rude.

As he slipped into his clothes, he thought again about the unpleasant confrontation he'd had over dinner with his now ex-boyfriend. And he recalled the conversation earlier in the week with his therapist as he acknowledged the failure of that relationship. Tim had remarked what a cruel joke it was that he felt unloved and unlovable because there were too many people who wanted him and he never knew if it were for his money, his body, or himself. "So I've just never believed in love," he said. "I guess I need to want somebody."

He glanced out the window hoping to find a cab waiting outside the building. He noticed a commotion on the street. A crowd had gathered down by the corner. A number of people were pointing up in the air. At first Tim thought maybe his building was on fire but, before he panicked, he realized they were pointing at something much higher than the building. He stuck his head out to see what was up there, but couldn't see anything.

His curiosity urged him to rush as he pulled on a jacket, locked the apartment door behind him, and waited anxiously for the elevator to let him out on the ground floor.

As he stepped out of the building, he saw people running past him toward the end of the block. He still couldn't see. *Whatever's going on is certainly causing a lot of excitement. Maybe the Empire State Building's on fire.* When he reached the corner and turned to see what everybody was looking at, Tim realized he should have gone up to the roof where he'd have had a much better view

Tim's worries about love and sex all seemed suddenly insignificant.

*G*reen light flickered over John Marshall's face. Around him in the darkened room of the Space Defense Research Facility at March Air Force Base in Riverside, CA, other crew-cut young airmen steadily watched the hypnotic radar screens sweeping the skies for signs of invasion by missiles or bombers or, potentially even more threatening, space objects, like asteroids or large meteors, or maybe alien spaceships. Sometime in the future—if the current research going on just down the hall, John knew, were successful—such signs would be the occasion for activating the space shield, a force field that would surround the United States stopping all invaders from entering our air space.

Some of the other faces seemed intent, but most looked bored. John had had the job of supervising the radar monitors of the experimental facility now for several months. Most of the time he too was bored. Tonight he was thinking about his girlfriend. Before coming on duty, he'd talked with her on the phone. She'd told him she was going to be away for a couple of weeks on a job assignment. He hadn't liked that. He was jealous. But he had been too tongue-tied to explain his feelings. *She's flying all over the world on assignment, hoping to reestablish her career with CNN after last year's fiasco. It was her own fault. And she's just too intent on this career of hers. But damn it. I can't talk to her about my feelings. If she'd just give me a chance…*

After his shift ended, John hung around for a while. He was reluctant to go home. He knew Joan would be there. Probably packing.

And he didn't want to face her. *I'll just freeze up and we'll both get upset.* He drank an extra cup of coffee to get himself alert enough for the forty-five minute drive back to Covina, the suburb they'd agree was halfway between his job in Riverside and hers in Hollywood. And he even smoked a cigarette. He'd quit smoking months ago and was not happy that he'd bummed one without thinking.

Finally he left the station, asking for another cigarette on his way out. He stopped just outside the door to light it. And then stood for a minute looking up at the sky. *If only Joan and I could communicate...*

It was a dark, clear night. The stars were brilliant. John was surprised how little haze there was. He gazed up at the stars, testing his memory of astronomy, as he smoked the cigarette. He forgot that he was peeved with himself for smoking it, for not being able to do what he really wanted. John was just thinking he'd identified the star Regulus in the constellation Leo, when suddenly it looked as if a hole had opened in the sky. The stars were blanked out in a circle almost directly overhead.

John blinked and then rubbed his eyes before he looked again. *Oh my God.* Just then he heard the horns go off signaling an alert.

Sister Margaret Mary Alacoque sang the words of Compline along with the other sisters at St. Benedict's Home. The elderly voices occasionally hit sour notes. Margaret Mary didn't think of herself as as old or feeble as the rest of the sisters around here. But then she thought, down inside, probably none of them thought of herself that way either.

Two years ago, when Sister Margaret Mary came to St. Benedict's she'd been happy to give up teaching and happy to get away from the cold winters back in New England. She'd been looking forward to the opportunity to spend her days in prayer. But by now she was feeling bored. Instead of a house of contemplation, St. Benedict's Home turned out to be an asylum for dotty old nuns. Margaret Mary might not have been so dissatisfied if she finally achieved the kind of mystical, religious experiences she'd longed for as a novice fifty years ago. It seemed like she had been waiting all these years for a chance to discover contemplation. And all she was getting were old women.

The world has changed too much. Nothing makes sense anymore. But better to believe in all those old stories, even if they were wrong, than to believe in nothing. Maybe I'd be better off dead. But, God, I wish just once You'd give me a vision, something to prove all these years of waiting on You were worthwhile.

After night prayers Sister Margaret Mary headed back to her room. As she often did, she went the long way around the outside of the building. She liked getting a little fresh air before bed. She was cantankerous enough herself that if the side door were already locked she didn't mind ringing the bell and making that young sister who was in charge of her wing of the residence hall come let her in, Sister Jennifer. *Not a proper name for a nun anyway. She needs a little discipline.*

The night air was cool, but not uncomfortable. Sister Margaret Mary sat down on a bench overlooking the convent garden. She was surprisingly out of breath and felt a sudden pain in her chest. *My heart?* she wondered, only half-afraid.

She looked up at the night sky, as if she could peer through the heavens into the celestial realms. In lieu of her vision, she reminded herself of the good she'd done in her life, of the success of the students she'd taught over the years. *Why just last night I saw that pretty Joanie Salado on TV.* Sister remembered Joanie clumsily reading Shakespeare in Speech class. She smiled with the thought that something she'd taught had prepared that young girl for being a TV commentator. And Sister remembered this morning getting an announcement from his mother of Kevin Anderson's upcoming graduation. *He was a sweet boy, a little bit of a sissy, but so talented.* She used to get him to draw elaborate cartoons on the blackboard to spice up the daily announcements. *You'd think he'd have made a better weatherman than an architect,* she chortled. And then coughed painfully. She strained to stand up.

She limped along the side of the old red-brick building. Coming round a corner, she saw the lights of Los Angeles spread out across the horizon. Just then Sister heard a roaring sound behind her. For a moment she felt afraid. She started to turn around when the sound overtook her. She looked up, thinking it was a jet airplane flying too close to the ground. Instead in the sky above her, moving in with ponderous grace, was a huge darkness. As she strained her neck to see better, a circle of amber lights flashed on above her. It was as though a golden halo opened in the sky. Her fear suddenly disappeared.

Margaret Mary sat right down on the sidewalk with a bump. She didn't feel the clutch at her heart. *My prayer's been answered,* she thought gratefully. She hadn't expected death to be like this. She hadn't expected God to open a hole in the sky and carry her soul up to him. But here it was happening.

She let her head fall back and she closed her eyes. She could feel the whistling wind blowing across her face and she imagined that now angels were descending from the golden circle in the sky, coming to carry her away. And, very gently, she gave up her soul to the Lord.

"This joint's about as short as it's ever gonna get, Joel. You sure you don't want the last toke?"

"Well, Bunny, since you put it like that," Joel answered, giggling. "Sure I'll take a toke." As he reached for the joint the older lady offered him, he added, "Wouldn't want the joint to get any shorter now, would we?"

"Huh?" Bunny responded quizzically. She had not quite understood the innocent fun Joel was making of her peculiar syntax.

"I'm just as happy with the moodie," Joel continued. "Since the doctor's been prescribing these for me, I haven't been smoking as much grass."

"So I've noticed." Bunny fell silent a moment, staring off into space. The two were sitting on the narrow deck of the Victorian four-plex they lived in on the edge of San Francisco's Mission District. "Look at all the stars," she mumbled under her breath.

"You wanna save the roach?" Joel asked struggling to hold his breath as he passed the joint back.

Taking a look at it in the dim light illuminating the deck from her kitchen, Bunny replied nonchalantly, "hardly enough to make it worth throwing away."

Joel giggled again as he flicked the roach over the railing. As a wave of euphoria rushed through him, he leaned over and gently hugged his friend and neighbor. He felt suddenly warm and affectionate toward her in spite of her eccentricity and occasionally maddening distortion of the English language.

Though now at least in her mid-sixties, Bunny lived just like the hippie chick she'd been as a girl. Her flat next door to his was mostly empty. Unless he invited her over for dinner, it appeared she ate nothing but carrots and brown rice. But in spite of her apparent poverty, she was always bringing homeless people around to share her carrots and brown rice and to get high with her—and, Joel imagined, probably to have sex. "Make love, not war," was one of her mottos.

Bunny frequently went up to Mount Shasta where she was connected with a band of UFO watchers who fervently expected and prepared for extraterrestrials to come rescue them just before the nuclear holocaust or the depletion of the ozone layer or the flood from the greenhouse effect devastated all life on Earth. Bunny herself called the group "fanatics" and had never moved permanently to the mountain commune, but added in her inimitable way that, "Still you never know when you might not want to be there—just in case. After all, you might get a chance to make love with an alien."

"Joel, you know, I'd worry about those moodies if I were you. I don't trust doctors. After all, Goddess gave us marijuana and peyote and magic mushrooms. They're organic. How do you know about these, uh, chemicals? ...what they might be doing to your mind?"

Joel laughed to himself for a moment. *Of all people to worry about what something might do to your mind! Bunny's taken enough drugs to burn out all the lights in Schenectady.* Joel stopped himself, thinking, *Oh God, now I'm starting to sound like her.*

"But, Bun, they're legal, they're cheap, they're harmless. They've taken the crime out of drugs. And they address the real problem."

"The real problem?"

"Sure. Drugs were a problem of technology. Technology created them, imported them, and sold them,. And the technologization of society got people so uptight they needed or wanted them. And like with all the other problems of technology, the only solution is in better technology. The answer to the drug problem was better drugs that provide euphoria and get you high without doing any damage, dulling consciousness, impeding judgment, or slowing response time."

"I still don't trust the government," she replied.

"Well, at least the government finally started telling the truth about drugs. That's what was necessary before anything could've been done. Now, if only they'd start telling the truth about nuclear weapons and international diplomacy and that force field they want to build in the sky..."

"...and UFOs," Bunny interjected one of her favorite subjects. "After all, the people deserve to know what we all know we know"

Joel was just thinking that Bunny's communication skills might have been a whole lot better if there'd been moodies back in the old days instead of acid, when suddenly Bunny's mouth dropped open.

She slowly began to stand, pointing up into the sky behind Joel's head. "Here they come," she managed to say.

"Oh, Bunny, come off it," Joel commented skeptically, thinking that as soon as anybody mentioned UFOs around Bunny she starts seeing things.

"No, Joel. I mean it. Look."

He turned around.

Joel felt the blood rush from his face. He wondered if Bunny had been right. *Maybe the moodies can cause hallucinations.*

"Oh my God," she said, "It's as big as if it weren't even there."

Called back to reality by Bunny's nonsensical phraseology, Joel did a little reality testing. He asked himself if what he were seeing slowly move across the sky could be explained as an airplane or maybe the Goodyear blimp.

But no, the flat dark shape, encircled with golden lights, was obviously not a blimp. *That just couldn't be anything else but a real flying saucer.*

"Damn," Bunny said, "here I am in the City. This is no time to not be at Mount Shasta."

"Yeah," Joel answered, feeling more euphoria than any combination of drugs could produce. "But you don't need to be at Mount Shasta. They're here, Bunny. They're right *here* ."

*J*oan Salado watched TV most of the night, switching through the five hundred and twenty channels the cable brought in looking for new news. She was excited and she was worried. It was almost 3 a.m. and John still wasn't home. She wasn't surprised that he might be held up on base, but still she worried. *What if more is going on than is getting reported? What if the Aliens, uh, Visitors—what should I call them?—are hostile? What if there've been attacks?*

She'd once read a story about a team of scientists who'd faked an alien invasion in order to get the conflicting countries of the world to see they could cooperate with one another. For a moment she wondered if this invasion had been faked. But she had looked out her own window only a few hours ago and watched the ship move slowly across the Southern California sky. She knew it was real.

Remembering the awesome size of that ship, Joan felt a surge of fear and respect pass through her. *The world is never going to be the same again.*

That was not an all together unwelcome idea. Part of Joan's upset this evening had preceded the arrival of those spaceships—or whatever they were. Joan was still trembling with the embarrassment of this morning's scene at the Air Force Base. And wondering if her career with CNN could withstand one more blow like that.

A year ago Joan had become suddenly famous as the CNN staffer to report from the Great San Francisco Earthquake. The public loved her and her down-to-earth reaction to and reporting of the disaster. She produced a series blending warm, "womanly" human interest stories with hard-hitting catastrophe footage, characterized by her use of compact, mobile cameras—in which she was sometimes shown climbing through ruined buildings or under collapsed freeways helping perform rescues as well as report on them. Her star was rising.

Just as the quake story was dying down, Joan discovered that a Department of Homeland Security project to generate the space shield had been going on in a facility in the Rumsfeld Research Park in San Francisco *and* that the experimental device had been turned on at the time of the earthquake. Joan accused Dr. Maxwell Humphries and the military of covering up the fact that this device may have been responsible for triggering the quake.

She'd made a splash in the news with the story, but then the story was squelched by the Pentagon and dismissed as ludicrous and Joan was professionally discredited. She'd been reassigned to the Hollywood office and given jobs reporting on celebrity weddings and fancy night club openings.

Coincidentally Dr. Humphries' research program also moved south to March Air Force Base near Riverside. The move was officially explained as a precaution to protect the delicate equipment which had been damaged in the San Francisco earthquake, but Joan fervently believed the lab was moved to get it away from a fault line so future experiments wouldn't cause another earthquake. In part to resurrect her career and prove she was right *and* to prevent further earthquakes, she'd continued on the sly to trace down stories about the space shield research.

She'd learned through her current boyfriend whom she'd met at one of those night club openings and whom she'd pursued in part because he was in the Air Force at March A.F.B., that Maxwell Humphries was giving a talk to Pentagon contractors at March just that morning. She'd sneaked into the talk—with her mobile camera tucked surreptiously over her ear like a wireless headset—hoping to get a clue about Humphries' work that could exonerate her.

As the lecture began, Humphries explained that even though the Terrorist War seems to have cooled with the establishment of the U.N. redress and reconciliation courts mandated by Al Qaeda, there was still threat against the homeland. Now it came again in the form of attack by air. The three missile attacks on New York City in the last few years was evidence.

The latest international hot-spot was the Nasserine Civil War. The Loyalists, Humphries said, were believed to control missiles capable of reaching the United States. He reminded the audience that recent intelligence reports indicated that Saudi space-based weapons and even old-fashioned, but still firable, Russian ICBMs had ended up in the hands of the Nasserinian rebels, and perhaps even former Iranian and Iraqi insurgents, South African Reactionaries, Korean Sovereignty Partisans, Russian Neo-Czarists, and who knows how many others.

His project, he explained, has been to create a "space shield" over the country which would prevent missile intrusion. Once expanded worldwide, the shield would be able to block unauthorized military actions anywhere on Earth. And he added that, theoretically, it might even protect the planet from collision with an asteroid.

Joan was just congratulating herself on getting into the lecture— and thinking about how to position her head so the camera would pick up Humphries' every facial expression, when the scientist recognized her in the audience and started shouting, "THAT woman, get her out of here."

She was surrounded by security guards and literally dragged out of the room. She'd never been so embarrassed in her life.

Her supervisor had left her an email notice that he was expecting to see her in his office first thing tomorrow morning.

All evening Joan had been worrying about getting fired *and* reminding herself that the arrival of the spaceships changed everything. But still John wasn't home. It was admitting to him what had happened this morning that she feared the most. John had never been sympathetic with her effort to undermine Maxwell Humphries' research. After all, he was now working in Humphries' own department. And he'd kept reminding Joan how careful he had to be to not let slip anything about his relationship with her.

Just then, Joan's DimeBox played a gentle ringtone, Edith Piaf's classic *L'hymne À L'amour (Let It Happen)*, resurrected as the poignant love theme for last year's Oscar-winning sci-fi tearjerker romance, *When Worlds Collide*.

The DimeBox, or just "dime" as they'd come to be called, was the all-in-one, hand-held phone, text and voice messaging device, satellite computer link, gamer, and audio-video save/play pod that, under a number of different brand names, had become the essential work and play tool of 21st century *DI*gital *ME*dia.

L'hymne À L'amour was the signal the call was coming from John.

"Hi, honey," he said. "Sorry I'm so late calling. The base was locked down tight till a few minutes ago."

"I guessed as much," she answered. "Hey, got any hot scoops for me?" She tried to keep the conversation light. She had no intention of mentioning this morning's embarrassing scene, at least not on the phone.

"I probably know less than you do. I haven't heard any news. We've been on red alert since the ship first appeared over the base…"

"Where's it now?"

"Still right overhead."

"Hmm? You think they're interested in the space-shield?" she asked.

"Look, Joan, I probably shouldn't be talking about this stuff. And don't mention the space-shield," he said coldly. "Anyway, the reason I called was to say I was late and to, well, apologize for what I said earlier, I mean, about resenting your assignment…"

"Well, that'll probably change anyway. Everything's gonna change."

"'cept us?" John asked sheepishly, hoping she'd understand the veiled import of his communication.

"'cept us."

Chapter Two

Kevin lay on the bed of his room in Dunster House, the dorm which until today had been his home most of the past five years he'd been a student at Harvard. Because he was in the architecture program his undergraduate career had spanned five years instead of the usual four. He'd been happy he could remain in Dunster House the extra year, if only because it had meant he could continue to room with his friend Tim Lewiston. There'd been a kind of unspoken agreement between them to protect one another's deepest feelings, not to pry into secrets each kept—maybe even from himself.

Today the room was bare and stark. The bed had been stripped. Several suitcases stood by the door. Kevin was staring at the ceiling. His heart was beating like mad.

Tim, sitting on the other bare bed, repeated his question: "Tell me the truth now. You've had the hots for me for years, haven't you?"

"I am not a pervert," Kevin answered defensively.

"There you go with that word again. I didn't say you were a 'pervert.' You are the kindest, sweetest, best-intentioned and most innocent person I've ever known in my life. But that doesn't mean you're not gay. I mean, Kevin, who do you think you're fooling?"

"Stop it, Tim. Just stop it! You've got no right to make fun of me."

"Oh, Kev, lighten up. I'm not making fun of you, I'm just trying to get you to wake up and listen to the music."

"Well, you're scaring me."

"What? With fantasies of child molesters and homosexual ogres? Kevin, there's nothing wrong with feeling what you're feeling."

"How do you know what I'm feeling?"

"Kevin, honey, we've been rooming together for three years now. I've gotten to know you. And, to be honest, I've gotten to know myself, too."

"Just 'cause you think you're gay doesn't mean everybody else is," Kevin retorted.

"I'm not talking about 'everybody,' I'm talking about you, my good friend, who I'm liable not to see again for a long time, and, if I don't get this conversation cleared up right now," Tim laughed embarrassed, "maybe never."

"You think I'll reject you 'cause you've turned queer?" Kevin sounded hurt and just a little angry.

"No. But I am afraid you'll get scared of me 'cause you think *you* might 'turn queer.'"

"Whaddya want me to say? That I've been out sucking cock in the Boston Commons?"

"Of course not. I know perfectly well you wouldn't be doing anything like that. What I wanted was, well, was for you to, oh you know," Tim was suddenly flustered, "say you like me."

"I do like you, Tim. Why else would I have roomed with you all these years? This past year I could've moved to my own apartment. I stayed here 'cause I liked living with you."

"No, I don't just mean like that. I mean, well, this is the last day. I'm going back to New York. You're going to San Francisco soon. This may be the last time we really talk. And I just want to tell you how much I really care for you and think you're cute in your goddamn Clark Kent sort of way…"

"And what do you mean by that?" Kevin interrupted.

"That you're a beautiful man. You've got a really pretty face and a good body. But you hide yourself behind those out-of-style glasses and keep your shirt buttoned up to your neck like a first class nerd…"

As Tim talked, Kevin took off his glasses and casually laid them down on the bedside table.

"…with that alabaster skin of yours, those blue eyes, and the five o'clock shadow… migod, you'd be so sexy. But you've got to stop looking so uptight and so, so innocent—I mean, Kevin, it really isn't innocence 'cause it's a lie. You may be a virgin, but that doesn't mean you don't have feelings. I know! And, besides, while I'm at it, you need to get your hair styled."

Kevin looked up sheepishly. "Thanks for telling me that," he said as he tried to surreptitiously undo the collar button of his shirt. "Go on."

"What was I saying? Oh yeah, look, I brought all this up to see if I could help you, you know, acknowledge your own feelings. 'Cause you'd be a lot happier if you did. And, frankly my dear," Tim adopted his best Rhett Butler tone of voice, "life in the ruins of San Francisco will be a damn sight easier if you do."

Kevin felt himself trembling. Just the words "San Francisco" sent a thrill through him. And at the same time a wave of terror.

As if he somehow knew what Kevin was feeling, Tim continued, "God, Kev, you're on your way to gay heaven. And don't you see instead of getting you all excited, it's scaring the shit out of you?"

"You mean AIDS hell, don't you?" Kevin answered.

"Oh come off it. I've been hearing you talk like that for years now and it just doesn't make any sense. You sound like your mother."

"Maybe the medical stuff has cleared up with the RNAi nanozyme treatment. But that's just started another crusade against homosexuals having sex. Being gay looks icky. Why would you want to identify with that?" Kevin challenged.

"And maybe the Church isn't so wrong," he continued. "I mean I just think, well, doesn't the fact that the disease started among homosexuals make you suspect that maybe there is something, uh, morally wrong about that kind of sex?"

"No. No more than I think there was something morally wrong about burning coal because coal miners got black lung disease. Maybe there was something wrong with forcing miners to work under unsafe conditions … and maybe there was something, uh, hygienically wrong with the sex some homosexuals were having back in the old days. But we're supposed to learn from their mistakes, Kev, not just blame them some more and make ourselves miserable today on their account. Things have changed."

"Look, Tim, when I was growing up…"

"I know about when you were growing up. I know all the horror stories about AIDS and then the religious backlash against same-sex marriage, all the mean things they said. That stuff certainly didn't make it any easier to recognize gay feelings."

"So maybe I *do* get some gay feelings sometimes," Kevin said staring down at the floor. "Look, I'm human and humans are bisexual. So what? That doesn't mean I have to devote my life to goddamn 'gay feelings.' Or to tell everybody else about it. My feelings are my own business, aren't they?" Kevin retorted. His voice was strained.

"But if they're there…"

"Then I can control them," Kevin answered, suddenly sitting up and glaring angrily at Tim.

"Okay, okay. I'm sorry." This time Tim looked down at the floor. Kevin reached out and tentatively touched his friend on the knee. "Look, Tim, I'm sorry too. I didn't mean to make you mad. You know, some of what you were saying, I guess, was kinda true. I mean, maybe a couple of years ago when we first moved in here, I guess I *was* in love with you…"

Tim started to take Kevin's hand that was resting lightly on his knee, then seemed to think better of it.

"…I guess I still get a little, uh, jealous, when you talk about your boyfriend in New York."

"Oh, don't worry about him," Tim answered, interrupting Kevin's emotional expression, "Didn't I tell you we broke up a week ago, the day before the Visitors arrived?"

Kevin sat back, pulling his hand away, then scooted himself back up on the bed and leaned against the wall, curling his legs together into a half-lotus. "You mentioned my going to San Francisco. You know, you're right that I'm scared. I'm scared of being all by myself. I'm not gonna know a soul out there. I'm scared of this gay life you talk about—I mean, I just want to keep all that stuff out of my life for the time being. Maybe I'd cop to a little bisexuality, but all the rest of that stuff—it's just not me. I've got too much else to worry about. I'm scared of the job. You know, damn it, I guess I'm even afraid of another earthquake."

Tim stood up and stretched, throwing his arms way over his head. As he did so, his short t-shirt pulled out of his jeans, momentarily exposing his tight-muscled, lightly reddish-haired torso. (Tim tried to catch Kevin looking, but wasn't sure whether he had.) Yawning, he replied, "Oh, Kev, don't worry about the earthquake. I've seen what the Big One did last year. I promise you it relieved *all* the pressure on the fault. It practically reduced whole areas of the city to rubble."

"What a tragedy!"

"Well, yeah, but look on the bright side. It got you a job, didn't it." Tim leaned against the window, looking out into the spring green yard.

"I hate to think of my good fortune coming from other people's disaster."

"Well, that's usually how it is," Tim answered. "You were talking about AIDS. Look at all the discoveries in immunology that came out of that… and the changes that happened in gay life—"

"I don't know," Kevin resisted what he feared was Tim's attempt to get the conversation back on sexual identity. "I'm just an architect… hey, I'm not even an architect, I'm just an intern."

"Yeah, but you've been hired by one of the most prestigious firms in the country and you'll be working on one of the most exciting projects in history: the Rebuilding of San Francisco." Tim said the last words with awe in his voice. "Besides, you're gonna be around all those gorgeous blond construction workers, toiling away in the California sun with their shirts off." Tim was still looking out the window. As he made that last teasing overtly sexual comment, he peeked around to see Kevin's reaction.

"Oh, stop it," Kevin answered. "I'm not going out there to have sex with construction workers."

"I just meant to tell you about the beauties of the City," Tim responded mock-innocently.

"You're teasing me."

"For your own good, my dear," Tim put on a shaky, grandmotherly voice.

Kevin suddenly jumped off the bed and started toward Tim. Tim, in turn, fearing he'd gone too far with his teasing, cowered back and then pulled the drape in front of himself. "Don't hit me, massa, don't hit me."

Kevin lifted the heavy drapery away from Tim and looked at him, gradually letting himself begin to smile. "I'm not going to hit you," he giggled. "It's just… Oh, Tim, I'm gonna miss you…"

Tim reached up and pushed the drape out of the way. The gesture allowed him to reach around behind Kevin and then let his arm drop onto his shoulder. At first Kevin flinched from the touch, but then he stepped closer to Tim and brought his own arms up and around him. They held one another silently. Kevin let his cheek slowly come in full contact with Tim's.

"Let's move away from the window, okay?" Tim said softly.

Kevin was trembling. With intentional effort he let himself relax into Tim's strong embrace. Gradually the trembling subsided. Kevin was surprised how comfortable and comforted he felt. Scenes flashed through his mind; some nostalgically sweet, others frightening.

...the smiling face of the boy he'd had a crush on in third grade—Kevin had to think hard for a moment to recall his name—Charley.

...the slightly leering grin on the face of the priest who'd been called to counsel Kevin the first day back after Christmas vacation when he'd started crying uncontrollably when the teacher explained to the class that Charley wouldn't be coming back because his parents had been transferred to another city. Kevin could still remember the odd sensation he'd felt in his stomach when the priest insisted on giving him a hug as part of "counseling" him about the inappropriateness of his youthful tears. How different Tim's embrace felt today.

...the angry, but devoutly Catholic, glare on his mother's face when she dressed Kevin and his brother up in their Sunday Mass suits, just little boys, to march in demonstrations against same-sex marriage and against priest pedophiles. (At the time, Kevin was too young to understand "pedophiles"; he thought they were demonstrating against those little counters that tell you how many steps you've taken in a day.) Later, Kevin wondered if his mother had been abused herself when she was a little girl. He never dared ask her, but she was always so judgmental about other people's sex lives.

...the serious look in his father's eyes when he struggled to explain to the burgeoning adolescent who'd suddenly come to life in Kevin's no longer boyish body about the dangers of "uh, certain forms of sex." He wanted to be a good son, but he could not remember his father ever mentioning any good things about sex or love.

...the innocent, joking smiles of the other boys as they changed into swimming trunks the first day Kevin was at summer camp when he was thirteen. It was the first time he had had to undress in public. He'd been scared of letting the other boys see the changes that had been occurring in his body, and fascinated with seeing that those same changes had been occurring in theirs.

...the disapproving and scornful look of the friend whose campaign for Student Body President Kevin had tirelessly volunteered in out of hopes the handsome, blond, and brilliantly blue-eyed young man would notice him. At the victory party Kevin had had too many beers—it was practically his first time drinking—and when he compulsively went to congratulate the successful candidate, he innocently and inadvertently kissed the boy on the lips. Even today in Tim's arms he felt the horror and embarrassment of that moment.

These and other images—his girlfriend from Radcliffe he'd tried so hard to love; the statue of the Blessed Mother in the Catholic Student Center chapel before which he'd prayed devoutly for guidance, confused and fearful; his mother ironically urging him to be careful about girls and not to marry too young—all flashed urgently through Kevin's mind.

Kevin started to fidget, then reminded himself to relax and enjoy the feel of finally letting himself touch and be touched. After a while he pulled his face away and looked at Tim. "What am I gonna do?"

"You're going to fall in love with a wonderful man who loves you as much as you love him," Tim said. "That's what you're gonna do."

"You know, technically I *am* a virgin, at least when it comes to actually making love with another person." Kevin stammered, pulling away from Tim's embrace, but holding his gaze. "I love *you*…"

This time it was Tim who stammered, "Yeah, and I love you too… but, well, this 'd be the wrong time for us to go falling in love with each other. And, Kev, I want you to have a wonderful first time with somebody you really can love. And I guess, I love you enough—you know, like a brother, or like a sister, as they say," Tim smiled, "that I want your, uh, first time to be real special.

"It makes a difference. If your first experiences are in the Lamont Library bathroom, that's what you're gonna think is hot. If it's with somebody you love and who loves you, that's what'll turn you on and what you'll keep looking for. I think that's the kinda love you deserve."

"Tim, you're sweet."

"Me, sweet?" Tim answered with feigned indignation. "I don't want you to get the wrong impression. Who do you think I was talking about in the Lamont Library john?"

"Oh, come off it," Kevin answered.

Tim grabbed him and pulled him close and kissed him full on the mouth. "It's gonna be great," Tim smiled and added, "I just got a rule against deflowering virgins."

Kevin grinned. "Well, thanks, I think."

"Look, Kev, uh, let's go eat… before we get too horny to quit."

$\mathcal{A}$s Kevin and Tim entered the Dunster House dining hall, they discovered an unexpected commotion. No one was eating. Instead everyone in the room was clustered at the far end where a large television screen hung on the wall. Taking the lead, Kevin headed straight for the crowd, "Let's see what's going on."

As he approached he could hear the mellifluous voice of a TV commentator.

"For the past week, the Visitors have been in lengthy negotiations with the Secretary of State and the President, but only by radio. They have not shown themselves. Speculation has run high that they suspect their appearance will be shocking to us—"

Kevin was close enough now to makeout the image on the 60 inch nano-adjusting diffusion screen TV, the newest imaging technology that produced color by reflecting ambient light off its nanofilament surface like a peacock feather. A huge crowd surrounded the fenced area around one of the ships. Kevin supposed the ship in Washington D.C. was the command ship for the squadron.

"As you can see," the commentator continued, "the crowd is waving banners welcoming the Visitors. I see one that reads, 'We don't care what you look like.'"

"I bet they're lizards," shouted a redheaded student close to the TV.

"Nah," answered somebody from in back, "they'll look like those little white dough men. Lots of people have seen them already."

"Whaddya mean 'lots of people'?" somebody else spoke up.

"I mean, there've been aliens abducting people for a long time and like taking them off for scientific tests. This is nothing new," answered the voice from the back of the crowd.

"I disagree. This is something new. Not the same thing at all."

"Maybe they'll look like those devils, like in *Childhood's End*." The movie of Arthur C. Clarke's famous science fiction novel had finally been made a few years before. "The way the ships arrived and all... just like in the movie!"

"That's right," somebody else spoke up. "Arthur C. Clarke was a prophet."

"Hey, that movie ends with the children all turning into poltergeists or something and the world ending," a fellow nearby rejoined.

Another spoke up, sounding annoyed, "They were fully evolved consciousnesses, not poltergeists, for god's sake. Didn't you understand the movie? And they returned the Earth to the Overmind. Like to God."

"Is that gonna be a self-fulfilling prophecy or what?" somebody else said.

"Shut up, you guys," shouted a young woman. "We can't hear the TV."

"You think the TV's gonna tell you the truth...?" another piped up. "All this is a scam. Those 'visitors' won't come out of the ship 'cause they're Russians—or Nasserinians or Chinese or something."

"Look, didn't you hear the lady?" another voice shouted very loud, "SHUT UP."

"...we're still waiting word," the reporter was saying, "of when the Visitors will leave their ship. In the meantime, let me repeat the summary of negotiations the Secretary of State announced this morning.

"Secretary FitzGibbons said the Visitors have come primarily for humanitarian reasons. They have expressed interest in scientific exchange and perhaps in commerce. The Secretary reassured that they seem to have no hostile motives. And, though of course such assessments are subject to change, Air Force weapons experts say their studies of the ships seem to indicate the Visitors are unarmed, as they say they are.

"The Visitors have asked to dispatch research teams to several locations, including New York, San Francisco, London, Amsterdam, Moscow, and Beijing. So far it appears foreign governments are willing to welcome them. The Russians apparently were reluctant at first. President Cernikov who is ailing announced through his press secretary that, in light of last year's Havanagate scandal, he wants reassurance that the Visitors are not another American C.I.A. disinformation plot. With proper evidence, he said, Russia will be happy to admit Visitor representatives. Adding to recent tensions between Washington and Moscow over development of the space shield, Cernikov questioned publicly what it suggests about the Visitors that they chose to land in a nation with what he called 'such a paranoid and defensive attitude.'

"Secretary FitzGibbons denied the charges of defensiveness, and explained that Visitor teams are welcome, under some degree of Homeland Security surveillance, to travel about the United States and to set up bases from which to observe life on Earth... Wait, now I see some activity in front of the ship..."

Kevin, with Tim right behind him, had crept up as close as he could get to the front of the circle round the TV. On the big screen, he could see the Visitor ship. It surprised him for a moment to see how small it looked. From TV coverage on the night of the arrival, he had thought the ships were much bigger. "Kinda small, isn't it?" he whispered to Tim.

"The ship I saw over Manhattan musta been ten or twenty times that size," Tim answered. "How did they do that?"

"Geometry," somebody whispered in answer to Tim's puzzlement.

"Huh?"

"Geometry. I mean, the Visitors must be able to warp the shape of space. Only way they could have come interstellar distances anyway. That could allow them to alter the shape and size of their ships..."

"Oh," answered Tim, more puzzled than ever.

"There seems to be a door opening in the side of the vessel," the reporter announced.

Kevin realized the room had become absolutely hushed. He'd stopped breathing himself. Intentionally he drew in a breath.

"President Arnold is approaching the ship now. If the camera can turn that way, yes, there it is, you can see the motorcade slowly coming through the crowd."

The picture flashed back to the ship. In the side of the curving wall an arch-shaped opening had appeared. Now a floor was sliding out from inside the ship to form a platform. And then two young men dressed in what looked like dark purple fatigues stepped out of the ship pushing a collapsed gangway ahead of them.

"Apparently military personnel were admitted earlier to help with the disembarking," the commentator said, a touch of perplexity in his voice.

"Aren't they cute?" Tim whispered in Kevin's ear, echoing a thought Kevin had already had, but had resisted registering.

The men in the purple fatigues attached the gangway to the platform, then turned and went back inside the opening while the gangway began to unfold mechanically on its own. The crowd had hushed. Now all of a sudden there was a groundswell of murmuring as some people began to suspect what they'd just witnessed.

As the President's motorcade pulled up at the base of the gangway and the President stepped out of his car, a shadowy figure appeared inside the doorway of the ship.

The crowd was cheering like crazy.

"This is the moment," announced the TV.

President Malcolm Arnold walked over the gangway and took a couple of hesitant steps up. The figure in the door stepped out into the light.

The crowd gasped.

"Oh my God," said somebody right next to Kevin.

The Visitor stood looking out at the crowd for a moment and then turned and extended her hand toward the President who, at first, seemed paralyzed and then got control of himself and stepped up to the platform.

The Visitor was tall and slender. Her almost translucent hair shimmered golden in the afternoon sun. She was dressed in a dark purple uniform that matched the color of those of the two men who'd come out earlier, though was more formally cut, with a short cape over the shoulders. One side of the cape was thrown back to expose a white shiny, satin-like lining.

"Well," said the reporter in what would be remembered for years as classic understatement.

Kevin was just observing that the Visitor was humanoid with two arms and two legs and a head when the redheaded kid at the front of the circle who'd suggested the Visitors would look like lizards shouted in a strained voice, "Why, they're people."

"As you can see, the President is taking the Visitor's hand," the reporter was continuing in a choked and awkward tone of voice. "The truth is," he blurted out, "everybody seems dumbfounded. The Visitors appear completely human. I doubt anybody was expecting this."

"Well, perhaps not absolutely human. You can see that the Visitor is somewhat taller than the President. And she looks female. Her hair seems abnormally blond and her skin looks almost metallically golden. But, indeed," sighed the reporter, "the alien looks human."

"See, I told you it was a Russian plot or something. Obviously a foreign agent," spoke up the student who'd scoffed earlier.

The redheaded kid countered, "The lizard face is camouflaged to look human."

"The President is about to speak."

There was a little static and the sound of wind blowing as the President's hand mike was turned on.

"Welcome to planet Earth and to the United States of America."

"We are grateful for your hospitality. We have made quite a journey to meet you," answered the Visitor.

"She's beautiful," a young man exclaimed. "Do you think they came here to intermarry?"

"If the guys working the gangplank are available, I'll volunteer," Tim whispered in Kevin's ear. Kevin blushed. He was himself perhaps a little more impressed with the Visitors' striking beauty than he wanted to admit to himself, but embarrassed by Tim's innuendo.

"We come in friendship and in curiosity," the Visitor was saying. "We are like you in many ways…"

"I think we're all a little surprised by that," the President said.

The Visitor smiled, enigmatically.

"We're very glad you're here. This is a wonderful moment for Earth and for the United States. I regret that my friend Mikail Cernikov is not with me here to greet you," the President said in his famous politically noncommittal manner.

"Our greetings are to all the Earth," the Visitor answered. "To the Russian people and the Chinese, to Earth people on every continent. We are looking forward to visiting you all.

"But now, let me introduce more of our people to you. And come, Mr. President, let us go down and meet the people who've come here today."

As the President looked nervously toward the head of his Secret Service force, a stream of Visitors began pouring out through the ship's door pushing the President down the gangway.

"Hey, look," somebody exclaimed near Kevin, "they're different colored." She was right, Kevin realized. Some of the Visitors seemed to be blue, some greenish, even some muddy gray, though most were the golden color of the leader.

"You think they have racial problems?" another voice piped up to a peal of laughter.

$\mathcal{K}$evin's plane was leaving in four hours. His mother was in the kitchen finishing preparations for the huge meal she was serving as his going away. He'd reminded her several times already that he could buy lunch on the flight from Boston to San Francisco, but that had not deterred her from what she perceived as her motherly duties.

Kevin, his dad, and his younger brother Jeff were sitting in the living room of their house in the Boston suburb of Medford. Mr. Anderson, a building contractor by profession, was gloating over Kevin's seemingly already successful start in the business.

"I'm really proud of you, son," Kevin's father said for the third or fourth time. "You've done remarkably well. Just think, you're not even twenty-five yet and you've got your degree in architecture and a job with Sutro Associates. My Lord, even back here in Boston, we've heard of them. You're gonna go so much farther than I ever did…"

"I'm just an intern, dad," Kevin murmured, embarrassed by all the attention.

"I bet you're gonna see Visitors in 'Frisco," Jeff interrupted. Kevin's teenage brother was much more impressed with such an opportunity than with the job at Sutro.

"You should come visit, Jeff," Kevin answered. "Maybe you can sneak into a Visitor ship."

"Hot damn," Jeff exclaimed.

"You watch your language, young man," their dad scolded.

"Sorry."

"And now you've got the time and the resources to settle down and start a family. You look so handsome with your new haircut. You'll have to fight off all the young women," Mrs. Anderson remarked, pushing her way through the swinging door from the kitchen. She had her hands full with a tray of hors d'oeuvres. "I'll certainly come out there and help with the babysitting."

Kevin felt a rush of embarrassment. He didn't know what to say.

"Well, we'll all be out for the wedding," his dad rejoined. "In the meantime, you watch yourself out there. You know about, er, those people in San Francisco."

"Remember what we think about same-sex marriage and all that, son," Mrs. Anderson commented as she placed the hors d'oeuvre tray on the coffee table. "Dinner's almost ready now. Jeff, why don't you bring these into the dining room?"

"Aw, mom, how come you serve the hors d'oeuvres the same time as dinner," Jeff complained.

Watching his family, Kevin felt a pang of nostalgia for his childhood and the things of family life—his mother's quirks, his brother's endearing peevishness, his dad's self-effacing pride in his sons. He also felt a burning desire to get as far away as he could from the family's expectations of him. And, indeed, San Francisco was about as far as he could possibly go.

"Maybe Kevin'll marry a Visitor girl. Bet they're all hot," Jeff said in a lurid tone of voice.

"I think it's so nice the Visitors turned out to be just like us." Kevin's mother was carrying bowl after bowl to the dining table. "Kevin, would you like to pour the wine. We have to toast your going away."

Kevin could sense emotion in her voice. It further embarrassed him. *Why couldn't I have just left quietly?* he thought, as he headed toward the refrigerator to get the bottle of wine.

What does she mean 'what we think about same-sex marriage'? She doesn't know what I think about same-sex marriage. Kevin wasn't sure himself what he thought about gay marriage. He was annoyed that the topic kept getting talked about. It was embarrassing. But he could understand men loving other men. And sometimes he feared he couldn't understand men loving women. He didn't like "gay marriage" because "gay" made it sound so frivolous. He thought, with a mixture of revulsion and envy, of Tim's weekends in New York City. He certainly didn't want to be gay like that, but he could understand two friends wanting to be companions for life.

He hated it that his parents thought they knew him so well. He knew he was keeping secrets from them. And damn proud of himself for doing so.

Kevin had been home now for nearly three weeks. After graduation he had a little time before he was to report for his new position as architect intern for Sutro and Associates, Architects. He'd originally planned to take a short vacation, maybe to Jamaica, during this time but the arrival of the Visitors had changed his plans. His mother, though now an avid fan of the beautiful people from the stars—some people were already calling them angels—had, a month ago, expressed dire concern about the safety of travelling anywhere, especially by air. So Kevin spent the time at home. Among other things it had given him a chance to get his eyesight laser-corrected, so he wouldn't have to wear glasses anymore.

Though, of course, he'd been in school in nearby Cambridge, he'd lived on campus—that was an essential part of the Harvard education. Even though he'd pursued an almost monkish existence, he'd known he didn't want his family prying into his personal life. So, except for summers, he'd really moved out five years ago. Even so, that move had never given him the freedom and final independence that this relocation to San Francisco was going to.

"Oh, now maybe this turkey really isn't done yet." Kevin could hear his mother fussing over her dinner as he struggled to get the corkscrew into the top of the wine bottle.

"Aw, mom, don't put it back now," Jeff whined.

"Don't talk to your mother that way."

"But, dad, if she doesn't serve the damned dinner, Kevin's gonna miss his plane."

"Mind your language, young man."

Kevin paused and listened to the familial sounds in the dining room. He sometimes felt embarrassed that his family was so normal. *They're like a cliche.* For a moment he wished his mother were a "fag hag" (he hated some of the words he'd learned from Tim), preferring to hang out more with her hairdresser than with the ladies from the Parish Auxiliary. And for a moment he wondered if, of course, she really did. After all, he realized, surprised, he probably knew as little about his parents' lives as they did about his. Maybe he'd always misunderstood.

Why dad might even be a C.I.A. agent for all I know!

"Kevin," his mother shouted from the dining room, "if you can't get the cork out, we could toast with 7-Up. There's a bottle in the ice box."

Kevin laughed. *I guess we really are the perfect cliche family, after all.* He shook his head. *How am I ever going to tell them the truth?*

"Kevin, come on with the 7-Up," Jeff complained.

Oh, thank God, I'm getting out of here, Kevin smiled to himself, as he pulled the cork out of the wine bottle with an audible pop.

Chapter Three

As he filed into the airport with the stream of passengers from the American Airlines flight, Kevin hunted through the crowd at the gate. *There he is,* he thought, spying a man a few years older than himself. Though he vaguely recognized the face from his past, he had no trouble at all identifying him, because, as planned, the man was carrying a small sign with the word SUTRO penned on it in impeccable architect's printing.

As Kevin caught his eye, the man stepped forward, "Hi, Kevin, I'm Will Salado."

"Kevin Anderson," he replied, shaking hands in a manly fashion. "Welcome to San Francisco."

In fact, Kevin could barely restrain his excitement. He'd been waiting for this moment for six months—and really for more than a year. The day the earthquake struck, Kevin had remarked "I want to work on the rebuilding." Now that declaration was coming true.

As they hustled along with the crowd toward the baggage claim, Salado pointed out how the airport terminal had been damaged. Through windows Kevin could see the ruins of one whole wing that had been abandoned. (As genuinely interested as he was in the effects of the earthquake and the pointers Salado was sharing with him on earthquake safety in California construction, Kevin was even more intrigued by the view of twinkling lights in the distance. Out there, somewhere—he wasn't sure where—was San Francisco.

"Down this way, Kevin," Salado led him to a set of escalators and down to what was obviously the baggage claim area. There were several rotating carousels with bags being loaded on them by porters. "The repair isn't finished. You can see they don't have the baggage conveyors working yet. Still doing that by hand."

Kevin stood beside Salado waiting. He thought he ought to be asking questions, but couldn't think of anything to ask. His eyes wandered through the crowd waiting for their bags. He noticed a young man about his own age. He seemed to look familiar: nice-looking, slim, longish hair—a cultured look. The young man was leaning against one of the thick pylons that supported the floor above. The cant of his hip, Kevin thought, gave him a sort of devil-may-care appearance that seemed simultaneously impertinent and appealing. As Kevin wondered for a moment if he might really recognize him as someone he knew, the young man noticed him and looked back.

For a moment Kevin found himself lost in the man's eyes. There was something magnetic about the gaze, something promising, alluring. Then a rush of anxiety ran through him; the gaze had obviously been held a moment too long… *Oh my God, what am I doing here?*

Kevin had no objections to people being gay. It was part of being human, he knew that. He just didn't want it to be about him.

"I'm sure these are the bags from your flight," Will Salado interrupted Kevin's anxiety attack.

"Oh, I'm sorry… I was thinking… uh, about being in California…"

Will laughed. "I remember that myself. Little bit of culture shock coming out here from the East Coast. But you'll like it. I promise."

I wonder if you know what you're saying, Kevin thought to himself. Then he saw his bag come around the carousel again. He felt a little stupid for a moment; the suitcase could've been jostling around for several turns. He reached out and grabbed it off the conveyor.

"That all you got?" Will asked.

"The rest of my things are coming by UPS next week. I thought I ought to give myself some time to find an apartment."

"Good thinking. *And* I think maybe I can help with that. One of the guys in the office owns a building over in Dolores Heights. Wasn't hurt too bad by the quake. Needs some work on the plaster. One of his tenants moved out recently. He said he'd be happy to let you have her apartment reasonable. Housing's pretty hard to come by, you know."

"Sounds great," Kevin answered as he followed Salado out of the baggage claim area.

"I've got a surprise for you. I borrowed this car so I could show you some of the sites," Will said turning off the freeway and heading down a bumpy road that must once have been the frontage road for another freeway, the elevated portion of which now lay in ruins. "You've never been here before, that right?"

"Nope. Guess I missed something, didn't I?" Kevin peered out the window at the broken and burned buildings.

"Well, there's been very little restoration down here on the peninsula. A lot of fires swept through here. Frankly this part of town was always an eyesore anyway. Once they get to fixing it up it'll be a helluva lot nicer than it was. Just last week we got asked to bid on a job down here that'd incorporate the structure of this freeway into a major shopping and apartment complex."

"Huh?"

"That's the newest thing out here. You'll be hearing a lot more about it. The City's being rebuilt around mass transit and superconductor trains instead of private automobiles."

"Oh yeah," Kevin answered quickly, "I've read about that."

"So the plan is to use the old freeway system as the foundation for new structures. The road spans broke in a lot of places, but the support structures held up pretty well."

"How come you're driving then?" Kevin asked innocently.

"Well, that's still way in the future. The light rail lines are just being put in now connecting the old BART and Metro systems with the surface buses.

"The first thing they did was get the buses running. With the cost of hydro so high these days and gasoline practically beyond the pale, people weren't driving. And for a while the roads were such a mess, who'd want to? Dump trucks were carrying away debris everywhere you went... To keep the City livable public transportation had to be working. And it is! And better than ever...

"Ah, now the road gets better," Will interrupted himself as he drove up a steep entrance ramp onto a stretch of elevated highway that was still intact. As their vantage point got higher, Kevin saw there were patches of city lights scattered all through the rolling hills.

"Is this San Francisco?"

Will laughed. "Not yet. I'm taking you in through the back way."

They rode along for another five or ten minutes in silence. Kevin was surprised how chilly the night was and how clear the air. He realized most of what he knew about California was based on his impressions from TV and movies of Los Angeles. San Francisco didn't seem anything like the crowded, smoggy beach city he'd imagined.

"Well, how's life in Medford?" Will interrupted his reverie.

"Oh, guess about the same as ever. You know Medford?" Kevin asked a little surprised.

"Grew up there myself. Thought I'd mentioned that on the phone the other day."

"Maybe. I guess I didn't remember. I was sort of nervous when you called."

"Oh yeah. Well, I suppose I know more about you than you know about me…"

For a moment Kevin's heart sank. *What did he mean by that?*

"I mean, I've seen your résumé. Know where you went to school and all that. By the way, you ever see ol' Fr. Shannon?"

Kevin had to think for a moment. Then realized Will was asking about the priest in the local parish. Kevin hadn't been to mass at the parish in a long time; when he'd gone with his mother during summers he hadn't paid much attention. At first the name didn't mean anything. *Fr. Shannon? Oh Lord.* It suddenly dawned on him who Fr. Shannon was. He felt that confusing upset feeling in his stomach. *What could Will know about Fr. Shannon? Why'd he bring him up?* "Guess I remember him from grade school. Haven't seen him in a long time."

"I was wondering if he was still alive. Had a big influence on me when I was a teenager back in the late '70s. He kinda kept me on the straight and narrow. These days I'm pretty grateful for that. Lot of my friends got into some pretty bad drug scenes. You know, back when I was growing up they didn't have the prescription moodies. Recreational drugs were all illegal and some pretty dangerous."

"I remember," Kevin answered, relieved that Will's recollection of the priest was apparently very different from his own.

"This is all San Francisco now," Will pointed out. They were driving through a residential district. Most of the houses appeared intact. Though scattered through the neighborhood were empty lots. "Lot of fires. Fortunately, they just hit individual houses instead of whole neighborhoods. The rain helped with that."

"Rain?"

"It was raining when the quake happened. That really was a godsend… Oh, but what a mess at the time! Well, I was saying, me and my kid sister grew up in Medford. Maybe you know her, Joan Salado. She's a reporter on CNN."

"Oh, yeah, I saw her doing some story about the Visitors."

"Right. There's a Visitor ship down near Riverside. She lives in that area. Nobody knows why that ship bothers to stay there. Sure seems kinda out of the way. What could be going on in Riverside that'd interest the Visitors?"

"I'm sorry, Will, you know I should have put your names together. My mom talks about Joan Salado all the time. I mean, I guess every time she comes on the TV. Mom always repeats the story about how we went to the same school. Every time Mom reminds me how Sister Margaret Mary Alacoque compared me to your sister and said I had a responsibility to the school to be a great success."

"Compared you to my sister, huh?" Will said jokingly. "I was Sister Margaret Mary's star pupil long before Joanie came along. And I'm probably a better example for you to follow than she is. I mean, you know, we're in the same profession and all that." Will seemed to realize he'd let a little sibling rivalry show. "Ever hear anything of Sister Alacoque?" Will turned off the steeply rising road they were on onto an even steeper road.

"Oooh, now this looks like the San Francisco I've seen in the movies," Kevin commented. "Oh, you know, my mom said she'd heard at church last week that Sister died recently. Out here in California some place."

"Hmm. That's too bad, I guess. Funny, you never think about nuns dying. I mean, even back when I had her she seemed ancient." Will made several sharp turns and then came out onto a flat stretch of road. Directly ahead were a couple of steep hills. One of them was crowned with a twisted mass of red and white steel girders topped with flashing aerial warning lights. "That used to be a big TV tower," Will anticipated Kevin's question. "This is called Twin Peaks. Now just wait."

A moment later Will turned the car around a horseshoe turn and suddenly one of the most spectacular sights Kevin had ever seen lay before them. "Tat-tah," Will announced. "The City of San Francisco."

It was like a garden of flickering gold and white and multicolored lights. They spread out from around the downtown center of tall buildings; some of the buildings were dark; some, even from this distance, were obviously broken and twisted. Dominating the skyline was a tall steeply pyramidal-shaped building that Kevin recognized as the famous Golden State Building. Angling out from the crowd of skyscrapers downtown was a broad, brightly-lit thoroughfare. "That's Market Street there," Will pointed out.

"It's all just beautiful," Kevin remarked. "And not as much damage as I expected."

"Let's get out. Notice the smell of the air. That's very characteristic of San Francisco. Here, I'll show you what the earthquake did."

"Try the chow mein sub gum with pan-fried noodles and, let's see, maybe shrimp with black bean sauce." Will was introducing Kevin to the exotic splendors and culinary delights of Chinatown. In the restaurant he'd chosen plywood panels were nailed up around the walls and the marble tiled floor bore deep cracks, but the place was appropriately dark and paper lanterns cast colored shadows that hid the trauma of a year ago. "This used to be one of the best places in Chinatown. The cook was killed during the quake and the food isn't quite so special anymore. But I still come here, if only for old times' sake." Will sighed. "I think we San Franciscans do a lot these days 'for old times' sake.'"

"You think of yourself as a San Franciscan?" Kevin asked, taking a sip of the Japanese Kirin beer.

"You will too. It may take you a while. But, you know, this city really grows on you. There's just something… well, something very special about the openness and acceptance of the people here. That's especially true since the quake. I mean all of us who lived through it are like a mystic brotherhood. There was a lot of talk last year about the survivors all being reincarnations of the survivors of Atlantis."

"You believe that?" Kevin asked hesitantly. It dawned on him that he really was in nutty California. He didn't want to offend Will—if only because he was probably going to be his supervisor—but that kind of talk sounded a little silly.

"If I were back home in Boston, I'd probably make fun of such ideas myself. But out here, well, especially if you'd been through it, it kinda makes sense. Oh, maybe not literally, but figuratively. Atlantis is a pretty good symbol of the idealized memories of the City we all share."

"Has it changed much?"

"Yes and no. A lot of the people died. The population's still less than half what it was then. Of course that's 'cause a lot of survivors moved away. I guess for some of them there were really bad memories here. Though, you know, no more earthquake danger. The fault is stabilized now for at least another hundred, hundred and fifty years. A lot of the people who stayed were the old time hippies. Most of them are pretty good people, some a little burnt out and spacey, but nice and friendly and easy going.

"A lot of gays moved here after the quake… I think some of them saw the quake as a chance to come reclaim turf… after AIDS and all."

Kevin wondered what he should say. He worried that anything he said would give something away. *Can Will see I'm nervous? Will he guess anything 'bout me? What in the hell is there to guess?*

"Besides," Will laughed, "there's a crying need for decorators these days. I heard a joke last week I don't remember, but the punch line was something like, 'you wouldn't believe what the queer eye can do with a few stalks of fennel, a broken wall, and some twisted track lights.'"

The word 'queer' burned Kevin. It was the labels that really bothered him. "Uh, uh, what was that about 'fennel'?" he asked nervously. He hadn't understood the joke at all.

"Fennel's a weed that grows all over everything out here. In Italian it's called *finocchio*, which is a slang word for homosexual. But anyway, the point of the joke is that, at least for a little while, there wasn't very much to work with here. But people—and maybe especially the gay men—were doing their best to fix up the ruins real nice."

"Do, uh, you, uh, mind all the homosexuals around here?"

"Oh, of course not. I don't suppose I'd want my sister to marry one of 'em," Will joked, taking a swig of his beer in an affectedly country red-neck gesture. "But, to tell the truth, I think Joan might do better with a Frisco faggot than that flyboy she's got now. But that's personal… Oh, and Kevin, don't you go calling San Francisco 'Frisco.' Faster than anything, that'll brand you as an outsider.

"And, quite seriously, for the sake of the firm and your own happiness, you need to learn to fit in. I mean in a way people here are grateful for all the help that's come to San Francisco by way of the recovery. But there're also a lot of hard feelings. You know, outsiders taking advantage of us, people trying to change the City, make it less diverse and multicultural. There are those preachers saying the quake was punishment for the City's openness; some of 'em, like that guy with the big tabernacle out by the Golden Gate, Billy McMasterson, are saying that since AIDS is about solved, God was having to take more desperate measures. Well, you know, natives around here don't like that kind of talk. This City was built on love-ins and rock 'n roll," Will laughed.

The waiter, a young Asian man dressed in a crisp white button up jacket, arrived with a tray of food. Setting it down on the corner of the table, he did a perfunctory little bow and then placed the covered bowls in the middle of the table. "Chow mein with pan-fried noodle. Shrimp with black bean. Steam rice. Anything else, sir?"

In spite of all he'd eaten today, the food smelled wonderful. And Kevin was feeling a little more secure tonight since Will's talk about acceptance and openness. *Maybe San Francisco*—he said the name to himself carefully, syllable by syllable—*isn't going to be so bad after all.*

As Will was serving himself some of the white rice and then topping it with the black bean shrimp, he looked up at Kevin, "You know, whatever they say, San Francisco couldn't be a bad place. After all, this is one of the cities the Visitors want to come to."

"*W*ell, Kevin, are you up for more of San Francisco tonight," Will asked as they walked out of the Chinese restaurant into the cold night air, "or are you ready to go back to the hotel?"

"I'm exhausted, Will. And I imagine you must be getting tired too. I'd be happy to get settled in my room."

"That's nearby. We've set you up in the Hyatt Union Square. Nice place. Real plush. And don't you worry about the cost. For the first two weeks the company's picking up the tab. Which—just between you and me," Will whispered conspiratorially, "—isn't going to cost the company a cent. We did the rebuilding and they give us a *very* good deal on rooms." He grinned. "Besides, it'll be a chance for you to see some of the firm's work. We're pretty proud of that job."

"Sounds good. And I hope I won't be in the hotel long. I'd like to get an apartment soon. I hope that place you mentioned works out."

"Remind me in the morning to talk with Sam, make sure the offer's still open. Maybe he can take you over there to see it tomorrow." Will looked at his wristwatch. "Speaking of the morning. It's time we both got some sleep. You're due in the office at 9 a.m. sharp."

"Will," Kevin grinned embarrassed. "Where *is* the office?"

Will laughed. "Good question. It's in walking distance. Let's leave the car here; we'll come back for your suitcase." Will started off down Grant Avenue with Kevin behind. Will continued to point out features of the rebuilding.

At one point they had to climb along a narrow path over piles of debris. "This used to be a tunnel," Will explained. "The whole thing collapsed. There's a plan now to build pedestrian walkways up there," he pointed up at the broken edges of the steep hills on either side. "And," he proclaimed as they came out onto flat ground again, "there is the hotel."

Rising above bulldozed lots and small mountains of debris, stood a graceful tower glittering with bright white and brassy golden lights.

"But we're going this way," Will said, turning left and leading Kevin on a few blocks further.

They soon came upon a modern six-storey building standing isolated in the center of a bulldozed tract. Even in the blue-white glare of the streetlights and distorted color of neon signs, the building, all chrome and marble, looked impressive. "Here we are. The main offices are up on the third floor there where the lights are on. Hmm, looks like somebody's up there. Wanna go see?"

"If it's okay, sure."

Will led Kevin through a street level garden under a graceful marquee-like structure which, in marble and bronze bore the name: "**SUTRO & ASSOCIATES, Architects**" and in smaller letters: "**Joining in the Rebuilding**." Beyond the glass-enclosed lobby was a concealed night entrance. Will waved his hand over a thin silver plate in the wall, RFID'ing himself by the implant in his wrist, and instantly a panel in the marble facade swung away.

"Neat," Will remarked as he ushered Kevin in. "The elevators are down this hall."

Kevin was impressed by the authority with which Salado waved them through the electronic security, but a little wary of having to get that kind of implant in his own wrist. Back at Harvard, in spite of Administration pressure to enable student tracking, he'd declined to get the radio broadcasting I.D. device inserted in his body. Even then he was aware that someday there might be places he'd want to go where he wouldn't want *anybody* knowing he'd been.

As the shiny brass doors of the otherwise all glass elevator slid open on the third floor, Will called out, "Hello. Anybody home?"

A moment later a well-dressed, slightly older and distinguished looking man appeared at the doorway leading into the office area off the elevator lobby. He had his finger to his lips in the familiar gesture.

Silently extending his hand, Will led Kevin across the expanse of the lobby. "This is Joe Sykes," he whispered, "one of the associate partners. Kevin Anderson, the new intern in my department," he added to Sykes.

Shaking Kevin's hand amiably, Sykes whispered, "We're having a meeting. You'll probably be interested in seeing this. Both of you," he added, obviously not intending Kevin to feel left out.

Kevin was grateful for that. He was feeling surprisingly anxious tiptoeing around this impressive, but stark building late at night.

"Wait'll you see who's here," Sykes grinned at Will as he beckoned for them to follow.

Kevin stayed right behind Will. Sykes led them past a couple of open doors through which, in the subdued light, Kevin could see tastefully decorated offices. As they entered the brightly lit conference room, Kevin recognized this as the room they'd seen from the street. There was glass on two walls through which he could see the buildings and vacant spaces Will had led him through. Rising above the nearby buildings was the graceful tower he recognized as the Hyatt Hotel.

Sykes gestured them to two dark maroon leather-upholstered chairs. Only after they'd sat down did Kevin begin to pay attention to the six men sitting about the broad glass table in the center of the room. Directly across from him he recognized the man who was speaking, Jules Domergue, the President of Sutro & Associates. He'd met Mr. Domergue at Harvard six months ago. That had been the occasion for his applying for this position.

"Of course, we'd be *very* interested in the project. This firm has long been committed to the future of San Francisco and we're very pleased you've decided to locate your, uh, uh, office here."

Only as the impressively white-haired Domergue stumbled over his words did Kevin look away from the familiar face to see the—he supposed—prospective client he was addressing. And as he did and just as the client began to answer in the accented speech Kevin had only heard before on television, Kevin's heart skipped a beat.

"We hope this association will bring success and good fortune to all of us," answered the Visitor sitting a couple of chairs down the table. Kevin's view of the impressive—though slightly unnerving—figure had been blocked by Sykes and another man sitting at the table.

The Visitor turned and looked around the room. "I will bring the plans over to you in the morning. Then I or my secretary will be in touch with you tomorrow evening regarding your understanding of our needs and specifications." As the Visitor noticed the two newcomers, he smiled, looking directly, first at Will and then at Kevin.

Oh God, Kevin thought excitedly and a little childishly he realized, *won't Mom and Jeff be green with envy when they hear about this! And,* Kevin thought, growing a little anxious with the private thought, *isn't he handsome!*

They're even more beautiful in person than on TV. No wonder people are calling them angels. Though, I suppose, he corrected himself, *people probably wouldn't call this one an angel. Wrong color. Too chalky gray to look like the usual angel.*

Chapter Four

"*C*mon, Kevin, you belong in this meeting too," Will Salado called to Kevin, distracting him from the careful and tedious calculation of steel girder specifications he'd been doing all morning as his first assignment as an intern for Sutro & Associates.

"I'll be right there," Kevin answered, not looking up from the display screen of the computer he was using.

Will walked over and slapped Kevin on the back. "It's okay. We can see you're committed to this job. You don't have to overwork yourself." Will reached down and fed the SAVE command into the console. "Besides, I think you'll find this meeting interesting. You already know more about it than most everybody else around here."

Kevin smiled as he stood up and followed Will. *Okay, I'll be happy to stop work and see what this is about.* He figured it must be about the Visitors, since that was the only thing about the company he had any inside info on.

"I think we're very fortunate to get this job," Jules Domergue was saying. "It'll pay very well. The Visitors are offering gold bullion and they've made a very generous offer. Someday," he added as an aside, "somebody's gonna have to find out whether this gold is a precious metal to them. For all we know they're paying us in what they think of as iron. It'll be interesting once we start buying things from them. What are they gonna want?"

"Mr. Domergue, you bring up a good point."

"Yes, Chuck, what is that?" Domergue answered Chuck Sperry, a thin, red-faced man who was sitting at the back of the room.

"How do we know we can trust the Visitors? I mean, what if this gold isn't real? Or what if they're flooding our economy with gold in order to ruin us? They could, couldn't they?"

"You've got a point. I guess we just *have* to trust them. Otherwise trade relations will never get started. But you're right that our economy could suffer if we let them devalue our monetary systems. But I think the real responsibility lies with us. We have to be honest in what we take from them. Say we charged them a billion for this one million dollar building. That'd make this firm a lot of money, but hurt the economy. If we're fair with them and equitable with our own competitors, well, then things'll work out okay."

"For the record," Sperry spoke up, "I don't trust 'em. I don't think they're human, regardless of what they look like, and…"

"Have you ever talked to a Visitor?" Domergue interrupted.

"Hell no."

"C'mon, Chuck, that's not a very good attitude."

"Sorry, sir."

Kevin observed Sperry's apology seemed based more of his fear of Domergue's power over his job than it was sincere.

"Well, I have. I mean, we have. Just last night we talked at length with a Visitor. They've obviously gone out of their way to accommodate themselves to us. I mean they speak our language. They're willing to do things our way. And everything about them just exudes trust."

"I think that's why we'd better be careful," Sperry answered.

"Well, okay, you've made your point. Now as I was saying," Domergue continued, "besides financial rewards, we stand to gain a helluva lot of knowledge from this job. And I want all of you to be looking for new technology incorporated into their plans."

"How come they're getting us to build their building for them instead of doing it themselves?" someone in the crowded room asked.

"Maybe this is precisely to avoid giving us their technology," someone else answered. "Once they leave we'll have only our own building, not something of theirs."

"You may be right about that, Jeff," Domergue replied. "But maybe they're just busy; maybe they didn't bring along any construction crews; maybe they just want to do business with us in order to establish good relations."

"What is this building going to be anyway?" another voice asked.

"The U.S. government has given permission for the Visitors to set up 'embassies' in a couple of the major cities they've asked to visit and study. They're apparently quite interested in learning how we live. They seem especially interested in San Francisco. I have a theory, by the way, that they're interested in how we cope with disaster. That's certainly something significant about this city."

"That sounds like they're studying how to defeat us," Chuck Sperry offered another negative viewpoint.

"Or they see they can learn something from us," Domergue answered.

"Maybe they're interested in how our different cultures interrelate," Will Salado turned the conversation back to positive speculation. "I mean, they must have some pretty complex racial dynamics themselves, with as many colors of them as there seem to be. San Francisco's a pretty good example of how different cultures get along together on Earth."

"Maybe they like nightlife. This is a pretty good place to party," said one of the men in back.

"Oh, George," somebody else groaned.

"No, I mean it."

"Well, look, everybody," Jules Domergue got the floor back. "Here's how I'm assigning this job…"

As Domergue read a list of names and duties that meant very little to him, Kevin peered around at the man named George. He'd heard something in his tone of voice that sounded, well, familiar. Indeed, there was something about how this guy looked, something that reminded Kevin of, of, he wasn't sure what. Maybe it was the same thing he recognized in that guy at the airport the other day. Maybe something that reminded him of Tim.

"Anderson," Kevin was pulled out of his thoughts by the sound of his name. "In case you haven't met our new guy, this is Kevin Anderson, everybody," Domergue announced. "Kevin, you'll be doing general go-fer for the time being. Give you a chance to see how we do things around here. But I know from our talk back in Boston you're especially interested in virtual design. The Visitors have given us some very detailed specs that'll need to be converted into standard design models; that virtual app you wrote oughta make that a snap. I bet you'd like to work on the Visitor project, so I'm going to assign you to the team. Besides, there'll be a lot of site visits, not just working at your terminal. That'll give you a chance to see more of the City too. How's that?"

"Thank you, sir," Kevin spoke up. He was pleased with how nice the people were around here.

"George Sanders, you take charge of the Visitor site team."

Kevin looked up to see George, the gay man, staring right into his eyes. *Uh-ho*, he thought. *What are they getting me into?* He wished he were still wearing his glasses.

"Louise, you work on that too."

Well, at least there's a woman, Kevin thought as he looked around the room to see who Louise was. *Hmm, pretty*, he thought, then felt the emptiness that was part of what had been bothering him for years.

"This is a pretty strange building," one of the architects was saying as he and several others stood around a drafting table in the general work room poring over the plans George Sanders had just brought down from Jules Domergue's office.

"What is this tower for, for instance?"

"For the view, Dick, what else?" George answered. "You take note of that, by the way, Kevin," George shouted over to Kevin who was back at his computer console finishing the steel support specs.

"What's that, sir?" Kevin spoke up, hearing his name.

"George, call me George," Sanders answered, "anything but sir." He put his outstretched hand to his breast, threw his head back, and rolled his eyes up into his head, "It makes me sound o-o-ld," he coo'ed. "I am *not* your father, young man."

Kevin blushed with embarrassment. "Okay, George. Sorry. I missed what you'd said."

"Oh, I said make a note that this tower ought to have a good view."

"Got it," Kevin answered obediently. He noticed that none of the other men had reacted at all to George's outrageous little act.

"Well, George, tell me what this here is for," Dick Jularian continued his critique of the Visitor plans.

"Good question," George answered, sounding serious again.

Dick was pointing at what seemed to be a spiral-shaped structure inside a small cubical chamber in the center of the building.

"Kevin, look at this. Maybe you'll recognize it," George called.

As Kevin came over, one of the other architects on the team observed, "Well, according to this legend down here that spiral-shaped thing is supposed to be completely mirrored. And, look over here at the horizontal projection, the floor and walls slope toward each other."

"It looks like a sea shell," Kevin commented.

"Yeah, but why?" Dick asked the obvious question.

"Could it be a loud speaker? Or some kind of surveillance device?" George queried.

"Seems to be stationary," Jularian answered.

"Maybe an antenna," Kevin spoke up.

"Good idea," George answered. "E.T. phone home," he said in a high-pitched broken voice.

"Huh?" said Kevin.

"George, you're dating yourself," Dick warned laughing.

George cleared his throat, "E.T. dime home!" he corrected himself with current lingo, and then winked at Kevin.

"And the specifications call for exact stereotactic placement of that cubical chamber," Jularian continued to express his bafflement. "They want it at exactly that spot. Why?"

"And where do these steps go?" someone else in the circle pointed out another peculiarity of the design.

"Look," Dick answered, "here's an obviously alien way of doing things. Each floor has its own stairs leading to it. They don't connect floor to floor."

"Maybe a security measure."

"I thought these Visitors were supposed to be so trustworthy. How come they need such security?" replied Dick Jularian.

"Maybe just to separate business areas from residential," Kevin spoke up. "They have a right to some privacy."

"I think there's something fishy about them," a man Kevin didn't recognize commented.

Kevin felt a little angry at those kinds of remarks. Especially now that he'd actually seen a Visitor up close, he was feeling defensive on their behalf.

"You know, I kinda did too," George responded. "I know better than to trust a pretty face," he tapped his temple with his forefinger as if to say I've gained some wisdom. "But when I was just talking with that Visitor up in Jules' office, well, I just couldn't help but like him. It wasn't just his looks—"

"Yeah, we know—" Dick teased George.

"No, I mean it. It was like there was something so magnetic and so natural about him. Well, well, it really was like talking with an angel or something. I mean, he was just so natural—except, I suppose, for that funny color, kind of bluish-green."

Bluish-green? Kevin wondered. *He was dark gray.*

Well, maybe this was a different one, maybe the secretary, he explained away the inconsistency.

"*It*'s such a pretty day. Why don't you roam around some out here? I need to get home. My kid's day care is closing early today. But there's no reason for you to go back to the office."

"Thanks, Louise. Sounds like a good idea. This really is beautiful."

"Yeah, I'm glad the Visitors picked this spot. Great view of the Bridge. You know, whenever you're feeling down, I say the best medicine in San Francisco is to come out here, maybe out to Fort Point, and gaze up at the Golden Gate Bridge. It's just so big and so grand, makes you forget about yourself. Especially at sunset, when the bridge color reverberates with the orange in the sun. Magical.

"I've been doin' it for years, even back when this area was Crissy Airfield. Just don't look up that way." She made a face and rolled her eyes, as if to show professional scorn for the huge, blocky church building, still surrounded with scaffolding from the quake damage repairs, that dominated the hillside above the Rumsfeld Research Park where the Visitors had insisted their embassy be located.

"You remember that, Kevin. The Golden Gate Bridge. Sunset. Now, you're sure you can get home okay?"

"Let's see. I take the 96 Seacliff Heights shuttle up there on Mason Street toward downtown and transfer at Lombard to the 45 Stockton or the 41 Union. Those would take me back to the office. But to get home, transfer at Fillmore, uh, going to the left?"

"No, going to the right," Louise answered. The two of them— sometimes the three of them, when George Sanders could come along— had been out here several times in the past week. It had gotten to be a joke that Kevin could not keep track of his directions. ("This is the most confusing city I've ever seen," he'd complain exasperatedly while Louise and George laughed and George consoled him that when he first moved out here he'd been lost most of the time too.)

"Oh, okay, then that'll connect with the Church Street line…?"

"If you got on the car that says '30th & Church,' otherwise you have to change at Market."

"Then I get off at Church and 22nd and walk down the hill and I'm home." Kevin rattled off the last leg of the trip with ease. He'd done that successfully several times now since he'd gotten settled in the apartment in Sam Long's building on Fair Oaks Street.

"Sounds like you can do it," Louise said cheerfully. Kevin grinned. He'd come to like Louise Hoffman a lot. He'd been disappointed to learn she was married. Even though he wasn't sure what good it'd do him, he'd wanted to maintain the fantasy, at least, that she was available to him for, *uh, possible courtship*. Bisexual was a label Kevin didn't feel so hemmed in by; it sounded sort of classical. Anyway, they'd become friends.

"Well, Kev, don't get lost now. If you've got time, take my advice and walk out to Fort Point under the ramps to the Bridge. But don't fall in. I mean that," she reiterated, seeing his nonchalance. "People have gotten washed over the edge by waves or they've slipped and fallen. And that was before the quake. It's worse now. The paths haven't been restored, so you don't know where they lead."

"Well, maybe I'll stay down here in the Research Park rather than go toward the Bridge. Think that would safer?"

"Probably not. Maybe it's even more dangerous around here. I mean some of these broken foundations might give way under you. But, hey, you'll be okay. Look, I gotta run. See you tomorrow."

Thirty minutes later, Kevin was wondering if he were lost. He wasn't sure where he was. He'd gotten on the Seacliff Heights shuttle, but, he discovered, going the wrong way. Instead of back to town, the bus took him around to the other side of the Bridge. *Maybe I'll do a little sightseeing.* From the bus he'd noticed a darkly tanned, muscly man in a bathing suit out among the trees off the road. When everybody else on the bus got off at the next stop, he followed them. The other riders all crossed the street and looked like they were walking up into a residential neighbor.

Kevin'd be the last one off. Hesitating, he must've looked lost or uncertain, 'cause the driver spoke to him. "Going down to Jackie O?" he asked, with a certain knowingness in his voice that Kevin didn't get.

"Jackie O?"

"The beach," the driver answered. When Kevin still looked blank the driver went on, "The Jacqueline Bouvier Kennedy Onassis Memorial State Beach. It's down at the bottom of the cliffs." He pointed towards a wooded path leading off from the street. "Over that way."

"Oh, I don't know."

"Well, then you should," the driver announced jauntily. "You'll like it."

"Thanks," Kevin answered, jumping off the bus. "Maybe I will."

"Have fun." The driver winked.

Kevin was on his own. He followed the path the driver had pointed out. Somewhere nearby there was supposed to be a beach, and the day was still relatively warm. Partly out of geographical curiosity and partly out of an urge he didn't want to put a name to, he was trying to find that beach and that bathing-suited man he'd seen earlier. He figured he couldn't get too lost. There were people roaming around in the woods alongside the remains of what must once have been a paved road.

As he reached the top of a rise, he saw he could see the beach below. There were several bodies lying on the sand in the sun. *But it's so cold*, he thought to himself, and zipped his jacket up to further shield himself from the strong wind blowing up the hillside from the ocean. *How does anybody manage to take their clothes off to get a tan?* But there they were, he could see, bare bodies lying in the late afternoon sun.

Still peering toward the beach, hoping to see where the broken roadbed led to, Kevin took a step forward and then felt the ground go out from under him. "Whoa-a-a," he heard himself exclaim. As he slid down a sandy slope he remembered Louise Hoffman's warning about broken concrete and managed to look back to see that the paved path had ended abruptly at the top of that rise.

He heard an accented voice calling out from the top of the slope he'd just slid down, "Are you all right?"

Kevin turned and looked up to see—to his surprise—a golden-haired Visitor crouched down and reaching out his hand in an obvious offer of assistance. As he tried to stand up, the ground slipped out from under him again. He wasn't sure if that was more nervousness than lack of agility. This time he reached up and took the Visitor's hand. The touch felt almost electric. With a little jump, assisted by the Visitor's pull, he climbed right up the slope, swung around, and in a moment was standing next to the Visitor, in fact, standing almost right up against the Visitor—who'd made no attempt at all to step out of the way.

Kevin took a step back and brushed himself off. To his surprise, as he pulled his hand out of the Visitor's, the tall, golden-haired, golden-eyed alien reached up and laid his hand on Kevin's shoulder in a gesture of what seemed like comradeship and concern. To Kevin the gesture was confusingly comforting, exciting, and frightening. He could almost still feel the "electricity" radiating through his jacket and shirt.

"Thank you," he said, taking another step back so the alien had to drop his hand. For a moment it looked as if the Visitor were going to move with him to avoid losing contact, but then he too seemed to think better of it and took a step back himself, stepping back right over the break in the path that had been the cause of Kevin's fall a moment ago. Losing his balance, the Visitor started to fall over backwards. There was nothing for Kevin to do but the spontaneous and the obvious. Lurching forward, he grabbed the Visitor around the shoulders with both arms and pulled him away from the edge.

Suddenly the Visitor started laughing happily. He clasped Kevin to his chest and hugged him tight. (Kevin was surprised at himself to see how spontaneously and unself-consciously he responded to the hug.) Then, guiding them both away from the precarious break in the path, the Visitor ceremoniously extended his hand. He nodded to Kevin, with a quizzical look in his eyes, to do likewise.

"I'm Tuarul, er, 'Belwyn Tuarul," the Visitor announced.

It took Kevin a second to realize the Visitor had spoken his name.

"My name is Kevin Anderson," he replied.

"Are you all right, Kevin Anderson? Were you hurt by your fall?"

"Oh no, I'm okay. Are you? You almost fell over too."

"That was fun, Kevin Anderson."

"Oh, just call me Kevin," Kevin corrected. He realized he'd come across a Visitor who didn't seem versed in Earth ways.

"Then I am just 'Bel."

"I'm glad to meet you. You know, you're the first Visitor I've met." He looked down at the ground. "I guess I'm a little nervous."

"I too," the Visitor said. "I'm only just becoming acquainted with your world. And I too am glad to meet you. Your look and color are lovely to me and appealing."

"Well, thank you," Kevin answered nervously. He hadn't expected a Visitor to be so, well, so forward. *Is he coming on to me?* "What are you doing out here?" he changed the subject.

"I am assigned to the Sociology Team. We're studying human behavior."

"What're you studying out here?" Kevin asked.

"I was going to see the beach."

"That part of your study?"

"An important part."

"Well, then, let's go," Kevin suggested, ill-at-ease with trying to make conversation.

As they climbed down the sandy incline between broken pieces of concrete, 'Bel reached out to take Kevin's hand. Kevin accepted the assistance, but immediately pulled his hand away. He didn't understand why the Visitor was being so touchy.

"What are *you* doing out here, Kevin?" the Visitor asked after a few minutes of silence as they wound their way down the hillside.

"Something to do with your people, in fact. I work for the architecture firm that's designing the Visitor embassy. It's over on the other side. Maybe you know. I was out here earlier with a couple of my co-workers. We were making measurements and stuff."

"You are an architect?"

"Well, I will be. I'm just an intern now. Uh, that means I'm just starting," Kevin explained.

"Me too. I'm also an intern," the Visitor used the word smoothly.

Noticing his tone with what he'd thought would be a new word, Kevin asked, "You know, I've been curious about how well you people speak English. Did you train a long time before you came here?"

"Yes, a little," 'Bel replied. He seemed distracted. Kevin noticed he was staring intently down toward the bottom of the slope.

"But doesn't it take a lot of effort to learn our language?"

"It's not all that different. I didn't…" 'Bel answered, then obviously changed the subject quite suddenly. "Look, aren't there men in the bushes down there?" He pointed.

Kevin peered in the direction of 'Bel's extended finger. He thought he saw somebody. *Probably one of the swimmers.* He could see flesh. As he looked closer, he realized that there were two men there. Naked.

Suddenly he felt embarrassed. This whole thing was proving very embarrassing. "You know, we shouldn't go down there."

"Why is that, Kevin?"

"Well, I mean, I mean, it's not polite. Here, let's go this way. We can get right down to the beach," Kevin said grabbing 'Bel's hand momentarily and dragging him after him—away from the men in the bushes. The Visitor followed obediently.

"What did you say you were studying?" Kevin asked, hoping to avoid an embarrassing discussion.

"I'm on the Sexual Behavior Team," 'Bel answered casually.

Oh my God, thought Kevin.

"We're studying homosexual behavior among Earth people."

"Why would you be interested in, uh, something like that?"

"Oh, it's very interesting, isn't it?" 'Bel answered innocently. "Aren't you interested?"

"Me? Why do you think I'd be interested?"

"You're out here."

"Whaddya mean?" Kevin blurted out.

"According to the guidebooks, this is the gay beach." 'Bel extended his hand, turning around in a circle. "The whole area west of here was once a major center for sexual and outdoor social activities. Since the earthquake, when that whole neighborhood slid into the ocean, the action's moved over this direction."

"I told you," Kevin said firmly, "I was out here on business for the firm. Maybe I should ask you the same question." He felt his heart racing.

"I can see why the gay community socializes out here. The view is beautiful, isn't it?" the Visitor said innocently. "It makes me homesick."

"Is your world like ours?" Kevin asked, glad to get the subject onto something else. He turned and looked out at the sweeping view of the windswept hills and crashing ocean.

"Yes, it is," 'Bel answered quietly, hesitantly.

Now Kevin was surprised by the alien's tone of voice. He turned around and started to ask if something were wrong. He was shocked to see that the Visitor suddenly seemed to have changed color. Where a moment ago, he'd looked beautifully golden in the afternoon sun, now he was greenish-blue. And getting darker even as Kevin watched. "What's happening to you?" he exclaimed.

"I said something I wasn't supposed to," 'Bel answered.

"But what's happened to you? You're turning green."

"I'm not supposed to talk about that either," 'Bel said, turning even darker. "I wasn't supposed to let this happen." He sat down on a rock near his feet and buried his face in his hands. "I promised I wouldn't let it happen if they'd let me not take the pills," he mumbled half to himself. He seemed to be crying.

Kevin reached out and touched him on the head in a cautious effort to comfort him. For all that he was unnerved, Kevin felt a rush of warmth and concern for the troubled Visitor. Kevin had always had a soft place in his heart for kittens and puppies and sometimes for people who seemed distressed or in trouble. Something about the Visitor seemed to trigger those feelings.

Kevin was surprised to see that where he touched him, the scalp under 'Bel's almost translucent straw-colored hair turned from the muddy bluish-green back to gold. "What's happening to you?" he repeated his question.

'Bel looked up at him sheepishly. "I've done everything wrong today. This is my first day out by myself. And I did everything wrong." After a moment, he added softly, "It was because I saw you, Kevin." The Visitor's face was lightening noticeably.

Kevin felt a wave of dread. *What's going on?* All of a sudden he'd learned more about the Visitors than he'd had any inkling. He realized 'Bel had inadvertently told him too much. He'd told him about English being easy to learn. He'd told him their world was like Earth. And he'd shown him that somehow the Visitors change color.

Kevin had been surprised at how many different colors the Visitors seemed to come in. But he'd assumed those were like different races. He'd had no idea they could change like, *well, like chameleons.*

"I didn't want to take the drugs to stop the change. They make me nauseous and I think they're wrong. They just create perversion… I, er, wasn't expecting to talk to anybody. I mean I knew I'd be in golden out here. That was the idea."

"What do you mean?"

"I spoke to you even though I hadn't intended to," the Visitor answered softly. "I, I couldn't just let you fall. And you reminded me of somebody…" His voice sounded wistful but strained. "And now I've even let you see too much." The bluish-green color darkened noticeably.

"You mean you'll get in trouble? Look, 'Bel, I won't tell anybody. Promise! You don't have to tell anybody that you talked to me."

'Bel smiled. His face turned golden again. "It isn't like that, Kevin. I mean, I could never, uh, lie. But it's so sweet of you." He reached out his hand toward Kevin who hesitantly took it for a moment.

"Uh, look, 'Bel, maybe we'd better be getting back. I mean, I've got to get back. You can go down to the beach if you want. But I gotta go." Kevin was feeling a very strange fluttering in his abdomen. He could feel his skin flushing all over his body. Maybe it was because of the strange transformation he'd seen in the Visitor or maybe it was something else. But suddenly he felt very self-conscious about blushing. And he knew he couldn't help it.

"Will you come here again?" 'Bel asked.

"I guess so," Kevin answered hesitantly.

"I hope I'll see you again." 'Bel replied. "I hope I haven't scared you."

"No, no." Kevin intentionally looked at his wristwatch—and then felt guilty about the subterfuge. "It's just that I've got to go now." He reached out to shake hands.

The Visitor, still sitting, took Kevin's hand gently in his and drew it to his cheek. "Goodbye, then, Kevin Anderson."

Kevin turned and started up the hill. Running. He didn't know what to make of that last gesture. Maybe that was just as common among the Visitors as shaking hands on Earth. *But, but… it seemed so wistful, so intimate.*

Chapter Five

Kevin's new apartment on Fair Oaks Street was a typical San Francisco Victorian railroad flat. The front door opened directly into a long hallway off which the two bedrooms, bathroom, water closet, living room and connected dining room were situated like compartments in a train car. At the back, the hall—the wainscotting along which was painted in brilliant kelly green—opened into the kitchen. Behind the kitchen was a small glassed utility porch which opened out to a redwood deck and backstairs that appeared to have been added since the earthquake. The building had survived both major San Francisco quakes.

From the deck, Kevin could look out into the backyards, separated by high wooden fences, of the other houses on the block. Used to the relative flatness of the Boston suburbs, Kevin thought these yards clinging to the steep backside of Dolores Heights a veritable hanging gardens. As he marvelled at the brilliant magenta of a bougainvillea that had completely overgrown a tree halfway up the block, he mulled over his experiences during the past three weeks.

Already, he knew, construction on the foundation of the Visitor embassy had begun. The Visitors were in a rush to get settled, it appeared. Kevin couldn't blame them. *For all that the design of the embassy seems strange to us, it'll seem just like home to them.* Kevin recalled how unsettled he'd felt in the week and a half he'd lived in the Hyatt, in spite of its luxury.

Actually he hadn't been thinking much about the Visitors lately. Though he was assigned to the embassy project, Will Salado had had him doing paper work and math calculations on a variety of projects that so far hadn't included anything in the embassy except the costing out of that still inexplicable shell or horn-like structure that was going up as soon as the foundation was completed.

Kevin did not mind being less involved with the project. He had been almost as frightened as he was intrigued by his meeting with the handsome Visitor in the woods above the beach. He was consciously avoiding thinking about that too much. Indeed he was consciously avoiding most everything except work and repair of his apartment. In exchange for a break in the rent, he'd agreed to repaint the walls, which had been recently patched where the plaster had been broken. The kelly green had been his idea—a daring one that proved to be very attractive. Kevin was proud of his taste in colors.

Tonight was practically the first time he'd come and stood out on this porch, the first time he'd paid much attention to the neighborhood outside his door. Now standing on the three-storey high deck, enjoying the chill of the early evening, Kevin felt pleased to have found such a marvelous place to live. But he was feeling lonely. He was already beginning to think it would be nice to find a roommate for the second bedroom. It would help pay the rent. And he'd have somebody to talk with.

He'd tried calling home to Medford a few minutes before coming out to the back porch, but he had not found anyone at home. He'd been disappointed. He missed his family, especially his mother. He missed her idiosyncrasies and occasionally inept expressions of affection and concern for her family. At the same time, he felt relieved that he wasn't going to have to deal with parental questions about his personal life— as though he had any personal life.

The only subject he'd felt comfortable talking about with them— especially because he knew it both excited and rankled his little brother Jeff—was his experience with meeting Visitors. Every time he called his mother repeated the speculation, widely proclaimed in the tabloids in the grocery store checkout lines, that the Visitors were really angels come to oversee the salvation of the Earth. Even so, he had been circumspect in reporting any details about his experience at that beach.

Tonight, thinking about the Visitors seemed to exacerbate his loneliness. He remembered how appealing that Visitor guy had been— 'Bel, he corrected himself, *after all, he's a real person and deserves to be called by name*—how easy and open. He wondered if he'd ever see him again. All of a sudden he felt foolish about how freaked out he'd gotten that afternoon. *Why did I run off? My God, what an opportunity! To talk face to face with someone from outer space. And I screwed it up by getting nervous and acting silly.*

- - -

Kevin's father had given him his first laptop on his fourteenth birthday. Before that he'd been expected to use the family computer in the back corner of the living room, where his and Jeff's computer use could be parentally monitored. The birthday present allowed him to take his wireless laptop everywhere he went. Kevin was turning shy and reclusive at that age and was grateful to have the cyberworld to escape into. Occasionally, late at night, under the bedcovers to hide the glow of the screen, he looked at porn sites on the web, but found them unsettling and creepy—especially the photos of women all painted and posed in contrived stances that were supposed to look sexy. He didn't think the women looked sexy; they looked unnatural. The men on the gay sites looked more natural, but just accessing the sites made Kevin nervous. He never went beyond the splash pages; he was under 21, after all, and there were warnings.

It was his playing with that laptop that got Kevin interested in computer-assisted design, and his growing shyness that turned him toward math and engineering. He sometimes thought it was his dad's gift of that laptop that later got him into Harvard.

That summer the family spent a couple of weeks in Maine at that backwoods resort his dad loved. It wasn't quite so backwoods anymore. There was a Starbuck's with a wi-fi hotspot nextdoor to their motel that allowed Kevin to watch web-cable movies on the laptop. He fell in love with old movies on the archive and nostalgia channels that summer. The black and white movies from the previous century allowed him all the escape a shy teenager could want.

A scene from one of those old movies—he thought maybe it was called "I Married An Angel"—came back to him now as he thought about 'Bel and the Visitors and the media hype that was likening them to supernatural messengers. 'Bel certainly had demonstrated the innocence and honesty that went with that identity.

Kevin pictured 'Bel in his favorite scene from the old movie. He imagined the Visitor meeting an elderly fat lady dressed in an elegant, but tent-like, evening gown. That was the set-up in the movie.

"I hope this dress doesn't make me look fat," the lady says.

"Oh no, Madam," 'Bel replies, just like the angel in the movie, "the dress doesn't make you look fat. You *are* fat."

As a boy, Kevin had longed for the chance to deliver that line. He longed to be that honest and innocent and straightforward. But the chance never came. And as he grew older he learned to hide thoughts like that... and *other* thoughts he knew shouldn't be spoken about.

Kevin became aware of cooking smells wafting through the evening air. He had just stuck a microwave dinner in the oven for himself. Kevin thought about inviting 'Bel to dinner, though, of course, he wasn't sure such a thing would be possible. He had no idea what the Visitors ate— *if they even eat.*

"Well, hello up there."

Kevin looked around. He was sure he'd heard somebody call. Just then he perceived the screeching of rusty hinges. He looked down to see the back gate be pushed open by a man with arms full of groceries.

"Hello," the man shouted again. "I saw you from the alley." He let the gate swing closed with a bang. "I'm Joel Horstman," he continued talking as he walked through the narrow yard and disappeared into the scaffolding of the deck and stairs under Kevin. "I live next door to you."

"Hello," Kevin answered, "I'm Kevin, uh..."

"Keep talking, I'm on my way up."

Kevin could feel the vibration in the stairs. A moment later a handsome, though windblown, blond-haired man, looking just a little older than Kevin, arrived out of breath at the top of the stairs.

"I tell you. Every time I climb these fucking stairs I say to myself, 'Honey, now is the time to stop smoking.' But," he said balancing the grocery bags on the top railing, "I just bought a new carton." He produced a carton of cigarettes from one of the bags. "Hav'ta wait till next week to stop." Sticking the cigarettes back in the bag, he reached out his hand to Kevin. "Welcome to the building."

"Thanks, I've been here a couple of weeks."

"I know. I've heard you over there working away. I knew it needed work. The previous tenant never did anything to repair the place. Good to meet you. Here, help me with this," Joel ordered peremptorily. He was losing his grip on one of the bags. "If you help me get this inside, I'll fix us a cup of coffee."

Kevin grabbed the grocery bag just before it slipped off the railing. He was about to decline the invitation for coffee with the excuse he had dinner in the microwave when he realized here was somebody to talk to. *No reason to be afraid of him.* Joel unlocked the back door to his apartment, right next to Kevin's door, and suddenly a wildly yapping little dog bounded out onto the porch and started jumping around Kevin's feet.

"Well, don't just stand there, c'mon in," Joel said smiling warmly.

"I went to a matinee of that new Rob Grant film today." Joel got up from the table as he talked to get the coffee pot. "Getting outed by the New York Times hasn't hurt Grant's career one bit—or his acting abilities." He poured the last of the pot into Kevin's cup and began clearing away the now empty plastic trays from the two microwave dinners Kevin had brought over to share with Joel.

Kevin was happy to have met his neighbor, and was impressed with having a real artist next door. He loved the highly ornate faux Japanese screens Joel painted. When Kevin praised the freedom of the artist's life, Joel had confessed he couldn't make enough money with his art to live in San Francisco, so was moonlighting as a bartender.

Kevin was enjoying the conversation with Joel, though it was hardly a conversation. Joel was doing most all the talking. He was a little high-strung for Kevin's tastes, but he was also marvelously funny and he'd quickly pulled Kevin out of his loneliness. "Grant makes a wonderful James Bond. Sexy! I bet you'll love the movie as much as if you miss it"

"What did you just say?" Kevin asked.

Joel grinned. "You caught that, didn't you? It's funny how many people don't even notice."

"You mean you did that on purpose?"

"Not exactly. I started mimicking the lady who used to live in your apartment. She talked like that all the time. Her expressions have sort of crept on little cat's feet right into my own speech. Sometimes I do it without even noticing that it's not happening at all."

"What?" Kevin answered. "You did that on purpose!"

"I should hope so. For both our sakes." Joel burst out laughing. "Seriously, she was a great lady. I love her dearly."

"What happened to her?"

"Moved up to Mount Shasta. She belonged to this commune up there that was planning to fly away in a UFO. After the Visitors arrived they all started preparing. Here, read this postcard she sent me last week." Joel reached up to the tackboard above the table and pulled down a card with a painting of an ethereal looking spacecraft flying among snow-covered mountains. He handed it to Kevin. "Read what she says."

"We're all waiting eagerly for the Visitors to find us. We're sure they've heard our prayers. Joel, it's beautiful up here. Love you. I miss you almost as much as if you were here. XXOX, Bunny," Kevin read aloud. "Sounds like a nut."

"Well, yes, but a really nice nut. Her name was Hazel Bunn. She was a real San Francisco hippie. Did a little too much acid over the years. I suspect that's why she talked like that. She'd changed her name to Pollen. You know, hippies took funny names like Clover and Forest and Butterfly. Bunny—I always called her Bunny—had got into Navajo myth and had read about the Pollen Path between earth and heaven. Being a real Age of Aquarius believer she thought she'd make herself such a path.

"Anyway, she developed the self-defeating habit of always explaining that her name was Pollen and not Honey. Which, of course, only reminded people of a pun they probably wouldn't have noticed if she hadn't mentioned it."

"Huh?"

"Her last name was Bunn."

"Oh, I get it," Kevin answered smiling.

"So everybody called her Bunny. Lovely, generous lady, but absolutely dingy…" Joel paused for a moment as though thinking up something. "…dingy as a wharf in London," he added. "Oh, that's not a very good one."

"How about 'dingy as a Hostess Ding-Dong,'" Kevin offered.

"Better," Joel answered, "but not comparable to Bunny. Anyway, you get the idea."

"I hope you don't talk like this all the time," Kevin answered. "You might get me doing it."

Joel just laughed. "Anyway," he resumed, "I was telling you that after the movie I went over to the St. Francis Hotel since I was downtown to see if anybody, you know, famous was in the lobby. And, lo and behold, I walked right into a Visitor."

"Their temporary headquarters are in the St. Francis," Kevin explained.

"Well, this guy was a hunk."

Uh oh, thought Kevin, *Here we go again.* He'd recognized Joel's sexuality, but so far the guy had not put the make on him he told himself, and indeed, Joel had seemed totally uninterested in a friendly, neighborly sort of way. Kevin had decided to calm down and not worry. He hadn't seen any reason to feel intimidated by Joel anymore than he had by Tim. *But I don't want to have to listen to this guy talk about gay sex.*

"The firm I work for is doing some business with the Visitors," he said to change the subject.

"Well, they may be gorgeous, but I for one don't believe in them," Joel announced smugly.

"Believe in them?"

"I mean, that they're real. I think it's some kind of Russian plot... or terrorist plot or C.I.A. plot... or maybe just a movie hype. I don't know. But, frankly, I just can't believe that aliens from outer space would arrive looking just like human beings."

Kevin felt a sudden rush of defensiveness. "But, of course, they're real. I mean, why'd anybody spend all this money on building an embassy for them if they aren't real?"

"C'mon, Kevin, use your noggin. If this is a conspiracy, it's gotta look real. Of course that's gonna cost some money. But spies always have money."

"But why?"

"Find out all our secrets maybe. Get us thinking about disarmament. I don't know."

"Well, I like them."

"You just fall for a pretty face."

At that remark, Kevin bristled. He wasn't sure he liked Joel after all. "No, I mean it," he said. "They seem very genuine. And, and, well, I've seen something about them that proves to me they're real."

"And what was that?" Joel asked, his tone revealing he was playing Devil's Advocate as much as he was expressing genuine doubt.

"Uh, I don't think I should say."

"You what?" Joel exclaimed.

"I mean, it was sort of in confidence."

"So, next door neighbor, you're part of the conspiracy."

"No, no," Kevin was suddenly on the defensive. "I mean, what I saw was just between me and the Visitor."

"You know one personally?" Joel asked. Now he sounded much less hostile and more intrigued. "What I'd give to get to know one of those guys!"

"At work a couple of weeks ago, well, I met a Visitor. His name was 'Bel."

"Tall, blond, and beautiful like the rest."

"Sort of. I mean he looked like the other Visitors. But—look Joel, just between you and me, okay—"

"Okay."

"They, uh, change color."

"They what?"

"Change color. I saw it myself. While I was talking with 'Bel, he turned from the golden color most of them seem to bluish-green."

"Whaddya get him sick or something?"

"No, not like that. He changed color, just like a chameleon. He said they usually take some kind of pills to stop it. I don't know. He wouldn't explain any further. In fact, he seemed to feel guilty that he'd let me see whatever happened to him. But, look, Joel, the point is, whatever happened to 'Bel that afternoon just wasn't human."

"Maybe so. Hmmm. Maybe they were just pulling the wool over your eyes, you know, tricking you, so you'd corroborate their plot."

"Oh no. I know 'Bel wasn't lying to me. I could tell."

"And just how friendly were you with this guy 'Bel?" Joel asked suggestively.

"Not like that," Kevin scolded. "We just met. We talked a little while. Then he, apparently by accident or something, turned blue. I told you he got upset about that. Then I left."

"You left him upset? Didn't you try to, uh, comfort him?"

"Well, that's a funny thing too. I reached out and touched his head. And where I touched him his skin turned golden again. It was like my touch affected him."

"Maybe the color change is sexual—like getting aroused."

"Oh, Joel, come off it," Kevin said annoyed. But at the same time, he realized he felt that strange fluttering in his stomach again.

"Honey, if I were you, I'd be high-tailin' my little 'hiney right down there to the St. Francis Hotel tonight. It's Friday night. Time to boogie."

Kevin didn't like Joel talking that way about 'Bel. And in that offensive sounding last century slang. It sounded cheap.

But, strangely, it seemed to make the feeling in his stomach that much more vivid.

*T*he underground Metro whisked Kevin toward downtown. As the walls rushed by, occasionally illuminated by the white or blue light of a work station, Kevin was glad he hadn't been down here when the quake hit. *My God, the people must've felt trapped.*

In fact, he knew, the underground tunnels had proved to be one of the safest places during the disaster. They were built to withstand enormous strain; in only one spot did the actual tunnel wall rupture when the earth sheared. And the tunnels protected people from falling debris, in the downtown area one of the chief causes of injury. "The Financial District," Will Salado had told him, "was raining plate glass after the first shock wave. People were getting cut to pieces as they tried to get out of the buildings."

The train was relatively empty this morning. It was Saturday. Very few of the riders were going to work. *Most of them,* Kevin surmised, *like me are going shopping or sightseeing or...* He didn't quite finish his sentence to himself.

Kevin had spent a restless night. Joel Horstman tried to convince him to go bar-hopping with him on his night off, but Kevin declined. He'd ended up staying around Joel's apartment till nearly ten. He hadn't wanted to go home. The idea of sitting alone in his apartment did not appeal to him. Even if he did have five hundred and twenty channels coming in on the cable, he'd still be alone. Besides, though Joel occasionally made him feel uncomfortable, he was genuinely getting to like him. Once he did come home, when Joel practically threw him out so he could get dressed to go out, Kevin couldn't settle down. He wasn't at all sleepy—though this morning he felt the fatigue. He ended up mopping and waxing the kitchen floor till almost three a.m. (He'd heard Joel come in about two-thirty; Kevin had been glad he'd come home alone; he'd been fearing he might have to listen to... *well, sounds.*)

Now it was just after ten a.m. Kevin had decided to go shopping. He needed a variety of things for the apartment: from linens to kitchen utensils to furniture. (Fortunately, the landlord had partially furnished the apartment.) He wasn't planning to buy very much today, but Kevin wanted to familiarize himself with the various stores. *And, besides*—the thought was lurking in his mind—*I want to stop by and see the hotel where the Visitors are staying.*

"I work for Sutro & Associates." Kevin was struggling to avoid sounding nervous. "That's the architecture firm—"

"Oh yes. Your company is designing the Embassy," the Visitor answered. She was sitting at the desk outside the elevator on the second floor of the newly renovated St. Francis Hotel. "Are you here to see Mr. 'Tarawan Horam? He is the liaison with Sutro and Associates." Her voice was rhythmic and melodic. Just like among human beings, Visitor females' voices were higher pitched and softer.

How funny "Mister" sounds in front of a Visitor name, Kevin thought. *That must be the name of the Visitor who was at the meeting that first night.* Kevin felt his heart pounding.

"Is Mr. 'Belwyn in?" he blurted out.

The receptionist looked through a list that Kevin assumed were of Visitor names. Of course, he was seeing the page upside down, but, though the letters seemed oddly formed and unfamiliar, the writing looked surprisingly human. "Are you sure you have the name right? I don't see anyone in Horam's department with a name like that."

"Oh, he's not in that department," Kevin answered hastily, regretting he'd ever come up here. *How am I going to explain why I want to see him?*

"Do you know what department he works in?"

"Sociology," Kevin replied abruptly. "I met him a couple of weeks ago when I was visiting the site of the Embassy," he added hoping to give his request legitimacy.

"Ah, of course, 'Belwyn Tuarul, the research intern. Very nice young man."

In spite of Kevin's anxiety about seeming to trespass into Visitor space, he couldn't help feeling amazed and, almost frightened, by the normalness of everything about the Visitors. *Shouldn't aliens from space be more different from us?*

Maybe this is part of their strategy when they come to another planet. Maybe they always imitate local styles to bridge the gap between cultures. I wonder if they realize how strange it makes them seem.

"'Belwyn Tuarul is out for the day, I see," the receptionist looked up from her notes. She didn't seem at all surprised that Kevin was looking for him. Recognizing that, Kevin felt much more at ease. "Would you like to leave word that you came by?"

"Yes, please. My name is Kevin Anderson."

The receptionist typed Kevin's name into the computer in front of her. "And he could reach you at Sutro and Associates?"

"Well, not today."

"Would you like to say what you came to see him about?"

"Oh, I think he'll understand. We, uh, were talking about something and, uh, I, uh, said I'd look something up for him." All of a sudden he felt very nervous. He wasn't a good liar. He worried that he could be getting 'Bel in trouble.

"I will leave this message for him. Thank you." Her tone was one of finality.

Kevin turned and pressed the button for the elevator. Almost immediately the door opened. "Goodbye," the receptionist said, sounding very friendly.

"I'm going to be downtown the rest of the afternoon. Perhaps I'll stop by later," Kevin said abruptly as he stepped into the elevator, not waiting for her reply.

He calmed himself down. He wasn't sure why he'd come looking for 'Bel. Though he knew it had something to do with Joel Horstman's comment, he told himself he wanted to impress his brother Jeff with the fact he knew a Visitor personally. Suddenly he realized that though the doors had closed, the elevator wasn't moving. He'd forgotten to push the button for the ground floor. As he did, he observed that the third and fourth floors had key slots instead of buttons—apparently to keep strangers out. It reminded him of the odd way the staircases in the Embassy were designed. *For privacy.* He wondered what went on in the Visitors' quarters. For a brief moment it occurred to him that maybe they eat human beings.

What am I doing? Why did I come up here?

- - -

By early afternoon, Kevin had forgotten his anxiety about talking with the receptionist. In fact, he was now feeling quite comfortable about walking right into Visitor territory. There didn't seem to be anything to fear.

He had his arms full of bags as he crossed Powell Street and headed back into the St. Francis. He'd bought more than he'd expected to, but was feeling pleased that he'd accomplished so much. By the time all the things he'd purchased were delivered, the apartment was going to be really livable.

He headed straight for the elevators and went right up without even thinking what he was doing. He was pleased to find the same receptionist on duty.

"'Bel picked up your message a while ago. I told him you might be coming by. He asked me to tell you he was going to be at Ocean Beach all afternoon and invited you to meet him for sunset at the Cliff House."

All of a sudden, Kevin's heart was beating like crazy again.

"Of course we eat," 'Bel said with a ring of laughter. "Don't you see we're really just like you."

"I guess so," Kevin answered, a little embarrassed by his own question. He looked away from the handsome Visitor sitting across from him and gazed out the wall of windows that overlooked the Pacific Ocean. The sun had just set and the western sky was still awash with reds and golds, oranges and magentas. As he had since Joel made him realize he wanted to see 'Bel again, Kevin felt a mix of comfortable excitement and near-panic. He didn't know what to say and was feeling even more ill-at-ease as the silence lengthened.

"My friend Louise told me that sometimes, just after sunset, there's a moment when the sun is actually directly across the ocean from us below the horizon and there's a flash of green light that happens when the sunlight passes through the mass of water."

"Really, do you think it's about to happen?"

"Oh, I don't know. I've never seen it. I guess for it to work there have to be clear skies in the western Pacific and maybe other special weather conditions..." The conversation fell into silence again.

'Bel seemed quite comfortable with the silence. (*I guess that's a real difference about them*, Kevin thought.) He seemed quite content to sit staring at Kevin.

"Hey, tell me what it's like in space."

"Oh, well. It is beautiful in space."

Kevin had been paying special attention to 'Bel's coloration, now he thought he noticed a slight darkening in the Visitor's face.

"I mean what do stars and galaxies and stuff really look like?"

"They're big and bright. Lots of light out in space." The color change was slight, but now noticeable—if one knew what to look for. Kevin decided to try to force the issue with 'Bel.

"I've always wanted to see what the solar system looked like from above. You know, can you see the planets going around the sun?"

Now 'Bel looked uncomfortably out the window. Just as he started to open his mouth, Kevin interrupted. "Did you take the pills to suppress the change?" he whispered conspiratorially.

'Bel took a breath and obviously relaxed. (Kevin thought he could see a general lightening in his complexion.) "Yes, Kevin, I did."

"Why?"

"Now you're asking something that demands too big an answer. Let me just say that we *are* very much like you. But there are a few things that are *very* different." He looked around the room, as if to make sure no one was watching, then leaned forward and whispered, "Maybe I'll explain all this later." Sitting back, he added, "For now, let me tell you that the way the, uh, drive system works in our ships, we don't really go *into* space. I don't know what planets and galaxies and the solar system look like. I've never seen them."

"You mean you're from right here on Earth?" Kevin exclaimed.

"Ssshh," 'Bel hushed him. "Oh no. We're obviously from another world. Look at me. But getting here isn't done by flying around from galaxy to galaxy. It's hard to explain, but let me say it's all done by warping space geometry. We started on our world. The drive system changed the shape of space and then we were here—without passing through space or time."

"Wow," Kevin responded. "But how come your ships appeared out in space?"

"We couldn't come through on the planet's surface without a

window already existing. It would cause distortion in the space of your world. So until we could build windows on the surface, we had to get up outside the atmosphere and come in from space."

"Wow," Kevin repeated himself. Now he looked around. He was feeling very special, like he'd just been let in on a very big secret. Though, of course, knowing such a secret had few practical uses, he realized.

They were sitting in a private party room at the recently rebuilt Cliff House at the tip of Land's End. 'Bel had earlier explained to Kevin that the Visitors kept this room reserved for their own use—especially entertaining Earth-people. Right now, there was only one other party in the room: a group of five Japanese businessmen in dark suits sitting with two Visitors—apparently discussing business ventures, 'Bel and Kevin had surmised. They were on the other side of the room, far enough away that their conversation was unintelligible and so that, presumably, Kevin's and 'Bel's would be also to them.

Basking in the closeness of the shared confidence for a moment, Kevin and 'Bel fell again into silence. This time there was no discomfort.

"Thanks for telling me," Kevin finally remarked.

'Bel smiled, then reached out and gently touched Kevin's hand. Kevin flinched and then relaxed. *These people really are different from us*, he told himself. *I don't have to be intimidated by their expression of affection.* Kevin let himself actually grasp 'Bel's hand. He could see the golden glow in 'Bel's face brighten.

"The changes in your complexion have something to do with your moods, don't they?"

'Bel laughed. "You want to find out everything all at once. I promise I will explain, but not yet—"

Just then they were interrupted by the arrival of their dinner. At 'Bel's suggestion, they had ordered the combination seafood dinner for two. The waiter arrived with several plates and bowls piled high with fried shrimp and oysters, a whole lobster, several pieces of fish and lots of french fried potatoes.

"You like seafood?" Kevin asked, adding "You better, 'cause there sure is a lot here."

"It's what I mostly eat at home," 'Bel answered, once more thrilling Kevin with another fact about the secret life of the Visitors.

- - -

There was no moon tonight—and in the new San Francisco, very little light pollution; the ecologists had won control of the rebuilding of the City and mandated that all outdoor lights shine down, not up. So along the beach a brilliant sky of twinkling stars was visible. This was Kevin's first experience of the beach at night.

"It's almost like being in space, isn't it? I mean, like what I asked you back at dinner."

"We are in space, aren't we? Even if we're on a planet, the planet's hanging in space. The universe is so big, Kevin, big enough for everything."

They'd been walking for over an hour. 'Bel had revealed no more "secrets," but had casually talked about daily life on his world and Kevin had responded with stories of his own life. They really didn't seem that different.

Kevin had grown comfortable with the Visitor's expression of affection. As they walked they held hands lightly. Kevin had reminded himself that in Europe men commonly walk together holding hands. *It doesn't necessarily suggest anything, well, sexual.* Though as the evening wore on, Kevin was feeling less and less worried about the sexual implications. The warm tingling in his abdomen didn't feel scary anymore.

"Shouldn't we be going in soon. It's getting late. I didn't get much sleep last night. I'm afraid I'm gonna conk out on you any minute."

'Bel turned and put both hands on Kevin's shoulders, but didn't pull close. He looked him straight in the eye, "Kevin, I think you can conk out on me anytime you want." Then he dropped his arms. "But I don't know what 'conk out' means," he laughed. And then, suddenly, he leaned forward and kissed Kevin on the cheek.

Kevin laughed too, out of embarrassment and miscommunication. "'Conk out' means fall asleep, I'm afraid."

"Oh. Well, I guess that's okay too."

Kevin had liked the feeling of 'Bel hands on his shoulders. The warmth had seemed to radiate into his body, relaxing what fears he had left, obliterating what thoughts still buzzed in his head. For all that those thoughts—now seeming so meaningless—told him he shouldn't, he liked the feeling in his cheek where 'Bel's lips had touched him. He could almost feel a golden glow spreading out through his own face.

He reached out and touched 'Bel on the upper arm. Then closed his hand on the long tight muscle. His hand felt so alive. Kevin thought he could feel a tingling in the air between them, as though the space all around him was full of those bright stars overhead. He'd never felt anything like this in his life. All of a sudden nothing from before mattered anymore. Something brand new was happening in his life.

For a moment he thought of Tim Lewiston. He remembered that moment back in the dorm when Tim embraced him—in some ways so similar to this, but oh so different.

'Bel seemed so patient. He stood still, not rushing Kevin, just letting whatever was pouring through his mind run its course. Perhaps he knew that, for Kevin, now it was too late, that now he'd discovered something about his own secret life. Kevin wondered what this beautiful man from the stars might be thinking. And then he released his grip on 'Bel's arm and turned to him and embraced him openly.

They held one another cheek to cheek for a long time. Long enough for the feeling of closeness to become so natural and comfortable it wasn't strange or frightening anymore. 'Bel gently turned his head and kissed Kevin on the lips.

The night wind blew cold off the ocean, but neither of them seemed to notice the cold.

"Are you going to conk out on me?" 'Bel asked.

"I don't think so." Kevin smiled, then whispered, "You're wonderful."

'Bel pointed up toward the Great Highway above the beach. "I think we're near a major street. I can see lights up there. Maybe we can catch a cab. It really is time to go home."

Chapter Six

*K*evin was struggling to keep his attention on the building specifications he'd been working on this week. His mind kept drifting back to Saturday evening at the beach. Here it was Wednesday and he hadn't seen 'Bel all week. He knew he shouldn't be worried—'Bel's goodnight had assured him of that. And he knew he shouldn't be surprised that he couldn't spend more time with his new friend: obviously they both had to work. But he had to admit he missed the intensity of those moments on the beach. And he missed the quiet pleasure of just looking at the beautiful golden Visitor.

"Oh Kevin," he was suddenly jerked back into reality by George Sanders cooing in his ear.

"Oh, yes sir."

"I've been calling you from across the room for the last five minutes," George said testily. "Where's your mind been?"

"Right here on these specs," Kevin fibbed a little.

"You must be quite a good concentrator," George answered. "Maybe you'd like to do a little concentrating on me sometime."

Kevin smiled. "Whatcha need, George?" Since the weekend, George's campiness and exaggerated sexual innuendo had stopped bothering Kevin. He'd come to realize it was just a style George affected and didn't have to present any threat at all. George carried on like that with almost everybody at Sutro except Jules Domergue.

"Meeting of the Visitor Embassy team in ten minutes in the conference room."

"I'll be there," Kevin promised. "Look I'm sorry if I seemed to be ignoring you. I honestly didn't hear you calling."

Thirty minutes later, the meeting had deteriorated from a planning session for the next stage of construction of the Embassy building now that the foundation was completed to a gossip session about the Visitors' intentions.

"I heard on the news last night that several Republican senators are strongly opposing the Visitor treaty," Dick Jularian said. "Blanchard from Ohio believes there's something sinister about them. He thinks they really want to conquer the Earth and the friendliness is a cover."

"That's just paranoia," Louise Hoffman objected.

"Well, you can call it paranoia, but that doesn't mean this whole thing isn't some plot to overthrow the country," Chuck Sperry remarked from his place leaning against the door frame. Chuck wasn't actually on the team, but he attended the meetings—usually with negative things to say about the project.

"Why would somebody come all the way across outer space just to conquer a world that's already over-crowded and polluted, maybe past the point of saving?" Louise replied.

"Do you really think they're from outer space? That's nonsense. Why wouldn't radio telescopes have picked up their arrival long before they got here? Radar only picked the ships up just inside the orbit of the moon. Besides, who really believes in aliens from outer space. They're Russian. I'll wager you that."

"We're friends with the Russians now," Louise scoffed.

"Well, they don't look Arab or Chinese. Who's the enemy now then? Chuck pushed his idea the Visitors were not what they appeared to be. "Maybe we're at war with Scandinavia!"

"What if their ships use some kind of matter transmission or space warp so they don't have to traverse distance?" Kevin countered Sperry's argument. He didn't want to acknowledge that a Visitor had told him that's exactly how it worked—from Sperry's point of view that would just further invalidate the explanation. And besides, it was a secret he shared with 'Bel.

"I think it *could* be some sort of elaborate hoax, though why anybody would want to go to so much trouble?" Jularian said.

"Movie promotion?" George offered.

"It's gone on too long for that," Dick answered.

"Look, why not just accept the truth? Why look for plots?" Louise sounded exasperated.

"Jules is going to walk in here any minute and ask how we're coming with the plans," Will Salado spoke with the voice of authority. "This company's business is building buildings, not uncovering conspiracies."

"If it's a conspiracy, Will, there's not going to be any of that precious gold Jules is coveting," Sperry said. "And," leaning out the door and checking both directions, "I'll tell you when Jules is coming."

"Well, let me tell you what I heard on the news last night—"

Kevin stopped listening as George Sanders started in on another rumor. He didn't like hearing all this. He knew more about the Visitors than any of them here. But he was just an intern. Who'd care what he knew? *Well, I know the Visitors are real. I've kissed one.* Even as he thought that, he blushed. He was sure that wasn't the kind of evidence he'd want to present to the architectural team.

Kevin's mind wandered back to that last long kiss. 'Bel had been right: they'd found a cab easily when they climbed up to the Great Highway above the beach. They'd sat silently in the shadows of the back seat, saying nothing, lightly touching hands on the seat between them. Kevin had kept looking at the driver to make sure he wasn't paying attention to them. Kevin didn't think he realized he had a Visitor in the back seat. In the dark 'Bel didn't look especially alien.

When they arrived at Fair Oaks Street, Kevin hesitantly asked 'Bel if he'd like to come up. With a warm smile and a tightening of his hand clasp, 'Bel declined the invitation. "Not tonight. I have to be back at headquarters very soon." Then he glanced at the driver and then stealthily pulled Kevin's head down below the back of the front seat. "Just so you don't worry about my intentions," he said, and he pressed his lips against Kevin's and then slowly, teasingly he opened his mouth and let the kiss grow deeper. "I'm sure glad I came to your Earth," he whispered after he finally pulled away.

As he remembered the warmth and passion and safety of that secret moment, Kevin felt himself go warm all over.

"The Book of Genesis doesn't say anything about Adams and Eves on other planets," Kevin realized Chuck Sperry had just said.

"Oh my God, is that what's bothering you?" Louise replied.

Kevin recalled the sweet sound of 'Bel's voice mixing with the sound of the waves under the brilliantly starry sky telling him about what he called their "Story of the Origins of People."

"In the beginning, God created man and woman in the Garden and gave them everything they needed to live in peace and harmony with all the other animals in the Garden, in its ponds and rivers, and its trees.

Only one thing did he forbid them: to eat of the fruit of the Tree of the Knowledge of Truth and Falsehood. They were tempted by a jealous and competitive spirit which disguised itself as a beautiful plumed bird and promised the man and woman mastery over the world if they would eat of the fruit."

"Did that really happen?" Kevin had asked, a little incredulous.

"It's a holy story," 'Bel answered. "...like poetry. It's not meant to be history; it's meant to teach a lesson about Heaven."

"Wow," Kevin exclaimed. "It sounds just like the story in the Bible. It's just amazing."

"Our races are very much alike," 'Bel responded. "That is why we can communicate so easily. We have much to learn from one another."

"I thought all these similarities were made up, I mean, that your leaders taught you all how to talk and act like us so our two planets could get along."

"That is partly true. But it is more true that our people are very much alike. After all, are we not creations of the same God that also made all this?" 'Bel extended his hand in a sweeping gesture toward the sea and the stars.

"You mean everybody in the universe is human just like us?"

"I don't know about everybody. I know that you and I have two arms and two legs and two eyes to see each other with and a face upon which to carry a smile of love. That's what God created us for. That's all God asks."

"You believe in God then?" Kevin asked.

"God is an image for the universe's joy."

Not understanding 'Bel's comment, Kevin continued, "I believe in God, I guess, but I wonder... I used to think he was somewhere up in the sky. Maybe you've seen him?" he asked playfully.

"Not in the sky. But all around. How can you question God? God is life. Are you not yourself a flower of God's consciousness?"

"I don't know. I don't know about God."

"That is a result of how our peoples differ, I suppose."

"How *do* we differ, 'Bel? Tell me what you know."

'Bel had stopped walking then and turned to Kevin and taken both of Kevin's hands in his and, sounding very solemn, announced, "That is a secret still. Maybe one day I can tell you. But not now."

"What's a secret?"

"I wish it were not so. The secret is about the difference between your experience of life and ours. It is really why we came here."

"And you can't tell me?"

'Bel grinned. He pulled away though kept hold of one of Kevin's hands. "Come on," he shouted and started half-running, half-skipping playfully along the beach. "Kevin," he shouted into the wind, "I'd get in so much trouble if I told you any more." And then laughing uncontrollably in a way that surprised Kevin because it made so little sense to him because it seemed so childishly innocent, 'Bel added breathlessly, "And I don't even know what 'getting in trouble' means."

"Here comes Jules," Chuck Sperry said, forcing Kevin out of his memories. "See you later." He exited down the hall.

"Okay, everybody, back to work," Will Salado struggled to get the meeting back on track. "I want a report on the construction timetable. When is that seashell-shaped thing supposed to be finished?"

*W*hen the doorbell rang, Kevin was puttering around in the kitchen trying to keep himself busy. He'd been a nervous wreck all day. *It's been four days since I heard anything from 'Bel.* Part of him was anxious to follow through with the connection that was established Saturday night. Another part wasn't at all sure he ever wanted to hear from the Visitor again. Now that the immediacy of the moment had passed, the sexuality of the relationship again scared and offended him. Those emotions had been reinforced this afternoon when, after the Embassy team meeting, George Sanders made a barbed remark about how sexy "and well-endowed" the Visitor men looked and then stuck its barb in Kevin by complaining that only a "cute young thing, like our Kevin here" would stand a chance with one of "Them."

The conflict between the two parts of him was leaving Kevin restless, unhappy, and, at the moment, compulsively hungry. Joel had invited Kevin over for pot-luck at his place, but Kevin hadn't wanted anything to do with Joel this evening. *That'd only make it worse.*

So he was pouring milk, bananas, eggs, protein powder, and ice into the new blender he'd bought last weekend at Macy's in an effort to satisfy his restlessness with something nutritious. He'd just turned off the blender to taste his concoction when he realized the antique bell on his front door was jingling frantically.

Kevin ran to the door. Peeking through the shutters over the window in the door, he saw a strange sight. It took him a moment to realize the tall figure under what looked like a floppy sun hat pulled down tight around his face was 'Bel. He swung open the door.

"Kevin, I'm glad you are home. I feel silly wearing this thing."

"What is it?"

"A radiation helmet."

"Why are you wearing it?"

"Look at me," he said agitatedly, as he pulled off what Kevin could now see was a heavy fabric shield. 'Bel's face was mottled. Kevin flicked on the hall light to see better and realized the mottling was varicolored.

"You look like you fell into an artist's palette," Kevin joked. "What happened?"

'Bel started to cry. "I found out what being in trouble was all about. And then I had to come see you. I've missed you."

Kevin reached out and touched 'Bel's arm tentatively. Then they quickly closed together in a tight embrace.

"I knew I couldn't come over here looking red, so I took those drugs. And look what it's done to me."

Kevin wasn't sure what 'Bel was talking about. What did he mean "looking red"? But he was sure he was glad to see his Visitor friend. The anxiety and ambivalence he'd been feeling a few minutes ago had disappeared instantly when he'd realized it was 'Bel at his door.

"Does your face hurt?" he asked solicitously, as he escorted 'Bel toward the living room.

"Oh no. The changes are normal. But not like this." 'Bel was looking at himself in the age-specked mirror built into the fireplace mantle. "It ought to go away if I could just relax." He looked at Kevin kind of helplessly. "This must not make much sense to you."

"You're right," Kevin said, trying to be joking about the remark. "I don't understand what's happened to you. Can you explain?"

"Well, that's what's happened. I mean, they think I've told you too much already."

"Who?"

"My superiors."

"How?"

"When I got in Saturday night, I was too bright. The guard at the desk saw and talked to my supervisor. She called me in to report to the whole team about what I was doing with you. They, uh, uh, scolded me, and then warned me about getting involved with your people."

"Didn't you tell them that nothing had happened?" Even as he said that Kevin knew it wasn't altogether true. Something had sure happened.

"They didn't believe me. That's what hurts so much. The whole crew is getting perverted. Being in this world is contaminating us, turning us all into perverts."

Kevin felt his stomach turn as though he'd just been punched. He started to tremble all over. *Perverts?* The word itself burned in his brain. *What if 'Bel's sexual come-on hasn't been sexual at all?* He suddenly felt guilty and dirty. *What if I've misunderstood?* "I don't understand," he stammered.

'Bel looked at him with such a sweet look. "Oh, Kevin Anderson, I don't mean you." 'Bel reached out his hand. When Kevin didn't respond, but just stood there staring at him, looking helpless, 'Bel stepped forward and took him in his arms. For a moment they clutched tightly to one another. Kevin could feel 'Bel's warmth penetrate his chest and flow through his whole body. He felt so safe. He started to relax, when, abruptly, 'Bel's saying the crew was getting perverted rang again through Kevin's mind. *My God, would he think I was a pervert if he knew what I was feeling?*

As 'Bel's warmth and closeness flowing into him was gradually interpreted by his body into affection and sexual arousal, Kevin felt himself trapped. He couldn't allow 'Bel to realize he was getting aroused. But he couldn't stop himself. He didn't know how to avoid showing his feelings. He felt so confused.

All of a sudden, the warmth of 'Bel's touch wasn't comfort anymore, but pain. Kevin was shaking like a leaf in a high wind. 'Bel, perhaps in response, clutched Kevin tighter. Uncontrollably, Kevin pulled away and then struggled to push 'Bel away. He had to get out of his arms. Now. He had to stop the feelings that were surging through him. As he pushed himself away, he actually struck out at 'Bel, pummeling him on the chest with open, impotent fists.

As he clumsily and almost violently extricated himself from the Visitor's arms, in an odd moment of detached observation, Kevin noticed that 'Bel's mottled color had resolved. His face was now uniformly and brightly golden.

"What's wrong, Kevin?"

"I, I couldn't breathe. I… please, 'Bel, just let me alone for a minute. I'm feeling so confused. I don't know what's happening."

"Neither do I," 'Bel answered despondently. The brightness of the gold in his complexion was fading now.

"Why don't you sit down?" Kevin finally said. "Over there." He pointed to a chair. He himself sat down on a stool in the far corner of the room away from 'Bel. He took a deep breath and signed. "Look, I don't understand what's going on. I mean, you came in here looking like you'd gotten rouge or something all over your face. And then you talked about perversion and then, uh, came on to me."

"Came on to you?" 'Bel asked. "I don't understand?"

"Don't understand? Oh my God. Now you're gonna use the language against me. You talk perfect English, just like an American—even though you claim to be from outer space—and then right when things get heavy, you say you don't understand. *I* don't understand."

'Bel was silent for a long time, his eyes downcast. His golden color turned ashen. Finally, he looked up at Kevin, "I'm sorry. I don't know what to do either. I mean, I'm not supposed to tell you what this is about. That's what my team ordered." His voice trailed off. He looked at the back of his hands for a long time, then at Kevin. Holding out his hands, he continued, "Look, the drugs I took earlier have ruined my color. It's driving me crazy. It's driving us all crazy. We're not showing color. Kevin, that's what I meant about perversion. I didn't mean to suggest that *you*'re perverted because you don't show color."

Kevin looked at him quizzically. "I don't know what you're talking about. Do you mean these drugs you're taking for your, uh, complexion are mind-altering, I mean, you know, get you high, like moodies?"

"The drugs are only for the color," 'Bel answered warily.

"Well, my God, what color are you then? I mean, why do you take drugs that you say drive you crazy if they're just cosmetics? You people look funny enough all blue and green. You mean that's just cosmetics?" Kevin felt a little sorry about how angry his tone was. He didn't really mean to attack 'Bel, but the confusion was getting to him.

"Oh, Kevin, I'm not supposed to explain." There was another long silence. "But it's not you. And it's not the drugs, I mean, not what you just said. It's, uh, the effect of the drugs that I meant was driving me crazy. I can't tell what's real anymore. And I know it's not your fault that you can't show color, but I don't know how to talk to you. I can't tell what you're feeling. It's like we're not speaking the same language."

"The same language?" Kevin was beginning to get angrier as he got more confused. He began to suspect that 'Bel was doing this on purpose. He remembered Joel Horstman's theory that this was all faked. *What if 'Bel is just using me, manipulating my homosexual feelings.* Even as he thought those words, Kevin felt a terror roar through him. He'd never dared called those feelings by name before. And now the Visitor's perplexing and maddening talk was driving him toward something he didn't want to know about or think about or... or... or.

"Look, tell me something." Kevin was managing to calm himself by literally suppressing his emotions. He could tell his voice was strained, but at least he was in control again. "Is this all a plot or something? Are you real? You said something about language just now. My God, 'Bel, you've got a funny accent all right, but if you're from outer space, how come you speak English as if it were your native tongue?"

'Bel looked at Kevin intently. From around his eyes—Kevin at least thought he saw—dark circles began to spread out across his face. His eyes looked so deep and so expressive, and Kevin felt himself being drawn into the depths. 'Bel extended his hand as if to reach out to Kevin, though of course on the other side of the room Kevin was way beyond his reach. "I'm not supposed to answer such questions. But how can I not? How can I, uh, lie to you?" He dropped his hand helplessly.

Staring down at the floor, he softly—hesitantly—continued, "Kev, I can speak English because it *is* my native tongue." Now Kevin's eyes widened. "Not the accent. I had to practice that. And not all the words. Before we came to your world I didn't know words like 'lie' and 'trouble.' Believe me, we are for real. I mean, we're not part of your world. But nobody thought you would believe us—I mean, your people. That's why we let you believe we came from space.

"Oh, Kevin, I guess there is a sort of 'plot.' But it's not what you meant. We came here for a reason. And we haven't revealed that yet. But, please, Kevin, I didn't come here tonight for any hidden reason. I came because I was scared and hurt and I needed to be with you." He held out his hand again, almost beggingly.

Kevin was dumbstruck. He just sat on the stool and stared at the strange, strange man on the other side of the room. For the moment, he was questioning his own sanity. *Maybe this is all a dream… that is turning into a nightmare. What does he want from me? And why me?*

Kevin said nothing in response to 'Bel's pleading. 'Bel seemed to get distracted after a moment. He began to look at his hands again. "Look at me," he said, more to himself than to Kevin. "I feel so blue but there's no color at all."

Kevin stood up. He started to walk toward 'Bel. Some place deep in his body consciousness he could feel the touch of the Visitor. He knew he longed to take 'Bel's hand and pull him close and let the closeness answer all the questions in his mind. But then the fear filled him again. And now he wasn't just afraid of his feelings, he was afraid of whatever the incomprehensible plot 'Bel was talking about, he was afraid of getting caught in something he couldn't get out of, something that maybe could drive him mad.

As Kevin came a step closer to him, 'Bel looked up from studying his hands and started to smile. "Please…" he started to say when Kevin interrupted him.

"'Bel, go home. Get out of here. Now." Kevin's voice was tight, the words pressured, as though they were about to explode into an open outburst. 'Bel uttered something that Kevin didn't understand. "Put on that stupid hat and get out of here," Kevin finally shouted.

Kevin stood looking into the fireplace, watching 'Bel covertly through the mirror, as the Visitor stood and walked toward the doorway into the hall. As he left the room, he turned, almost catching Kevin's eye in the reflection. But Kevin was too fast for him. And the alien turned and disappeared into the hallway.

He stood staring sightless into the empty fireplace until he heard the front door softly close behind the departing Visitor.

Kevin lay awake long into the night worrying about 'Bel, wondering what had happened to him after he left. He hoped he was okay, that he got back to the hotel safely, that he'd come back again.

For a while he slept. In his dream he thought 'Bel *had* come back and had sneaked into the room and stripped off his clothes. He remembered somehow being able to see and admire the Visitor's body even in the darkened room. Then 'Bel slipped into the bed and pressed his long, smooth body against him. He could feel his own body respond by growing taut and hard against the golden muscles. He felt the Visitor's lips against his own, and he felt his mouth slowly open. He felt the warmth of the other's body pouring into him, like fire.

And in the dream he believed that somehow the two of them, clutching so close, had indeed caught fire. And the fire was not pain but pleasure and it filled his whole body and consciousness and seemed even to light up the room. He felt the golden flames radiating out from his loins. In the dream the Visitor seemed to be standing over him with his lower body pressed hard against his own, and he could marvel at the look of 'Bel's chest and abdomen illuminated by the fire that jumped between them. Kevin could feel 'Bel pounding against him as his own spine seemed to pound and quiver in time to the Visitor's thrusts.

Then suddenly Kevin awoke. The dream was gone. In an instant. But the biological, psychological process that had been initiated continued. And almost without his being in touch with what was happening—after all he was just struggling to regain full consciousness— the rhythm in his spine ran down into his groin and he felt a sudden, embarrassing wetness spread out onto his abdomen. As the pleasure coursed through him a part of his mind that seemed half-awake and yet still half in the dream looked down at his clenching muscles and observed that his own body had turned to bright shining gold.

The dream—now tinged with the sexual guilt that had haunted Kevin's pleasure all his life—was still clinging to the edge of consciousness when the radio alarm in his laptop went off in the morning.

"…announced today a major policy speech on Visitor relations," a newscaster was saying. "The President will address the nation at noon today. Speculation is mixed on the content of the speech. In other news, an American Airlines plane was forced to land…" Kevin shut off the radio as he finally woke for the morning.

As he padded down the hall to the bathroom, pulling his robe on to protect him from the cold, he wondered if that newscast about the President was part of his dream or if were real.

Real? he thought again. And remembered the strange meeting with 'Bel last evening. *Oh God, is anything real anymore?*

Chapter Seven

"*D*id you see this?" Joel asked, opening his back door and coming out to the deck to join Kevin who was just finishing a last cup of coffee before leaving for the office. Joel was holding up an epage tablet showing a headline announcing: "President Changes Tune on Visitors."

"What does that mean?"

Ignoring Kevin's question, Joel continued, "I heard, uh, 'commotion' around your place last night."

"Huh?"

"Your Visitor friend was over here, wasn't he?"

"Why do you think that?" Kevin asked defensively. He'd been getting to like Joel, but all of a sudden was discovering the problem with nosy neighbors.

"I happened to be passing by the front door when your 'friend' was ringing the bell. I noticed 'cause he rang for so long— "

"—I had the blender running."

"Yeah, well, I looked out the window and saw this really tall guy. And I guess, well, I remembered you knew a Visitor. And I thought maybe it was him."

"It was," Kevin answered matter-of-factly.

"You getting along okay with him?"

"Why do you ask that?" Kevin was trying to remain calm. The questions really weren't that out of line. It was just that they were hitting a sensitive point.

"Well, later on it seemed like maybe you all were arguing or something?"

"What did you hear, Joel?"

"Oh, not a lot. But I could hear you shouting, Kevin. Look I'm not asking just to be nosy. I thought maybe I could, oh you know, help you somehow. I know what it's like to lose a boyfriend."

"Look, Joel, I understand you mean well. But he is not my boyfriend." Kevin's manner was icy.

"Anymore, you mean?"

"He was *never* my boyfriend."

"Okay, okay. I can take a hint." Joel was suddenly more meek than Kevin had ever imagined he could be. "Well, anyway, there's this article on the enews."

"I've got to run to work. But tell me what it says real quick." Kevin tried to sound friendly and appreciative.

"I didn't follow all the links, but it sounds like some of the President's advisors are warning him that there's something suspicious about the Visitors. He's gonna make a national address this afternoon in which, it says here, he's liable to side with the anti-Visitor sentiment."

Kevin was conscious that Joel was not embellishing the news report with any snide remarks about the previous night's visit from 'Bel. "We'll just have to wait and see what happens."

"Guess so. Well, you have a nice day at work," Joel said as he folded the epage shut. "Don't do anything I wouldn't do for a wooden nickel." When Kevin didn't laugh he went back into his apartment.

Kevin glanced at his watch. It was time to be leaving. He drank down the last of his coffee and headed inside. He locked the back door, put the empty cup in the sink, and grabbed the jacket he'd earlier tossed over a wooden folding chair he was using in the kitchen.

I am worried what that's all about. Maybe that's what 'Bel had on his mind last night… and I never let him get to it. As he locked the front door of the apartment behind him, Kevin decided he wouldn't think about the Visitor question anymore this morning. *After all, what can I do about it?*

But he was only half-way down the steps when he started worrying that maybe he'd never have an opportunity to apologize to 'Bel for how he treated him.

Nobody was saying much around Sutro and Associates. There was obviously a pall over the place. The firm had put in a lot of time and effort on the Visitor embassy project. A major change in government policy toward the Visitors could mean a loss for the company. In the coffee room Kevin had overheard Jules Domergue remarking to Joe Sykes, "We passed up some pretty good contracts to get this Visitor thing. If that damn fool in Washington screws up this project, it might be hard finding anything new."

On the other hand, though Chuck Sperry never said a word out loud, Kevin could easily tell the broad grin on Sperry's face was a satisfied I-told-you-so.

Just before noon, Jules' voice boomed out over the paging system. "Everybody's welcome to join me in the client conference room to watch the President's speech."

Kevin had not been going out for lunch most days anyway. He'd usually grabbed a roll or piece of fruit from the vending machine in the coffee room and spent his lunch break reading. Today he was happy to spend the time with the rest of the staff. In fact, he'd been a little worried how he was going to get to hear the speech. He'd thought maybe he'd have to go over to Macy's and hang around the electronics department. Now that was settled.

When you assemble all the employees of Sutro and Associates, Kevin was surprised to see, *you get quite a roomful.* The client conference room, the largest room in the building, was set up like a theater with seats arranged on tiers in a semi-circle around a central podium. The room was designed for teleconferences and video presentations. Today it was practically full.

Most of the employees Kevin had never seen. Only a few worked on the third floor where he had his space off Will Salado's office. The rest were apparently part of the support staff: the people who built the architect's models, designed and produced the blueprints, programmed the roboconstructors, updated the web, typed the reports into memory, and managed the business's finances. Kevin was flattered when Will signalled to him to leave the seat he'd taken in the back row and come down to the front to sit with the partners and associates.

He was just thanking Will when the lights in the room dimmed and the projected image flickered on above the podium. CNN's popular White House correspondent was explaining, "…House rumors have caused many of us in the press corps to expect this address to be full of surprises. Up till now the President has taken a dim view of the anti-Visitor factions in Congress and in his Cabinet. He has publicly declared several times that the arrival of the Visitors has offered unparalleled opportunity for technological exchange. And he has specifically silenced skeptics, warning that debate over the issue of cooperation with the Visitors could easily sour relations.

"Thus the announcement last night of today's address suggests a major shift in policy toward the Visitors that must be based on information heretofore not released to the public." The reporter looked away from the camera for a moment, then, "Here's the President."

The camera shifted to the familiar scene of the White House press room. The President strode forcefully down the corridor at the head of which was positioned the lectern bearing the Great Seal. He looked stern as he put his papers down and then looked up into the camera.

"Ladies and Gentleman, fellow Americans, the last few months have been a time of great excitement and great confusion on our planet. For the first time, it seemed, we had been visited by members of another race. The news of their arrival that night in early June brought fear of an attack from space. Human beings all over the planet drew together in recognition of our common concern for the birthplace of our species. Had there been hostilities, it appeared, we would have joined together East and West to protect the cradle of humanity.

"We seemed fortunate to discover in only a few days that the Visitors did not come in an attacking armada, but came in peace and curiosity. We were surprised—and most of us relieved—to discover they were fundamentally human, like ourselves. Though many were skeptical precisely because they did seem *so much* like ourselves. Perhaps they were imposters.

"I spent a great deal of time with representatives of the Visitors. We discussed how our two races might assist one another through trade and exchange of scientific discovery. I came to trust them and their intentions." The President paused and looked out over the audience.

"I am sorry to say," he began, his voice slightly tremulous, "that during the past week the negotiations for our mutual benefit broke down. In spite of our explanations and reaffirmations of peaceful intentions, the Visitors have objected to our research on the development of the space shield.

"My fellow Americans, I believe all of you understand the historical significance of the shield. Since my esteemed predecessor Ronald Reagan first initiated the Strategic Defense Initiative over half a century ago, this country has poured money and talent into the creation of an effective shield against air or space attack.

"New threats have arisen since President Reagan's time. The Terrorist War that started in the first year of this century made us aware we could be attacked by our own airplanes or by a sole individual carrying a vial of anthrax or a suitcase size nuke. Even though we're actively cooperating with the U.N.'s redress and reconciliation process, the same axis of evil still threatens us, though the names and causes of the terrorists have changed.

"The missile attacks on New York, though causing little damage, showed our enemies still sought to attack us by air. And now, most recently, U.S. intelligence has discovered international terrorists have likely gained access to ICBM's, those missiles from last century's Cold War that can travel round the world to deliver nuclear payloads. And we suspect the Nasserinian rebels may even be able to fire orbiting weapons certain rogue elements were able to install in industrial satellites without the world's knowledge.

"Bio weapons and suitcase nukes notwithstanding, we need space defense. And we need it now!

"In recent years, as you know, we have been most fortunate that that research has shown that the original plans for space-based weapons or lasers cannons that could shoot down attacking missiles were clumsy and inefficient. A much more elegant and simple solution was discovered: the matter-field shield.

"Homeland Security scientists have developed techniques for subtly shifting the basic forces that hold matter together, changing slightly the values of fundamental constants. Thus they can create what in science-fiction were called 'force-fields' that can shield the United States from above so that no attacking missile can enter our air space. Matter field technology has become the bulwark of our defense program. You all know this, I believe. I repeat it, however, because it has become the source of contention with our extraterrestrial guests.

"Last week the Visitors asked us to stop all research in this area. They have been adamant in their objection, though they are only able to give vague justification.

"These actions have given support to the position of skeptics. Frankly I am still a believer that the Visitors are from outer space—though the astronomical data they have provided our scientists has not revealed anything which would support the notion that they've viewed the universe from any perspective other than the surface of this Earth.

"Many in our government are concerned the Visitors are actually foreign agents. Again I say I am sorry to admit that such an explanation now seems plausible. Even if it is not true, the fact that they are asking us to stop research on a defense mechanism that would, indeed, protect us from attack *by them*, if they proved to be actually hostile, forces me to reconsider the invitation I previously extended in good faith.

"We are, of course, willing to reextend that invitation to remain on our planet if the Visitors will refrain from meddling in our internal affairs. We cannot leave ourselves vulnerable to them anymore than we can leave ourselves vulnerable to our enemies on this planet. Therefore, as of noon tomorrow, I am withdrawing the invitation to the Visitors." He sighed noticeably. Apparently the formal address was over.

"Mr. President, Mr. President." Hands shot up all around the room.

The President pointed toward a reporter in the first row, a man from the *New York Times*. "Does this mean the Visitors must leave Earth?"

"Apparently so," the President answered as though he were surprised that his intentions had not been more obvious.

"What have we learned from them already?" Another reporter shouted out. The President looked at him quizzically. He continued, "I mean, have we learned enough from them before we drive them away?"

"I'm not fond of your choice of words there," the President responded. "But, yes, I think we have learned some things from them. Though to be candid, I must admit that their scientific sophistication does not seem all that advanced. What they tell us about their science sounds more like art composition than hard science—shapes and designs rather than forces and energy. This, of course, is part of what makes many skeptical of them. They don't seem to be the master race we expected."

"Mr. President, what have the Visitors said to support their objection to matter-field research?"

"Their major objection has been what we might call 'religious' or aesthetic. I mean they have said that tinkering with the constants of space is unnatural. That may be a laudable sentiment, but given the reality of hostility on Earth and the possibility of hostilities from space, it seems naive."

"Is that all they said?"

"Well, no. They also said the matter-field would not work. But our research shows they are wrong in that assessment."

"What did they mean it would not work?"

"Well, you should probably ask them that. But my understanding of their position was that the field would disrupt the space within it. Our experiments show that this is false."

"How do you intend to enforce your demand that they leave?"

"Apparently, we won't have to. Their leaders have agreed to depart peacefully if the invitation is withdrawn."

"Follow-up," the reporter announced, remaining on his feet. "If you are concerned about the Visitors being potentially hostile, aren't you concerned about provoking attack?"

"Our armed forces are going to yellow alert at this very moment," the President announced. He seemed distracted by something off-camera. "Yes, that's right."

"Do you mean we're at war?" Someone shouted out of turn.

"Let's keep this press conference organized," the President scolded, ignoring the content of the question.

"Mr. President," a young man bolted out of his seat when the President pointed toward him. "Let me go back a moment. I believe you said the Visitors said the matter-field would disrupt space within it. Do you mean they told you that if you turn this thing on over the United States, it will destroy us?" He said the last two words very dramatically.

"Well," the President hesitated for a moment, "well, yes, that's what they said. But, but—"

All of a sudden the room was in an uproar.

The same was true of the client conference room at Sutro and Associates in San Francisco.

Jules Domergue sat forward in his seat and turned toward the partners to his left, "Well, there goes *that* contract."

For a moment Kevin wondered about his job. Then he wondered about 'Bel. A wave of relief passed through him. Then a wave of grief.

A crowd was forming outside the St. Francis Hotel when Kevin arrived only a few minutes after the broadcast ended. (Will Salado had assured him no more work was going to get done today and it'd be okay to run out for a while.) Inside the hotel police were stationed by the elevator.

Ignoring his fear—and surprising himself—Kevin went right up to the first policeman and explained he was with the architecture firm employed by the Visitors and that he had to talk with one of them right away. The policeman started to brush him aside. "Only official government business allowed."

"But wait," Kevin hastily objected, "my boss sent me over here to collect on a bill. If they leave we won't get paid."

The policeman looked at him for a moment, then smiled. "That's a real patriotic American reason if I ever heard one." He pressed the call button on the elevator for Kevin.

The Visitor sitting at the receptionist desk was not the one Kevin had spoken with the other day. Today that place was occupied by a dark-haired, dark-complected woman with an obvious scowl on her face. When Kevin asked to speak with 'Belwyn Tuarul, she replied, seeming to turn an even darker color, "He's busy now and unable to speak with you."

"May I wait here?" Kevin asked politely.

"No, you may not," the receptionist replied. "You must leave now."

"But how—" Kevin started to ask a question he realized was not going to have an answer.

For a moment the receptionist seemed almost to smile. "I'm sorry," she said. Kevin noticed that her complexion seemed to lighten. "But you have to leave." She resumed her previous stern demeanor.

Kevin suddenly felt totally lost. *Maybe the only thing to do is forget this whole thing. But I can't. I just can't.* He stood looking helpless in front of the desk. Finally the receptionist asked him again, "Please, just get in the elevator and leave before we both, uh, get in trouble. You are not supposed to be here."

This time Kevin did as he was told. Once in the elevator his will seemed to come back to him. Just as the door was opening into the lobby, he decided he'd stay here at the St. Francis. 'Bel was bound to come by sooner or later. At least he'd have a chance to see him before he left Earth. *Forever,* he thought forlorn.

The lobby was teeming with people. Most of them were reporters, Kevin surmised from the electronic equipment some of them were carrying. He noticed the police were diligently keeping them away from the elevators. Outside the plate glass doors of the main entrance he could see demonstrators with signs: some seemed to be pro-Visitor, others angrily anti-Visitor.

No wonder the Visitors don't want people around. They must be afraid of violence.

For a while Kevin milled around in the crowd, not sure where he should go. He didn't see any Visitors, so what he was doing didn't seem like it would help him find 'Bel. He found a utility hall near the elevators which led into the kitchen. He wandered around in the innards of the building, thinking maybe there'd be a back way the Visitors would be using by which to avoid the public. But there was nobody back there except a cook who told him he shouldn't be there either. He made up what he himself thought was a lame excuse that he was looking for the men's room. The cook politely gave him directions to the facilities off the lobby. Not knowing what else to do, he followed those directions to the public restrooms.

Kevin was surprised. Though very big with lots of stalls and a long row of lavatories, the men's room was deserted. Perhaps by coming here through the utility halls he'd bypassed a security barricade that was keeping the public out. Kevin washed his hands and face, and then stood leaning against the lavatory wondering what he was going to do. He certainly couldn't stay here and milling around in the lobby wasn't going to do any good. *I guess I might as well go back to work,* he was thinking when he realized he wasn't alone in the bathroom. He heard a shuffling sound coming from one of the cubicles. Apparently somebody was hiding in there. *What in the world?*

Kevin slowly walked over toward the row of stalls. He didn't want to surprise somebody who might be armed. *What if an assassin or something has gotten in here?* Passing the first stall he saw that by looking quickly and holding the motion with his eye, he could get a glimpse through the crack in the door jamb into the cubicle.

He glanced down and saw that no feet were visible. *That means whoever's in there has got his feet pulled up so I won't see him.* His heart was beating hard. As he passed by the stall in question, he managed to glimpse the top of a head. Something looked familiar. He turned and walked back by again. And then started laughing.

What he was seeing was the top of the radiation helmet 'Bel had worn to his house last night.

He knocked on the door. "'Bel, it's okay. It's me." Just as he was saying the words it occurred to him that 'Bel was not the only Visitor who might be hiding under one of those helmets.

"Oh thank you," 'Bel answered. "I wasn't sure what I was going to do. I wasn't expecting to find you in here."

"Well, what are you doing hiding in the men's room?"

Opening the door, 'Bel answered, "Kevin, I was sure you'd come when you heard the speech. I didn't dare call direct on your dime device; the call could be traced and I'd been ordered…" His voice trailed away and his eyes turned ashen.

"So I called your office from Horam's desk," he went on. "And learned you'd left. I knew you wouldn't get through the receptionist upstairs to find me. So I came down to the lobby to wait. But it was full of people and some guards shouted at me to get out of there. And I ended up in here. I've been huddling in that stall now for almost twenty minutes wondering how I was going to find you or, at least, get out of the hotel." He smiled and his face radiated a golden glow, mixed with a kind of rosy blush that made him look so innocent and loving.

Kevin's heart melted. *How sweet!*

Such a rush of joy filled Kevin. He opened his arms and 'Bel embraced him smoothly. They held each other and then slowly brought their cheeks together and finally their lips. Kevin pulled back and looked at 'Bel's now blazing gold face and deep into his emerald eyes. Then looking away and placing his cheek against 'Bel's he said softly, "I'm sorry about last night."

"I know you are."

After another pause, during which the joy began to turn to anxiety, Kevin asked, "What are we going to do? What's going to happen?"

"I don't know what's going to happen. And I think what we need to do is to live fully in the time we have."

"Are your people just going to leave?"

"That's what it sounds like, doesn't it? But we can't. I mean, we just can't give up on the mission. It's too important."

"What do you mean?"

"Well, I guess I can talk about it now," 'Bel said warily. "Our mission was to stop the matter-field research. And there's just too much at risk to give in."

"Then why are your leaders just conceding? Can't they explain?"

"I think they *did* explain, but your President didn't believe them. And I think that just devastated them."

"That the President didn't believe them?" Kevin seemed incredulous. *Doesn't everybody know that negotiation always involves mistrusting each other?*

"You can't understand what believing in each other means to us. It's just so basic. And coming here we've found all the rules changed. We don't know who to believe or how to tell. And it's driving us all crazy."

"I don't understand. What did you expect?"

"Maybe we can get out of here," 'Bel said, changing the subject. "Then I'll explain everything to you."

"Where do you want to go?"

"Your apartment?" 'Bel said and the rosy blush flickered across his face again.

Kevin grinned. The very idea excited him and scared him. He could feel himself starting to tremble. But he realized the guilt that usually seemed associated with that excitement was gone. "Okay."

"I can wear this helmet, that'll hide my face. Then how about changing clothes with me. You won't look like a Visitor even if you are wearing my clothes." He was right. The Visitors usually wore jump suits that looked pretty normal anyway, and in fact among fans of the Visitors the colorful jump suits had become a style fad. With his dark curly hair and fair complexion Kevin would look perfectly human.

"Won't you look like you're wearing high-water pants?" Kevin joked as he pulled off his wool dress slacks. After all, he was several inches shorter than 'Bel. "And with a sun hat?" he started laughing, growing giddy from the excitement of the day and the anticipation of the upcoming flight through the crowd of demonstrators with a ridiculously disguised Visitor.

"High water?" 'Bel looked quizzical. "What are you talking about? There's no water around here." Then more seriously he explained, "We only have to get as far as the garage. I've got keys to one of the automobiles we're using."

"Great," Kevin answered. He was thinking about the fact that 'Bel obviously hadn't gotten the idiom about high-water pants. *That doesn't prove anything. Foreign spies might not know that reference either.* With that thought he was reminded, however, that 'Bel seemed to use common expressions like "lying" and "getting in trouble" as though they were foreign words he'd had to learn. There was certainly something peculiar about his use of English.

But suddenly Kevin's linguistic speculations were interrupted by a rush of physical sensation as his body reacted automatically as 'Bel pulled his arms out of the jump suit and bent down to free his feet. For the first time, Kevin was seeing the Visitor's body naked. He was a little surprised to realize how close that dream image that had clung to the back of his mind all day was to the reality. Though, in fact, 'Bel's shoulders were more developed and the muscles of his upper chest more defined than in the dream and light blond, almost colorless hair spread across his chest. 'Bel seemed a perfect blend of masculinity and femininity, strong but gentle, manly but sweet—beyond the dualities.

"Wow," Kevin exclaimed, "you're the most beautiful man I've ever seen."

Continuing to pull the jump suit off his legs and then standing up straight, 'Bel smiled warmly. The rosy blush spread over his face and down his body. Even the hair on his chest and the brush of hair at his crotch seemed to change color slightly. "I'm glad you like how I look."

Kevin averted his gaze from 'Bel's groin, though his curiosity and rising sexual urge fought against this effort.

"I want to see your body too, Kevin Anderson, and admire your color," 'Bel said reaching out to part the white dress shirt Kevin was struggling to unbutton as fast as he could.

"But let's get out of here," Kevin pulled them both back into the reality that they were standing in the middle of a public restroom with a hoard of crazed demonstrators probably only a few dozen yards away on the other side of the wall.

Chapter Eight

"And I guess I love you enough—you know, like a brother, or like a sister, as they say—that I want your, uh, first time to be real special." Tim Lewiston's words of that day in Dunster House last June echoed in Kevin's mind as he lay exhausted, breathing slowly and deeply, letting himself recover from the passion that had just roared through him. June had been such a long time ago. So much had happened since then. *I'm barely the same person*, Kevin acknowledged.

Lifting his head from the pillow and opening his eyes, he felt the exhaustion as cleansing and joyful, as though he'd finally put down a terrible weight he'd been carrying, even though he hadn't even realized he'd been carrying it. He looked down at his own body. For one of the first times in his life he felt he liked his body; he felt relaxed in his flesh in a way he never had before. Now he saw the smooth curves of his muscles as lines of definition and not signs of being a ninety-pound weakling. He saw the dark hair that curled about the center of his chest as a symbol of his manliness and not an embarrassing exposure of his sexuality to be hidden behind buttoned-up shirts. He saw his pale color as a flush of love and not as a symptom of his hiding from the sun. And he thought he saw—though he was sure it was just an illusion—that, just like in his dream, his chest and torso were glowing with golden fire.

He turned his head toward the figure languishing next to him. "Hi," he whispered. "You okay?" He asked because as he looked at 'Bel he realized the golden color was gone. The Visitor's long, slender body was almost purple.

"Of course," he answered as he rolled over to face Kevin and to crane his long neck to kiss him lightly on the cheek. "I was thinking about home."

"Is your home planet beautiful?"

"Just like yours," 'Bel answered and the color in his face darkened.

"Look, 'Bel, you promised you'd explain what's going on. I don't want to pressure you. I mean, I know you told me you weren't supposed to talk about, uh, certain things, but at least explain to me what all the strange color changes are in your body. I mean, uh, sometimes it gives me the willies."

"The what?"

Kevin laughed at his childish expression. "Oh, never mind. Will you explain?" He sat up in the bed and turned to face 'Bel, folding his legs tailor fashion and pulling a blanket over his shoulders. 'Bel raised himself up on his elbows causing his abdomen to flex and tighten. Kevin was trying to be rational and find answers for his questions, but his sexual and affectionate urges overwhelmed him again and he reached out and stroked 'Bel's torso. His fingers tingled. And then he bent down and kissed 'Bel just below the navel.

As he sat up, he saw that where he'd kissed the Visitor, the skin had lightened and turned golden again, radiating lines of color that ran down into his now soft but still full penis. "See!" Kevin announced as though he'd just made a startling discovery. "You do that to me and I don't change colors."

'Bel laughed heartily. "You do deserve an explanation." He reached out and tugged at the blanket Kevin had wrapped around himself. "But right now I'm turning blue because I am cold," he said. "Come here." He pulled Kevin down out of his sitting position so that were cuddled together under the blanket.

"It must be obvious to you, by now, that my pigmentation changes with my moods and thoughts."

"Yeah, I guess so."

"It's really just like what you call blushing, only it's more developed as a medium of communication."

"We don't have very much control over blushing," Kevin objected, "so it really isn't communication. It's more like a give-away."

"You means it's autonomic," 'Bel corrected. "So's ours."

"You don't have any control over it?" Kevin pulled away a little so he could look into 'Bel's face.

"Very little. One can control one's thoughts, but the pigmentation change—our 'color'—is autonomic."

"But isn't that like being emotionally and mentally transparent all the time. How can you keep a secret?"

'Bel smiled and orangy-red highlights spread through his cheeks. "We can't."

"Oh my God," Kevin exclaimed, beginning to realize the implications.

"That's why we developed those awful pills before embarking on our mission here. The drug pretty much stops the pigmentation change, though it sometimes turns people funny colors. Your color just freezes in mid-change. It's very disconcerting."

"Did you have secrets to keep?"

'Bel's face turned dark then light then dark again in fast successive waves. "More than we should, I think." He smiled at Kevin and his face goldened again. He kissed him lightly on the lips. "You just discovered at least one of them."

"You mean about the color changes?"

"Well, that…"

Kevin was still reeling emotionally from the idea of being that psychologically transparent. He remembered how all his life he'd been struggling to hide *uh, certain feelings* from everybody, including himself.

"Don't you have any privacy?"

"Of course we do. But probably in a different way from what you mean. Privacy is something we grant to one another out of respect, not out of a need to hide the truth."

"Everybody accepts everybody else's, uh, desires and things?"

"Sure, at least if it's the truth."

"You mean you can't lie?" Kevin spoke the words slowly, carefully, one by one.

'Bel smiled. His hand still pressed to 'Bel's abdomen, Kevin could feel the muscles in his chest and belly quiver a little as the smile became a deep chuckle. "No, Kevin. That's why I had to learn that word to come here. We don't even have the concept."

"But, but," Kevin came right to the point of his amazement. "'Bel, we just did something that people—I mean, my people—have to keep very secret."

"You mean make love?"

"I mean have 'homosexual sex,'" Kevin surprised himself with the intensity of his voice. "My God, 'Bel, up until right now I've been denying these feelings all my life. This is supposed to be the most shameful thing human beings can do. If I couldn't keep any secrets, why, everybody would know!"

"That's why my people are taking drugs to suppress the truth," 'Bel answered. "Your whole race, unfortunately, can't accept the truth." He fell silent for a moment. "But it's destroying us. I don't mean the pills, but what they do. It'd be like going blind and deaf. All of a sudden we can't tell what each other is thinking and feeling. We've started to mistrust one another." He'd turned a kind of dirty blue. "That's another word we had to learn. At home we never had to 'trust' each other, we just always knew...

"Last night, Kevin, when I got home, practically everybody on the team was red."

"Red?"

"Angry," 'Bel answered. "Tempers are running high because we're all going crazy. And now your President is demanding we leave the planet," he said, suddenly bringing reality down around them.

"Oh, 'Bel, can't you stay with me? Or take me with you?" Kevin blustered. "Discovering you and feeling good about myself, making love with you—it's too wonderful to give up. I *can't* give it up now."

'Bel looked into Kevin's eyes and he turned a deep sad ashen grey. "Kev, I fell in love with you that first day. You were the first Earth person I'd seen whose color looked right to me. I mean, I know you all don't show color like we do. But you do, it's just much more subtle. That's another part of what's driving us crazy: being around people who are blatantly lying to us and showing it, but apparently not caring—because they don't know. But you didn't seem like that. Your face was full of, of what you call innocence, not-hurting. At the same time you looked so easily hurt, so, uh, vulnerable.

"That's why we were so interested in your gay culture. At least for a while it seemed like gay men in your world display just the traits that are so basic to our personalities."

"You mean you could tell I was gay?" Kevin asked.

'Bel's face glistened golden again. "Well, of course. How else do you think we'd ever have gotten into this bed?" Then gently he added, "My love."

Kevin buried his face in between 'Bel's neck and shoulder and clung tight. "What are we going to do?"

"Kevin, there's more at stake than just us two. I mean I really do love you and I, uh, believe you love me—I can see your color when you smile at me. But what's at risk is two whole worlds. And my people's trying to keep our secrets—mainly the one you just found out about," he stroked Kevin's cheek with his finger and then let his hand follow the line down Kevin's neck to his chest and torso, and let his open hand rest lightly around Kevin's penis. "—has led us into a stupid, stupid position and we're going to leave here and let everything be ruined."

"I don't understand what you mean. What's going to be ruined?"

"Both our worlds."

"Can I help? I mean, can you and I do something to change it?"

"What?" 'Bel's color darkened. "It seems like we're powerless before all the lying and deceit. You and I are just insignificant interns. What can we do?"

"No, 'Bel, we're not insignificant. 'Cause we love each other. Maybe I can teach you something about living in this world where people lie and cheat and play power games. One of the major themes of our culture," Kevin was feeling a surge of power, "is that love can't be conquered, that lovers can beat any odds. Maybe our love for one another can change whatever the problem is between our two races."

'Bel's color turned rosy. He grinned. "You got golded up."

"Now look, you gotta tell me more. There's still so much I don't understand. If we're gonna save the world, we gotta get straight with each other."

'Bel's hand was still resting against Kevin's thigh. As he smiled, starting to say, "I'll show you about getting straight" and to tighten his fist around Kevin, an electronic chime sounded in the room.

"What's that?" Kevin asked, feeling suddenly pulled out of his romantic, magically powerful world.

"My communicator."

'Bel leaped out of bed and rifled through his jumpsuit thrown over a chair in the corner. He pulled out a small metallic box and held it to his ear. Kevin could hear what sounded like oddly intonated English, but he couldn't quite understand the meaning.

"I've got to go. That was a priority command. I can't disobey."

"No, you can't go. The ships'll take off and, and I'll never see you again," Kevin was almost screaming. "What about saving the world?"

"We can still do it. Even if the ships take off. I mean, there's another way. The geometry window…" The communicator chimed again, as if to reiterate that this was a priority command. "…at the site."

"I don't believe you," Kevin exclaimed.

"Look at me then. Kevin, I love you. I have to go. But we'll see each other again." 'Bel's face was bright yellow, his eyes deep blue. He pointed with one finger at himself. "Look, Kevin, this can't lie."

Kevin suddenly wasn't sure what to believe anymore. He didn't know one color sign from another. Not accurately anyway. But he'd have to trust.

"If I don't go, they'll come after me. They can find me. There's no way to hide." His whole body was quivering. He was struggling to pull on his jumpsuit. "I can't hide. I'd die, Kevin, I'd die." His voice was strained, his color darkening toward somber maroon.

*K*evin was still lying in bed when his dime rang several hours later. He'd been half-sleeping, his feelings alternating from joy and excitement and anticipation of adventure to anger and loss and despondency.

"Kevin," 'Bel's voice was instantly recognizable over the phonelink, "you were right about the ships' leaving. But there *is* another way. I'll try to get back to you. But if I don't, you can come to me… Look, there are too many people around. I can't explain it now. I shouldn't be telling you this at all. But remember, we talked about it once. It's a matter of geometry."

'Bel's voice faltered slightly. "And remember I love you," he said.

Kevin started to answer when the connection broke. He felt angry at 'Bel for giving him a riddle like that. What an awful thing to have as a last memory! But maybe he could figure it out.

That night on the beach, he recalled, 'Bel had talked about the stars as floating or sinking in an ocean of geometry. Kevin hadn't understood what he meant and 'Bel had explained about Einstein's theory of gravitation as a distortion of space-time geometry. *Is that what he's talking about? What good could that do me? How's Einstein going to help me get to his space ship?*

*J*oel had offered to bring dinner over. He'd fried a chicken and made potato salad. Now the two of them were sitting in front of Kevin's little laptop in his still fairly empty living room, watching TV news , as the reports of the Visitor's departure were run over and over.

"Visitor teams in the major cities were recalled today following President Arnold's early afternoon address. By nightfall, all Visitors in New York City, Boston, and elsewhere along the East Coast had returned to their spaceship in Washington, D.C." As the newscaster recounted the events of the day, news footage showed Visitors hustling into automobiles and vans, which then drove off at breakneck speed, most led by police escorts.

"On the West Coast, the evacuation was apparently somewhat slower and quieter, but by this hour the team temporarily quartered in the St. Francis Hotel in downtown San Francisco has been escorted to the former Presidio Military Reservation to await arrival of a ship.

"It remains unclear at this time what decisions have been reached about the future of relations with the Visitors. The White House has remained officially silent, though rumors abound that the negotiations may be continued by electronic transmissions once the Visitors have returned to space. It is not clear whether the sudden evacuation was ordered by President Arnold specifically or if this dramatic reaction to his speech came from the Visitors themselves."

Kevin stared intently at the small screen hoping he might see 'Bel among the Visitors leaving the hotel and later standing around in a crowd on the landing field at the Presidio, quite near where he himself had been at the embassy construction site. He worried about the Visitors' vulnerability waiting in the open field. *If only I were with 'Bel,* he kept thinking irrationally, realizing it really wouldn't make any difference. The evacuation was happening with or without him and with or without his agreement.

The video switched to shots of now-deserted Visitor headquarters. "All over the planet, apparently even in Russia and China," the newscaster continued, "Visitor bases have been abandoned."

The half-built embassy nearby at the Rumsfeld Research Park appeared on the screen. "That's the building I was working on," Kevin remarked halfheartedly to Joel.

"You seem pretty depressed," Joel responded.

"Yeah," was all Kevin could answer. He kept remembering 'Bel's saying they could still reunite, that there was another way. But it all seemed so fanciful now. The fact was the Visitors were leaving, being driven off the Earth, apparently, because of President Arnold's hardnosed policy of building that space shield of his and because of the Visitors' internal psychological difficulty dealing with Earth people. Kevin wasn't sure who to blame. *If* there was anybody to blame at all. He couldn't help feeling a little like Romeo or Juliet, his love soured by a feud between families that made no sense at all to him but that was ruining his life anyway.

The video image continued to pan over the scenes of the embassy construction site as the newscaster recounted the brief history of positive expectations of the Visitors' arrival on Earth. In spite of his mood, Kevin couldn't help paying attention to the footage of the building he'd been working on. He noticed the strange architectural features—the oddly designed stairways, the nautilus-shaped chamber. He saw them as evidence of how alien the Visitors really were. Though in the tissue of his own body he knew how similar they were as well. His body literally ached with the teasing memory of 'Bel's touch.

"What's that supposed to be?" Joel interrupted his sorrowful musing. "...that thing in the middle?" He was pointing at the screen as the TV camera moved through the deserted building and looked right into the mirror-lined opening of that odd-shaped central chamber. The Visitors themselves had already done the finishing out work on that room, Kevin noticed. He recalled hearing they were planning that.

"Funny, isn't it?" he answered Joel. "It's sort of shaped like a seashell inside a cube. Somebody at work thought it might be an antenna of some sort."

"Looks as much like an antenna as a high school solid geometry project," Joel joked in one of his confusing Bunnyisms.

Kevin was annoyed that Joel could make a joke at a time like this. Then all of a sudden he realized Joel had inadvertently said the magic word. Kevin's blood ran icy. *Yeah, there is something about that structure that's like a geometry project. Was that what 'Bel was talking about? What could he possibly have meant?*

Kevin's thoughts were interrupted by the newscaster's excited announcement, "We have a news bulletin. The Washington, D.C.-based ship has just lifted off. And, simultaneously, the ship that's been hovering mysteriously over the Southern California city of Riverside has begun to move north, probably toward San Francisco. The Visitors at the Presidio have fallen into ranks apparently in expectation of imminent departure. We are awaiting confirmation that a Moscow-based ship has also lifted off."

The screen showed the ship that had been resting gently in the Ellipse in front of the White House slowly rise and then with increasing speed ascend into the light-hazy night sky over Washington. After a moment, the image changed to show a similar ship hovering and then landing on the broad expanse of grassy field at the air station at the Presidio.

Though, of course, he could not tell which of the Visitors filing into the ship in formation was 'Bel, Kevin's heart burned with the fear he'd never see his lover again. At the same time, he knew something had changed dramatically in his life and that there'd be no going back to the fear and guilt. And he also clung to the hope that there really was something in that "high school geometry project" out at the Research Park that could reunite him with 'Bel. Kevin's vision of the video screen grew misty as tears filled his eyes.

"You're really in love with that Visitor guy, aren't you?" Joel observed with not nearly enough reverence for the intensity of Kevin's feelings, but with a certain "sisterly" concern that Kevin accepted warmly.

"Yes, I am," he answered, feeling the pride in his voice.

Chapter Nine

"Think we can convince anybody this is the newest fad in luxury housing?" George Sanders joked sardonically. "Maybe we can still salvage the firm's investment."

"I'm glad to see you have your employer's interests at heart, George," Jules Domergue replied as he jumped down from the rough concrete foundation, balancing himself by grabbing hold of a vertical stud in the half-completed staircase on the outside of the building. "We made a calculated gamble when we took on this project. If we lost, well, we lost."

"Look, the foundation's fine. The walls are in the right places. This'll be easy to redesign. It'll make a great office building. It's got a wonderful view," Morton Lau, the general contractor, observed, obviously trying to take a realistically positive view of the turn of events of the last three days.

Jules laughed. "I guess you're right, Morton. *You*'re lucky the project stopped before the building got any further along. But, you know, *we* had the blueprints completed. That work is lost."

"I disagree, Jules," the intense Asian-American contractor answered. "Most of the specifications will work fine. Of course, there'll be a few changes. We'll restructure the stairways—that'll actually give us more room. And we'll have to get rid of the, uh, statue here," he pointed up at the only part of the building that seemed anywhere near finished: the nautilus shell structure enclosed in a cube.

"I propose we go ahead and complete the building on speculation. I'll bet we can sell—"

Kevin tuned out the business conversation. He looked at those staircases on the outside of the building that didn't connect the floors to one another. He thought he'd been right that that was for privacy. *But what would the Visitors being doing in their quarters,* he wondered, *that'd require such privacy.* He turned his attention to that strange structure the

Visitors had placed in the center of the embassy building. No one had ever figured out what it was for. The most recent hypothesis among the members of the team was that it was some kind of Visitor religious icon or talisman. Kevin had another suspicion entirely.

Ever since Joel gave him the clue, he'd been reliving in his mind every conversation he'd had with 'Bel. He realized that he'd been so emotionally involved with his infatuation with the Visitor and his abject fear of what those feelings meant that he really hadn't been paying attention to the technical discussions they'd had. But he did remember that 'Bel had said something about how the space drive had worked, how their arrival did not require movement *through* space, how the Visitor ships simply jumped from one location to another by what, Kevin assumed, was called in science-fiction movies a "space-warp," and how they'd had to arrive outside the atmosphere *"until we could build a window on the surface."* Kevin was sure he could remember 'Bel saying something like that. *Isn't this just such a window on the surface? But how does it work?*

"I'm convinced this is a weapon," Chuck Sperry announced as he climbed around the shell-shaped structure.

"Why do you say that?" Jules asked. There was an edge to his voice that suggested Domergue was almost as annoyed as Kevin with Sperry's paranoia. Kevin wondered what Sperry was even doing out here. He wasn't actually on the team. He'd just tagged along this afternoon when Domergue announced the embassy project was temporarily suspended and invited the team to drive out with him to the site to "assess the damages" and "brainstorm ways to salvage the investment."

"Well, look at this mirror-surface the Visitors installed," Sperry answered Jules. "This is not just decorative. The surface is polished like a scientific instrument. And there's this coil of copper wire running along the opening. That's to create some sort of electromagnetic field."

Kevin was truly angry at Chuck Sperry. He realized that Chuck was harmless. And he was a good engineer—an asset to the firm. But... *It's people like him that scared the Visitors in the first place. That caused them to think they had to keep their secret—whatever that was! And that drove them away.* Kevin felt a wave of anger and pain pour through him. He knew it wasn't fair to blame Sperry for the Visitors' leaving or for his own separation from 'Bel. *But...*

"It'd be useless as a weapon. It's aimed in one direction and can't be moved," Dick Jularian spoke up. He'd been sitting on the foundation doing some sketching for the redesign. "I've always said it was an antenna. I think Chuck's point about the copper wire corroborates my hypothesis. Look, it's aimed across at Marin. What were they going to do, Chuck, shoot out the marina in Tiburon?" Dick joked, pointing across the Golden Gate toward the upscale towns of Marin County on the other side.

"How about ships going in and out of the Bay? From here you could control *all* the traffic to the San Francisco and Oakland ports." Chuck suddenly made sense.

"Yeah, but the weapon itself would be pretty vulnerable," Dick answered. "From the top of the hill anybody could take it out with a round of mortar fire." They all automatically looked up to see the black glass and marble facade of the Seacliff Heights Tabernacle of Jesus' Love imposing above them. Who'd doubt that Reverend McMasterson would be happy to allow the mortars to be fired from his rooftop?

Kevin didn't like this kind of talk at all. It just stirred up his own anxieties about the relationship with 'Bel. *What if he was using me? Trying to manipulate me into whatever plot they had going on?* After all, 'Bel admitted *there was something they were hiding.* It was bad enough that Kevin wasn't sure he could trust the Visitors. He knew he was in love with 'Bel. But wasn't that just a sign of his emotional immaturity? Sure, it was neat to have befriended a Visitor, especially since he was working with them. But what had he done letting himself get mixed up with 'Bel sexually? Years of homophobic anxiety echoed in his mind. He thought about how he'd let himself get into homosexual situations. And even though he'd never done anything, how guilty he'd felt later, how full of recriminations and regrets.

Kevin thought about the AIDS nightmare that had haunted all his boyhood notions of sex. He remembered his father warning him about body fluids (it was humiliating just remembering that happened). *What if 'Bel was trying to contaminate me with something.* He thought about the sex they had. *It was perfectly safe. I mean, there was no exchange of body fluids. But what about next time?* A shudder ran through him. *I mean, what if there'd been a next time. Maybe he was going to plant some kind of parasite or monster in me!* Kevin thought about old Sigourney Weaver movies he'd watched on TV as a kid. He suddenly felt disgust for his body.

"Hey, I got an idea," Morton Lau spoke up. He was examining the copper coil Chuck had pointed out. "Maybe we can get this thing to vibrate or something, then sell it to a faggot bathhouse. Tell 'em it's the latest sexual fad. Uh, you know, crawl inside this orifice…"

Kevin cringed. He hated that kind of humor. It didn't even make any sense. And it just exacerbated his sexual anxieties.

"Morton, that isn't very funny. Gay people wouldn't be so gullible…" George Sanders said sternly, the correction of Lau's choice of words obvious in his voice. He started shoo'ing them all towards the door.

Kevin felt proud of George. It occurred to him that his own misgivings came from the secrecy he demanded of himself. His mind was aswim with emotions. Even as he was cringing with homophobic guilt, he was admiring George's forthrightness and wishing he had the guts to talk with George about his feelings for 'Bel.

Almost as if he knew he was upset by all this talk, as George locked the door, he turned to Kevin, "You haven't said anything at all. What do you think that is?" He pointed at the shell structure back behind the glass windows of the now locked embassy.

Kevin had to get hold of himself for a moment. He was surprised by George's sudden attention. Without deciding whether he should have censored himself, he answered ingenuously, "It's a matter transporter unit, so they can get back and forth from their spaceship."

Kevin had politely declined George's offer of a ride home. He said he had some errands to run and would take the bus. "After all," he justified, "I need the practice. That's the only way to learn the system."

In reality, he wanted to be alone with the strange device, but he hadn't wanted the others to know of his interest. He was afraid to let them see what was really on his mind.

Earlier in the day, back at the office, Kevin had surreptitiously reloaded the specs for the Visitor embassy into the design app he'd created at Harvard, then tweaked the parameters for that "geometry project" that stood at the center of the building to include the mirrored surface and the copper wire that Visitor technicians had installed after Sutro's part of the job was completed. The gimmick of his computer creation—that got him his degree with top honors from the University *and* this job at Sutro & Associates—was that it graphically animated force and energy flow in the virtual design. The point of such a graphical representation, at least as Kevin first conceived it for his senior thesis, was to plot heat loss in large structures; that was a very practical need for architects and engineers designing buildings.

But this morning Kevin had had a different use in mind. The same functions that would model heat flow would also model electrical, magnetic, and even gravitational forces at play in the design. Kevin wanted to know what would happen if the "geometry project" were energized. He hoped the app would be even more perspicacious than its creator and would virtually model all energy flows, even of a type he hadn't anticipated.

The digitized specs had been sent by the Visitors directly to Sutro's main server. If the Visitors had included the full range of data on the building and its contents, the app might very well display exactly what Kevin was looking for. As the digitized information was loading into Kevin's Macintosh Scribe, the new laptop his dad had given him for graduation, he wondered again how it was that the Visitors' computers were so compatible with ours. Of course, there'd had to be a translation program, but even the fact that such a translator were possible indicated surprising compatibility between computer platforms designed lightyears apart. (He still didn't understand what 'Bel had meant by saying they weren't really from outer space.) *Even computer manufacturers, all in the U.S., can't accomplish such smooth transition.*

It made Kevin wonder just how long the Visitors had been watching Earth. *Is this really their first trip here? Have they been spying on us for years in what we've called UFO's? Do they really look like those little white and gray doughboys? But I've touched 'Bel. He's not a doughboy!*

Kevin brought up the plans for the site, selected the nautilus-shell-looking device, and set the app to assembling the 3-D model in virtual space. The computer screen flashed a dialogue asking for a name for the modelling sequence; Kevin entered 'Bel's enigmatic phrase "There is another way." Presently what Kevin had concluded was a transporter unit appeared as a green three dimensional wire-frame figure on the screen. Kevin pressed the key combination to initiate force replication.

As he anticipated, the wait cursor whirled for nearly a minute, then a series of bands of color composed of small vector arrows appeared showing various energy patterns the computer calculated would affect the model. Red arrows represented heat; they were uniformly radiating out. Dark purple arrows represented gravitation; as expected, they were all pointing down. *The thing's heavy*, Kevin thought. Blue arrows represented electric and static electric forces; they were smoothly chasing each other in a circle marquee around the mirrored aperture. There were also white dots swirling around the whole figure, like blank spots in the display.

"Undefined input" read the error message when Kevin tried to click on one of the moving dots. Nothing like that had ever showed up in any of his models before. *Is the information about the mirrored surface interfering with the calculations? Why would there be an undefined field? Could that be the Visitor data that the app doesn't know how to process?*

Kevin selected a couple of commands from the pulldown menus, "Reformat Forces> Other" and "Use Block Modeling." Inadvertently, he double-clicked the Execute key, so that he bypassed the dialogue about naming the sequence. The app automatically chose the previous text string he'd entered.

The wait cursor spun for a moment. Then the green wire-frame figure reappeared on the screen. The various bands of colored vector arrows had been replaced by a series of small blue boxes with the words "There is another way" inscribed in them. The boxes began to assemble a sphere around the whole figure.

Kevin tried several different combinations of parameters to see if he could understand what the computer was showing. When he selected "Electrical>On," the sphere of blue boxes began rotating, indicating there were electric circuits. It began spinning faster and faster. Then suddenly a pucker appeared right over the slightly trapezoidal opening of the transporter unit. The cursor, now showing as a larger yellow box with the words "There is another way" emblazoned inside it, spun once around the whole sphere and then inexplicably contracted to a point and shot right into that opening. To Kevin's amazement, the whole sphere of blue boxes then seemed to be sucked into the pucker and pulled right down behind the cursor. The energy field disappeared. And the cursor was gone.

Now, how did it do that?

Kevin had to abort the sequence to get the cursor back. He wasn't sure what it all meant. But he was now committed to investigating this phenomenon with the real machine. *That thing is powered. Somehow the electrical field must be able to be turned on.*

- - -

After the others had left him at the bus stop up at Mason Street, Kevin walked the couple of blocks back to the site. Though Jules had locked the half-constructed building as they were all leaving, Kevin had anticipated that and earlier disabled the make-shift fastener on one of the back doors , a stub of 2x4 nailed to the frame and turned sideways to hold the door closed. He could get back inside easily.

He climbed all over and inside the mirrored nautilus-shell enclosed in a cube, hoping to figure out what turned it on. But there seemed to be no power entering it at all. *Maybe it can only receive. Maybe it isn't finished. Maybe there's no way 'Bel could come back even if he wanted to.*

Not immediately finding a way to activate the transporter—*if that's what it is*—left Kevin feeling alone and desolate once again. He wanted to find 'Bel, to get himself transported up to the Visitors' ship—he was sure that was the purpose of this strange device. He certainly didn't want to go home. He didn't want to be alone in that apartment, in that bed. He knew he'd remember what it had been like to be with 'Bel in that bed. And he knew that then that mind-boggling confusion of thoughts would start again: *Am I? Do I want to be? Do I have to be? Why can't I just be myself without having to choose labels? Do I really love 'Bel? Does 'Bel love me? Does anybody love me? What if they knew?*

Remembering Louise Hoffman's prescription for feeling lost and lonely in San Francisco ("Gaze at the Golden Gate Bridge"), Kevin made his way out of the building, making sure to keep the back entrance unfastened. The late afternoon was getting colder as the sun was dropping. He huddled out of the wind in a cranny behind some construction equipment and curled up to watch the orangy rays of sunset illumine the towers of the great bridge that loomed over this whole end of San Francisco. *What next?*

The evening was beautiful. Overhead huge clouds turned gold and orange and magenta as the sun slipped down toward the horizon. The colors reminded Kevin of 'Bel. One particular shade of reddish-gold, Kevin was sure, was exactly the Visitor's color of sexual affection.

Louise had been right that the Bridge was beautiful and the view would be relaxing. It seemed to take away Kevin's worries. Its grandeur and total unconcern for human cares made his worries feel insignificant and soothed his troubles. These same thoughts also made him feel irrelevant and useless.

It occurred to him that many people had seen the Bridge as a usually foolproof method of suicide. Just then he heard the groan of a fog horn, a familiar but always poignant sound in San Francisco. Already Kevin had come to recognize the lonesome, plaintive sound. *Fog must be blowing in from the ocean around the other side.*

As he listened to the fog horn, and the roar of waves (or was it traffic pouring over the bridge), it seemed to him he could quite easily plunge from off that beautiful stately span right into those waves. And, after a moment, well, his worries would be over. Nobody would ever have to find out that he had *those* feelings. His parents would never have to be embarrassed by the truth about him. And he'd never have to worry about 'Bel anymore or the Visitors and whatever their secret was. It'd all be over. He could rest.

For a while the suicidal thoughts seemed comforting. There was a way out. No matter how pressured things got. But after a while they began to worry him. *What if I can't stop these feelings. What if they overcome me? What if maybe I want them to?*

The sun had just dropped below the horizon. The twilight would soon be growing darker. And the fog would be pouring over the bridge. *It's about to get cold.*

Just then he heard sounds. He looked back toward the construction site, having to stand up so he could see over the roboconstructor that had been shielding him from the wind. Indeed in the gathering darkness, a tall figure was swiftly making its way along the side of building. Kevin's heart started to pound. *A Visitor. Maybe it's 'Bel come back for me.* He crouched down behind the machinery to stay out of sight.

The figure went right up to a tall plate glass window unit on the side of the building. It fiddled with something on the side of windowframe, and then what had looked like a stationary window rotated on its vertical axis, so the mysterious figure could slip right through. *A secret entrance. Another way,* Kevin thought, *to get past the locked front door!*

Kevin jumped up from his hiding place and ran to the closest window so he could see in. He started to call out, then realized the figure was heading right for the, uh, transporter. He stayed hidden. Maybe he could find out something he needed to know.

As he looked closely at the opening to the nautilus-shell, he could see a kind of glow. At first he thought he was seeing the sunset sky reflecting off the mirror-surface. But as he looked closer, it seemed like the light was actually coming out of the inside of the shell. The Visitor, who as he had got closer Kevin could see was disguised with a hat and a heavy coat that made him look much thicker and heavier than the Visitors, walked right up to the opening of the shell and stepped inside. He bent down a little, crawled past the first turn of the spiral, and then was lost to Kevin's view.

A minute or two passed. The Visitor hadn't come out. Kevin went in through his own secret entrance. He raced to the transporter—he was now sure that's what it was, since it seemed obvious that that Visitor had just disappeared into it. He was less than three feet from the opening when the faint glow flickered out. As he reached the device—as he feared—he found it deactivated. *But,* he had an insight, *it had been energized at exactly sunset. Maybe it's on a set schedule!*

*I*n his backpack, Kevin took a change of clothes to the office. *How do you dress in a spaceship?* he'd wondered as he was packing this morning.

Right at five, he left Sutro & Associates in the Financial District downtown, and caught a bus on Columbus Street out toward the Marina. He arrived at the construction site a little after five-thirty, still early for sunset. Now he was waiting expectantly in view of the transporter chamber. He'd huddled down in the shadows behind a pile of lumber and building materials against the back wall of the room where he wouldn't be seen just in case the transporter was used again tonight by another Visitor, *uh, spy*—he realized that was the proper way to describe the undercover agent he saw yesterday. He didn't like that word. It sounded sinister. He didn't like the idea of thinking of the Visitors that way. *I am paranoid enough. But,* he consoled himself, *it's President Arnold's fault they've had to hide.* Then he remembered that 'Bel acknowledged the Visitors had something to hide long before Arnold and the government got suspicious.

Kevin tried reading a magazine he'd carried along with him, but he just couldn't concentrate. Every few minutes he'd check his watch, check the angle of the shadows outside, and then check the opening to the transporter. He didn't want to miss the opportunity if the gate to the Visitors' ship was activated again tonight.

Orangy light flooded through the windows illuminating the room with the colors of sunset. *Now's the time.*

It was just thirty seconds after the sun set when the opening to the chamber began to glow softly. Kevin took a deep breath, slowly counted to ten to calm himself, looked around to make sure nobody was watching, walked right over, and then stuck his head through the opening. Nothing happened. The inside of the chamber looked exactly like it had from outside. He leaned in a little further, getting more and more nervous. Finally, he just climbed up into the helical-shaped, mirrored chamber and crawled on his hands and knees around the first bend. It was darker inside, though the soft yellowish glow was more apparent. He sat quietly. He'd crawled completely inside. The walls were narrowing so that he couldn't really get much further in. But still nothing was happening. He kept expecting to feel himself "transported," though he wasn't sure what that would feel like. He suspected that at least it would tingle. *It looked that way on TV.*

He checked his watch. It had been almost five minutes. Still nothing had happened. He waited a bit longer. Then the soft glow flickered out. Downcast, Kevin turned around and started to climb back out. *Maybe you have to have a communicator to let the control room in the ship know you want to beam up.*

Going out wasn't quite as easy as going in. After all, the walls sloped pretty steeply and the inside surface was slippery. Kevin was afraid he was going to slide right out headfirst and fall onto the hard concrete of the foundation.

He turned around so he could back out of the shell and lower himself to the ground. As he extended his right foot, he felt something unnerving. The shell had been situated about two feet above the foundation. That had been to allow a floor with crawl space under it to be constructed below the chamber. But as Kevin reached out with his foot toward that floor, the drop was much less than two feet. The thing seemed to be sitting right on the ground.

Oh my God.

Sliding out and turning around quickly, Kevin found himself standing on a wooden surface outside a duplicate of the shell he had crawled into, but he wasn't in the empty hall of a half-constructed building. As he looked about him and gathered his wits, he realized he was inside a translucent dome.

But he did not seem to be in a spaceship. He could still hear the muffled sound of waves, just as he had before. And through fabric of the dome, he could see the same orangy glow of sunset, just as before. It seemed like he was still in San Francisco.

Kevin peered around the side of the cube he'd just stepped out of. Behind it was a glass case full of crystals that glowed softly like the light that had surrounded the opening of the transporter. *The controls*, Kevin surmised. Further, along what Kevin could now easily see was the far wall of the dome, was a small cubicle room with a door on the near side.

Seeing that there was apparently no other opening in the wall of the dome, Kevin assumed the way out must be through that room. He wasn't sure he liked the idea of going anywhere. After all, he didn't know where he was—how could he know where to go to? Or when he was. Things sure seemed to have changed abruptly during the five minutes he was in the chamber.

He was just remembering that 'Bel had said he liked the area around Jackie O Beach because it reminded him of home and Kevin was beginning to suspect the transporter had actually taken him all the way to the Visitors' home planet, when a naked man stepped out of the doorway Kevin had been heading toward. The man startled when he saw Kevin. Almost simultaneously they both emitted a muffled little scream. The man dropped what he was carrying—something that looked to Kevin like a bottle of Windex. In the other hand he had a wad of paper towels. He wasn't exactly naked. He was wearing a six inch wide strip of brightly colored fabric in front and back that hung from a loose-fitting collar of the same fabric. The scapular-like strip which reached almost to the ground was cinched around the waist with a belt from which hung a small pouch and a couple of tool-like instruments.

"I was going to wipe down the surface of the geometry window. You startled me," he said as he bent over to pick up the bottle. He was obviously speaking English. Kevin could make out the words. But the rhythm was strange and the intonation and value given to the vowels different. Kevin had never heard an accent like it. Except from the Visitors, of course, but they never sounded this strange.

"Where am I?" Kevin asked the obvious question.

"Who are you?" the man replied. "How did you get here?"

"Through that thing," Kevin pointed at the chamber he'd just exited. "My name is Kevin Anderson. I'm from Earth. I came looking for 'Belwyn Tuarul."

"Oh dear me," the man seemed to Kevin to have said. "I'm just a gatekeeper. I had better get somebody over here. You just come here and sit down." He pointed toward the cubicle he'd come from. "There are seats in the waiting area."

"Where am I?" Kevin repeated his question.

Kevin waited only a few minutes. Then a vehicle arrived that looked pretty much like an ambulance. The Visitor attendants were very polite, but firm. They spoke English with the same heavy, just barely intelligible accent as the gatekeeper. They insisted Kevin lie down on a gurney to which he was loosely strapped. "You need to lie down. You may have trouble breathing," one of the attendants said. Kevin objected to the restraints, but the attendant assured him they were only for his protection and showed him how to release the straps in case of emergency.

The ride had been fast, occasionally bumpy, and up and down hill. Kevin was glad he'd allowed them to use the straps. He wouldn't have wanted to be rolling around on the floor of the van. Unfortunately, he couldn't see anything. *Maybe that's why they wanted me to lie down.*

They took him to what might have been a hospital. At least it was stark and the Visitors—*though now I'm the visitor and they're the natives,* Kevin reminded himself—were dressed in gauze gowns. A woman "doctor" came in and examined him and, speaking in that same strangely accented English, reassured him nothing was wrong.

It was only while she was talking that it dawned on Kevin that the Visitors were all showing color. He was trying to focus on her explanation of why bacteria in the air might be harmful to him and why he needed to take some sort of herbal antibiotic/immune stimulant potion she offered him, but he was marveling at how sudden and fluid were the pigmentation changes in her face. Though he couldn't appreciate the full complexity of the signals she was conveying, he knew that sometimes she was displaying compassion, other times sternness, other times humor, and even annoyance at him. It totally amazed him.

For the first time, he understood why 'Bel had found it so difficult to communicate with somebody who didn't show color. It was as though the pigmentation added a whole new dimension to communication. *But why had the Visitors NOT wanted us to know they communicated this way? What are they hiding?*

The doctor suggested he sleep. "It's getting late, you know."

"What about my friend 'Bel?"

"He has been contacted. He will certainly come in the morning."

In fact, it wasn't the morning. It was less than an hour before 'Bel arrived. *The doctor underestimated his feelings for me,* Kevin told himself.

"How did you get here?" 'Bel asked, sounding incredulous and turning quickly from green to reddish-gold as he rushed into the small room and immediately hugged Kevin tightly.

"You gave me a clue and I figured it out," Kevin answered nonchalantly.

"They weren't supposed to allow traffic through the geometry window. That was opened only to let stranded agents get back across."

"You said you'd come for me."

"I was hoping I could. I tried to get permission to cross back, but my supervisors absolutely forbid it. Even when I insisted maybe I could do something to save us, they said it was too late. They told me to go home and prepare to return to the Sea of Bliss—"

"To what?" Kevin exclaimed.

"Oh, Kevin, you don't know what's happening, do you?" 'Bel turned a sickly downcast purple. "Both our worlds are on the verge of destruction. That's why we went to warn your people. But we couldn't get them to listen. We couldn't figure out how to talk with them. I mean, we ended up going crazy over there. We were all fighting with one another. Our people were getting stuck in red or gray and couldn't get out. One of the leaders stayed red so long he hanged himself out of shame. After your President Arnold told us to leave, well, everybody just gave up and came back here to prepare for the Sea of Bliss."

"Sea of Bliss?" Kevin again quizzed.

"Consciousness will go on, on course. But not for us. For us it means death, Kevin, death."

"I don't understand. What's going on?"

"We've got an appointment tomorrow morning with the High Court of Judges. They're like our, uh, rulers, if you can call them that."

'Bel turned a quizzical bluish-green. "They'll explain it to you. I've been warned…" His face darkened. "But they said you can stay with me in the meantime, unless you want to be in the hospital here—"

"Of course, I'd rather be with you."

'Bel smiled. "Me too." They hugged each other again. "They'll explain all this to you. You deserve to know. And in the morning, I'll give you a tour of my world."

"Is *that* where we are?" Kevin sounded confused.

"Where did you think?" 'Bel answered and they both started laughing.

*K*evin awoke early. He lay cuddled spoon-fashion against 'Bel's back and, nuzzling his face into the Visitor's neck, he relished his recollections of last night's lazy romance.

In the restful early morning revery he relived the night's events— their departure from the hospital in an odd little vehicle that looked a lot like an old-fashioned VW bug which 'Bel said he'd borrowed for the occasion; the drive through the quiet streets of a large but surprisingly calm and softly lit city; their arrival at 'Bel's apartment in a building that looked almost like a San Francisco stick Victorian, though the proportions were a little different; their smoking a pipe of a sweet-tasting herb that lifted Kevin's spirits reminiscent of marijuana without the harshness and disorientation he associated with drugs at home; and their alternatively playful, passionate, and deep-felt love-making, occasionally interrupted by long pauses for nostalgic conversations about past loves and disappointments.

"I'd been really confused when we first met," 'Bel had confided. "Remember I told you you reminded me of somebody? That was my first boyfriend, Alain. We were both very young, and very much in love. I think I learned how to love from him…"

"What happened?"

"Oh, nothing happened. We got older and went to different schools. We were always friends." There was a long pause. "He was killed. That's why I volunteered for this mission: to honor him. When I saw you that day at the beach, I thought somehow Alain'd come back in your world."

"Why would you think that?" Kevin asked, trying to be gentle but also trying to figure out all the strange things that seemed to be going on in his life now.

"The Judges will explain," 'Bel answered enigmatically, as though "the Judges will explain" was an adequate answer to everything.

"You *do* look like him, Kev. I'm glad I broke the rules and spoke to you. It really is a little like my first love coming back. I think you are a lot like him, a lot like all the things I loved in him."

What struck Kevin as he recollected that conversation in the morning—with noticeably no hangover—was that for all 'Bel's acknowledgement that relationships he had had sometimes failed to meet his expectations or just didn't work out, he never recounted any bitterness or disappointment. How unlike Kevin's own experience in which relationships of every sort had been fraught with anxieties and fears, occasional bitterness and, ultimately, frustration.

In part out of sorrow for himself and his impotent sufferings and, in part, out of his admiration for 'Bel and his joy in finding such a wonderful change in his own destiny, Kevin sobbed softly into the back of 'Bel's long neck. The warmth radiating from the Visitor's body, seeming to glow golden, salved Kevin's pain in a way that made the tears come easily and comfortably.

"Are you all right?" 'Bel whispered, rolling over to face Kevin and to wrap him in his arms and pull him against his chest. "You're crying."

"Out of happiness," Kevin fibbed just a little. He tightened his arms around 'Bel and realized that even a fib had no place in this world. "And, I guess, a little out of self-pity."

"I understand. Your world must sometimes be very painful." 'Bel pulled his head back so he looked right into Kevin's eyes. And then kissed him on the mouth.

Kevin started to pull away, his mind full of distracting memories of commercials for mouthwash. *Morning breath!*

"Is something wrong?" 'Bel asked.

Kevin felt terribly embarrassed. He didn't know what to say. He stammered for a moment and then said, "Can I brush my teeth?"

'Bel suddenly started laughing. He rolled over on top of Kevin, taking his wrists in his hands. Rising up on his extended arms, he pinned Kevin to the bed. "We're in my world now, honey. Everything's perfect here!" He blew a long steady breath into Kevin's face. For a moment Kevin resisted, thinking he'd be grossed out. Then he realized 'Bel's breath was fresh. And his own mouth tasted sweet and clean.

"How did you do that?" Kevin asked, marvelling.

"It's all in your mind," 'Bel answered, glowing all golden. He slowly relaxed his arms, allowing his torso to gradually press against Kevin's, till his face was right up against his.

"I want to surprise you," 'Bel giggled playfully as he loosely tied a lavender silk scarf around Kevin's eyes, just as they were preparing to leave the apartment for the promised tour of the city. "Now, I'll lead you to the car. Promise you won't look."

"I promise," Kevin answered. "This had better be good."

"Just you wait." 'Bel sounded gleeful and childlike as he gently guided Kevin through the front door, down a flight of stairs, and out to what Kevin remembered from the previous night was the street, though he'd noticed last night the streets had looked deserted. He'd assumed that was because it was night and the people were at home with their cars safely parked in garages.

"After this, we'll use the transport system. It's faster and more efficient anyway. But it won't take us where we're going. That's why I got this car."

"You borrowed it from a friend? Or rented it?" Kevin asked, partly just to make conversation. The blindfold seemed to tongue-tie him.

"Oh, they're available. The cars are left at the transport stops. Whenever you want one, you can just take it."

"Don't people steal them?" Kevin answered, incredulous.

"We're in my world now," 'Bel repeated the phrase he's been saying off and on all morning. They both laughed.

Kevin could tell they were going uphill, though since there were occasional downhill jaunts as well, he couldn't really tell the overall effect until the last few minutes of the drive. Then it was all practically straight up it seemed. It reminded him of some of those truly intimidating climbs in San Francisco.

"We're here," 'Bel announced. "You can take off the blindfold."

As Kevin pulled the scarf away from his eyes, 'Bel continued, "Tattah, the City of Franchestiano."

Kevin looked out at the vista. Suddenly he began to tremble. *Something is wrong. Terribly wrong. This can't be. This doesn't make any sense. Am I going crazy?*

"Well, isn't it beautiful?" 'Bel asked ingenuously.

Kevin struggled to speak. He felt almost as if he'd been kicked in the chest and had all the air knocked out of him. He just couldn't manage to get words to come out. Instead, he just kind of groaned.

"Oh my, Kev, I'm sorry," 'Bel suddenly became very solicitous. "I wanted to surprise you. I guess I should've warned you, shouldn't I? Are you all right?"

"I, I don't understand. What is this?"

"It's my home, Kevin, the city I live in. Like the city you live in."

"Well, I mean, yeah. I mean, that's the problem. I mean, how?"

Still dumbfounded, Kevin looked out at the vista. He turned round and round, making sure this was all real and really looked like what it looked like. From their vantage point atop one of the two peaks that rose right in the middle of the city, he could see the densely packed white houses that clustered on the sides of the rolling hills. To the west—he knew it was west!—stretched out a great expanse of ocean. To the north, close by he could see a swath of green, dotted here and there with ornate buildings. "That must be the park, huh?" he asked rhetorically of 'Bel. Beyond, the ocean swept into a narrow, steep-walled channel cutting off the city from the land on the other side where a mountain rose up green and beautiful; on its top sat a line of little white domes.

"Holy Anderu's Straits," 'Bel identified the landmarks. "And Mount Blissful on the other side."

As he continued the slow turn Kevin could see that the ocean swept in through that channel into a huge body of water—*the Bay*, he thought. On the far side a verdant forest stretched toward a row of hills at the base of which was obviously another city.

Around the base of the peak they were on lay what 'Bel had called the city of Franchestiano. Directly beneath this vantage Kevin could see a broad thoroughfare that cut diagonally through residential areas and headed into the tall buildings that formed the center of the city. His eyes followed it downtown to where it ended in front of a square building with a tall spire. To the left, rising higher than all the other buildings, was a tall steep pyramidal structure.

"Amazing, isn't it?"

"Market Street?" Kevin pointed toward the broad thoroughfare.

"We call it Bazaar Promenade," 'Bel answered softly.

"But how? I mean, how can there be a city that looks this much like San Francisco, but on another planet on the other side of the galaxy?"

"It's not the other side of the galaxy," 'Bel answered, his color darkening.

"Fuck it, 'Bel," Kevin shouted. "What's going on? This couldn't be a coincidence, could it?"

"I've told you there is much similarity between your world and ours. We look practically the same. We speak a similar language. But there are lots of differences too. Notice, there are no bridges."

"Yeah, how come no bridges?"

"You'll see. We've got a simpler way to get from one place to another."

Kevin pointed out toward an island in the middle of the bay. "Yerba Buena," he said under his breath. But, of course, the familiar spans of the Bay Bridge that connected through Yerba Buena Island were missing.

"Ille Maria Janus," 'Bel corrected, smiling. "Almost."

"So our worlds are 'very similar,' you say?"

"The differences are actually even more interesting than the similarities. Look at that," 'Bel pointed due east.

In the near distance, rising up out of the mists beyond the Berkeley hills was the impressive cone of a mountain that—if he'd been a member of Bunny Bunn's UFO cult, instead of being the now hopelessly infatuated, but very confused, lover of an alien even stranger than Bunny's cult could have imagined—Kevin would have recognized as Mount Shasta.

"Quite a difference," 'Bel commented. "We've wondered about the significance of that…"

"Back in my world, there's a mountain over there called Mount Diablo, but it's much smaller."

"Yes, that smaller mountain for us is in the area in your world called Death Valley. We call this mountain that overshadows Franchestiano Mount Divole ," 'Bel explained. "Divole is the name of a mythological character who brought fire to human beings."

"Like Prometheus?"

"Right. Sort of means the same thing as your idea of devil, diablo, but from a different perspective."

"How can this be?" Kevin sputtered. Then turned to 'Bel. "You said the name of the city was...?"

"Franchestiano. After Franchestino Berdoni. He was a religious teacher during our, uh, 'Middle Ages.' He said God is the deepest part of the human mind and can be reached through simplicity of life."

"St. Francis."

"Franchestino was more like your Buddha. He taught that afterlife ambitions and mythical thinking and all that were distractions from the beauty of this world."

"Still sounds like St. Francis," Kevin answered. "I don't understand."

'Bel's color was noticeably off. He looked muddy grey. "Kevin, I'm sorry. My effort to delight you with my world has only upset you more. Look, we're going to see the Judges this afternoon. I ought to let them explain."

"There is an explanation, then? This really isn't 'just coincidence'?"

'Bel smiled widely, turning bright yellow. "Yes, there *is* an explanation, Kev."

Chapter Ten

As 'Bel led him into the heart of the city, Kevin found that the differences began to outweigh the similarities.

"I guess I'd better warn you," 'Bel said as they were driving down the slopes of the Visitor world's equivalent of Twin Peaks. "You don't like surprises."

"That depends," Kevin answered. He was smiling now. The shock had worn off, but not the curiosity.

"I should explain about clothing," 'Bel said.

"Am I dressed wrong for meeting the Judges?" Kevin asked.

"That's part of it, honey," 'Bel laughed. "Look," he pointed at a group of people they were approaching as he maneuvered the car onto a wide street.

Kevin noticed most of the people walking along casually were wearing long capes. As he looked closer, he realized that's about *all* they were wearing. Many of them wore the colorful scapulars he saw on the gatekeeper last night. A few wore something like kilts. Most of the females had short capes over their shoulders and loose halters to support their breasts. But that was all. "Oh my Lord," Kevin exhaled nervously. "They're all naked."

'Bel reached over and affectionately massaged Kevin's thigh, as if to reassure him things were not threatening. "In a world in which skin pigmentation is part of communication, it doesn't make any sense to wear clothing. It'd be like your people wearing ear-muffs to the symphony."

"Well, when it's cold, we *do* wear ear-muffs," Kevin answered. "Clothes are for warmth and protection."

"That's what the cloaks are for. And if it were colder today, you'd see people in heavier robes, but, well, it's a pretty day—"

Kevin was just amazed. He was a little embarrassed by the distraction all the naked bodies caused him. He was having a hard time paying attention to 'Bel. Most of the people on the street, male and female, looked relatively young and in good physical shape. It occurred to

Kevin that in a world without clothes there was an obvious incentive to keep in shape. "Isn't it hard to, uh, to concentrate?" he giggled with embarrassment.

"You'll get used to it. We got used to wearing those overalls in your world."

"Did you really? I thought you said the communication problems were driving you all crazy," Kevin answered, intentionally turning his attention back to 'Bel and the business at hand of inter-species relations.

"Maybe you're right," 'Bel acknowledged. "It hadn't occurred to me that our ways might be as hard for you to adjust to as your world's ways were for us."

They drove on in silence a few more minutes. 'Bel's color was kind of greenish. Kevin worried he'd said something that hurt him. Finally 'Bel broke the silence. "We need to make a decision. We can go back to my house and change clothes, I mean, if you'd prefer to look less, well, conspicuous. Or we can leave the car here and take the subway system on downtown. Or—we've still got more time—we could eat or drive out to the beach... You're the guest of honor. What would you like?"

"I'm not sure I'm ready to, uh, change clothes, quite yet. I think I'd rather be conspicuous. And I'm still so confused," Kevin answered. "Look, 'Bel, if you want me to wait for an explanation till we see these Judges, then let's do that as soon as we can. I know I'd feel a lot better if I wasn't a little afraid I had gone crazy or something." For the first time an unsettling thought occurred to Kevin: *What if I've died and gone to heaven. That would explain all this.* He recalled a story he'd seen on some TV series about a character who'd died without realizing it. *Maybe Chuck Sperry was right about that thing at the embassy. Maybe it was a weapon. Maybe it killed me. Maybe this is all some kind of dream. What if I wake up any minute and discover I'm dead!*

"The transport system's going to seem a little strange to you at first. It works like the geometry window you came through to get over here."

"Geometry window?" Kevin asked. "You mean the transporter?"

'Bel grinned. "It's probably much simpler than whatever you've imagined. About a hundred years ago our technology took a radical departure from the direction it—and your world's—had been going. We discovered how to very simply and subtly shift the shape of non-spatial dimensions—"

"Huh?"

"Well, what that does is like creating passageways in time so you can move from one place to another without having to pass through the distance between them."

"You explained that to me about your space ships," Kevin answered. "A space-warp!" he said as though using the science-fiction jargon made it understandable. "You mean, the subway works the same way?"

"Exactly. Quantum compression. The travelers' intention to go someplace puts them there without having to pass the intervening time," 'Bel answered, but in a way that didn't really seem to Kevin to explain anything.

They'd been walking about a block from the storage lot where they had parked the surface vehicle. Soon they came to a glass kiosk. As they entered, 'Bel stepped back to allow Kevin to go ahead of him down the long escalator. Below, Kevin could see, groups of people—most wearing cloaks, though some wearing virtually nothing but shoes or sandals—queueing up in front of geometrically-shaped portals surrounded by flickering colored lights.

'Bel called Kevin's attention to the large electronic sign suspended in the center of the station. The lettering looked vaguely like American English and Kevin thought he could make out a few words. Most of the sign was apparently a diagram of the city.

"This map shows what jumps to make to get to your destination and which windows to go through," 'Bel explained. "See each door is color- and shape-coded according to which line of jumps it'll take you through." He pointed toward one of the longer queues about halfway down the length of the station. "We want the red trapezoid down there.

"Just like the T in Boston," Kevin answered.

As they walked toward the window, 'Bel continued with the instructions. "Notice that people are coming out the same windows they're going in. The opening keeps changing direction so long as there's somebody on the other side wanting to come through. You have to wait for the light above the window to flash, then you walk through. And then keep on walking. I'll go first, okay? You can follow me. There's nothing to it. You might feel dizzy for a moment since you're not used to this, but you probably won't notice the change at all."

One by one the people at the head of the line were entering the trapezoidal doorway. Because it looked dark inside, they seemed to disappear. A moment later somebody else came out. It reminded Kevin of a department store revolving door. Soon it was their turn. "Remember to wait for the light to flash, then walk through confident you'll come out at your destination," 'Bel said as he stepped away from Kevin and entered the geometry window.

Kevin felt a surge of terror. *What if it's a disintegrator.* And then, as the light came on over the portal, he pushed the fear aside and stepped through. On the other side was a queue of people facing him. For just a second, he hesitated wondering if he'd been turned around and was facing back the way he came in. Then 'Bel called to him and he realized he must be in the destination station. *Just like that.*

"Up this way," 'Bel gestured. The station they were now in looked very different from the one they'd been in only a moment before.

Wow, thought Kevin. *That's the neatest thing I've ever seen.*

"This is Civic Center station," 'Bel explained. Taking Kevin's hand, he pulled him along through the crowd. "Most of the public administration buildings are around here. That's why it's so crowded."

They were having no trouble getting through the masses of people streaming through the station. A space in the crowd was opening around them as they made their way; people stopped to stare at the odd sight. For the first time Kevin realized 'Bel had been right about being conspicuous: 'Bel in his Earth-going jumpsuit and him in jeans and long-sleeved shirt. He wondered what the Visitors thought of him.

'Bel led the way through a short tunnel and then up another escalator to the surface. They stepped out into a lush green park, full of trees and flowering gardens. Here and there, buildings were visible through the trees. "This is lovely," Kevin exclaimed.

"Getting rid of the surface vehicles was a great boon to the cities," 'Bel explained as he led the way along a winding path. "There are tunnels underground to supply this part of town—we still use vehicles to carry materials from place to place inside the city. But around here there're no streets, so it can stay landscaped like this."

For just a moment, Kevin once again had the suspicion—less fearful this time—that he'd died and gone to heaven. *If so, heaven is turning out pretty neat.*

'Bel pointed toward a large stone building, the dome on top of which rose above the trees ahead of them, "That's where we're going."

All morning Kevin had been imagining that this meeting would be primarily a briefing for him on what the secrets of the Visitors were. All of a sudden it struck him that it might be just the opposite, that he might be interrogated about his life and his world. For the first time, he felt afraid of the meeting. "Uh, 'Bel, what's, uh, going to happen at this meeting? I mean—"

"I imagine they'll ask you some questions. And answer some of your questions. I'm sure it will go smooth."

A new anxiety hit Kevin, "What am I supposed to say if they ask me, oh you know, about how, well, how we know one another?"

"You and me?" 'Bel responded innocently. "Why, tell them the truth, of course."

"What's the truth, then?" Kevin asked tentatively. "You don't mean you want me to admit that we've, uh, gone to bed?"

"Of course. I mean, you wouldn't want to seem like a pervert."

Kevin's anxiety surged. Then he reminded himself that whatever this misunderstanding was it was the same as they'd had that awful night he'd thrown 'Bel out of his apartment. He knew he didn't want a repeat of that. "Look, 'Bel, sit down." They happened to be passing a wrought iron bench. "Before we talk to these Judges, we need to have a talk about what the word 'pervert' means."

Kevin felt a little awkward wearing only the belt and narrow floor length scapular. But 'Bel explained it would be in bad taste to appear before the Judges clothed. "After all, they could only assume you were trying to hide something."

"Well, I would be," Kevin answered, half-humorously, half-embarrassedly. "I mean, you know, I don't know that I want to show my body. I'm not as—"

"Kevin, you've got a beautiful body. You're little thin, perhaps. But you should be proud. *I* love you."

"Thanks, 'Bel. This is just all so new." Kevin stood gazing into the mirror. He had to admit he did look kind of good in the Visitor garb. The wide collar and strip down the front of his chest made his shoulders look broad and highlighted the definition of the muscles along his ribs. He realized he stood up a little straighter than usual.

"I agree," 'Bel smiled.

"Huh?"

"Weren't you thinking you look good?"

"'Bel, is the secret that you can read minds?" Kevin asked excitedly.

"Oh no. That didn't take any mind reading. I think you look great. And I could see by your smile that you do too. Well, come on." 'Bel led the way out of the dressing room into the grand foyer of the building.

Tall stone pillars formed an arcade along either side. Between the pillars the walls were made of richly parqueted wood. In the center of the inside wall was a high arch in which was set an ornately carved doorway. As 'Bel led Kevin toward that door, he gave a last word of encouragement. "Now, don't be afraid. These people won't hurt you." 'Bel pushed open the doors and stepped back to allow Kevin entry.

The room was huge. The high ceiling was domed and painted sky-blue. Along the walls, stone pillars, also painted blue, seem to uphold the sky. The room was surprisingly empty. There was virtually no furniture. Far across the room, behind a massive table on a raised dais, sat four men and four women.

"Who are you who enters?" someone shouted.

Kevin looked back at 'Bel. "It's okay," he allayed Kevin's anxiety. "It's just a ritual. Announce your name. They're expecting you."

"I am Kevin Anderson." Then he added: "From Earth."

"Join us, Kevin," one of the men on the dais said and came out to meet him in the center of the room. As Kevin approached, the man bowed deeply. "We are the citizen Judges of the High Court," he proclaimed, apparently still executing a ritual. Kevin returned the bow. "We welcome you and assure you that no harm can befall you in our presence." He pointed up at the ceiling. "You are under the protection of the Firmament of Truth whereon all justice is founded."

Kevin understood the speech, though the man's accent was thicker than most he'd heard so far.

"Come, come," the man gestured to Kevin, now speaking almost perfect American English. "I was on the visiting team who met with your President," he added quietly to Kevin as he escorted him toward the raised table at which the other judges sat. "If you have any problem with the language, I'll be happy to assist you."

"And who presents the petitioner?" A woman behind the table stood and announced.

"I am 'Belwyn Tuarul," 'Bel answered and the ritual was repeated.

Once both Kevin and 'Bel were standing in front of the Judges and the two who'd come out to escort them had resumed their places, the woman at the center of the table proclaimed, "Let us meet to discover our sameness before Heaven." At that the Judges all bowed.

"Now, we bow back," 'Bel whispered.

The central Judge then cleared her throat. "I am Judge Robul," she said, dropping the tone of ritual formality. "Kevin, you have been very daring. We admire your courage. As 'Belwyn may have told you, our people came to your world in hopes of convincing your leaders of a serious and dangerous error they are about to make. They would not listen. Our envoys found your world very difficult to live in. And so we retreated. I think we were not as brave as you.

"For a number of reasons we failed. Yet the mission remains. Both of our worlds are threatened.

"Now you have come across to our world. You have already discovered something about us that we had thought had to be kept secret from your people. Your friend 'Bel has assured us it has been no problem for you. We think you may understand something about your culture we do not. Perhaps you may be willing to help in our mission."

"There are so many things I don't understand," Kevin answered. "Of course, I'd like to help you, but you need to help me. I mean, 'Bel has explained about how you, uh, color. I guess that's what you mean by the secret I've already learned about. There's so much more…"

"The physiology of color," another of the Judges spoke up, "is only one small part of what we felt we had to conceal. And that was merely for practical reasons. We did not think your people would be offended by our development of communication through pigmentation. But we recognized that if we showed color obviously we could not conceal anything else about ourselves."

"You mean color is not the secret?"

"Not at all." The Judge looked over at 'Bel. "You said he understood."

"I don't think he realizes what you're talking about," 'Bel answered.

Judge Robul reclaimed the floor. "Kevin, do you understand how the 'space shield' works?"

Kevin was surprised by the question. Of course, he knew the shield was a point of contention between Earth and the Visitors, but he really didn't understand why. "No, ma'am," he answered. "I think it has something to do with creating a force field that distorts the structure of atoms or something that pass through it."

"Ah, you do understand a great deal. What your world does not recognize—and which we have been unable to convince them—is that the force field is actually destructive to matter *within* the field, not simply *across* it. But there is more. The particular technique that your technology uses to distort space directly affects *our* world."

"You mean it's like the geometry window?" Kevin exclaimed, feeling a burst of insight.

"Exactly," answered Judge Robul. "The field creates a window within its entirety."

"And is that bad?" Kevin asked. "What does it do? Move it all some place?"

"It moves everything within the field into *our* world," one of the other Judges proclaimed.

"You mean we could all come across to here?"

"No, Kevin, by itself that might not be so bad. If everyone in your world were as innocent and attractive as you, such a possibility might even be desirable." (Kevin felt a little embarrassed by the unexpected flattery.) "It means the two worlds would be superimposed; they would both exist in the same space."

"How is that possible?"

"It is not. That is the problem."

"Let him see the results of his world's experiments," another Judge spoke up forcefully. His face was bright red.

The Judges took Kevin and 'Bel to a morgue-like room in the back of the building to show them an exhibit of charred and blackened bodies. "These were people who happened to be in the places of coincidence when tests have been run of your space shield," the red faced Judge said angrily. "They had done nothing. They were simply enjoying the evening, listening to the crashing waves at Holy Anderu Park, when your terrible weapon was turned on. The shock wave rocked the whole city."

'Bel was ashen and faintly lavender. There were tears in his eyes. Kevin wondered if he had friends among the dead.

"I'm sorry," Kevin answered helplessly. "I don't think we knew." Before the Judge could scold him again, he asked, "Haven't you explained this to the President and the scientists?"

"They would not believe," Judge Robul answered. "They insisted their tests were correct and that what we said happened could not have happened. That is why we need your help, Kevin."

"Why do you think they'll believe me?"

"Because you have seen our world," she answered. "Because you have loved one of us. You have touched our truth in a way no other on your Earth has."

Suddenly Kevin felt exposed. *They must know about 'Bel and me. But they seem to think it's an advantage.* "I'm sorry. I do not understand. I can't go back to the President and tell him I know his space shield is dangerous because I, uh, uh, am in love with a Visitor." He turned and looked helplessly at 'Bel. "I can't do that. They wouldn't believe me… about the shield, I mean."

"But they have to," 'Bel exclaimed.

"You see," another of the Judges said, "even their own people keep the secret."

"*O*h Joel, I just don't know what to do. I mean it all happened so fast," Kevin said.

"Where's your boyfriend now?"

"He's not supposed to come across. Apparently they promised there would be no Visitors coming through. And they said they can't break their promise."

"Even if the future of the world depends on it?"

"That's something that's funny about them. I mean, it's like they're so moral and ethical and innocent, they're… they're like children. Look how helpless they got when President Arnold wouldn't believe them about the space shield. Instead of trying to prove to him they were right, they just retreated with their tails curled behind them."

"You mean they have tails?" Joel exclaimed.

"Oh no," Kevin laughed. "That was just a figure of speech. But, you know, they *are* like puppy dogs. Have you ever seen a dog that's been highly trained. It'll always stay obedient, even when its own life is threatened. Maybe that's admirable—"

"Maybe it's stupid."

"Anyway, for the time being at least, I'm on my own. I promised I'd try to get the government to rethink the space shield policy."

"That's a big order," Joel said with mock-consolation.

"Well, this morning—over there—it made sense. Everything made sense. It was just so lovely… But now, oh, Joel, I don't know."

"Do you really believe their story?"

"It sure made sense. I mean, I understand why they couldn't reveal the truth about how they live. I think it would be shocking enough to most Americans to find out they don't wear clothes. Just wait till they've heard the rest of it. And, to be very honest, Joel, I'm not sure I still understand the whole story. The Visitors seem so much like us AND so different. For one thing, they seem, well, very religious. They must have taken Earth religion very seriously. That's why they decided they would never be believed about the space shield if the whole truth about them was known."

"I can imagine. Just from what you've told me about 'Bel and your relationship, I know if the truth were found out the preachers, like that guy McMasterson, would have a field day. They'd declare the Visitors demons right away."

"And they couldn't keep their secret without having to cover up the color change. You know, they really *can't* lie. They turn a sickly gray color. It's just obvious."

"So what are you going to do?"

"Well, I tried calling the White House this afternoon. This guy I talked to said he'd call me back. But I don't believe he will. I think that's a dead-end that way. I mean, you know, you just can't call up the President of the United States to discuss policy—"

"How about going to the media?"

"Are they going to believe me? How many articles have you seen in the Enquirer already about people who claim to have been whisked away in a flying saucer or taken to the Visitors' home world! I'd just be one more. I mean *I* did it and *I* don't altogether believe it really happened."

"Maybe you can start at the bottom. You know, go see your Congressman. What's the rush?"

"But there is a rush. I mean, they told me there's a test of the space shield scheduled for next week. I promised I'd try to stop it."

Kevin tossed and turned all night. He kept remembering the tone of that Presidential Aide he'd talked to, Mr. Fairchild: at first interested, and then condescending, and finally politely rude as he gave Kevin the brush-off. "Don't call us. We'll call you."

How am I going to get anybody to listen to me. I've got maybe the most important information of the century, maybe of all time. My God, this could change everything. I mean when people find out who the Visitors really are and why they came, it's bound to change everything we think we know about reality... and, certainly, about religion and God. The thoughts kept swimming in his head. He almost felt dizzy. This was really the first time he'd let himself think about the implications of the news he carried.

Early in the evening Joel had given him one of the mood adjustors he got from his doctor. The powder inhalant came in a unit dose crushpac that was squeezed between thumb and forefinger then sucked on, a little like a marijuana roach. "Moodies" contained an aromatherapy component so they always included a flavor. The lavender scented relaxant had put Kevin into a blissful, peaceful state of mind in which the adventures on the Visitor planet had seemed to him a little like Alice's adventures in Wonderland. The geometry window had struck him humorously as a high-tech version of Alice's looking-glass. He'd joked with Joel for a while and then decided to go to bed.

Kevin had refused Joel's offer of another moodie. "I can't depend on drugs to get me through this," he insisted. But now that the night-anxieties had overcome him, he couldn't help thinking better of that noble sentiment. In his mind, he kept imagining that he was getting up and walking down the hall and then going outside and knocking on Joel's door and asking for another crushpac. And then just after he'd sucked the powder, he'd realize that he was still in bed with his eyes shut tight and his forehead wrinkled, and that it had all been a fantasy.

Alternating with that fantasy of going next door to Joel's was a fantasy of going out to the Research Park and going back through the looking-glass to find 'Bel. *I could stay there forever.* But with that romantic thought, he'd remember it wasn't true. *If I don't do something, that world is going to be destroyed. The only way I can manage to save 'Bel is to do what I promised, to get to President Arnold and stop the matter-field research.*

In his troubled half-sleep he imagined himself finding the geometry window in the nautilus shell activated and waiting for him. He climbed through, right into 'Bel's waiting arms. But almost no sooner than he felt safe, in his vision, 'Bel would be suddenly pulled away by President Arnold's Secret Service men who would then drag him into some sort of testing chamber. There'd be a bright light and then the men would open the door and show Kevin all that was left of his beautiful lover. And it would be one of the charred and deformed bodies the Visitor judges had shown Kevin as evidence of what the matter-field experiments did in their world. And Kevin would begin to scream.

The first time that fantasy haunted him, he almost jumped out of bed thinking the screams had been real. He lay in bed half-listening for echoes. But, of course, there were none. Though he almost wished there had been and that Joel had heard him and would come over with a moodie.

He lay back down and started thinking through the fantasy once again, but this time, just as that awful image of the devastated carcass started to surface, he jumped out of bed and went to the bathroom. After using the toilet in its own little closet down the hall, he went to the lavatory and splashed cold water on his face. Heading back to bed, he checked the illuminated clock face on the sidetable: 3:30 a.m.

Telling himself he was just curious, he went back out into the hall and peered through the shutters of his front door in hopes that maybe, just maybe, Joel's lights were still on. But the bright light at the top of the stairs outside the door obscured his seeing any faint light that might be showing through the shutters in Joel's front door.

Kevin went down to his own kitchen and found a can of beer in the refrigerator. He sat down at his make-shift kitchen table and drank the beer in several long gulps he was hoping would make the alcohol hit him hard enough and fast enough to put him to sleep. At the same time, he tried to logically think through a plan of action.

Joel suggested going to the media. Maybe that's the only alternative I have. But what am I going to say? How am I going to explain why the Visitors trusted me enough to tell what they wouldn't tell the President of the United States? I'm not sure it would make any more sense to tell them about my relationship with 'Bel. But that's the only justification I've got. And it's the truth.

Truth. Who believes in the truth anymore? What does it even mean? The Visitors seem to think it's so important, but even they couldn't bring themselves to admit it. And now they expect me to! And telling this truth is bound to force me to admit my—uh—admit being—uh—acknowledge having had—uh— homosexual sex with 'Bel.

Kevin could feel himself getting woozy from the beer. *Maybe I can get to sleep now.* Walking slowly down the long hall, he felt himself weaving. He knew he could probably fight the effects of the mild amount of alcohol, but tonight, that was the last thing he wanted to do. After all, he needed to get to sleep soon. He had to go to work in the morning. Remembering that, he stopped in the lavatory and drank a glass of water—his mother's, usually effective, home-remedy for preventing hangovers.

Then in a few minutes he was back in bed, the covers pulled up tight around his neck. He did indeed feel sleepy now.

The earlier hypnogogic sleep images that had troubled Kevin were now replaced by a somewhat less anxiety-provoking image. Kevin saw himself standing side by side with 'Bel in front of a TV camera at a news conference. He was explaining the truth he'd learned about the Visitor's origins and about the nature of their warning. After his long speech, a reporter asked him the question he'd been dreading about why the Visitors would have entrusted him with this knowledge.

From his objective stance in the fantasy, he could see that 'Bel was glowing bright yellow with traces of rosy gold playing across his countenance. He heard himself start to say something about how being an architect's intern had brought him into close contact with the Visitors so that they were willing to trust him. Then all of a sudden he realized that, in his fantasy, his face was turning muddy gray. And he realized he couldn't lie anymore. Loving 'Bel and having been to the Visitors' world and acknowledging to himself the truth about his feelings, he just couldn't lie. Anymore.

Okay, he managed to think rationally through his alcohol-induced light sleep state, *how am I going to get to the media to tell the truth? How can I call a press conference?*

All of a sudden, the obvious answer came to him like the proverbial flash of lightning. Kevin committed himself to talking with Will Salado first thing in the morning.

After that, sleep seemed to come easily.

Chapter Eleven

Kevin had been working at Sutro and Associates now for about six weeks. He'd become a regular member of the firm. And while the intrigues of the last week had taken him away from work unexpectedly and Will Salado had cautioned him during their talk this morning about his absences, at the same time he complemented him on his work and assured him the firm was pleased with him.

Nonetheless, Kevin was quite surprised in mid-afternoon when George Sanders shouted at him, "Hey, Kev, sweetie, outside line for you." He didn't have time to take offense at the new appellation, "sweetie," George had started using because he was so surprised to be getting a call from somewhere outside the firm itself.

"Hello."

A muffled voice said abruptly, "Kevin Anderson?"

"This is Kevin Anderson."

"Hello, Kev," the voice answered in Visitor tones. "There are so many levels to go through to get to you! I was afraid somebody would recognize my voice."

"'Bel, where are you?" Kevin answered in hushed tones.

"I just came through the geometry window. I'm at the embassy site. I found a deskset phone here in the contractor's office."

"Oh, Lord," he exclaimed. Then realized he needed to make his intent obvious, "I'm glad you've come. I've had an idea and I need your help."

"Can you come get me? I can't be seen in public."

"Of course. But, look, can you hide out there till after five. I just can't leave early today. It's important." Kevin remembered Will's words of caution.

"Yes, I can. And, Kevin, I've brought keys for a couple of the cars that had been loaned to the team if we can find them…"

"Hey, that's good," Kevin was thankful for 'Bel's good sense. They weren't going to be able to get around by public transportation. 'Bel would just be too obvious.

"I can probably borrow Joel's car or get him to drive. He's okay. He's on our side. I'll be there—" he calculated in his mind for a moment—"by six. You better go hide now. Can you go back through the window?"

"No, it's deactivated now. I wasn't supposed to come over here," 'Bel seemed flustered. "I can hide. I'll be watching for you."

"See you in a while. And, 'Bel, thanks." Kevin thought the word "hide" sounded unfamiliar in 'Bel's mouth.

Kevin's heart was beating like crazy as he switched off the connection. He made a quick call to Joel to confirm he would be willing to give him a ride. For the time being he didn't explain where they'd be going.

Kevin tried to turn his mind back to his work. He was still calculating stress figures for the building Sutro was contracted to work on following completion of the Visitor embassy. Since the embassy project had been cancelled, there was a rush put on the new project. Kevin didn't mind the work. He was good at math and liked doing the calculations. In fact, he was developing an almost symbiotic relationship with his computer terminal. But this afternoon, he realized, he wasn't going to get anything else done but give the appearance of being at work on schedule. After all, the adventure he'd been contemplating was about to begin.

There was barricade tape strung across the front of the half-constructed building and a sign with the notice: "No Trespassing. By Order of the Federal Government." The key Kevin had stealthily borrowed from George Sanders' desk didn't fit the door anymore.

They went around to the back. Kevin tried the door he'd left unfastened, but found it now nailed shut. Then he went to the glass pane he'd seen the Visitor rotate open. He examined the frame for a moment and found a tiny secret catch that when released allowed the glass to swivel. "Come on, Joel. We can get in here."

As they entered the empty space of the now darkened building, Joel asked, "What's that thing?"

"That's the geometry window," Kevin answered. "Don't you recognize it? You know, it was your comment that made me realize just what it was."

"Everything looks different on TV," Joel replied.

"'Bel," Kevin called out. "'Bel." He felt a rush of anxiety when he feared the Visitor wasn't there waiting for him. "Where are you?"

"Kevin, here I am." 'Bel called out as he rose up from behind the same stack of lumber in the back corner of the big room Kevin had used for a hiding place.

"I didn't think I should be too close to the window. It's opened at this end at sunrise and sunset. I didn't want to risk being seen."

"By who?" Joel asked.

"'Bel, this is Joel, my next door neighbor," Kevin interrupted to make proper introductions. "We can trust him."

"I am pleased to meet you," 'Bel answered. Kevin felt a rush of excitement and validation when he noticed 'Bel's color shift noticeably. *That's the first time Joel's seen that. That'll sure convince him.*

"There are still observers over here," 'Bel answered Joel's innocent question. "They're not supposed to interfere, just watch. But now they're all being recalled."

Kevin's excitement turned to jealousy as he realized the shift in 'Bel's color to bright yellow as he spoke to Joel was followed by a blush of amorous rosy-gold across his cheeks.

"That's why the window still gets opened regularly," 'Bel was saying. "So they can get back. The Judges are convinced we shouldn't allow anybody to stay over here at all. It's just too stressful."

"Does that mean you're not staying?" Kevin snapped. His voice betrayed his jealousy, disappointment, and annoyance.

'Bel reached out to take Kevin's hand. "I'm not supposed to be here at all. I disobeyed. I wanted to be with you, Kev."

All of a sudden Kevin felt so stupid. *Of course, 'Bel would have a sexual response to Joel. Joel's a good-looking guy. And, of course, it'd show. That's the nature of telling the truth all the time. And it doesn't mean 'Bel doesn't love me.* Kevin realized he was still discovering the full implications of living with total transparency and honesty.

"I knew the job you'd agreed to was going to be difficult," 'Bel continued, his face now glowing the soft orangy-pink Kevin recognized as the color of support and comfort. "I didn't want you to have to be alone."

"You're staying, then?" Kevin answered.

"Of course," 'Bel smiled and held Kevin's eye an extra long moment as his face turned golden with just a delicate trace of rose shimmering along his high cheek bones that made Kevin's heart melt.

"'Scuse me for being personal or something," Joel broke the intimacy. "Kevin told me you guys don't wear clothes. How come you're all covered up in that jumpsuit? I'd had gotten my curiosity aroused."

"I didn't think it was your curiosity that was aroused," Kevin answered playfully.

"Well, we need to cover up in your world," 'Bel answered innocently, seeming not to get the double entendre. "Besides, it's cold over here."

"Yeah, let's get home," Kevin responded and started to hustle them all out the secret portal and back to the car.

"I'd be happy to show myself to you," 'Bel continued, "when we get home. That is, uh, if it's all right with Kevin. We're in your world now."

For a moment Kevin started to feel the annoyance once again. 'Bel's caveat reassured him. But he was again aware of how strange it was to be with somebody who lived in openness and innocence.

"I'm sure Kevin wouldn't mind anymore than I would," Joel answered in a Bunnyism, laughing with mock-guilt as he ran ahead a little.

Kevin managed to laugh himself. *Love is a big mess if you can't keep your sense of humor*, he reminded himself.

*P*anting and out of breath, Kevin rolled over. "Whoa," he laughed. "I gotta slow down. 'Member I'm kinda new at this."

'Bel's laughter answered Kevin's as he raised up on his elbows, leaned over and kissed Kevin on the top of the head, then slipped his arm under Kevin's shoulder and pulled him over so his head was resting on his chest. Kevin purred and cuddled up closer against 'Bel as he relaxed into the warmth of the calm affection.

Kevin ran his hand gently across the tight muscles of 'Bel's abdomen. There was just the thinnest layer of subcutaneous fat under the skin that made his body feel soft and pliable at the same time that he felt and looked tight and hard. The way 'Bel was lying with his head propped on the pillows, his torso flexed so Kevin could feel the ripples of muscle. *He's so beautiful. And so sweet and kind and good. I don't think I've ever felt so happy. In spite of what anybody thinks.*

"You said your first boyfriend was killed and that's why you joined the team that came to our world. He was killed in one of those collisions caused by the matter-field machine, wasn't he?"

"You're right," 'Bel answered. "I knew your world was like a different dimension of ours. When I saw you that day I thought maybe the same people lived in both, and that he hadn't died on your side."

"That isn't how it works, is it?"

"No, I guess not. But it is a little like my love for him generated you. I'm glad."

"I'm glad too," Kevin whispered. "I love you."

'Bel's abdomen lightened as bright yellow replaced the rosy color of sexual arousal. "I, uh, believe you."

"You hesitated?" Kevin answered warily. He still couldn't help feeling insecure, even when he was totally enraptured.

"I had to remember the word. 'Believe' doesn't mean anything in my world. I mean, we always know."

"Oh." It took Kevin a moment to realize that 'Bel was talking about something much broader than their relationship. "You mean you don't have things like 'trust' and 'faith' and 'fidelity'? Those are such important virtues to us."

"We have different virtues. They don't involve truth-telling because there's no such thing as not telling the truth. For us the virtues you mentioned have to do with what you might call confidence in our own or someone else's abilities."

"You all seem so innocent."

"Innocent means not causing harm. We sometimes do cause harm to one another. But it's always by accident, certainly not on purpose."

"Unfortunately," Kevin answered pensively, "we seem to cause harm on purpose."

"But, you know Kevin, the greatest harm your people cause one another is also by accident."

"What do you mean?" Kevin turned his head and lifted himself on his arm so he could face 'Bel.

"Even good people sometimes have goals and intentions for themselves that clash with those of other people. Your stock market is an example. I doubt people want other people to lose money, but the fact is in order to buy stock low somebody else has to be selling it, and that's probably at a loss to them."

"Not necessarily," Kevin answered.

"Well, let's not debate the example. I don't understand your money well enough. The point is that one person's intention to be rich inadvertently includes the intention that somebody else be poor."

"And you think that causes the other people to be poor?"

"Indirectly. And sometimes directly. Let me use a different example: the reason my people contacted yours in the first place. Your country feels threatened and wants to create the force field defense. That sounds okay, doesn't it? But the fact is that that apparently good, though perhaps short-sighted, intention has a terrible consequence attached to it. And that consequence is liable to be terrible not just for your people, but for mine—unless we do something."

"We will, 'Bel. I promise."

"Unless one is very careful, the fulfillment of their immediate needs and desires implies frustration and suffering for someone else."

"It wouldn't have to. I mean, my desire to be happy and close to you right now doesn't necessarily mean somebody else is unhappy."

"It takes a lot of consciousness to recognize that, Kev," 'Bel chuckled. "That's why I love you. Happiness isn't quite so limited as the amount of money or food or clean water. *But* from what I've seen of your people, the fact is that there *are* some who don't want other people to be happy."

"Who, for instance?" Kevin quizzed.

"People who'd disapprove of you and me making love with each other right now, Reverend McMasterson, for instance."

"Oh, yeah, I know who he is. That big church up there above the geometry window. You—the Visitors, I mean—know about him?"

"There are some people whose notion of their own righteousness requires calling other people wrong."

"I guess…"

"You'd think there'd be enough rightness in the world—like happiness—for everybody to share it. But this world seems full of people who don't want other people to be right too."

"That's because we believe in non-contradiction. I mean, if you and I disagree on something, we can't both be right."

"That's true about mathematical logic," 'Bel answered. "But it's probably not true about consciousness and perception and abstractions like right and wrong and even true and false. And it certainly isn't true about subjective feelings. A minute ago you said you needed to rest from our love-making; I was ready to keep going. But my feelings didn't make yours wrong. We were both right and we were able to negotiate a way to handle both our needs."

"I guess you're right—"

"So are you," 'Bel interrupted.

Kevin grinned. "—maybe especially about the people who would call us sick or sinful or criminal for loving each other. "

"And isn't it obvious that their doing that has caused you a lot of psychological harm?"

"It's called internalized homophobia," Kevin answered. "You said your people sometimes cause harm by accident. Did you mean the same thing?"

"I didn't mean about making love."

"I love talking to you. You make me think." Kevin rolled over onto his stomach and pulled himself up against 'Bel's long body and then hiked himself up so they were face-to-face. "And I love touching you. And kissing you. And feeling you touching me."

Kevin slowly lowered his mouth to 'Bel's and the surge of passion swelled between them again. In moments Kevin was lost in the feelings in his body and in his mind. The love and fascination he felt with this apparently young, but so wise, alien seemed of one piece with the sensations he felt pouring in through his skin and surging through his muscles. He'd never thought sex was like this. He'd always thought it was some kind of performance skill you had to practice to learn.

It wasn't as though they were acting out some prescribed postures or practices of sex. Everything seemed to swell up out of the innocence and naturalness of their feelings and their excitement of being with one another. Kevin found himself struggling—intermittently relaxed and frenzied—to get so close to 'Bel they'd become one being. And indeed sometimes Kevin couldn't tell which intertwined limbs were his and which were 'Bel's and he couldn't tell whether the pleasure that suffused his every muscle was originating in his own body or in 'Bel's as they pressed themselves tighter and tighter together.

As the pleasure and the closeness mounted higher and higher, Kevin found himself kissing 'Bel so deep that his whole consciousness seemed to explode gloriously as reflex conquered volition and a great surge of love and joy and physical pleasure and emotional relief and release overwhelmed them both.

As he was starting to come, Kevin heard 'Bel whisper, "Open your eyes." And he raised his head just a little and looked into 'Bel's eyes and rosy golden light seemed to erupt from the pupils and plunge deep into Kevin's heart and soul. And then he could feel his body melting into 'Bel's and the orgasm seemed to radiate from every point along his spine and he felt like he was turning into the rose-colored light. For just a moment he felt the top of his head open and brilliant white light poured into him. And for just a moment he remembered Dante's vision of the multifoliate Rose. And the Rose became 'Bel's eyes. And the white light suddenly shot back up his spine and pierced right into the center of the gradually opening Rose. For a moment he wondered if this would ever end, if he had died or somehow left his body, if he'd ever be able to remember who he was again. And then his whole body seemed to turn to jelly that flowed into the golden warmth of 'Bel's love. Kevin closed his eyes and was engulfed in darkness and sweet unconsciousness.

"Hey, excuse me. But I heard you guys, uh, finishing up a while ago. My God, everybody in the neighborhood probably heard you. You know you all shouldn't make so much noise. Remember this isn't the only house we're in."

Kevin felt embarrassed by Joel's bawdy innuendo, especially since he was still standing naked in the front doorway clutching a blanket around himself. "Well, come in. It's cold."

Joel was following Kevin right into the bedroom.

'Bel's face was purplish. "What did he say?" he asked Kevin.

"You don't want to know. He'll drive you batty with his funny expressions."

"Well," 'Bel spoke up with innocent good humor. "If you were listening, Joel, I hope you felt comfortable joining in with our sexual consciousness on your own."

"Whaddya mean?" Now Joel sounded embarrassed.

"You know perfectly well what he means?" Kevin scolded laughing. He was pleased to see the sexual embarrassment shift to his next door neighbor whose wit he'd so seldom been able to keep up with.

"Well, I, uh, guess I do. And, uh, well, I did."

"Did what?" Kevin pressed.

"You know perfectly well what I mean." Joel rejoined.

"I hope you enjoyed yourself," 'Bel responded.

"Hope it was as good for you as it was for us," Kevin continued to kid Joel.

"Well, look, I'm sorry to barge in. I mean really. But it's getting late. You said you wanted to get started around midnight. It's almost that now."

"Thanks, Joel," Kevin said, his tone obviously forgiving. "You still willing to give us a ride down to the St. Francis to see if the Visitors' cars are in the garage?"

"Of course. I promised, didn't I? Fact is, I wish you'd take me with you. I mean, uh, I'd sure like an encore performance of whatever was going on in here. With maybe a better seat, uh?"

'Bel burst out laughing as he pulled Kevin close. Kevin was again cringing with embarrassment.

"Joel, if all goes well, we'll meet you in about twenty minutes at 6th and Bryant and get our stuff from you. We can catch the freeway south there. If for any reason we think we're being followed, we won't stop. I don't want you in trouble."

"Me neither," Joel answered nervously.

"—besides, we may need your help in the future," Kevin continued.

"Anything I can do," Joel averred. "But what if the cars aren't there anymore?"

"Oh, right. We need a contingency plan. How about waiting at Stockton and Geary? We'll flash the lights as we go by. If we don't go by, just wait a few minutes and we'll be there on foot. Will that work?"

"Sounds good," 'Bel spoke up from the back seat of Joel's little sports car where he'd scrunched in, in part, so he could keep his head down and avoid being seen.

"You nervous?" Joel asked.

"Of course," Kevin responded immediately. "But this is too important to chicken out now."

"What are you planning to do once you get the car?"

"You shouldn't know too much, Joel, just in case you do get caught.

Let me just say we're going to follow your advice and go to the media. I think I've got a connection with a pretty high placed reporter. I hope she'll believe us. We need to stop that test."

"Is it going to be dangerous?"

"I don't think—"

'Bel interrupted Kevin, "Yes, it will be. If we fail, it may be the end of the world…"

They'd been working out plans since before leaving the apartment. Joel had warned Kevin to drive south on 280 and not cross the Bay Bridge in order to avoid the car being registered by the RF monitors billing toll charges.

"Remember, leave your dime device here. That's a way you could be traced—*if* they're after you.

"And, look," Joel said, pulling down a tattered cigar box full of cash from a shelf in his closet. "I've been stashing old bills that I've gotten in tips from bartending. Even if they've got the new RFID tag embedded in them, they came out of an ATM machine on somebody else's card. They're not linked to me—or to you. Don't take your credit card or use your ID for anything, remember. Pay cash. You won't show up anywhere in the system, and they can't trace your movement.

"Here's nearly a thousand bucks. That ought to get you to L.A. And have a little play money."

"Gosh, Joel, that's so kind of you. I promise I'll repay you."

"If this mission is as important as you say, a thousand dollars is a minor investment."

'Bel's assertion of danger echoed in Kevin's mind as they turned onto Powell Street. The hotel garage was only a block away. For a moment he wished he could just forget this whole thing. *What am I doing trying to be a hero? I'm not the type. I'm an architect, for God's sake.*

Just then, as if understanding his anxiety, 'Bel touched him on the shoulder. "But we won't fail."

Joel stopped the car a little ways down from the back of the St. Francis. The parking garage loomed above them. Half the concrete structure was obviously still under construction; it was dark. At the far end of the block, a bright light shone over the exit ramp. Above it several lights illuminated the floors.

"You know what to do?" 'Bel quizzed Kevin.

"Sure. Nothing to it," Kevin answered bravely as he opened the car door. He turned toward the driver. "Joel, thanks. Thanks very much."

As he got out, Kevin could hear Joel saying something in reply, but the words were lost in the cold wind whipping down the dark street. *Can I really pull off this little acting job?*

Without looking back, he sauntered slowly and clumsily toward the lighted booth at the exit ramp. He trusted that, as planned, 'Bel had more quickly headed into the construction area and was already climbing up the ramps to the third level where the cars had been parked that, at least up till five days ago, had been on loan to the Visitor team. In his mind's eye, Kevin imagined that the cars were still sitting there, now surrounded by a bright yellow police barricade tape and signed with a notice like the one out at the embassy site at the Research Park. He prayed the Feds had been satisfied locking up the cars and sealing them with a strip of tape. *After all, as far as they know the Visitors are gone — up into the sky.*

"'Scuse me," Kevin slurred the words as best he could without sounding too phony. "Hey, 'scuse me." Kevin remembered how last year Tim Lewiston had cajoled him to join in a skit for a Dunster House Talent Show. Tim had coached Kevin for hours on how to sound drunk. Finally that Harvard training was coming in useful.

The attendant looked away from the micro TV screen placed just out of sight to the left of the desk. "Yes sir," he answered smartly.

"Can you help me? My wife and I went out for a drink. And now she's too drunk for me to make it back here without her." (Joel's fractured syntax was coming in handy too.) Kevin paused to allow the attendant to feel confused.

"I don't understand, sir. Are you and your wife guests of the hotel?"

"I walked back here to get the car. Wanna go pick her up now."

"Perhaps you should get a taxi, sir. Maybe you shouldn't be driving..."

"I said I wanna go pick her up now."

"Your car is parked in the garage?" the attendant asked trying to be polite.

"We walked over to Chinatown. Now I want to drive back to get her. You know where my car is?"

"Is your car parked in the garage, sir?"

"Red Ferrari. Parked it myself. Up there." He gestured drunkenly up the ramp. *Might as well make it sound fancy,* Kevin thought. *If he falls for it, it'll be 'cause he's expecting a big tip.*

"You're welcome to take the elevator up."

"You get it for me." Kevin scratched the side of his head and stared down at the ground looking dazed.

"The valet parking is around front, by the lobby entrance, sir."

"Don't think I can make all those turns down the ramp," Kevin answered, reaching into his pocket and pulling out a hundred dollar bill. He held it up between both hands. "Make it worth your while," he mumbled.

"Well, yes sir. I mean, sir, I'm not allowed to leave my post."

Stumbling to the center of the exit, Kevin slung one arm over the yellow and black striped barricade. "I'll hold down the fort for you."

The attendant looked a little nervous. Kevin could tell he wanted the hundred dollars. He looked around as if to assure himself that the garage was deserted. Then quickly he jumped up and came out of the booth. "Keys?" he held out his hand.

"Under the front seat."

"How am I going to tell which car it is?"

"Fourth, no, maybe fifth level up. Let's see we're in room six something. My wife has the room key in her purse. Damn it. Shouldn't gotten that drunk…"

"You said a red Ferrari? Do you know the license number?"

"Nevada plates. Uh, 555—something. You'll see." Again he pointed up the ramp. He peered up into the half-lit darkness above. He was hoping to see 'Bel in the car up there somewhere. "I'll guard the gate." He patted the barricade. "Oh, and hurry up. What if my wife has another drink? She'll pass out on the floor and they'll send her home instead of to the hotel. And it'll all be your fault," he waved the hundred dollar bill in his free hand. *Oh God, I hope this is convincing.*

"Yes sir," the attendant suddenly snapped to and ran toward the elevator.

Kevin hung onto the barricade nervously, hoping 'Bel would be appearing any moment. Just as the time seemed to be stretching too long, a small blue compact car rolled silently down the ramp. *Success!*

Scolding himself for not having figured out sooner how to open the barricade, Kevin jumped away from the gate and hiked himself up over the window in the attendant's booth. It took him a moment to see what to do. Then he pressed a button on the back of the desk and was gratified by the sound of the gate raising.

In a minute, he was in the car. 'Bel had jumped out and climbed into the back seat so he could hide. Kevin took the wheel.

"What took you so long?" Kevin asked, still trembling from the adventure of the ruse.

"I switched the ID plates with another car's up there," 'Bel answered. "Maybe that'll help keep us from being caught."

You're catching on to life on this planet pretty fast, Kevin thought. As he drove out and turned toward Geary and his rendezvous with Joel, he looked back at the garage. The gate was lowering automatically. He hoped the young attendant wouldn't be too annoyed that there was no red Ferrari up there since when he got back to his station there *was* going to be that hundred dollar bill waiting for him. *A little deception certainly has its place.* Kevin congratulated himself and 'Bel on successfully accomplishing the first step of this adventure.

Two hours later with 'Bel at the wheel, they turned east at Gilroy onto the cross-over to Interstate 5. Kevin was curled up in the back seat struggling to get some sleep. They had a long drive ahead of them through the central valley, down to Los Angeles, and then east to Covina or maybe out to Riverside and March Air Force Base. Kevin figured it was safe to let 'Bel drive at night.

"Nobody will recognize you as a Visitor in the dark. And tomorrow," he'd said, much to 'Bel's chagrin, "we'll get some dye and pancake make-up and see if we can't disguise you."

Kevin was half-sleeping as the car raced through the night. Occasionally he'd be aware of the roar of road, of the jumble of sounds coming from the radio, of the presence so near him of this strange and alien, but wonderful man whom he'd begun to think of, boldly, as his "lover." Occasionally he'd drift into fantasies of their passionate and intense love-making earlier and occasionally of the uncertain future.

Kevin dreamed he was back in Massachusetts, driving home from Provincetown from what had been a very awkward and unpleasant holiday with Tim Lewiston and one of his boyfriends who kept insisting Kevin "needed to relax more." Kevin had known what that was supposed to mean and wasn't having any of it. Tonight he was glad, though, he'd finally "relaxed." In the dream he was trying to explain to Tim why he'd needed to wait so long, when he was jolted into consciousness by bright fluorescent light pouring into the car.

"Where are we?" Kevin asked sleepily.

"Coming into Los Baños," 'Bel answered mutilating the Spanish pronunciation. "I crossed over the freeway a few minutes ago. But we need fuel."

"Should you let me drive?"

"I'm okay. It's dark. But I'll let you handle the service station."

Soon 'Bel drove into a Pennzogen station, pulling the car up to a set of pumps furthest from the office and away from the brightest lights. Kevin got out, inserted a fifty dollar bill into the cash-pay slot on the pump, pulled out the retracting snorkel, and attached the locking clamps to the tank connection on the car. He was watching the register clicking off the amount of hydrogen being delivered when he was startled by the approach of a heavy-set teenager. A Pennzogen baseball cap proclaimed his officialness.

"Hi, there. Out late. Anything you need besides hydro?"

"No thanks."

"My mom runs the coffee shop over there. Open twenty-four hours. Why don't you go over and have a piece of pie or something." He had apparently been instructed by his mother to drum up late-night business.

Kevin looked over at the warmly-lit coffee shop across the street. The idea sounded appealing. He was hungry, he realized. "We're sort of in a hurry."

"Get it to go, then. Mom makes a great apple pie. I eat lots of it myself," he patted himself on his oversized tummy. "Hey, your friend's probably hungry too." The boy walked around to the driver's side.

As he started to lean over, Kevin called out to him, "You got a pressure gauge for the tires? Need to check that."

"Go get yourself a cup of coffee and piece of pie and I'll check it for you," the boy offered real friendly.

Just what we don't need now.

The boy crouched down at the front tire, then looked up at 'Bel and started in on his advertising spiel for his mom's apple pie, when all of a sudden his eyes got very big. He looked up and pointed right at 'Bel and wagged his finger. "Hey, mister, you look just like them space monsters President Arnold ran off last week."

Kevin quickly put the snorkel back into its receptacle on the hydrogen pump. The meter showed he still had a little credit from the bill he'd fed in, but at this point that was expendable.

"I, uh, don't know what you're talking about," 'Bel answered the boy, as Kevin jumped into the front seat. Just as Kevin started to say, "Let's go," he realized that right in front of this affable, but very likely redneck, teenager 'Bel's face had turned dark greenish-gray.

'Bel started the engine and in a moment they were squealing out of the station. Kevin looked back to see the kid standing there looking dumbfounded, his arm still outstretched pointing after them.

"I'm sorry, Kev. That was my fault."

"It'll be okay. Give the kid a story to tell tomorrow at school." Kevin made a noise like an old fifties sci-fi movie soundtrack. "The Night the Space Monster Filled Up at the Pennzogen Station." 'Bel didn't get the joke at all. "Look, we've got to do something about a disguise for you as soon as possible."

About a mile down the road, Kevin added wistfully, "You know, I was just about to give in and go get us some of his mom's pie."

Chapter Twelve

*A*bout ten minutes down the interstate, Kevin who was now in the driver's seat hit a late night traffic jam. A string of trucks in both free-drive lanes was blocking the way of several passenger cars. Though the trucks were moving pretty fast, the drivers of the cars seemed to be wanting to pass but were not finding opportunities to do so.

When he first came upon the snag, Kevin was annoyed. But he soon satisfied himself that the whole stream of traffic was travelling nearly twenty miles over the speed limit and he might as well just follow along.

He switched on the bumper radar and locked his car into the traffic-train in the center lane. He wouldn't have to pay attention to driving now. The stream would carry them along electronically. The only time things bogged down is when several cars entered the train ahead and the fixed distance between vehicles had to adjust or the traffic-train slowed to climb an occasional rise in what was otherwise a very flat highway.

It was at just such a slow-down that Kevin happened to notice a car coming slowly the other way down the inner service median of the divided highway shining a searchlight into the vehicles coming toward him. "'Bel, get down, quick," he managed to say as the car with the light passed by directing its bright light directly into the passenger compartment of their car. "That's probably the Highway Patrol."

"Do you think they're looking for us?" 'Bel asked as he unfolded himself from the cramped space under the dash he'd managed to crawl into and peered out the back window to watch the patrol car continue on down the highway.

"Maybe that kid in the service station reported us. He might not have gotten the license plate number, just told the Highway Patrol he thought he'd seen a Visitor. On the other hand, of course, maybe they're looking for illegal aliens. Vehicles heading south on this highway are liable to be transporting Japanese refugees that sneaked in along the Oregon coast."

"I think *I'm* an illegal alien," 'Bel answered. "We've got to be careful." He was still half-kneeling on the floor looking back over the seat. "Hey, here comes another car with bright lights."

Kevin could see in the rearview mirror that a Highway Patrol car with its blue and red roof lights flashing was racing up toward them in the free-drive lanes.

"Stay down," he urged.

The Highway Patrol car shot by at breakneck speed.

"Maybe there's a road block up ahead. We gotta get off this highway."

"Can you turn around?"

"If they saw us, that'd be a dead giveaway, wouldn't it?"

"Let me out. I could hide out somewhere while you went on."

"No, you'd die or get killed. Besides, I don't know what to do. I need you." Kevin reached over and touched 'Bel's cheek.

"Me too."

"What if we pull over and see if we can wait them out?"

'Bel didn't answer. And after a moment Kevin answered himself, "How would we ever know when it was safe?"

"Look, there's an exit coming up," 'Bel announced. "Rest stop."

"The police are liable to be there. But I guess we'd see if they were. Maybe we could hide there a while without being noticed."

As they neared the rest stop set on a raised hummock alongside the road, both Kevin and 'Bel agreed there seemed to be no police cars parked in the lot—"unless there's one over on the other side leading back to the highway," Kevin acknowledged as he pulled off the highway onto the entrance ramp. The only vehicle there appeared to be a sixteen wheeler parked with its lights and engine off.

Cautiously Kevin drove up toward the two small buildings which he assumed held restrooms and vending machines. He certainly hoped for the latter. He'd been craving sweets ever since he started thinking about that apple pie he never got to eat.

"You know there could be nothing to any of this," Kevin remarked as he parked the car. "But you stay down and let me look around."

Except for the truck, the driver of which was probably sleeping in the cab, the place was deserted. Kevin even checked in the ladies room. In his search he found a candy machine and brought several different treats back to the car to share with 'Bel.

He was getting more and more nervous.

"Let's just wait here," 'Bel suggested. "At least till daylight. We'll both feel better then. We need sleep."

"What if somebody looks in the car and sees you?"

"Do I really look that different?"

"When you're changing color you sure do."

"Let me sleep in the back compartment."

"The trunk? You wouldn't fit."

"Oh yes I would. You'd be safe. Nobody would even suspect."

"Maybe you're right. But it's sure going to be tight back there."

"I can curl up. I'll pretend I'm in your arms."

"That's sweet," Kevin smiled.

"Let's see how you feel in the morning," he added humorously, but ironically, a few minutes later as he closed the trunk.

Alone in the front seat, Kevin kept waking himself up fearing if he fell asleep somebody would find them in the car and kill them both. He tried telling himself that sleep was necessary and he had to conquer that paranoid fantasy. But it wouldn't go away. Though finally, in spite of his fears, just a little before sunrise he fell into a very deep sleep.

The sun was warm on his face when he was awakened later by the sound of doors slamming right outside the car. At first he couldn't remember what he was doing scrunched up on the front seat of a strange automobile. Then suddenly the whole scene came back to him. And with it, the realization 'Bel was still in the trunk.

Kevin peeped up over the edge of the window. He could see that another car had pulled up alongside theirs. The people were gone now. As he looked out, he realized the parking lot of the rest stop was full. *Something's strange about this.* He rolled down the window. He could hear sounds coming from far away.

Sitting up, Kevin saw there was a crowd gathered at the far end of the parking area. An older man was standing in the back of a pickup truck talking to the crowd. *Maybe he's a preacher or something.* Kevin watched, struggling to hear what the man was saying. But the wind whistling by the open window blew the words away.

All of a sudden a chill clutched at Kevin's heart and he broke out in a cold sweat. Right in front of the crowd someone had a sign. It had been turned so he'd been seeing it edge on. He'd thought it was some sort of cross or religious banner. But as the wind caught the sign and swung it around, he could see it was a placard with crude hand-lettering:

STOP THE NEO-COMMIE VISITORS. USA FOR AMERICANS

Oh my God, I'm in the middle of a vigilante crowd.

Almost as if to confirm Kevin's worst fears, the teenager from the Pennzogen station climbed up onto the bed of the pickup truck and gestured wildly.

There was no time to try to alert 'Bel. The only thing to do was to get out of here quick before he was noticed. *What if that kid recognizes me or the car!*

Kevin started the engine. He let it warm up just a moment, then backed up and slowly started toward the exit. Through the rearview mirror he could just see the kid on the bed of the pickup pointing out his direction. *He's seen us and is calling to the crowd to chase us.* Indeed, he could see the crowd was dispersing toward their cars.

In a panic, Kevin floored the accelerator and sped down the exit ramp onto the freeway. The engine was roaring with the strain of the sudden acceleration. He didn't turn the wheel fast enough as he entered the highway and started to shoot right into the traffic-train, but managed to right the car just in time. Through the mirror he could see that other cars were leaving the scene of whatever that meeting was. But none of them seemed to be chasing him—in spite of his obvious speedy exit. *Maybe they think I was just enthusiastic.*

Still he kept up his speed. *I hope 'Bel's okay back there.* In fact, he just realized 'Bel was knocking on the back of the seat to get his attention. "It's okay," he shouted. "I think I outran them. You okay?" He heard a muffled "yes." He tried to relax.

Partly to calm himself, he switched on the satrad. There was a talk show on. He started to change the station—he was looking for classical music—when he recognized that the gruff voice coming through the speakers was saying something about an invasion force on its way. From the sound of the connection it was clear the man was calling in on an old-fashioned landline telephone.

"Why last night, right here in Los Baños," Kevin heard him say and realized that, of all things, they were talking about him and 'Bel.

"Police won't help. Highway Patrol says we're crazy. Says the Visitors left in the space ships. My grandson saw 'em in the service station last night. A whole carload. I tried to get the police to chase down the aliens last night or put up a road block. But no way. Wouldn't believe me."

Hooray, thought Kevin.

"Funny, there's a news story on the wire this morning out of San Francisco," the trained voice of the D.J. broke in. "Seems one of the cars that had been loaned to the Visitors was stolen last night."

Uh-oh.

"We're gonna have to protect ourselves. My grandson's out there right now with friends o' his puttin' together a posse. They're meeting at the rest stop south on I–5. We'll scour the highways from here to Bakersfield. They won't get away. We'll find 'em damn 'Visitors.' Maybe string 'em up. At least scare them away from this town."

You're sure right about that last one.

Kevin passed up the next couple of exits. It was just too close. But after that pulled off at an interchange of what on his map looked like farm roads. He climbed into the back seat and called to 'Bel.

"What's going on? Can I get out of here?" 'Bel answered.

"Maybe not yet. I'm sorry. We had a real close call back there and I'm still scared. There's a posse out after us."

"A what?"

"Oh, I'll explain. Look, for now, can you handle staying back there till I can find a town. There's a place called Shafter coming up. It's off the Interstate a ways. We need to get some makeup for you."

"Whatever you say," 'Bel's muffled voice answered. Kevin felt a pang of sorrow for his wonderful friend—and for himself. This adventure he'd been looking forward to as exciting and romantic was turning sour already.

Two hours later, now about mid-morning, 'Bel was sitting on the rickety chair pulled into the bathroom from the bedroom of the rundown motel Kevin had selected as unlikely to have people watching what was going on.

Kevin had just combed dark brown dye through 'Bel's hair. "It has to sit now for ten to twenty minutes, then we can wash it out and see if at least some of it will stay. Your pigmentation's so different, you know, it may not work."

'Bel stared at himself in the mirror over the sink. "Don't I look awful! I realize, Kev, we have to do this. But I can't help feeling terrible about it. Look at me: this is the color of lying and deceit."

"Yeah, but around here it looks perfectly normal."

"Will it come out?"

"Sure. This is not permanent color. We may have to repeat it, but at least we can get rid of it if we need you to look like a Visitor again."

'Bel looked so sad. His face was a dark grayish green and his ordinarily full almost translucent blond hair was plastered to his scalp with the dye.

"Are you hungry?" Kevin changed the subject.

"Oh, yes." 'Bel's color brightened some.

"While we're waiting for this to set, let me see if I can get something to go in the cafe next door. One of the reasons I picked this place was cause the cafe looked good."

"Will you be safe?"

"Oh, no problem. I don't know whether it'd be a good idea for you to appear in public even when we do get you made up. From what I heard on that radio station this morning, everybody around here is up in arms about the 'alien invasion' they think is happening. They'll probably be seeing Visitors everywhere."

"I'll be okay. Go get us something to eat," 'Bel smiled at Kevin through his reflection in the mirror, then turned around and, half-standing up, kissed Kevin lightly.

The small cafe was empty except for the cook who was scraping the griddle in the kitchen and four women sitting at a table in the corner. Kevin sat down at the counter and picked up a menu. When the cook, a tired looking middle-aged woman, turned and looked up at him through the window between the kitchen and counter area, he asked if she could fix him something to-go.

"Anything you want. I mean, off the menu."

"How about, uh, four cheeseburgers, two orders of fries, two large cokes... Can I have a cup of coffee while I'm waiting? Oh, and you got any pie? Maybe apple?" To her nod of affirmation, Kevin replied, "Two slices, please." There was a grin in his tone of voice.

"You can help yourself to coffee. There're cups over by the pot at the end of the counter."

Kevin saw that the coffee set-up was right next to the table of women. They were all dressed in simple dark blue dresses and each wore a black veil in her hair that identified them as nuns. Three of them looked very old. The fourth was quite young and rather pretty, though she was not wearing make-up and looked a little plain. Kevin was reminded of the sisters that had taught at the parochial school he attended in Medford. *How long ago and far away that all seems now.*

As Kevin poured himself a cup of coffee, he turned slightly toward the sisters and saw that the young one was looking at him. Slightly embarrassed, he smiled at her. "Good morning, Sister."

"Hi," she replied sprightly. "How are you this morning?"

"Okay," he replied.

"You look tired. Been driving all night?"

"Something like that. Had a hard night. Didn't realize it showed."

"Here, sit down then," she gestured toward a chair at the empty table between Kevin and her.

"Thanks, I'm waiting for a take-out order."

"I know," she answered. "Might as well sit down." As Kevin did as the young sister ordered, she continued, "This is Sister Magdalene, Sister Aqualina, and Sister Calasanctious." The three old sisters looked up from their breakfast plates momentarily and nodded, then resumed their slow eating. "I'm Jennifer."

"Sister Jennifer?"

"Well, sure. But you can just call me Jennifer. I don't so much go by the old ways."

"You sure have a different sounding name from the others," Kevin answered.

"My mother named me after an actress." She grinned sheepishly. "Turned out sort of appropriate," she added. "I do clown ministry with hospitalized children. The sisters here have been at the hospital our Order runs in Sacramento. I came up to get them and drive them back to St. Benedict's Home in Westwood where I live." She turned in her seat and whispered in a kind of aside, "The sisters aren't very good conversationalists."

Kevin grinned. He'd just caught on to the reason for her friendliness.

She'd probably been alone with these very old women for at least a day or two already and was happy to find somebody younger to talk to.

"Where are you going?" Sister Jennifer asked.

"L.A."

"Downtown?"

"No, not really. Uh, I'm hoping to see somebody in Covina."

"Who's that?"

Kevin started to think Sister Jennifer was nosy, but then quickly forgave her. After all, it seemed like she was just trying to make conversation. "Well, in fact, somebody you might have heard of, Joan Salado. She's a reporter for CNN."

"Oh, yeah. I recognize the name. I think I even know which one she is. I don't get to see a lot of TV. Though the last few weeks, what with all the news about the Visitors, we had the TV going all the time. The old sisters were real interested."

"How come?" Kevin asked, mainly just to keep up the friendly if superficial conversation.

"Everybody was, weren't they? I guess one reason the old gals got especially interested was cause the night the Visitors arrived one of the sisters in the house died. She'd been talking earlier in the day about God coming to get her. At first some of the sisters thought maybe the Visitors had killed her when the ship flew over the house. Some others suggested the Visitors were angels who were coming—"

One of the old sisters looked up and interrupted, "Sister Alacoque was a nut, always talking about mysticism."

"I rather liked the Visitors. I didn't exactly think they were angels, but I sure did believe they were aliens and I think President Arnold was crazy to run them off like that. I think there was more going on than we know about."

Kevin didn't want to touch that subject. "I had a nun in grade school named Sister Alacoque—Margaret Mary Alacoque."

"That's pretty common. A saint's name. She's the one who got the promise of the Nine Fridays from Our Lord."

"Have you made the Nine First Fridays, young man?" Another of the sisters asked.

"The sister I knew belonged to the Benedictine School Sisters of the Incarnate Word."

"Really?" Sister Jennifer asked excitedly. "That's our Order. Where did you go to school?"

"Medford, Massachusetts. St. Joseph's Parish."

"Isn't that amazing?" Jennifer replied. "We teach at that parish and the sister that died last month had been there for years."

"Small world," Kevin answered tritely, but excitedly. "She died the night the Visitors arrived? My mom said she'd heard Sister had died. She always kept in touch with her. She'll be interested."

"In fact, Margaret Mary was outside at the time. She must have watched the ship come over. Must have been a dramatic sight. I wonder what she thought." Kevin noticed that Sister Jennifer avoided the nunnish-sounding names and titles. "I'm real sorry the Visitors went away so fast. I never even got a chance to see one of them in person, much less talk to them. Big mistake Arnold made."

If only she knew. Sister would shit a brick. Kevin couldn't help laughing at his irreverent thought.

"Are you laughing at me?" Sister Jennifer pretended offense.

"Just something I thought. About the Visitors."

"I think there was so much they could have told us about religion. In fact, I think maybe it was really the Pope that was behind driving them away. You know how he is about women's rights and celibacy and sex and all that," Jennifer dropped back into her whisper to Kevin. He felt a wave of conspiratorial affection for the young woman. "What if it turned out the Visitors had women priests? Or what if Jesus had been a woman on their planet?"

"Hey, mister, your cheeseburgers are getting cold," the cook called out. "Been waitin' for you for over five minutes," she scolded.

On impulse, Kevin grinned widely. *Maybe here's just the cover we need to get out of here.* "Jennifer, would you trust me enough to come back with me to my room. I've got something I think you'd like to see."

"Well, young man. I might very well like to see it," she answered indignantly. "But just because I said I didn't necessarily agree with the Pope's position on celibacy doesn't mean you can proposition me."

All of a sudden, Kevin understood what she'd heard. His face reddened. He realized the three other sisters were staring intently at him. "Oh no, I didn't mean that, nothing sexual. I was responding to your comments about the Visitors."

"And you've got a Visitor in your room, I suppose."

"Ssshh," Kevin leaned over and whispered in her ear, "Well, yes. And I really mean it."

"And he eats cheeseburgers!" Sister Jennifer was still mocking.

"Well, look, Sister, I'm sorry. I guess I spoke out of turn. I'll just go now." Kevin backed away from the table feeling very foolish.

He paid for his order with one of the bills Joel had given him and picked up the bag, checking that everything was there. As he turned to leave, Sister Jennifer got up and followed him to the door.

"You were serious, weren't you?" she said nervously. "I mean about a Visitor."

"Please, Sister. Don't broadcast this." He looked around to see if the cook could have heard. *Probably not.* She had the water running in the sink in back.

"I'm sorry I made fun of you just now. It's… well, you know."

"I know." Kevin pushed open the door and started out.

"Can I come too?"

Kevin took a deep breath. He'd made a mistake in telling her. But maybe it'd be a worse mistake to fail to bring her into his confidence now. Maybe she could help them. They were on the run. As he thought a moment earlier, a nun might be good cover. *And besides, she'll be more liable to talk if I keep her in suspense.* Kevin tilted his head as if to say, "C'mon."

"Sister Jennifer," one of the older women called out, "You come back here now."

"I'll only be a moment, Sister," Jennifer answered as she followed Kevin out the door. Excitement was obvious in her voice.

As they started down the sidewalk toward the room, Kevin tried to set some conditions. "Did you hear the radio this morning?"

"There's no radio in our car. Vow of Poverty, you know."

"Well, somebody saw us in a service station last night and there's a posse forming to chase us down. I don't think they even know what kind of a car we're in. But we're getting in more trouble than I know how to handle. I mean, I could use your help. If you'd be willing."

As the two of them approached the door to the room, the nun held back. "You are telling me the truth, aren't you?"

Would I lie to a nun? Kevin decided not to say that thought out loud.

Instead he continued with his explanation. "We're trying to dye his hair so he won't be so noticeable." He stuck his key in the lock.

"Is that you, Kevin?" came an accented voice from just inside door. The nun's eyes lit up.

"It's me," he answered. He could hear the chain being disengaged inside. He turned to Sister Jennifer. "His name is 'Bel," Kevin explained as he swung open the door.

*K*evin followed the big station wagon Sister Jennifer was driving up the curving driveway to the front of St. Benedict's Home. He was grateful for a safe and uneventful trip. Of course, Sister Aqualina had not been much of a traveling companion. She fell asleep about twenty minutes out of Shafter—and she snored. But, if indeed the car was seen by any of the vigilantes, it certainly wouldn't have been recognized with an old nun in the passenger seat. And if the vigilantes had taken any notice at all of the lumbering station wagon full of sisters, they probably would never have looked twice at the dark-haired, dark-skinned young man in the front seat talking animatedly with the wimpled driver.

"Oh, Kevin, this has been one of the best days of my whole life," Sister Jennifer gushed dramatically after she'd hustled the three older women inside. She smiled at 'Bel and took his hand affectionately, "I've learned so much from you." She looked back at Kevin and in her characteristic aside whisper said, "I think maybe the sisters were right when they said the Visitors were angels coming for Sister Margaret Mary."

"Well, thank you, Jennifer," Kevin replied. "I don't know if we really were in any danger, but you sure provided a good cover."

Sister Jennifer laughed. She tugged at her veil with one hand, "These are good for something."

"Your virtue and kindness are good for many things," 'Bel responded very seriously to her joke. She blushed.

Under the dark brown makeup 'Bel was glowing bright yellow Kevin could see looking close. *Good disguise.* He thanked whatever gods arranged coincidences like these: not only was Sister Jennifer a welcoming chauffeur for the visiting fugitive, she was also a drama major at nearby Loyola Marymount College and her specialty was makeup. In fact, she'd been carrying her makeup kit with her for her clown ministry to kids in the Children's Unit at the Order's hospital in Sacramento.

"Thank you, 'Bel," she said warmly. "Look, you guys, stay here and eat with us. I mean, I'll bring dinner up to the parlor—no use getting all the old gals around here too excited. You're welcome to make phone calls. You can use my dime, whatever you need." The young nun surreptitiously pulled one of the little contemporary electronic devices out of her pocket to show she had one as though it were a piece of contraband. "And you're welcome to stay the night."

"Thank you, but—" Kevin started to decline politely. But he was interrupted by 'Bel.

"We are grateful for your hospitality and assistance. I think Kevin needs to call the reporter we are hoping to see. And I'm sure we're both hungry, and looking forward to getting to bed." 'Bel grinned.

"Joan said Will had called yesterday and told her to expect us, though, of course, she didn't know about you." Kevin explained to 'Bel over a postprandial cup of coffee in the delicate, old-fashioned parlor of the convent. Jennifer had gone back to the kitchen to get a sampling of liqueurs—several of which, she'd said, they brew right here in the house.

Kevin and 'Bel were discussing their plan of action.

"What did you tell her?"

"Well, I didn't say I had a Visitor with me, though I hinted that I was with somebody who had inside knowledge about the Visitor's concerns. She might have guessed what I wasn't quite saying. I told her I had important information that would prove the President wrong and that might make the Air Force reconsider the matter-field test. She sounded real interested."

"Good."

"Fortunate coincidence: her boyfriend, she said, works at March Air Force Base and has something to do with the test. You must have good karma."

"The best," 'Bel answered matter-of-factly.

"I think that's why she was so interested. If there's really a danger, it might affect him."

"Kevin, there really is a danger."

"I understand. Well, I also explained we were in a car that might have been reported stolen and that I didn't want to be driving around L.A. She said she'd come pick us up here tomorrow afternoon when she finishes with the noon news. You know, she went to the same parochial school. She didn't know Sr. Margaret Mary Alacoque had died or was even living here, but she's got the same connection to this place as me."

"Small world," 'Bel commented. Kevin wondered if he'd learned that expression from his time on Earth or if that was also a hackneyed, but often appropriate, cliche among the Visitors at home.

"I also called my friend Tim Lewiston in New York. There was no answer. I called my own number in San Francisco and found a message Tim had left this morning saying he was coming out to visit his parents up in Nevada City. I think he could be a big help to us. His folks are very well-connected."

"Connected to what?" 'Bel replied quizzically just as Sister Jennifer pushed open the door with her hip and entered carrying a tray full of fancy-shaped bottles. Kevin smiled to himself as he realized he'd caught another idiom that 'Bel hadn't known.

Chapter Thirteen

John Marshall extinguished his fourth—or was it fifth?—smokeless cigarette in the ash tray on the kitchen table around which the four were sitting. He looked over at his girlfriend Joan with a twinge of guilt as though he knew she didn't approve of the smokeless cigarettes anymore than the regular.

John had been getting more and more nervous as 'Bel explained the reasons for stopping the upcoming test of the matter-field. "You're sure the field effect will extend beyond the experimental chamber?" he asked for the second time. He obviously did not want that to be true.

"We don't know your exact technology. But we think that the field expands logarithmically in relation to time. At least it does where it impinges into our world. The tests that have been run so far have all had larger locuses of effect in our world than in yours. Though they've been damaging, they've been relatively small. But so far the field has been more confined than planned for this next test. So far the field's only been turned on instantaneously."

"Even so, the upcoming test is only supposed to stabilize the field right around the chamber," John interrupted.

"Well, we think the field collision echoes back into your world by another logarithmic expansion. In the past when the generator has been turned on instantaneously, that caused some extra energy but probably just seemed like greater efficiency than expected. But if the generator stays on over time, the field will keep growing and pull the space in our world back over here. "

"I'm sorry, I'm lost," Joan Salado spoke up. "I know I'm not a physicist and can't expect to understand all this talk about Planck's constant and parallel universes, but if you want me to report on this, I've got to understand it better."

"The explanation isn't as important," 'Bel answered, "as the fact that these tests of the force-field generator in your world create disturbances in ours. Already your preliminary experiments have killed hundreds of people."

"But, 'Bel, I just don't see how what happens on Earth affects anything on your planet. Aren't you light-years away someplace?"

"Look, Joan, I understand what he's saying about that," John answered her. "Right now, we need to get clear on whether this test is really a danger to *us* ."

"You mean you don't care what it does in the Visitor world? All you care about is whether it endangers you or your Air Force base?" Kevin broke in angrily.

"No, Kevin, I don't mean that. It's just that I'm not sure anybody's going to believe any of this. The Visitors apparently already tried to convince President Arnold that the test was harmful to them and he interpreted that as a ploy to dismantle our defense system. But I think if we—I—can convince the scientists that leaving the field on in stable mode threatens to blow up the whole base, maybe they'll do something."

"I think John's right, Kev, that we've got to make the case that *this* world is threatened, not just ours." 'Bel reached over and touched Kevin gently on the arm as if to say he appreciated Kevin's loyalty to his people. "Joan, what separates our worlds isn't space. It's the value of this quantum constant h…"

Kevin was feeling annoyed with all the questions and he was tired of hearing this explanation about parallel universes. *Why can't they just trust the Visitors? They don't have to understand all this physics to see something important is going on and they ought to be listening.* Kevin was tired of talk. *It's time to do something.*

As an escape mechanism for coping with the strain of the long conversation with Joan Salado and John Marshall, Kevin's mind wandered back to his remarkable experience with 'Bel last night. Ever since he'd met 'Bel, he'd found himself occasionally spacing out like this. *Being in love,* he explained to himself.

He grew warm all over again with the memory. *Even if we are all killed this week, it'll be okay. The past few days with 'Bel have satisfied every need I could possibly have.*

Soon after she brought the liqueurs, Sister Jennifer had excused herself to join the other sisters in praying Compline. Since Kevin and 'Bel were staying in guestrooms outside the sisters' cloister, Jennifer explained, they could stay up as long as they liked. She urged them to go out and look at the view of L.A. at night.

Taking her suggestion, 'Bel and Kevin walked around to the side of the convent. The lights of the city spread out as far as the eye could see. The night was clear and the lights flickered like a million candles. "Let's climb up there," 'Bel said, pointing up toward a classic-looking gazebo on the summit of a small hill behind the building.

As they climbed, the horizon opened out even more. And now their view extended in three-hundred-and-sixty degrees. To the west the Pacific Ocean lay like a great blanket of darkness.

'Bel leaned against one of the concrete pillars that held up the wrought-iron dome of the gazebo. He pulled Kevin to him so that Kevin's back was pressed against the front of his body. Kevin let his weight sink back against 'Bel. He stared out at the beauty of the night.

"Let me show you something," 'Bel whispered.

"What's that?"

"Just close your eyes and imagine you're sinking backward into me. Think about my color. I'm pale yellow right now. Feel that color surrounding your own body. Now imagine that the top of your head is opening up—"

"I felt something like that yesterday when we made love."

"Good. See if you can recall that feeling. And then let white light shine up out of your head."

"Okay."

"Now let the white light surround your whole body." He paused. "And let the color you imagined from me mingle with the white light."

"Okay."

"Now, keeping that image in your mind, open your eyes slowly."

"Oh wow." To his amazement, Kevin could see colored light flickering around him. "'Bel, it's real, isn't it?" The lights reminded him of what he thought auroras looked like: wisps of transparent color moving slowly through empty air. "What is it?"

"You're seeing what some people in your world call your aura, Kevin, the energy field around your body. It's there all the time, but you just don't see it."

"Is this mine or yours?" Kevin whispered as though the vision might be scared off by talking too loud.

"Well, right now, it's both. Mine is stronger than yours. I mean we experience ours stronger. This is the source of the color in my skin. The pigment responds to the energy field. Your people have the psychic energy around their bodies, but you are discouraged from seeing it."

Kevin saw the light was flickering a rosy magenta, a color he sort of recognized. "Is that, uh, sexual arousal I see?"

"In part. That's my love for you. And yours for me. Be aware of your feelings of love, let your mind go, and just feel the feelings."

Kevin allowed his eyes to close gently. In his mind's eye, he could still see the colors wafting round him. As he felt affection for 'Bel, the light brightened. He could feel even more light pouring into the aura from 'Bel behind him. He could feel the touch of 'Bel's body all along his back. He relaxed a little and then something remarkable happened.

Suddenly Kevin felt his body was gone. He felt like he'd turned into the auroral light. And 'Bel was gone. He too had turned into light. And suddenly time was gone. His consciousness was flooded with joy and bliss. The suddenness and the involuntariness of it reminded him a little of orgasm, but there was none of the strain and pressure than went with that physical pleasure. And there seemed to be no limit at all on this spirit pleasure and joy. Kevin felt himself opening wider and wider. He could feel 'Bel's love for him and his love for 'Bel. He could feel the importance of their joint mission. He could feel the pleasure of their success. And it all merged into a great rainbow of blissful light.

Afterwards, 'Bel held Kevin's hand and led him back down the hill since he was still in his daze.

Now, as he sat at the table in Joan Salado's kitchen, the recollection soothed Kevin's annoyance with Joan's and John's insistence on rational explanations. Kevin understood that he'd experienced the magic of the Visitors in a way most other people hadn't. Reminded to feel empathy for Joan's incredulity, Kevin brought his mind back to the conversation.

"I think I'm getting this," John was saying. "It makes sense. The whole universe is just vibrations, yeah? And the human senses pick up some of those and generate the appearance of the world in our minds. But what's really outside is lots more vibrations than we can perceive." He turned to 'Bel for confirmation.

"The physical world exists within consciousness, not consciousness within the world. There's so much more in the cosmos than just what appears to be the world the senses show. The five senses experience the five dimensions of spacetime. But we think there are actually eleven dimensions of consciousness itself. "

"Explain it one more time," Joan said, annoyance and frustration in her voice.

"I know. I know," exclaimed John. "It's like the signals coming through a TV cable. All the channels—and all the TV and telephone and webnet signals—are all coming through at the same time. They're vibrations in the electrical pattern in the wires. Modems and receiver boxes tune into these by synchronizing with one set of vibrations and filtering all the others out."

Kevin understood John's simile of the TV cable. It had always amazed him that there could be so many different channels coming in all through the same wire. *Maybe all of this does make sense.*

"I did an interview once with a scientist who talked about how matter isn't as solid or real as it looks…"

"The appearance of materiality is in the mind," 'Bel concurred.

"This guy said atoms are almost all empty space. Maybe there can be atoms from your world vibrating at different frequencies or something right inside the atoms of our world. This scientist hypothesized that what they call 'dark matter' and 'dark energy' is other matter that coexists with what we can see."

"…but that isn't vibrating at the same frequency as ours," John broke in.

"That's our universe," 'Bel said." It's right here," he extended his arm in a circle. "I think your scientist is right, Joan, but we'd call it Deep Consciousness not dark matter. Matter is a secondary artifact of consciousness sorting patterns of vibrations that come through the senses.

"Your universe and our universe are just different dimensions of the same vibrations. But we don't experience you and you don't experience us because we're moving at different frequencies in the second dimension of time."

"Second dimension of time?" Kevin questioned.

"Yes, 'celerity,' the time that time moves through, 'long time." 'Bel answered. "Interesting coincidence: your great scientist Albert Einstein called the speed of light *celeritas* from the Latin, like in E equals mc squared. We call the second time dimension celerity . We wonder how he knew…

"It's like how speed is measured in miles per hour—we call that fast time—and acceleration in miles per hour per hour. That second 'per hour' is celerity, long time, the dimension of time that speed itself is moving through. We all experience it as inertia, as mass. That's why heavy things seem to move slow to start get going or if they're in motion take time to slow down. They're moving at a different angle to fast time in celerity."

Kevin could not quite get his mind around that.

"And what you call Planck's constant, h, the size of the quantum, is the measure of that second degree frequency! It's what your world's perception is tuned to."

"Hmmm," John said, also not quite seeming to get it.

"What's important is that the matter-field collapses the difference in frequencies of Planck's constant and brings the two worlds into collision. If the generator is left on continuously, we think, it will create an expanding disturbance in spacetime geometry that could wreck a large area around it."

"Any idea how big?" John asked. Kevin could tell by his tone of voice that John too was happy to get back to practical matters.

"It depends whether the generator creates a geometry window around itself. John, have you seen the apparatus itself?"

"Yeah, sure. Why?"

"Because the shape of the space the machine itself is in makes a great difference. I'm not an expert on spacetime geometry, but I know that a cube shields a geometry window more efficiently than a sphere..."

"That's why the transporter in San Francisco was inside a cube?" Kevin observed questioningly.

"Right."

"And the transport system in your world had those different shaped doors?" Kevin continued.

"Well, the test chamber is hemi-spherical... you know, a small dome," John offered. "The generator itself is inside a metal box— probably either rectangular or cubical."

"Is there any way you could remove the metal box?" Joan asked. She looked at 'Bel. "Would that help?"

"Probably. Enclosing the apparatus in a sphere instead of a cube would reduce shielding and speed up the self-destruction of the generator."

"What do you mean?"

"If the generator isn't shielded geometrically, it will be destroyed itself in the collision and the bubble of coincidence'll remain relatively small."

"What does 'relatively small' mean?" Joan asked.

"It expands very fast." 'Bel looked down at the map of the eastern half of the L.A. metroplex laid out on the kitchen table. "I'm just guessing. But the logarithm has the reciprocal of h as a base. Remember h is the point of divergence between the two worlds. Well, h is equal to point-zero-zero-zero—uh, twenty-six zeros—six-five-four-seven. That makes the curve very steep. If the generator survives even a couple of seconds…" With his finger he made a circle with the research complex at March Air Force Base at the approximate center.

"That's the whole city of Riverside *and* San Bernardino," Joan exclaimed.

John caught his breath. "And if the generator *is* shielded and doesn't destroy itself?"

'Bel answered calmly, but Kevin noticed that under the makeup his skin darkened significantly and his eye color changed to red. "With nothing to stop it, the field will grow indefinitely… Well, maybe not indefinitely. We discovered that our space ships couldn't cross over into your world if they were inside the orbit of the moon…"

"That's why it looked like your ships were coming from outer space," Kevin interjected.

"That's also what we needed you to think," 'Bel answered Kevin enigmatically, then continued to John. "Our engineers think there must be a slight distortion in the value of h within the earth's gravitational field caused by the mass of the moon. If so that would probably limit the size the field could impinge into our universe. Maybe that would stop it."

"But you mean this could destroy the whole planet?"

"That's why we decided it was worth coming over here to warn you. And if it destroys your Earth, it will take ours with you."

"*I*t's just terribly important I get this information to President Arnold or to somebody who has got the power to stop that test."

"Mr. Anderson, you say the test could possibly destroy the whole planet Earth?" Joan asked Kevin in that calm reporter voice that sounded as though she might have been asking if he was planning on having dinner out this evening.

"*I* don't say that. The Visitors say that. And I think we just have to trust them. Their whole technology is based on a different approach from ours. I'm not a physicist, but I understand that they caught onto Einstein's notions and quantum physics a long time ago. They have a very developed science, but it looks different from ours."

"You've seen evidence of their technology?"

"I've been to their world."

"Excuse me for being skeptical, Mr. Anderson, but you sound just like a lot of people who claim they've been abducted by flying saucers."

"I realize that. But I'm not claiming I was whisked away in a flying saucer."

"Can you explain how you got to the Visitor planet?"

"This is going to be hard to explain, Joan, as you know. The Visitors don't come from another planet, I mean, like out in space. They come from another universe that exists side by side with ours."

"What does that mean?"

Kevin repeated the simile John had proposed of the different channels coming through a TV cable. He thought he did a good job of articulating it.

"The Visitors' universe is just like ours except for a tiny difference in what's called Planck's constant. That is a measure of frequency of a single quantum. It's a very small number: 6.547×10^{-27}. But it's the basis for atoms existing altogether.

"And what's that got to do with the upcoming test of the space shield?"

"The matter-field the shield creates shifts the value of Planck's constant. It's like shifting everything inside the shield into a slightly different universe. You can see how that would stop enemy missiles from getting through.

"The problem is that there's already somebody living in that universe."

A voice in Kevin's ear announced, "That's the end of the disk. Let's take a break."

Kevin reached up and removed the earphone and, as Joan stepped forward to help him take off the microphone, he stood up and stretched. "How was that?"

"This is hard stuff to grasp. I finally understood it yesterday after 'Bel explained it a second time. I'm going to get his explanation on disk, by the way, so don't worry if you don't think you said it well enough. Maybe together with 'Bel's explanation, it'll make sense."

Kevin was not with 'Bel this morning. He'd come into Hollywood with Joan to the studio to record an extended interview. They agreed it might not be safe for 'Bel. Joan planned to bring home a portable camera tonight to get his side of the story.

"Joan, while there's a break, can I use a phone to make a call? I left mine back in San Francisco."

"Sure," she answered. "You want some privacy?" She escorted him to a small parlor off the studio and showed him the deskset phone.

Kevin punched in the number he wanted. A moment later a familiar voice answered.

"Hi, Tim, this is Kevin. I guess you're in California."

"Yup. I tried calling you last night but didn't get an answer. Where are you?"

"In Los Angeles. I left the dime at my apartment. Look, I can't talk long right now. Something very important has happened. I want to ask you for a favor. I need to get to President Arnold. Maybe your dad can help."

"Maybe. What's this about?"

"Tim, I'm telling the truth and you can either believe me or not. But if not, I want you to come down here and see for yourself."

"I've known you long enough to believe you. Whatever you say."

"Well, wait till you hear."

Thirty minutes later, Kevin was back still answering Joan's questions. They'd covered the Visitor's autonomic commitment to truth-telling, their utter confusion in trying to communicate with the people of Earth, and the gradual psychological deterioration of the ambassadors who tried to deal with human politics.

"But why didn't they just tell us the truth?" Joan asked. "And why hasn't your friend 'Bel gone crazy around you."

Oh God, here comes the big question. Kevin's heart started to pound. "Uh, Joan, you promised you'd edit this interview. I mean that you wouldn't necessarily use everything."

"Right," she answered. "I'd like to get as much of the story as you're willing to tell, but we can decide how much to use. I presume you're asking 'cause we just got to a question you don't want to answer."

"It isn't so much that I don't want to answer. Though, yeah, the truth is I don't want to get into this. But beyond my feelings, this is what the Visitors didn't want anybody to know."

"You mean they've got a secret?"

"They listened to radio transmissions that were coming across from our world through a hole or something that got punched between the worlds by the first tests of the space shield. And they heard all these religious broadcasts…"

"You told me before the interview," Joan interrupted. "'specially that preacher Billy McMasterson. You said you think his radio broadcast was beaming right through into their world."

"Well, yes, exactly. The radio signals were how they discovered the point of collision between the worlds. And they believed everything they heard. They thought that if they let us know the truth about themselves, we'd think they were devils and they'd never accomplish their mission."

"Like in that movie *Childhood's End*?" Joan quizzed, reminding Kevin of that innocent moment only a few months ago in Cambridge when the Visitors were first arriving and somebody in the audience suggested parallels with the hit sci fi movie of a couple of years ago. *Maybe Arthur C. Clarke is proving to be even more a prophet than anybody'd suspected.*

"Sort of," he replied. "So they had to keep a secret. And that meant they had to hide their color change so we wouldn't know there was a secret." Then hastened to add, "But this isn't a movie. This is real."

"And you know the secret?"

"Right."

"And your friend 'Bel knows you know and it doesn't bother him."

"No."

"Why is that?"

Kevin could feel his face redden with embarrassment. "Because we're in love with each other."

Joan gulped audibly. "What's that got to do with the Visitors' secret?" She tried a quick recovery.

Kevin smiled. "The secret," he said calmly—and just a little proudly, he realized—"is that the Visitors are all homosexual."

"*W*ell, my God, let's blow the place up then."

"Listen to what you're saying, Kevin. Even if that were possible, it's not reasonable. The research facility has got people in it twenty-fours a day. Somebody might get hurt."

"Somebody might get hurt? John, listen to what *you*'re saying. The whole planet might be destroyed if that test happens."

"Now, look, I talked to Dr. Humphries—he's the Director of the project. He assured me there was no way this test could have that kind of consequence. There just isn't enough energy involved, he said."

"It doesn't require much energy to open the window between universes," 'Bel answered.

"I explained to Humphries what you said about parallel universes. He said all that stuff is just speculative cosmology and belongs more in metaphysics. But, look, he did agree to remove the metal housing from the generator. He said it would be a good idea anyway, allow him to watch for overheating. He seemed to think the geometry stuff was interesting, said he'd like to talk to a Visitor scientist someday, but didn't really put much stock in it."

"But he did say he'd remove the cube-shape around the generator?" Kevin said. "That'll help, won't it, 'Bel?"

"Probably. But I don't know. It may still destroy the planet."

"How can you be so calm about this?" Kevin asked. "How can your people be so resigned to dying?"

"It's all just change. Everything and everybody dies sometime, even universes. The truth is the truth," 'Bel answered. "It is foolish to fight the inevitable. We tried and failed. Now the best we can do is embrace the truth as an expression of creative wisdom…"

"You people sure seem wacky spiritual," John observed. "Reminds me of some friends I used to know who were into Buddhism. No wonder some people call you angels… but it's still wacky."

"But what about Riverside?" Joan spoke up for the first time in this tense conversation. "Isn't there a danger being too close?"

"It seems to me if the thing is going to destroy itself, it'll just do that and the test will fail and nobody will get hurt," John said. "You know, I think Dr. Humphries' right. I bet nothing's going to happen."

"Then how come you talked to Humphries about removing the cube around the generator?" Kevin challenged.

"Let's say I was hedging my bet a little."

"Okay, but please, John," Joan said emotionally, "hedge it a little more and get as far away from the experiment as you can."

"I'll see," he replied.

"My estimate of the area of collision is pure guesswork. You may be right that the generator will shift its own space so quickly it will stop itself. I don't know."

Kevin was still extremely agitated. "John, can't you just use your own authority to stop the experiment?"

"My authority? Look, I'm just a technician monitoring radar waves produced by the generator. I may be a supervisor, but I don't have any authority. And whatever credibility I might have had I probably lost this morning when I talked to Humphries. He'll probably have my ass out of there anyway."

"That might just save your life," Kevin answered snidely.

"Well, maybe so." John turned his attention to Joan. "You know, Humphries said they'd already been warned to expect this kind of thing. The F.B.I. and C.I.A. and who-knows-what-else were out there last week talking about attempts to stop the experiment. They're convinced that if these 'Visitors' really are from outer space, the reason they want to prevent us from developing the space shield is 'cause with it we'd be invulnerable to *them*."

"We're not from outer space," 'Bel reiterated a point he'd been making over and over again. "If we were, we probably wouldn't care whether you blew your planet up or not."

Kevin noticed that as 'Bel said those words his face darkened noticeably. *That isn't true, is it? Not the part about not being from outer space, but about not caring.*

"I don't know how you do that chameleon act," John said. "It sure looks real. And, you know, I like you two guys. But, I don't know. This whole thing just doesn't make sense to me. I have to admit," he gestured toward 'Bel, "I think you're probably an enemy agent, maybe Russian, neo-Czarist, who knows?"

"Oh, come off it," Kevin answered. "I told you what I saw in their world. That was not Russia."

"Then maybe we can't trust you either," John answered plainly.

"Wait a minute," Joan implored. "Let's not break up this little foursome with personal accusations. At least not yet. I still believe you guys think you're telling the truth. I mean, I've been on assignment in Russia and I never saw any Russians who could change color like that."

"Harry Houdini," John answered smugly.

"Houdini was not a Russian," Joan answered irritably.

"I know that. I mean, people can do all sorts of magic tricks."

"What about the interview we made this morning? Are you going to show that on the air?" Kevin changed the subject.

"I don't know," Joan answered weakly. "My producer said it was an interesting story. But—you're not gonna like this, Kevin—he said it sounded more like a pilot for the All-New Twilight Zone than a news story. He said the F.B.I. had warned the network heads to expect attempts to stop this research. Besides, he didn't like the gay stuff. Thought it spoiled the story."

"But are you going to warn Riverside and San Bernardino to evacuate?"

"Kevin, that would be like shouting fire in a crowded theater. More people would get hurt in the panic than if the research facility just self-destructs. But, as I promised, I sent a copy of the interview to my contact at the White House. She's got enough pull to get Arnold to watch it."

"The whole thing?" Kevin asked nervously.

"Sure."

"But you promised you'd edit it… at least the part about the Visitors' sexuality."

"That was for the air. Don't you want President Arnold to understand what's really going on?"

"Oh my God," Kevin turned sheepishly to 'Bel. "I think I told her too much." At the same time that Kevin felt he'd betrayed the Visitors' secret, he also felt exposed himself. His account of his romantic relationship with 'Bel had just been forwarded to the White House. He wasn't sure whether his rush of anxiety had as much to do with betraying the Visitors as exposing himself.

'Bel stood up. Very calmly he said, "It appears our mission has been only partly successful. But, John, your intervention with Dr. Humphries may make the difference and you've given me important information. I should return to my world and warn the people who live in this area," he gestured around himself, "to get away from here. Especially if the field's going to be contained, it makes sense to evacuate the area on the other side. There's still hope."

"Sure I'll take 'Bel back to San Francisco to find this window—whatever that is," Tim answered.

"Go to my apartment first and meet up with Joel," Kevin said. "He'll know what to do from there. I really appreciate this."

"I'll do anything you ask… within reason, of course," he joked. And then, smiling lasciviously toward the Visitor who'd just gone into Joan Salado's kitchen to pour the three of them each a cup of coffee, Tim added, "And I'd be very pleased if *he* were within reason."

"Tim!" Kevin scolded. "We're talking about saving the world."

"I'm sorry," Tim answered, "I guess I shouldn't make light of what you said. It's just, well, all of a sudden you're talking about this stuff that's like right out of a cheap science fiction movie."

"You think he's science fiction?" Kevin answered sharply.

"I think he's gorgeous," Tim replied, with tones of Mae West in his voice. "Congratulations, Kev." He dropped the affectation. "I mean, I really am happy for you. I mean really."

"Okay. Thanks. Look, I know I'm pretty touchy. It's just we've been through a lot lately. And maybe it's all just starting."

'Bel walked back into the room carrying a tray. As he offered a cup to Tim and then to Kevin, Kevin kept talking. "I asked you to ask your dad about helping us talk with the President."

"Yeah. He said he couldn't promise anything, but if I trusted you he'd make the call. I think he did that after I left this morning. I reminded him at breakfast."

"Thank you, Tim," 'Bel commented as he sat down. "Kevin has very good friends."

"I could say the same thing," Tim answered, "I mean about you."

This time Kevin was easier on his friend; the news Mr. Lewiston had probably intervened in his behalf with the White House had improved his mood. "Are you flirting with my boyfriend?" he scolded jokingly.

"You're welcome to flirt with *my* boyfriend anytime," Tim rejoined.

"Since when do you have a boyfriend?"

"Well, I'm sure I will. My luck's not so bad. Though maybe these days not as good as yours."

'Bel changed the subject. (Kevin noticed his face reddened as he did so; he wasn't sure what that meant, but he appreciated the privacy of the communication between himself and 'Bel.) "I am grateful to you for offering to help us. I realize it is quite an imposition to ask you to drive all the way back to San Francisco."

"I'm sure I'll enjoy the chance to visit with you."

For a moment Kevin felt a wave of jealousy and distrust of his long-time friend. Then he realized that he could see that 'Bel's color was bright yellow, without the slightest trace of rose or of gold. And he knew that whatever was going on in Tim's mind, he could certainly trust 'Bel. That's the beauty of always telling the truth.

But what if the truth had been that 'Bel was showing all sorts of rosy-colored signs of attraction to Tim? Kevin answered himself. *Then we could have talked about it and reached a decision about what was possible. I know he wouldn't hurt me.* He looked at Tim for a moment and realized the same thing about him. *He wouldn't hurt me either.*

"I want to wait till Joan and John get back. As Kevin told you, we, uh, argued, with them this evening. It ended amiably but they decided to go out to dinner to let all the feelings settle. I wouldn't want to disappear now. I'm not sure how helpful they can be. Your father may prove more so, Tim. But I don't want to appear to reject their help."

"You're going to stay here for the test?" Tim asked Kevin.

"Joan promised that if there is some kind of accident, she'll get me on the air immediately. We're sure something's going to happen here. And I want to be around to explain it."

Chapter Fourteen

The view was beautiful. The air was clear and bracing. The rich scent of recent rainfall and dark fertile humus, autumnal leafmeal and pungent evergreen forest filled Kevin's nostrils and enlivened his senses. But he felt guilty about enjoying the morning. After all, they were here to watch for something potentially horrible and deadly.

For a moment Kevin wondered about death. *What if the field gets up this high?* He realized that if 'Bel were dying on the other side then he wouldn't mind dying. *Maybe that's crazy. Maybe that's love. Anyway, it's the truth.* Of course he certainly hoped he would not die—though if the whole world were ending, what difference would it make? *Funny, this isn't what I expected the end of the world to look like.*

Kevin was standing next to Joan's car. To his left, just behind a stand of evergreens, he could see the sun rising over the eastern horizon. He checked his watch. It was still almost twenty minutes before the scheduled time for the sunrise test. *We're up so high here the sun rises much earlier,* he explained to himself.

Stretched out in front of him lay the populous plain at the base of the San Bernardino Mountains on which were situated the cities of eastern Los Angeles: San Bernardino, Colton, Redlands, Riverside, and the numerous suburbs of the suburbs of the sprawling metroplex of L.A. that was too far west and too shrouded in urban haze to be visible even from this high point at Baylis Park on Rim of the World Drive near the ski resorts of the Southern California Mountains.

It's like I'm on the rim of time. We all are!

In the distance Kevin could see the terminator line slowly sweeping toward his right: dawn marching east to west. The line, of course, was diffused by the earth's atmosphere so that what he saw was less a distinct line than a gradual and blurred lightening of the Earth and a glow suffusing the air on the plain below.

Here and there, as he watched, the fingers of sunlight sparkled off water or glass or metal surfaces. The golden glow in the air and the rosy hue that streaked the eastern sky reminded Kevin of 'Bel's wondrous way of showing eros.

"Kevin, can you come here now," Joan called from a few feet below the road where she'd climbed down to find both an unobstructed view and a reasonably flat place on which to position her camera tripod. As Kevin scampered down, she explained, "Look, I've got the camera aimed right at what I'm pretty sure is the research facility. This is a really strong telephoto lens. I'm going to start it recording in a minute. But what I want you to do is to be ready to turn this knob here on the zoom to widen the frame just in case this, uh, collision you're expecting gets bigger than what's in the picture."

"What are you going to be doing?"

"I am going to be talking to John. He promised me he'd make some excuse to get away from the test site and call me."

She sounded so matter-of-fact. But Kevin couldn't help thinking she must feel awfully ambivalent herself about what might happen. It was her idea to come up into the mountains to get out of harm's way and to give her camera a bird's eye view of the collision—or whatever it was that might occur when the matter-field generator was activated. *She must believe something is going to happen.* At the same time, she was leaving John down there on the base, blithely believing he was perfectly safe doing his job as usual. *She must be worrying about him.*

The dime device in her pocket started to ring. "The Love Theme from *When Worlds Collide,*" Kevin recognized, for the first time noticing the coincidental pun: worlds really were about to collide. "That's John. I hope he got away from the building. It's getting close to time."

"Hi," she answered, "I hope you're clear." She turned to Kevin, "Hey, pull the trigger on the camera and press in the lock to get it recording."

Kevin did as he was instructed. The camera started smoothly humming. "Is he safe?" he called out.

"He's out of the building. Said he'll be in terrible trouble if nothing goes wrong. Oh God, I hope he'll be far enough away."

Kevin peered into the camera viewfinder. It all looked so peaceful. For a moment he hoped nothing was going to happen. He was humming that song to himself that Joan's dime had played. *How appropriate the words.* He remembered in the movie they're sung in both French and English. *If the sky should fall into the sea and the world collapse all around me, peut m'importe si tu m'aimes, it won't matter if you love me,* Kevin translated the French for himself, *really love me.* He felt a wave of affection and passion. He thought about 'Bel and hoped it was all true. Maybe their love for one another could actually help stop the imminent disaster. *Let it happen, I won't care.* The words and melody seemed so poignant.

"John says it ought to be activating any time now," Joan shouted.

Kevin looked up from the camera into the silent distance. Suddenly a brilliant blue-white light erupted below. Kevin quickly looked into the viewfinder. A small dome of light was rising out of the roof of the research facility. *The force field.* The dome was growing. It was expanding bigger than the camera's frame. Kevin fiddled with the knob to enlarge the lens' field. The dome of brilliance had now completely surrounded the building and was still expanding.

Suddenly the high mountain silence, filled only with the rushing of wind and the gentle rustling of leaves, was pierced by Joan Salado's terrified scream. "The dime made a high pitched whistle and went dead," she whispered to Kevin shakily, as the two of them watched the field grow.

"Are you getting this?" she said.

"What happened to John?" Kevin exclaimed in horror.

"I don't know. He could've been caught in the field. But maybe the cell towers just got zapped."

The dome of blinding light wasn't expanding as fast as 'Bel had predicted, but it was continuing to expand. They must both have been remembering 'Bel's warning that the zone of collision could encompass all the cities on the plain below. "How big is that gonna get?" Joan said with a hush of awe and genuine fear.

Then just as suddenly as the blue-white light had come on, it winked out. Through the viewfinder screen, Kevin could see that clouds of smoke were rising from where the bubble of interference—the research facility—had been.

"Thank God 'Bel was wrong," Kevin exclaimed

"It doesn't look like it expanded much beyond the building. Oh, please, let John be safe," she prayed aloud. Then she turned to Kevin, "Damn you," she shouted. "Why did you do this to me? It's not fair."

"I didn't do it," Kevin answered timidly. "I warned you about it. I'm sorry, Joan. Maybe John's okay. Let's get down there."

- - -

Joan let Kevin drive the car. "I'm liable to get hysterical and drive off the road," she excused her sudden weakness. About halfway down the curving mountain road, her dime rang again—this time with just the ding-dong of an unknown caller. Joan answered it, and listened breathlessly for a moment. Then her demeanor changed suddenly. "He's okay," she hurried to assure Kevin.

"Looks like he was close to the edge," Joan explained once she'd disconnected. "Said he thought he was going to get it. He could see the light of the field advancing down the street toward him. It stopped about a hundred yards away. He said everything's a smoking mess."

A moment later Joan had the camera in her lap as she changed lens. "Let's do the interview as we drive. I've got a pretty good exclusive on this. Don't want to waste any time."

"Okay, Kevin," she said lifting the small camera and framing the handsome, but harried-looking young man in the viewfinder. "How did you now this was going to happen?"

An hour later, Joan was still maneuvering the camera. But now she wasn't capturing Kevin's explanation or his frustration at having had his warning ignored. Now Joan was focusing on the burned and broken bodies that lay strewn in the remains of the buildings at March A.F.B. Few of the bodies were intact. Most seemed to have been exploded from inside; some were just shapeless masses. Many were blackened and charred from heat generated in the air when suddenly two atmospheres crashed into one another.

The strangest thing was that right in the middle of the devastation was what appeared to be the front half of a Visitor spacecraft. The rounded semi-circle of a flying saucer cut off cleanly just behind the pilots' cockpit lay slightly askew and smoking just a few feet from where Dr. Humphries' matter-field generator had once stood.

The two bodies, still strapped in their seats, though charred and also still smoking slightly, clearly looked like Visitors, tall, thin, finely featured. *How many more of the bodies might be Visitors*, Kevin worried. *Might 'Bel be among the dead.* But he kept reminding himself 'Bel went back to call for an evacuation, not to get caught in the collision.

Even stranger was that all around the broken spacecraft seemed to be a thick coating of melted lead. It looked as though there'd been some large pile of elemental lead positioned just between the two pilots, that had turned molten in the collision and flowed out all around the center of the disaster site.

"The fact that any of the bodies are Visitors," John Marshall said to Kevin, "goes a long way to prove your explanation. How else did they get here? They must have been in that craft on the other side when the field opened."

"Yeah, I'll bet the President's going to be looking for you now," Joan said. "The interview material we got is great."

His worry about 'Bel was making Kevin very high-strung. "Joan, please don't release that stuff I said yesterday. I don't know what had come over me. But don't run that part about me and 'Bel..."

"Now, Kevin, it's okay. It's all fascinating. And it makes a much better story if it's told in a way that makes sense. It really was important to tell the truth, regardless of how it might be misunderstood."

"*I* think we're heroes," John Marshall said as he proffered the burning joint to Kevin. Kevin shook his head. The marijuana appealed to his feelings of anxiety, but he knew he wanted to keep a clear head. For a moment he remembered the herb 'Bel had given him in the Visitor world. It had made him euphoric without blearing his mind. *Things are so much better over there.*

Apparently recognizing Kevin's seriousness, John amended his comment, "I mean, I guess *you* are. You saved my life."

"You're the hero, John. Getting that cubical shield removed from the generator may have saved the world. Though I still don't understand why the field expanded so slow and extinguished as quickly as it did."

"Well, let's just be glad it did. Too bad I couldn't get old Dr. Humphries to believe a little more: he wouldn't have been vaporized."

"I'm sure they'll believe now," Kevin answered turning his attention back to the TV screen.

The familiar CNN fanfare played over a graphic of the spinning globe. As the stylized map of the United States slid into the center of the picture, a drawing of a dish antenna appeared over Atlanta and, as the dish appeared to scan rapidly back and forth across the screen, the words "The News in Depth" were ticked out. "Tonight's big story on

'The News in Depth,'" a voice-over announced, "is the mysterious and tragic failure of the force-field test President Arnold announced last week." The handsome young anchor appeared on screen. "And now, reporting from Los Angeles, is CNN West Coast reporter Joan Salado."

The screen filled with a sight too familiar to Kevin: the blackened remains of the Air Force base, scattered here and there with smoking remnants of human—and Visitor—bodies and, of course, the broken half of the Visitor craft slumped in the center of the devastation. "It was a tragedy of major proportions, lessened only by the fact that it might have been much worse," Joan's voice rang out. "Early arising residents of Riverside report they saw a strange bright light shining from the direction of nearby March Air Force Base. One man I spoke with told me he could see the light from what military officials here have downplayed as 'an accidental explosion' advancing up the street toward him."

"Hey, that's me she's talking about," John exclaimed.

"The number of dead still remains unknown. The 'explosion' and subsequent fire completely destroyed the research center where the test of the space shield technology was scheduled for sunrise this morning. A body count has been almost impossible, though the Riverside Coroner's Office and a special military disaster emergency team are on hand now investigating the extent and the cause of the 'explosion.' Estimates are that as many as a hundred Air Force personnel and civilians may have been in the building at the time of the 'explosion.'"

Kevin was pleased that he could hear the quotation marks in Joan's intonation every time she used the word "explosion."

The anchor broke in to report another facet of the story. "What appear to be the remains of bodies of the outer space Visitors who left Earth last week at the President's request were found among the wreckage of one of their spacecraft. Now high-ranking Administration officials are suggesting Kamikaze-style sabotage.

"The Visitors' objection to research into the matter-field technology is what sparked President Arnold's change of attitude toward them. There are reports from local residents of lights in the sky and Visitor ships last night and this morning. Joan..." he threw the story back to her.

"While that would support the Administration's hypothesis of sabotage, there is no hard evidence for the sightings. Neither Air Force nor Weather Service radar showed anything unusual in the skies over Riverside any time in the last forty-eight hours."

Joan pushed on with the story. She was about to spin it the other way. "That is not to say, however, that this disaster was totally unexpected. Indeed, this reporter was given advance warning of the danger of this morning's test—a warning that, though it appeared to have been totally unheeded, was conveyed to the White House yesterday by this reporter. Because of that warning I was able to cover the event from a unique vantage point."

The picture changed from the scene of Joan in front of the smoldering wreckage to the lovely mountain woods where Kevin had been this morning. The camera panned from the stands of evergreen trees dark and still in the early morning, across the plain hazy with the coming dawn, and then, abruptly, to Kevin standing solitary gazing out into space. "This young man, Kevin Anderson, a Harvard-trained architect, contacted me earlier this week to request assistance in convincing President Arnold to stop the scheduled test."

The scene changed to what Kevin recognized as the Hollywood studio. He was in the middle of explaining how the matter-field generator would force collision of the two worlds. "The matter-field creates the shield by slightly changing the value of a constant in physics—called Planck's constant, abbreviated h—which measures the activity in a single quantum of energy. The Visitors' world is linked to ours in quantum space by the value of that constant. In their world, h is slightly different from in ours. When the matter-field is activated, it causes the two worlds to coincide."

"That's pretty esoteric stuff, Kevin," Joan replied. "Can you simplify it by explaining what will happen?"

"I don't know… a collision of matter with widespread destruction within the space of the field… loss of life… a fire, maybe."

The scene jumped back to the mountains. With a gesture Kevin did not remember making—and which he certainly did not make at the time of the collision when he was looking through the camera's viewfinder for Joan—he raised his arm and pointed. The scene flashed to the sudden brightening of the expanding dome of light.

"How do you know this?" Joan's voice asked over the scene.

"The Visitors told me."

"Why would they have told you something they apparently didn't tell the President of the United States?"

The scene shifted back to the studio interview. "They did. But I think they made a tactical mistake. They were afraid of how we on Earth would react if we knew the whole truth about them." There was a quick break in his movement that Kevin recognized as a point where Joan had edited the interview. For a moment he wondered what she was going to have him say.

"They listened to radio transmissions," the image on the TV screen was continuing, "that were coming across from our world through a hole or something that got punched between the worlds by the first tests of the space shield..."

There was an editing flicker as something had been left out. Kevin remembered Joan's mentioning that anti-gay preacher Billy McMasterson. He was glad she'd left that out. It might have given something away about the content of the radio transmissions that Kevin would just as soon see overlooked.

"A hole got punched between the worlds by the space shield tests?" Joan asked in a question Kevin did not remember her asking. "In San Francisco?" He surmised she was emphasizing that aspect of the story for her own purposes. "Could that have caused last year's earthquake?"

He was surprised to hear himself agree with her emphasis. "Well, yes, exactly. The radio signals were how they discovered the point of collision between the worlds. And they believed everything they heard. They thought that if they let us know the truth about themselves, we'd think they were devils and they'd never accomplish their mission..." Flicker. "So they had to keep a secret."

She's made it sound like the secret was the earthquake!

Another editing flicker.

"And you know the secret?" Joan was asking.

"Right."

"And your friend 'Bel knows you know and it doesn't bother him."

"No."

Kevin felt a rush of dread of what was about to follow—and a surge of anger. *I asked Joan not to use this part.*

His anger abated abruptly when the scene shifted. 'Bel's image filled the screen. He was speaking, but he could not be heard. "This is

'Belwyn Tuarul," Joan's voice-over explained. "As you can see he is one of the Visitors. Apparently he remained—or returned—after the main force left a week ago. He has befriended Anderson and revealed to him several things about the Visitors that had previously been kept secret."

"Our people do not lie to one another. We cannot lie," 'Bel's voice got loud enough to hear.

"What about the secrets you kept from us?"

"It was very hard on my people. We thought the success of our mission—which meant the survival of our world and yours—depended on your, uh, believing in us. And we feared you would not."

"Why?"

"Because some of your religious teachings seem to conflict with ours. And because your science understands the structure of the universe very differently. We did not think you would grasp our message. So it was decided to simplify the message to what we thought you would understand, that is, your own safety.

"It was decided we would tell you as little as possible about ourselves and simply tell you that the technology of the space shield was dangerous to your own world. We expected that you would be so grateful for that news you would welcome us. And then, gradually, we could reveal more to you."

"What happened to that plan?"

Why doesn't Joan ask about the color change? Kevin thought, feeling helpless as the TV program continued. *That's the most important thing about them.* Kevin could see 'Bel's coloration changing from bright yellow to pale green to reddish. But he realized to most viewers it would just look like interference in the color of the TV image.

"Your President did not believe us. That was something we were totally unprepared for. He thought, along with many others of your people, that we were lying. That and the pressure of hiding our way of life caused some of us to have what you call a 'nervous breakdown.' Our Judges decided we had erred and that we should give up and accept the consequences."

"You said your world is threatened too?"

"The High Court Judges prayed and meditated over this and determined that we could do no more, that if our world was destroyed along with yours it would be a consequence of our hiding the truth."

"That sounds pretty fatalistic and passive."

"A society that lives with the truth *is* very accepting, Joan."

'Bel's face was replaced with Joan's. "Kevin, why would 'Bel reveal to you all these secrets?" she quizzed.

Kevin did not remember her asking exactly that question, but he dreaded what he was sure she was going to edit in as his answer. He felt his face redden in embarrassment and anger.

"Because we're in love with each other."

"What's that got to do with the Visitors' secret?"

"The secret is that the Visitors are all homosexual."

"How is that possible?"

"Their sexual biology is a little different from ours. Their females ovulate as part of orgasm. So whenever male and female Visitors have sex, and both of them, uh, reach climax, well, the female conceives a child."

"You mean every time they have sex they have a baby? Wouldn't that create terrible overpopulation?"

"Apparently. So they had to develop an adaptation early in their cultural and religious evolution. Heterosexual intercourse became a sacred act for them—engaged in in a ritual context—and homosexual sex became the basis for relationship and for recreational sex."

All of a sudden it hit Kevin that his mother and father just might be watching this program. He felt his blood run cold.

"What about families and child-rearing?"

"From what I have learned, I understand they do not have nuclear families as we know them. They live in small communities of like-minded individuals, fluidly moving from one household to another as their interests change. To some extent the sexes live independently of one another. Men are artists and philosophers. Women are craftsmen and executives. Children are raised by the opposite-sexed parent: boys are raised by mothers; girls by fathers. That's partly so that heterosexual relations will be perceived as parental, not sexual. Most of them only have one child so the population remains stable."

"What if a woman gives birth to two girls in a row?"

"I don't think that happens. I mean, I think they control the sex of their offspring by their loving intention and expectation. So it almost always works out right. But one of the most interesting—and for us controversial—things is that during pregnancy a woman can feel directly what's going on with her fetus. She knows whether it's healthy or not. If, for some reason, the developing fetus isn't wanted, 'cause it's deformed or sickly, it will be spontaneously aborted."

"Spontaneously?"

"Yeah. I mean they don't do invasive medical procedures like we have to do. They're all so in touch with what's happening in their bodies that, to some extent, they can control their body chemistry by conscious decisions—except, of course, for their coloration."

Kevin observed that that was probably going to be the only reference to the pigmentation differences.

"Hey, that stuff's pretty interesting," John said, breaking into Kevin's annoyance that the thing that most convincingly proved the Visitors were not Russian spies or Nasserinian operatives or whatever people were most afraid of wasn't being touched on.

"Remarkable," Joan commented about the maternity process.

"You can see why they thought they'd run into conflicts with our religions!"

"And you say they do not control their coloration?"

"Recently they've developed drugs that suppress the change and, apparently, some of them could learn to control it intentionally. But in their world that's considered perversion."

The scene shifted back to 'Bel sitting in the same living room in Joan Salado's apartment that now Kevin was in watching the show. He couldn't help feeling a little dismayed by how, in the name of presenting "the news in depth," TV was able manipulate reality.

While in the background 'Bel's voice could be heard faintly, Joan continued her narration. "Sex is apparently not the only difference between us and the Visitors. 'Belwyn Tuarul spoke about his people's commitment to telling the truth. This is perhaps the most remarkable thing I have learned about the Visitors."

Thank God she's finally going to explain. While Joan's voice continued to drone on about the Visitors' pigmentation change, Kevin gazed wistfully at the TV image of 'Bel. It was only after Tim and 'Bel had driven off two days ago back to San Francisco and the geometry window that it dawned on him that he might never see 'Bel again.

"*Y*ou got 'Bel taken care of and everything?" Kevin asked into the phone.

"Just as you asked," Tim answered. "And it looks like he was successful."

"What do you mean?"

"I mean the world didn't blow up."

"I don't understand."

"After we left you, 'Bel got an idea about how to destroy the matter-field generator from the other side. I assume that's what happened."

"I thought it was John's getting the shape of the container around the generator changed."

"Maybe it was both," Tim answered. "Anyway it's a funny story."

"Funny?"

"Yeah, when we got to San Francisco we came right over here to your apartment... by the way, this is a nice place you got... and connected with Joel. 'Bel was getting anxious to get over to the other side and start the evacuation and sort of despondent. So while we were driving out to the Research Park, Joel was trying to cheer him. You know Joel!"

"I can imagine," Kevin answered.

"Bel and I were talking about the parallel worlds and Planck's constant and the field collision and all that. Joel kept making jokes—those things he calls Bunnyisms..."

"Uh-huh."

"'Bel was taking them all very serious and getting pretty confused."

"He has a different sense of humor," Kevin said, "gentle and loving, but kind of literal. Maybe it's the difference in idioms..."

"Anyway, 'Bel was saying how sad it was that, even if he could manage to get them to evacuate all the people, this beautiful city was going to be destroyed 'cause it's on their side of where March Air Force Base is. He was telling us about his world, that it's like ours, but that his people don't get caught in the delusion of some things being better than others and so everything is perfect there...

"So Joel says in that charmingly nitwit way of his, 'Well, as they always say, if the grass is greener on the other side of the forest, the cow can't get over the fence for the trees.' As you might imagine, 'Bel was confused by that."

Kevin chortled.

"'Bel asked him if he meant cows showed green when they were frustrated. Now Joel gets all flustered saying you can't explain a Bunnyism, but then starts to explain what these proverbs mean that he's just slaughtered. He talks about how greener means the grass looks lush and dense and the cow wants to come over to eat but can't because the trees are in the way.

"Then 'Bel says, 'So what does the cow do?' And, of course, there's no answer to that and Joel just gets more flustered and says, 'It's a joke, 'Bel. Maybe the cow jumps over the moon.' Well, Joel starts apologizing for constructing a bad Bunnyism, when all of a sudden 'Bel lights up. It was like he was glowing white-hot. 'You mean, it can't fit... unless it goes over the moon,' he says and starts laughing."

"I don't get it," Kevin answered, but then recalled how it was one of those Bunnyisms that had given him the idea about the geometry window.

"Neither did I. I asked him what was up. Well, with this look of joy on his face he said something that I think went like this: Inside the orbit of the moon Planck's constant is collapsible between our two worlds. But the collapse can only happen within a gravitational field if there's room in both worlds. When there's mass accelerating in what 'Bel called the second time dimension the other side can't get in."

"That second time dimension idea is confusing, isn't it," Kevin responded.

"Well, you could hear the insight in his voice. He was just exultant. He was literally colored white and it was almost like there was a bright light shining all around his body. It's hard to describe. You know what I mean?"

"I know," Kevin replied, the image of the night time experience in the gazebo filling his mind's eye. He felt a pang of love and wondered if he were ever going to see 'Bel again. *What if, now that the mission is completed, the Visitors don't come back...*

"I think what he said," Tim continued, "was that if there's a mass on the other side accelerating toward the point of collision, when the generator shifts the two worlds together it is going to collide with the inertial mass and destroy itself immediately."

"...especially if it isn't shielded from the spacetime shift by having a cube around it," Kevin added, putting together the two factors that seemed to have combined to prevent the massive destruction they'd feared.

"Apparently. Anyway, 'Bel was going to get his people to propel something massive into the area of collision. And it must've worked cause the field barely started expanding. That's why there was only the front half of the Visitor spaceship. Those Visitor bodies in the wreckage must have been driving that mass of lead that was accelerated into the collision. They were real martyrs."

Just then it occurred to Kevin that 'Bel himself might have been one of those martyrs. After all, he'd said he joined this mission to honor his friend Alain who'd been killed in the first of these collisions between worlds. Kevin told himself 'Bel wouldn't have done that to him. But still he worried.

He tried to keep up the conversation with Tim. "You should see the damage to that Air Force base."

"I did, I mean, on TV. Just saw Joan Salado's program." Tim's voice changed quality, "Kevin, I'm real proud of you."

"Frankly, I was embarrassed. I mean, I didn't think she was going to run that whole interview like that."

"Well, we both thought you did well. You told the truth. And that was the right thing."

"That's still not all the truth yet. But, listen, you just said 'both.'" Kevin's pulse quickened. He wondered if Tim meant 'Bel had come back over.

"Me and Joel," Tim answered. "He's real nice."

Suppressing his own disappointment, Kevin couldn't help noticing the innuendo in that assessment. "And...?" he asked leadingly.

"You mean Joel and me?" Tim answered with mock offense. "Well, we did, uh, play around a little. Nothing real serious. Though, you know, Kev, I was thinking maybe we could get serious."

"That sounds strange coming from you."

"Now it shouldn't. Well, maybe you're right. But you know I guess I was feeling kind of envious of you and 'Bel. I don't mean jealous, I mean, uh, impressed... with what you two feel. I had a great talk with 'Bel on the drive up here. You're real lucky."

"Thanks, Tim. I think I have you to thank for that a little. I remember that day last June in our room you said you hoped I'd find true love. And maybe I have. That is, if we can manage a relationship from two different worlds."

"I understand the dilemma. But, you know, like I was telling 'Bel the other day I think his people took our homophobia too seriously. They made a mistake thinking that official religious doctrine is believed so literally."

"Apparently it is on their side."

"Apparently, they take everything literally. And, thank God, that's why 'Bel took Joel's crazy joke literally—and saved the world. But, you know, they must lack creativity or something. I mean, how come this never occurred to them before. Maybe that's the good side of our being able to lie and fake communication. I mean we learn to be a little more subtle and insightful."

"That's an interesting observation."

"'Bel said his people thought we really acted on all those rules in the Bible about stoning homosexuals and that Fundamentalists like Rev. McMasterson really represent what human beings are about. I told him no way. Lots of people talk about the 'evils of homosexuality'—especially after AIDS and all—but that doesn't mean they don't like their gay friends and don't respect their relationships and wish them well. Human beings have all sorts of opinions they report to the opinion polls, but they don't actually believe them in real life. I told 'Bel he's got to take us with a grain of salt."

"Did he understand the 'grain of salt'?"

"Well, I did have to explain the concept of skepticism," Tim laughed.

"That was good advice. Probably better than I gave him." Kevin confessed. "I mean, I've been pretty freaked out at this gay thing— "

"I know," Tim interrupted affectionately.

"Maybe I steered him all wrong."

"No, I think because you let yourself fall in love with him and admit to your confusion he could see how complicated human beings are. And that made him trust *you* in a way all the diplomats and ambassadors talking to the President couldn't."

"I hope so."

"That's why he hasn't gone crazy, you know. But, my God, Kevin, maybe you two just saved the world. Or at least Riverside, California. Hey, but that reminds me, the reason I called is to say that I just spoke with my dad after that show. I'd told him to watch it. And he did. And then he called Malcolm Arnold again. And Arnold's agreed to meet with you."

"Oh God, Tim, why didn't you say that earlier?"

"'Cause you were asking me about what kind of sex I had with Joel," Tim joked self-righteously.

"No I wasn't. Well, I mean, when and where?"

"Joel and me?" Tim teased. Then continued, "Let me be honest. Arnold didn't like the gay part. Though apparently he admitted it made the whole story make sense— "

As Tim said that, Kevin felt his anger at Joan Salado melt. *She was right.*

"—but he wants to keep the meeting a secret. At least till he can see what kind of reaction people have. So... he said he'll meet with you on my dad's turf. Make it look like a social visit to an old friend in California, not say anything about meeting with you. You're not supposed to tell Joan about this either. Okay?"

"Okay, I guess."

"Sure. It'll be okay. Now, rather than have to get up to Nevada City, the President's going to fly into the Alameda Naval Station in Oakland and then look like he's driving down to Hillsborough to visit Mom and Dad at the condo. But he's really going to get on dad's yacht. Then they'll come meet us in the Marina."

"Why all the intrigue?"

"Secrecy, my friend. We're human beings, after all. Couldn't possibly do anything straight," Tim joked.

"You said 'us.' I take it that means you and me?"

"And 'Bel, if we can get him."

"When?"

"Tomorrow afternoon. Can you make it?"

"If John or Joan can get me to the airport..."

"Take a taxi. We're talking about the future of planet, aren't we?"

"I'm still not as rich as you are," Kevin reacted.

Chapter Fifteen

"*I* wish *I* were going to have dinner on a yacht with the President," Joel remarked archly as he turned left from Fillmore Street onto Geary.

"I wish you were too," Tim answered affectionately. "I'm sorry this is all happening so fast."

"I'm not," Kevin remarked from the back seat. "And if you don't hurry up we're gonna be late. 'Bel said the geometry window is only open at sundown for a couple of minutes."

"When is sundown?" Joel asked.

"Look," Kevin answered sharply. The car was just cresting the hill at Masonic. The view to the west opened up suddenly. A bright golden sun was just slipping into a cloud bank resting on the horizon. "Ten minutes, maybe? Joel, where *are* you going?"

"I was gonna take the Arguello entrance."

"That'll take too long," Tim asserted. "Here, turn here. You can cut through behind the Digital Arts Center."

"Okay, okay. I thought Arguello *was* going to be a short-cut. I'll go as fast as I can." He made the right hand turn onto Presidio Ave, and pressed the accelerator to the floor.

"We're supposed to be meeting dad in the Marina in thirty minutes," Tim added.

"I can't be in two places at once," Joel snapped.

"Didn't mean to criticize," Tim answered, placing his hand on Joel's leg in a gesture of atonement. "I was just reminding us of the schedule."

"What if there's nobody at the geometry window on the other side? I mean, if there's nobody to contact 'Bel, what am I going to do?"

"Come back, Kevin. Whatever you do, don't get stuck over there."

"Well, I guess I'm expecting a gatekeeper. There was last time I went through. I hope they can find 'Bel for me quick."

"You can't keep the President waiting," Joel observed.

"He's going to have to wait," Kevin answered. "I mean if he wants to talk with 'Bel." Kevin suddenly felt a rush of pride. He realized he *was* quite prepared to make the President of the United States wait on him if that's what it took. *A year ago I'd have been quaking with fear. I mean not only because of the President, but because of being in the closet and all that.*

The threesome fell into silence as Joel sped through the new neighborhood where Pacific Heights had expanded into the old Presidio. Kevin sat back in the tiny rear seat and affectionately studied his friends in front.

He felt glad that Tim and Joel had hit it off. At first, he'd thought their alliance just a sign of the kind of casualness about sex he tended to disapprove of in both of them. But as he saw them together he realized there was obviously real affection between them. It occurred to him that his disapproval came out of the social conditioning and fear that had surrounded sex when he was growing up and that it was that disapproval that had made him doubt real affection and interpret it as lust. His fear and disapproval of Tim's burgeoning sexual identity in college had caused him to see his friend as promiscuous and faintly unwholesome—and to spoil his own experience of affection. Now that 'Bel's innocent truth-telling had allowed him to experience love and affection himself, he understood that Tim was feeling feelings just like him.

From what Kevin had come to learn of gay history, he knew it had often been just such anti-gay biases that produced the problems that occasionally beleaguered homosexual populations—like the spread of the AIDS virus—and that ironically were used to justify further negative bias. *What a really tragic cycle!*

My distorted perceptions made me see something that wasn't actually there. And, I suppose, in people who've bought into those perceptions about themselves the "promiscuity" and "unwholesomeness" become self-fulfilling prophecies. He remembered a notion from a course he'd taken in psychology: what we expect we tend to get because our expectations bring it about. *We see what we're looking for.*

Kevin felt a great affection for 'Bel. And a great sense of anticipation and anxiety as he observed Joel turning into the Rumsfeld Research Park and heading down the side street that led to the embassy site and the geometry window.

"Uh-oh," Joel was the first to comment. "This place doesn't look deserted at all."

Indeed there was a large crowd milling around in front of the construction site. Some people were carrying signs with slogans like: "Keep the Aliens off our planet," "God hates homosexuals," "The

Visitors are devil possessed," "No more abortions," "Capital Punishment Now," "Earth for Earthlings," "The Bible Says Stone 'Em."

It was just like the crowd he and 'Bel had escaped at the reststop outside Los Baños, Kevin realized. He imagined they'd gathered up at McMasterson's church and then come down here on the funicular tramway the Tabernacle had built to convey its massive congregation between the street level parking lots and the hilltop church. Indeed, Kevin thought he saw Billy McMasterson. And to add to his shock, he thought he saw his fellow co-worker at Sutro & Assoc., Chuck Sperry, also among the demonstrators. *How can I get to the geometry window?*

"What do I do?" Joel asked as he slowed the car to a snail's pace.

"It's sunset right now," Tim observed.

"What if I drive around the block and come up from the back?"

"That's a good idea, but I doubt there's time now," Tim said.

"Well, I've got to do something. Joel, look can you park right in front?" Kevin pointed toward an empty space.

As Joel pulled up toward the parking space, he asked, "How exactly do you plan to get 'Bel out to the car anyway?"

Just as he was finishing, someone outside shouted, "Faggots. There in that car!" Suddenly the crowd was swarming around Joel's little automobile, pounding on the sides and ragtop roof with their fists and hitting with their signs.

As the car was rocked back and forth, Joel shouted, "They're liable to turn it over."

"Get out. Fast. Now," Tim ordered.

Joel gunned the engine and—almost running over the demonstrators in front of the car, who just barely managed to jump out of the way—shot down the street.

"I guess the President's going to have to do without 'Bel," Kevin said, suppressing his nagging concern about just where 'Bel was. "Maybe Arnold can do something about the crowd. Those are the people who voted for him, after all."

"At least we won't keep him waiting," Tim remarked.

Malcolm Arnold was a surprisingly goodlooking and affable man, Kevin thought. On TV he seemed stiff and overly formal. Kevin had always assumed he was a humorless stuffed shirt. In fact, when they arrived at the meeting spot in the Marina to find the Lewiston yacht already moored and Tim jumped out and ran over to make sure the plan was still on, Malcolm Arnold himself had climbed out and come over to the car to meet Kevin and, probably at Tim's suggestion, to greet Joel and thank him for chauffeuring for this mission. Of course, there'd been two Secret Service men following close at hand, but Arnold showed himself to be friendly and unreserved.

After Joel left and Tim and Kevin went aboard the yacht, explaining excitedly and apologetically that they'd been unable to get 'Bel for this meeting, Arnold had shown real interest and concern for their welfare. And then laughing easily, suggested it was time for everybody to have a drink and relax. "We'll talk business after dinner." While he was waiting for his Scotch and soda, he turned to Kevin and suggested, "What about us heading up there in the middle of the night when the demonstrators are gone and see about getting your friend?"

Kevin was impressed with Arnold's daring. He liked the fact that the man said "what about *us*." "Unfortunately," he had to reply, "the geometry window is only open at sunrise and sunset."

"Well, how about sunrise then?"

"Okay," Kevin answered simply.

With that President Arnold changed the subject to his trip out and some sort of political debate he was having about some Senator who was also a friend of Porter Lewiston, Tim's father. Kevin sat back, nursing a bourbon and 7-Up while Arnold and Lewiston talked politics. Kevin had met Tim's father a couple of times. Porter Lewiston had seemed genuinely interested in him and his progress as a student and as a roommate for his son. Today Lewiston seemed a little distant, *more interested in talking with his old friend than with the new-comer, trouble-making kid,* Kevin couldn't help thinking. *But I'm not surprised. And the fact is this thing is probably forcing Lewiston out of the closet as the father of a homosexual.* All of a sudden Kevin felt admiration for Porter Lewiston.

Just as a young man in a steward's uniform came on deck to announce dinner, Arnold turned to Kevin, "Say, about that expedition to get your, uh, friend in the morning. Let's decide about that after we've had a chance to talk after dinner. You know, let's see what the issues are."

"Yes sir," Kevin answered, partly understanding Arnold's hesitance.

"I thought you did a good job on that TV show," Arnold went on as he gestured for Kevin to precede him out of the cabin. "I think there are some things we still need to talk about. The story you told was very impressive—and believable," Arnold emphasized. "It's just that there are some very serious issues to consider."

"I understand that, sir," Kevin answered as he followed Porter Lewiston into the dark mahogany-panelled dining room. He saw that Tim and his mother, Esther Lewiston, were already sitting at the table chatting animatedly. For a moment, Kevin wished his own mother were here as he realized he was probably more frightened and intimidated than he had ever been in his life.

"We'll have a good long talk after dinner," Arnold said softly to Kevin as he took his seat.

Kevin slept fitfully. The rocking of the boat kept him mildly seasick. At about three a.m., he'd climbed out of his tight berth and, pulling on his jeans and windbreaker as silently as possible to avoid waking Tim, his cabin partner, he went up on deck. He was surprised to find one of the Secret Service agents standing watch, though, of course, he supposed that is exactly what they'd do. He nodded to the agent, who came over to check on him as he came up from below, then, seeing the man was quite willing to let him be, he went up to the bow and curled up against the superstructure of the luxurious yacht.

The wet ocean wind cut right through the light windbreaker Kevin was wearing and chilled him to the bone. But there was something inspiringly beautiful about the night. The sky was clear. There were more stars than Kevin could remember seeing since he was at that boys' camp in the Berkshires when he was twelve. Even though he now understood, of course, that the Visitors were not really from another star at all, still the starry sky reminded him of 'Bel. *Maybe everything reminds me of 'Bel.*

Kevin found himself feeling sexual and the thoughts of boys' camp and of 'Bel exaggerated those urges. He wondered how many sailors had satisfied such urges on late night watches, alone under starry skies. He wondered how many of them were fantasizing their shipmates as they did so, feeling secretive and conflicted about those feelings. For a moment he wondered if only a little while ago the Secret Service man back there might have been doing the same thing up here out of sight.

But the night was too cold to allow him to do anything more than imagine committing such a secretive and boyishly-rebellious act.

While he shivered then and felt the blood run warm in his belly, he stared out across the water at the distant city of San Francisco. They'd come surprisingly far out. He wondered if they'd make it back in time for sunrise and the activation of the geometry window. The conversation with President Arnold had ended, as Kevin hoped, with a decision to pursue the plan to get 'Bel and perhaps another Visitor official to come across and explain again, more forthrightly, why the Visitors urged the termination of the space shield research.

Arnold had been extremely interested in what Kevin had to say. He was only a little skeptical. He could not quite grasp the notion that the Visitors were from a parallel Earth, He thought that must be a metaphor for the "space warp" Kevin himself had envisioned at first. Arnold kept using that sci-fi word as though it really explained something. Fortunately he never seemed to doubt Kevin's veracity in describing his experience of crossing over, perhaps because Kevin had also used sci-fi lingo for what the geometry window did—that second dimension of time, for instance. Arnold thought that very interesting.

The President was even willing to accept that the Visitors were actually threatened themselves by the matter-field technology. What he wouldn't or couldn't understand is how what happened in this world could affect something in another world. He just didn't believe one world could be quantum superimposed on the other. And, most importantly, he didn't see why we should trust the Visitors. He reminded Kevin that the Joint Chiefs were urging him to create a matter-field shield around the whole planet and that he was going to have to be convinced that the Earth wasn't in immediate danger of attack to disregard that advice.

Arnold was fascinated by Kevin's description of the Visitor pigmentation changes. Arnold acknowledged he'd seen something of that himself but had interpreted it as a chameleon-like camouflage mechanism that, in fact, had made him even more suspicious. He was willing to talk about the Visitors' sexuality. In the abstract he seemed to think it rather elegant and biologically efficient. But he avoided any talk of Kevin and 'Bel's relationship. He certainly didn't seem to want to hear anything about actual sexual intercourse.

The President seemed to accept that their somewhat alien styles of sexual behavior were something the Visitors had reason to keep secret. He didn't like the fact they had done so, but he agreed it made sense—especially after Kevin insisted on explaining how he himself had felt he had to keep his sexual feelings secret... even from himself for a while.

Kevin's recollections of the conversation with Arnold were interrupted by the sound of the yacht's engine starting up. For a moment, he was startled. *Maybe we're being highjacked.* Then he realized that, of course, if they were going to make it back to shore well before sunrise they needed such an early start.

As the boat swung round, water splashed up onto the bow and Kevin decided it was time to go in. He scurried back to the cabin and climbed back into bed, pulling the covers tight around him.

"Is it time to get up?" Tim asked groggily from the upper bunk.

"Go back to sleep," Kevin answered. For just a moment he wondered if he'd be able to sleep himself. But he was fast asleep even before the thought was fully formed.

*F*rom the front seat Tim Lewiston was pointing out changes in San Francisco as a result of the Big Quake just over a year ago. Kevin was sitting quietly in back next to President Arnold. He was barely awake; it was very early in the morning and he hadn't slept much last night. One of the Secret Service agents was driving Porter Lewiston's Rolls-Royce. It was a compact sports model, luxuriously spacious, of course, but there was only room for the four adults, leaving space (if everybody crowded) for 'Bel and possibly one other Visitor.

The Secret Service agent who'd been left behind had objected vigorously to the arrangement, but Malcolm Arnold dismissed his arguments. "After all," he boastfully asserted, "even if any of the demonstrators are out there this time of the morning, I'm their President. I mean, they are my constituency. I'm not afraid of them. Besides," he added realistically, "I'm not planning on getting out of the car."

The plan was for Tim and Kevin to jump out quickly and stealthily at the embassy site. Tim would act as lookout while Kevin went through to get 'Bel. The Secret Service agent was then to take the President on a tour of the Research Park and the northern tip of the San Francisco Peninsula. Arnold had not been to the City since the day after the earthquake when he'd declared the disaster officially and announced Federal support for rebuilding. This morning, while waiting for the Visitor or Visitors to come across, he was going to get to see the fruits of that rebuilding.

There was really no need for Arnold to have come along himself—the Secret Service agent had reiterated that. But Malcolm Arnold had been in a hot-shot Delta Force unit in Afghanistan. In spite of the fact that he was actually from Dallas blueblood stock (that's how he knew Porter Lewiston), learned to ride on an English saddle, and attended Exeter and Yale before being forced into the military by his ultra-patriotic father, during his Presidential campaign he had styled himself as a Texas cowboy and macho roustabout. After returning from overseas duty in the military, he'd been ordained a deacon in Dallas's biggest non-denominational Evangelical Christian fellowship and as a politician championed religiously-inspired government policies. Though he'd identified as a post-Fundamentalist progressive and claimed to support separation of church and state, his campaign addresses sometimes sounded like sermons. As a politician he'd been an odd contradiction in identities—something the voting public had loved, and put him in office to demonstrate.

Arnold had said it was appropriate for him to come greet the Visitors and, besides, he liked the idea of going along on this adventure himself. He wasn't afraid. Last night, during the planning, he'd commented, "Frankly, Kevin, I think I ought to go through that window with you. 'Beam me up, Scotty,'" he joked, inappropriately trying to mock a Scottish brogue, in a reference Kevin didn't understand in spite of his fascination with old movies. The Secret Service bodyguards had had no sympathy for that idea at all.

Tim was pointing out a row of newly reconstructed Victorian houses as they came up to the turn off toward the embassy site. In the early morning light, the white wood frame houses practically glowed. The air was crisp and slightly damp. Dew glistened on windows. "According to Naval Observatory time, sir," the agent spoke up, "sunrise will be in three minutes."

"Perfect timing, Jeff," Arnold commended his man. "Looks calm, doesn't it?"

"Well sir," answered Jeff the Secret Service agent, "I don't exactly like the looks of those three campers up there."

Kevin spoke his first words since they'd left the nearby Marina where the yacht was docked waiting for them, "The entrance to the construction site is clear," he pointed out. "That's where all the cars and picketers were yesterday. I think we'll be okay."

"That's the attitude, boy," Arnold encouraged. "Go get 'em."

"I'll be waiting inside ," Tim repeated the plan. "As soon as Kevin comes back through with 'Bel, I'll call you." He confirmed he had the Secret Service agent's number in his dime. "We'll be ready to jump in the car just as soon as you get back here. Right?"

Jeff agreed and swung the car around to let the two young men out. Tim climbed out the front door. He stood waiting just a moment while Kevin shook hands with President Arnold in what seemed, especially to Kevin, an unnecessarily formal ritual.

"I'm planning on twenty minutes," Jeff announced as Kevin gently closed the door.

Kevin stood up straight and looked around for just a moment. He hadn't had any worries about this at all till Jeff mentioned the campers parked down the road. Kevin glanced their way. *They seem harmless enough. Anyway, this'd be a beautiful place for tourists to park.* Indeed, it was a beautiful place. Kevin turned away from the street to admire the view for just a moment and to orient himself before he headed in to the construction site. As he glanced back toward the campers a chill ran through him. Leaning upside down against the side of the nearest one was a crudely-lettered sign that read, "Outer space faggots go home."

"Better get going," Tim whispered loudly just as the car started to roll quietly away.

Suddenly everything seemed to go into slow motion. Kevin's attention was caught by the flash of the headlights of that nearest camper. A man got out the passenger side and started to walk toward him. Kevin was momentarily stunned, sure he recognized the striding figure as Rev. Billy McMasterson.

A voice shouted from somewhere, "It's the queer lovers." The voice was followed almost immediately by a loud explosion. It took Kevin only a second to realize that was a gunshot.

"Get down," he shouted to Tim. The slowly moving Rolls-Royce accelerated. As Kevin threw himself to the ground he thought he saw that the front window on the driver's side had shattered. Another shot rang out. And the rear window became suddenly opaque.

The car sped right over the curb and the sidewalk and down the slight embankment toward the side of the half-constructed building. Kevin and Tim jumped up and were running as fast as they could behind. Kevin could see figures clambering up the outside staircase as if to get into the building by an alternate route. *They'll get a surprise when they discover there's no connection between floors.* As the car stopped, Jeff jumped out of the front door and, ducking down behind the car, ran around to the back door. He was shouting, "I told you so," as he swung the door open. Blood was running down the left side of his face.

Kevin peeled off to the left and up to the side of the building. "This way," he shouted, as he released the hidden catch on the swiveling window. He knew exactly how they were going to get out of this.

The Secret Service agent was arguing with President Arnold over the wisdom of Kevin's suggestion, when another shotgun blast exploded somewhere close outside the building.

"Let me go first," Kevin said, "so you can see what to do. I'll come right back just to prove to Jeff I wasn't disintegrated."

Kevin was pleased to see the faintly glowing yellow light surrounding the opening of the geometry window. He wasn't sure what he'd have done if the window were inactive. *Thank God, it's on.*

Kevin disappeared into the mirrored chamber. And momentarily stepped out into the Visitor world. Remembering that the controls for the window must be in the little office halfway up the slope behind the cubicle structure, he ran in that direction. He was greeted by a Visitor stepping out of the office who, almost immediately turning blue all over, asked in the heavily accented English of the Visitors' home world, "What's the matter?"

"I'm Kevin Anderson," he called out. "The Judges asked me to speak to the leaders in my world. I've got the President with me. Will you please keep the window open?"

The gatekeeper, now going red, asked "What're you doing here?"

"I told you," Kevin shouted. "Please. Let me go back and get them. Look," he added, "we're in danger on the other side."

The gatekeeper seemed to recognize the emergency. He started turning orangy-yellow as he ran toward Kevin, "I'll help." Kevin turned around and headed back to the window.

- - -

"Well, where are we?" Malcolm Arnold asked a few moments later after he'd stepped out of the translucent dome that surrounded the geometry window. "It looks like we're still in San Francisco."

"No, it doesn't," Tim exclaimed. "Look," he pointed across toward where Marin County would be.

"There's no bridge," Jeff answered.

"That's what I told you," Kevin said.

They were all so excited about President Arnold himself coming through the geometry window, and the gatekeeper so obsessed with polite and proper protocol that none of them noticed that the geometry window had been left energized. And none of them saw that soon after they'd been whisked off to meet the Judges, none other than Billy McMasterson, showing himself a true heir to the 007 legacy, came through the window and set out to discover the Visitor world on his own.

"Welcome to Earth," Judge Janesse Robul said warmly. The handsome middle-aged woman came out from behind the bench on the raised dais and, with outstretched arms, met President Arnold as an equal.

"You'll have to excuse me," Arnold answered. "This is all very new to me. Have we met before?"

"You and I have not," the Judge answered. "But my colleague here," she turned as one of the other judges stepped forward, "was on the negotiating team that met with you in your Earth."

Arnold smiled, "You look different."

"Perhaps it is my color," he glowed warm yellow. "When you last saw me I was dark brown, a natural color in your world, but in ours a stressful one."

"You didn't like our world?" Arnold asked, perhaps meaning to sound informally affable.

"As I imagine young Kevin here explained," Judge Robul spoke up, "our people had a difficult time in your world. We made what we now see were serious errors in how we presented ourselves to you."

"Yes, Kevin explained." Arnold turned toward Kevin who was standing proudly nestled against 'Bel. "We have a lot to be thankful to these two youngsters for," the President continued. "I understand it was their idea that prevented a much worse disaster for both sides."

"They are a fine example of cooperation between our two worlds," said Judge Robul, who reminded Kevin of the older Sigourney Weaver, remembered this time with all positive associations. "Looking back, it seems like such an obvious idea—though it did turn out to be more complicated when put in action. We were proud of young 'Bel for making us aware of the obvious. We trusted he was right because we saw that his intention was clear."

Kevin wondered what she meant by that. *I hope she means the Judges trusted that 'Bel and I love each other, and want true happiness for each other.*

Almost as if she'd read his mind, the High Judge continued to President Arnold, "It seems we misunderstood your people. We doubted your ability to understand honesty and love. It has been a costly lesson."

"I see why you would have perceived us as a threat. I guess I'm here right now because such a threat was just aimed at me. I am grateful that that window to this world was open and allowed me and my, uh, companion an escape." He gestured toward Jeff the Secret Service agent who was now wearing a bandage on one side of his face.

"Is this handsome man your beloved then?" the second Judge inquired solicitously.

"Oh no," Arnold answered too quickly, blushing embarrassedly. "He is, uh, uh, a bodyguard."

"It's okay, Mr. President," Kevin spoke up. "I think he was paying you a compliment."

To prove their account of the danger of the space shield, the Judges arranged for Arnold and his party to assess the damage on this side.

Kevin enjoyed the flight along the California coast in the saucer-shaped craft. He was glad somebody on this side had realized they shouldn't travel solely by geometry window. Unless President Arnold really saw the lay of the land beneath he was going to be skeptical of what he was seeing. The lush scenery of a California unspoiled by urbanization and modern pollution rushed below at breakneck speed and yet the ship gave virtually no experience of speed or acceleration.

"Are your ships UFOs? We've been seeing them for years."

"No, we're not the source of those sightings. We'd never visited your side before. And we have UFOs on our side, too. We don't know what they are either. It's a cosmic mystery... But this ship *is* a flying saucer, isn't it?" 'Bel laughed. "See how the front edge is energized. The ship is propelled by a gravity engine in back, but slips along the surface of spacetime geometry through a window it projects in front of itself, so we're sliding across time as well as space." Kevin didn't fully understand, but could see they were in Southern California in a flash.

As 'Bel had predicted, the damage here was much larger than the 500 foot diameter circle on the March A.F.B. side. The field eruption devastated an area nearly a mile across. But then, it was *only* a mile across. The damage was even more noticeable than at March because on this side, instead of desert, Southern California was lush with evergreen forest. The city that had been most immediately threatened with destruction was built among the trees.

Tim made a joke that the trees were so thick a cow couldn't even get across the fence. 'Bel laughed appreciatively, glowing bright yellow, and gave Tim a friendly hug.

The President was moved to tears by the destruction and, not getting the significance of Tim's remark, scolded the young men for being less sober than the occasion demanded.

In the middle of the devastated area, which they flew slowly around as if honoring a sacred place by circumambulating it, lay the back half of the broken craft that had accelerated the mass of lead bricks into the field collision. It had indeed been a "Kamikaze-style" flight, but not as an attack. The ship must have been severed—and the pilots killed—when the field intersection collapsed, leaving the ship half in one world and half in the other.

"They were trapped inside the bubble of the field at the leading edge of the collision," the pilot commented from the steering console.

"Why didn't you use an unmanned drone?" President Arnold asked. "Why did the two pilots have to die?"

"Our technology requires the presence of consciousness to collapse the quantum probability wave. We don't have drones. But we hadn't expected they would die," Judge Robul explained. "We thought they'd emerge on your side and collapse the field behind them. We are grieved by their deaths, but honor their generosity. They saved many lives."

"In retrospect," the pilot added, "it appears they should have had the mass in front of them as a shield instead of between them *and* they should have flown into the collision from the other side."

"You're saying they should have been on our side?" Jeff asked.

"If the mass had collided with the generator in front of them, it would've shut down the field and they'd have flown right through and away from the explosion," the pilot continued, "instead of into it."

The other Judge whose name Kevin had never learned spoke up. "The two had volunteered knowing there was danger. They had both lost their partners in the first collision disaster." He turned to Kevin and 'Bel, "Those were the remains we showed you before to convince you of the urgency of your mission."

Judge Robul added, with a touch of sadness in her voice, "The pilots were man and woman. They and their lovers had borne two children and were raising them all together. Both children were also killed."

"I fear we made a mistake letting them take on the mission," the other Judge said. "They had lost everything they loved. They may have wanted to return to the Sea of Bliss."

"You mean they let themselves be killed deliberately?" Arnold asked. "They could have come out the other side, stopping the collision, but not been hurt?" he added, almost presciently.

"Intention and expectation open doors you never dreamed existed," the Judges said simultaneously, apparently quoting a familiar aphorism. "They can close doors, too," Judge Robul added, bowing her head.

Soon the ship was bound back to Franchestiano for an official ceremony of peace between the two worlds.

"The Judges' craft is equipped with a gravity engine as well as the geometry drive. So ships like this one are capable of short jumps into space," the pilot was explaining to President Arnold and Jeff who were standing on either side of the console in the center of the flight deck. "The ship's pressure sealed so it can maintain internal atmosphere. You know, we have to go outside the orbit of the moon to cross over to your world by ship. We use this kind of craft to do that."

"Can you fly us to the moon," President Arnold asked excitedly.

"If the Judges don't mind our taking the long way home," the pilot answered looking over at Judge Robul and her associate, both of whom smiled golden, as if to give affirmation to the scenic detour.

The pilot reached out and touched his console. Suddenly the landscape below dropped away. There was no perception whatsoever of motion, but in the viewscreen it was clear the craft was heading straight out away from Earth. Malcolm Arnold groaned and then laughed deeply. "I've always been jealous of those astronauts…"

Kevin felt a rush of excitement. *Another adventure. And just for fun!*

At that moment, a communicator in Judge Robul's scapular chimed. She pulled the little metal box out of its pocket and held what Kevin recognized as the Visitors' equivalent of the all-purpose dime to her ear.

As she listened, her color changed from golden to dark purple with red blushes pulsing in her face. She looked at President Arnold with glaring eyes.

"There's just been an announcement in your world that you have been captured. Your assistant…"

"Vice-President Malloy," Arnold filled in.

"…thinks an attack has begun and he has ordered the matter-field generator at Oak Ridge be brought online immediately."

"Oh my God," almost everybody said simultaneously.

It hit Kevin that they hadn't been in time. They hadn't gotten Arnold back to Earth on the other side to stop the next phase of the defense against a Visitor "attack." Vice-President Malloy was about to bring on the planetary catastrophe they'd all thought they were preventing by bringing Malcolm Arnold over to the Visitor side to show him how real it was.

"Can you get me back to Washington?" President Arnold asked urgently. "I'm sure I can stop Malloy just by showing up."

"If we take the jump over the moon," the pilot answered.

"There isn't time," Judge Robul said. "The report relayed from your world through the geometry window in Franchestiano said the Oak Ridge facility is ready for activation. The field may initiate any minute."

"Well, God damn it, you've got to get me back," Arnold shouted. Then he questioned, "Look, can *this* ship be used to crash into the collision and stop it, like before? You said you knew what went wrong."

"Use the Judges' ship?" the pilot and copilot asked simultaneously, turning a shade of bluish green, and looked quizzically at Judge Robul.

"This ship? Of course," she answered. "Whatever it would take." But then turned the question to 'Bel. "It was your inspiration to seal the collision zone by accelerating mass into the generator. We trusted your inspiration. What does your inspiration tell you now?"

'Bel flushed dark red in embarrassment. "I'm just a Sociology Team intern. That idea came to me cause I misunderstood a joke Tim and Joel were pulling on me. Now you want me to make a decision on something as important as this? How do I know?"

"Now's the time we need that genius app you were always working on," Tim whispered to Kevin. "Wouldn't it model the energy fields?" Kevin could feel Tim's anxiety. Suddenly they were all being asked to risk their lives. He reached out and pulled his friend to his side. "That's what your senior thesis was, wasn't it?" Tim jabbered nervously.

"The High Court trusted your inspiration, young man," the Judge answered 'Bel's humble demurrer, "because we saw that your intention was clear and motivation was good. Your heart was open. The collective consciousness of which we are all flowers communicates through those whose intention is clear and heart open. Your inspiration was coming from a deeper place in you than your job on the Sociology Team. And, besides," she added, "the engineers were in agreement."

Kevin felt such a bond with 'Bel, he wanted to help. He thought through everything he knew about the matter-field technology. Tim's offhand comment about his senior thesis got him remembering the computer simulation he'd run that had convinced him power could be turned on to the geometry window. *This isn't the same thing, but maybe there's a clue here for how to turn the generator off.* The cursor—with those evocative words "There is another way"—had appeared to shoot right through the quantum geometry opening and suck the field in behind it and then lock up the computer. *Maybe we could repeat that.*

"Collective consciousness? Hmmm," Tim kept whispering to Kevin. "Sounds like Jung was right." Kevin recalled Tim had taken an honors' seminar a few semesters back in Jungian psychology and literature.

'Bel's complexion lightened noticeably as Judge Robul attributed his idea of how to close the matter-field to a greater mind than just his own *and* revealed the scientists had approved it.

"Why me?" 'Bel asked, "I'm no hero."

"We were already considering various options to block the collisions. An engineer was just presenting a plan to accelerate mass into the opening when you burst into the Hall shouting out the same plan. You were welcomed because you'd brought Kevin Anderson to see us. You were in the right place at the right time to be the person the High Court would listen to. The Judges saw a sign in your inspiration. Everybody's a hero when they follow their inspiration."

The second Judge added, "Coincidence and inspiration are the manner of doors opening. The bliss you long for attracts you into its future, and shows itself in meaningful coincidence." He sounded like he was reciting from some sacred text.

"That's what the Jungians call synchronicity," Tim said. Kevin had seen Tim obsessed with finding symbolic patterns in everything for a while when he was taking that class. He was a little annoyed with his friend's constant demanding of his attention, but Tim had given him an idea. *Maybe this is synchronicity too!*

"Do we have enough mass to make the difference?" 'Bel asked with a tone of authority—and a flash of orange across his face—that signified he'd accepted Judge Robul's assignment. "The previous attempt carried a load of lead bricks."

"This ship is bigger and it's got an aft-mounted gravity engine," the pilot answered. "I could fly the ship in backwards so we'd have the mass of the engine in front of us."

"Can I offer a suggestion?" asked Kevin. "I was listening to what the pilot said a minute ago about flying in from the other side. Maybe he's right. Look, the previous mission accelerated that mass of lead into the matter-field to plug the opening from your side. That meant forcing the mass to collide with the generator to stop it. And it meant flying *into* the explosion. But, remember, John Marshall got the shape of the chamber changed the way 'Bel suggested. The generator was unshielded so it could be collided with."

"I think we have to assume that won't be so this time," 'Bel interjected, his glowing yellow color showing he was happy to be actively involved in this decision *and* to be getting some help.

"Right. Well, what if we come in from the other side—our side—so instead of capping the opening, we go through it and push the generator over to your side. We wouldn't have to smash into it to turn it off. It just wouldn't have any power source. That would shut down the field and suck the opening closed behind us. And we'd come through unscathed?"

"Yes, yes," the pilot agreed. "The accelerating mass will push the matter-field intersection back in on itself. And if I activate the geometry drive as we go through, it would actually capture the window that's shielding the generator and drag it behind."

Kevin was pleased to have somebody knowledgeable about Visitor technology confirm his idea.

"Well, do it," President Arnold declared.

"And we're already far enough out to jump the moon and come in from your side," the pilot kept on with his logistics analysis.

'Bel excitedly announced, "Yes, this is going to work."

"As before, 'Bel, we agree too," the two Judges answered. "Do it."

"Wait a minute," Arnold's Secret Service bodyguard broke in, "Mr. President, I can't allow you to risk your life, sir. The last attempt to do this resulted in the deaths of all the people in the ship." He turned his attention to the pilots, "Can we drop Mr. Arnold off before we try this?"

"Ignore my young friend here," Malcolm Arnold said to the Judges. "He's just being officious and protective of me."

"Sir, you're President of the United States. You can't risk your life."

"Wouldn't Malloy get a kick out of hearing that?" Arnold joked. "Seriously, son, I want to do this. I *have* to do this."

"What do you mean?" asked Tim.

"Don't you all know your history? The Presidency was humiliated by the global warming disasters in the two-thousand-zeros. I'd be as good as dead politically if this matter-field research I backed causes a fireball to consume the eastern half of the United States. Maybe the rest of you should get off. But I'd be better off dead, like those pilots on your last ship, than the President who destroyed the country with his ill-conceived defense plan." He looked at the Judges, "Can I command this operation?" And to the pilot, "Could I fly the ship?"

While the pilot steered the craft on beyond the orbit of the moon, the copilot was directing the rearrangement of mass on the deck. "The gravity engine will be in front of us since we're going to fly in backwards. Let's get as much other mass as possible in front of us too to sheild us." There were heavy metal chairs around a massive conference table set up ceremonially in front of the steering console that needed to be moved.

"Is that the real reason the pilots didn't survive before?" Tim asked.

"Partly. The mass should have been in front of them. But the *real* reason the pilots were killed is that they were grieving. I don't think they wanted to survive. That they positioned the lead bricks between them shows, whether they knew it or not, that they were intentionally including their own bodies in the accelerated mass," answered the copilot. "I think they were honoring their loved ones by giving themselves to save others."

"I thought this was physics," rejoined Tim. "What does intention have to do with it?"

"It's the physics of quantum consciousness," 'Bel answered. "Intention is a quantum dimension of the spacetimeconsciousness continuum. Force exerted along that dimension collapses the quantum probability wave out of all possibile outcomes. And of that is created the future." It sounded like he was citing the same text the Judge just had.

"Like Schrödinger's cat?" Tim interjected, remembering a class he'd taken in superstring theory and cosmology.

"I don't know this cat," 'Bel answered.

"Yes, Tim," Jeff spoke up. "I think you're right. That's what it's called on our side. Consciousness paying attention determines outcome."

"You know quantum physics?" Tim sidled over to Jeff.

"Physics major at M.I.T.," Jeff answered proudly.

Kevin felt relief that Tim's nervous attention had shifted to the Secret Service agent. *Tim's my best friend, but I want to be beside 'Bel.* He felt his allegiance torn. And even as he had that thought he wondered what such conflicted feelings would show like in his color—if he showed color. *And if I showed color, would I feel such conflicted feelings?*

'Bel went on, "This is how our transport system works. Movement through the geometry windows is determined by your intention for the future. You get where you're going to be without have to go through the intervening time. Choosing is what makes consciousness unfold."

"Intention creates the future?" Tim quizzed. "Then how come it never turns out the way I want? How come there can be airplane crashes and disasters that nobody intends?"

"Good explanation, young man," Judge Robul commended 'Bel. "And good question," she turned to Tim. Her face taking on a soft bluish color, she addressed his challenge, "This *is* the problem on your side. We've been trying to understand your cultures. We perceive that conflicting, competing, and self-sabotaguing intentions cause the probability waves to collapse haphazardly. This whole process is driven by the dualistic view of consciousness in your world which arises from how you polarize male and female. It looks like all your world's divided into opposing forces, like good and evil, self and others, God and the world because for most of your people it *is* divided between man and woman, and they are seen as opposites and opposing forces..."

"...meaning straight people," Tim quipped, as he and Jeff grappled with one of the heavy chairs.

"...then the intentional force gets transferred to the time dimension and causes population to expand and everything seems to speed up, but doesn't happen as anybody intends. "

"I guess, we're fucked then..." Tim concluded, "...on our side."

A blush of annoyance passed over Judge Robul's face, as if in reaction to Tim's disrepectful slang for sexual love. "Not at all. The union of male and female propagates consciousness. It manifests collective intention. That's not the problem. It is the polarization—and fear of bridging the polarities—that creates the dualism. But that dualism can be overcome. Nonjudgmental regard of others, unselfish awareness, and mindful consciousness of one's own intention all exert the force directly. That is so for all of us in both worlds.

"Universal Mind arises from the harmony of intentional force. This is how planet Earth becomes conscious. This process is experienced by human beings as compassion and interpersonal love. These bring harmony. This is what your world's religions are about, isn't it?

"What about the religious homophobes?"

"We are confused about that too. How can they misunderstand love? They must need their fear assuaged."

"Wow 'em with gay sweetness and wit?" Tim answered irreverently.

"Maybe not wit, so much as sweetness and insight. Isn't that what those you call gay represent? Transcendence of duality. Perhaps that is your heroic duty, Tim. Just as 'Bel was motivated to come to us with his plan, so perhaps you are called to heal the polarization in your world. Remember each of you is entirely responsible for all the others."

Wow, Kevin thought, *this is like physics and religion rolled into one.*

"But now, we must hurry. It's almost time."

While they were sliding the chairs to the back, 'Bel pulled Kevin aside to ask, "Are you sure you want to do this? We might be killed."

"You said our love could save the world. That's the source of our intention, isn't it? Let's do it. Whatever happens, it won't matter if you love me, really love me," Kevin answered bravely, and surprisingly unafraid. That song *When Worlds Collide* was playing again in his head.

The copilot kept up his instructions. "Now, we need to get this conference table to the back of the flight deck. It's solid lead."

As they gathered round to pick up the heavy table, Kevin questioned 'Bel why the ship's furniture would be made of lead.

"This ship was built for the leaders of our society. So their conference table is made of our most honorable materials."

"Lead?"

"Lead is the breakdown product of the nuclear life of stars. It is our most precious metal."

"You mean, on your side lead is like gold?" Kevin was reminded of the discussion at Sutro and Associates a few months ago in which Chuck Speery had questioned whether gold was precious to the Visitors. *Who'd have thought it would be lead instead?* "But isn't it poisonous?"

"Nothing's poisonous on our side," 'Bel answered cryptically.

"We'll stand the conference table up on end," the copilot instructed, "and we can all get behind it to shield our bodies. Look, slide it up behind this bulkhead beam, then it can't fall over on us under gravity acceleration."

"The medieval alchemists tried to turn lead into gold," Kevin commented as they all heaved in unison to up-end the heavy table. "Looks like they had it backwards." He noticed how, so mundanely, their united, harmonious effort—and intention—to lift the table made the task so easy. *That's how life should always work.*

Tim commented, "Jung said transforming lead into gold was really a metaphor for creating a golden spirit body out of mortal flesh."

Tim's reference to the spirit body reminded Kevin of his experience with 'Bel at the Sisters' gazebo. He'd certainly experienced his "golden body" in that moment of sharing color. He wished he were back there instead of on this spaceship careening toward disaster.

"How will you know when it's time?" Jeff asked the pilot.

"The ship's sensors can tell when the first disturbance of the field constants starts," the pilot replied. "We've got to let the opening get just big enough for the ship to pass through." As he was explaining, he clicked switches on his console so the sensor read-out, including a graphic representation of the ship in relation to the field size, appeared in the corner of the viewscreen monitor overhead.

"We've already passed over to your side. Look," he pointed to the monitor. The ship was speeding down toward the crowded eastern seaboard of the United States. "I'm turning us around." The image on the screen rotated so they were now looking out at deep, empty space.

"Even with the inertial dampers on, we'll need to sit on the floor so we don't fall over when the ship accelerates," explained the copilot.

"All of you line up behind me," Judge Robul called out as she assumed a position facing the upended conference table. There was another viewscreen at the rear of the deck just above the rectangle of the table. It was showing eastern Tennessee. "Let us gather our intentions."

"She means we'll share color," 'Bel explained, causing Kevin to wonder if somehow they'd just read his mind.

"Share color?" President Arnold questioned.

"You'll like this, sir," Kevin said.

Somewhere down below, the components of the high-tech devices that would shift the value of Planck's constant over the entire United States—inadvertently bringing about the destruction of the planet on however many levels of consciousness it existed as a living entity— were being activated as the countdown reached completion.

In the Visitor spacecraft, now a mile or so overhead and turned around so its rear engine was in front, the crew and passengers were lining up behind the High Judge, kneeling or sitting down on the floor tailor-fashion so they could lean back against each other. She instructed President Arnold to get in front of her so she could clasp her arms, and her aura, around him from behind. Then in back of her was Jeff, the Secret Service agent, and the associate Judge who held Jeff close to him, then Tim and the copilot, then Kevin and finally 'Bel. The pilot stayed in his seat, but was himself already beginning to go into that meditative state of heightened consciousness the Visitors called sharing color.

Judge Robul instructed President Arnold to relax and let himself begin to see light around them all with the eye of his mind. Kevin could feel 'Bel beginning to glow behind him and the copilot in front of him.

"We're going to plunge through the opening between your world and ours," she said confidently, "and shut down the generator and close the matter-field collision. AND we're going to live." She added the last with firm and deliberate intention. "Live."

Just then it occurred to Kevin that the generator could have a self-contained power source and his plan might mean they were going to just carry the operating generator *and* the collision into the Visitor world. *What if I 'm wrong about it turning off?* He reminded himself to let go of fear. He could only hold his intention and expect the best. *LIVE.*

At first Kevin could feel a golden-tinged white light beginning to surround them all. It seemed to be brightest around Judge Robul, but was coming out of all the Visitors. He wondered if these people actually gave off light like a neon tube. He thought the glow that seemed to fill the room must really be an illusion for something happening in the mind. But the light sure seemed real. And bright.

Seeing how they were lined up before the dark metal rectangle reminded Kevin of a scene from one of those movies he'd escaped into as a boy: the apes in *2001: A Space Odyssey* gazing up at the rectangular monolith and the sun and moon lining up as the alien device turned on to transform the apes to human. This seemed almost like that: the eight of them, Earthman alternating with Visitor, facing the dark rectangle, that was both a shield for them and a portal to the future, while the light of consciousness and creative intention grew in intensity around them. Kevin could almost hear the kettle drums of the *2001* theme music.

"I love you," 'Bel whispered in his ear. And Kevin felt a surge of rosy golden love strike deep into his soul.

"I love you too, 'Bel," he answered, noticing the mystical light was changing to a resolute steely silver color. He could feel the intention growing sharp and keen.

"Live with me," 'Bel spoke. "Kevin, live with me."

Kevin knew, of course, that 'Bel was giving word to the intention they all held that quenching the matter-field would save both worlds and that they would all survive their plunge through the breach. "Yes, 'Bel, I will live with you," he answered feeling a rush of joy in the double meaning of the words. *We will live. And we will live together.*

The ship's pilot had explained to them all that because they'd be passing through the zone of quantum transposition without the benefit of an already established geometry window, they'd feel the shock wave in their bodies. Kevin tried to stay relaxed, but prepared for the sensations whatever they would be.

Malcolm Arnold wasn't going to get to fly the ship himself, of course, but by previous agreement, he was going to be able to declare his role in saving the day—and saving face for the Presidency—by being the one to give the order to commence the plunge. The pilot had set up the display so Arnold would know just when to give that order.

Kevin was so aware of the steel-white color around him and the bliss in his heart that he hardly had room in his mind for fear. He relaxed back into 'Bel's glowing aura, and counted his breath. *One... Two... Three...*

"Now," declared Malcolm Arnold, usurping the hero's role, of course, but being able to tell the truth when he'd say later he'd led the mission. After all, he was never going to be able to tell political lies again—not after his sojourn in the Visitor world.

For the first time in their travel in the craft, Kevin felt real acceleration. He braced as he was forced back against 'Bel. The geometry-shifting mechanisms had been shut down; they were flying with only the gravity engine now. And, he knew, they were flying virtually straight down toward the Oak Ridge laboratory. The ship would come hurtling in and then level out just at the last minute so that it could go through the opening between worlds and then pull it closed behind it with the generator in tow, and disconnected. *If it all works the way we think...*

Scared to death, but equally blissed out, Kevin watched the monitor. President Arnold had heralded the moment the matter-field was reaching optimal size. Now Kevin saw that blue-white light—the same light he'd seen from the Rim of the World over San Bernardino—blossom out from the distant outline of a building below.

The light suddenly burst around them as the ship accelerated into it at dramatic speed. Already Kevin's mind was full of light from the telepathic-like aura-sharing of the Visitors; now his eyes were blinded by the explosion of light from the monitor.

Then starting at the tip of his nose and moving millimeter by millimeter through his body, like some cosmic CT scanner, he felt the shockwave of the matter-field transposition. He knew what that meant: the value of Planck's constant was being shifted in each atom in each cell of his body. He was being forced from one world into the other.

The shockwave produced a sensation of intense sharp pain. Kevin worried he was being torn apart by the cosmic forces. As the line of pain moved through the space of his eyeballs he thought he couldn't bear this and would be better to just die and have it all over with.

And then just as suddenly as it had started, the pain had passed through him and was gone. He was filled with a surge of pleasure and relief and a great sense of loving and being loved. Indeed, he thought once again his recurrent question, *Have I died and gone to heaven?*

Kevin could feel the warmth of 'Bel's body pressing against his back. "We made it," he heard one of the pilots exclaim. "Yee-hah,"—or something like that—he heard President Arnold shout in triumph and redemption. "Live with me," he heard 'Bel whisper again in his ear, and this time he knew his beloved meant not only the cosmic, metaphysical state of surviving beyond threat, but also the mundane, but ever so romantic, reality of sharing a home and a life together.

The sense of acceleration stopped. The geometry drive must have come back on again. They were no longing falling. The ship was still flying backwards, but now was sailing gracefully and smoothly over green forests. It made a great sweeping circle. In the monitor Kevin could see a rectangular box, slowly spinning in space, being pulled behind them. *The matter-field generator caught in the field of the ship's geometry window—unpowered and harmless.*

"Look," reported the pilot with thanksgiving and relief in his voice, and bright white-shining gold in his face, "there's no damage at all. We closed the opening before the collision ever started."

"Congratulations, Malcolm," Judge Robul said, her eyes sparkling with glints of ironic laughter. "The mission you led saved both our worlds."

$\mathcal{M}$alcolm Arnold insisted on wearing a full cold weather cape over a short kilt. He had partially given in to the Visitors' dress custom because he must have realized he'd look odd and untrustworthy fully clothed.

The Visitors had arranged a ceremony to welcome President Arnold and to further introduce their world. Kevin, Tim, Arnold, and Jeff were assisted in choosing ceremonial garb; for all of them but Arnold this meant only the ornamental strip of fabric and a ceremonial cincture.

Jeff, the Secret Service agent, had seemed quite reluctant at first to follow along with custom. But once he got his clothes off, he seemed to take to the idea quite well. "I wonder if ol' Malcolm might just be rethinking his relationship with Jeff now," Tim joked to Kevin. "Jeff's been keeping quite a body under that black suit."

"Now you keep your hands to yourself," Kevin replied, also in casual jest. "What would you tell Joel?"

"What Joel doesn't know won't hurt him," Tim answered and then seemed to catch himself.

"I thought we'd learned a lesson about that," Kevin observed sagely.

- - -

After the initial formalities of welcome and Arnold's brief speech of acceptance to the assembly of some two hundred or more individuals, with lots of applause for the President's role in stopping the final disaster, the Chief Judge introduced a video presentation. It was a sort of travelogue of Earth on this side.

What amazed the four from the other Earth was that the picture seemed to float in mid-air and, while obviously framed within a specific rectangle, it possessed clear three-dimensionality.

"There'll be a real market in Hollywood for that technology," Arnold commented as the film was starting.

Among the scenes of stately cities, beautiful landscapes and happy, healthy people, mostly in same-sex couples, some with children, frolicking on beaches and ski slopes, hiking mountain trails, or dining in lovely restaurants, there were occasionally shown scenes from churches, as on Earth on the other side a travelogue of Europe might show pictures of the great cathedrals. Kevin noticed there was an absence of statues and crucifixes from the Visitors' version of cathedrals. And a couple of shots, during which obviously religious music was being played, were clearly scenes of men and women in sexual intercourse, apparently in those very churches. Kevin understood that was the nature of their religion. *Seems a little strange, but what a good idea! I wonder if President Arnold understands the religious nature of this video.*

Following the presentation, the Chief Judge addressed the assembly, looking directly at the front row where sat Jeff, President Arnold, Kevin, 'Bel, and Tim. "To us, your ways of relating to one another and of reproducing yourselves appears much more uncertain and difficult. Indeed, to us, your whole lives seem more difficult, so painfully polarized into male and female, light and dark, good and evil. We acknowledge you have developed a much more complex world than ours and a much more complex consciousness. In some ways we seem like children, innocent and naive, compared to you.

"We understand we have much to learn from you. The technological advances that our two cultures have made in the last centuries have challenged the survival of both of us. We also have much to teach you."

Malcolm Arnold stood up. And in what Kevin realized was a dramatically meaningful gesture, he pulled off the cape he'd been wearing. "I have something I'd like to say."

"Nice body for an older man," Tim whispered in Kevin's ear.

"Please," the Judge replied and the assembly began to applaud.

"I am still trembling with awe," Arnold began, "to understand who you people are. And what your world is like. I have to admit I think it's strange that you have same-sex marriage and don't have heterosexual families. You're different from us. But I also have to admit," he laughed, "I've wondered if I've died and gone to heaven.

Then, sounding like the Evangelical deacon he sometimes was, he continued, "Speaking of heaven, I have been reminded of a verse from our Holy Scriptures: 'For when they rise from the dead, they will neither marry nor be given in marriage, but are like angels in heaven.' That was said by Jesus, one of the great teachers of our world.

"Maybe what he meant by not marrying in heaven was being free to love and to give and receive pleasure without incurring the obligations and responsibilities of family life. Sexual pleasure isn't just for reproduction and making families. Pleasure is for the joy of life.

"Jesus said very little about sexuality. He didn't seem to think it was important, yet I see that it is your sexuality—and *our* rigid opinions about ours—that caused you to fear us. That is a shame. For I think you are indeed like those angels Jesus was talking about."

Well, Kevin realized, *Malcolm Arnold did get the religious significance. And he had the same thought as me about having died and gone to heaven!*

"I regret our failure to communicate properly before," the President said. "Of course, I want to see more of your world. This video has stirred my interest in your ways. All our people will want to see your world. And I promise you now, when I return to my world I will stop the work on the matter-field weapons altogether. There is no reason why you should fear us nor that we should cause you harm.

"Indeed, when we get home and explain what we found here, well, maybe *we* won't be needing any weapons at all any more ourselves either."

Kevin clutched 'Bel's hand tighter. He was so full of emotion. Tears of joy were coursing down his cheeks. His heart was pounding, his chest almost exploding. *God, I wish I had the gift of color*, he thought, *wouldn't it be wonderful to show how great I feel.*

'Bel squeezed his hand tighter and then put his arm around Kevin's shoulder. "Do you think we saved the world?" he whispered.

Epilogue

Kevin Anderson was sitting at his desk in his new *private* office. A week ago—with great fanfare, corporate meetings, and press releases—Jules Domergue announced that Kevin had been put in charge of the renewed Visitor embassy project. With George Sanders' enthusiastic approval, Kevin had taken over leadership of the team and been given his own office. George had taken to calling him "Sir," though he almost always winked slyly when he did so—and occasionally it was "Sweetie, sir." All of a sudden Kevin was finding George's blatant campiness amusing and affectionate.

Kevin, of course, was still an intern, in spite of his sudden ascent to success. Will Salado remained his supervisor. And this morning he was back calculating stress points and weight load values. But now he was doing it in his own office.

Coming to a logical stopping point, Kevin sat back in his chair and surveyed the room. It wasn't that it was all that big or luxurious, and what it represented had really little to do with skill or success as an architect. What the office meant to Kevin was that it was okay to be himself, that the message the Visitors brought to this Earth was really not so new: it had always been a part of human wisdom. It just hadn't been applied as simply or as totally as it could have been.

That message about being oneself and speaking the truth—even when it seemed embarrassing or socially unacceptable—had not been missed by Kevin's parents. One of Kevin's now most prized possessions was a quickfax from his Mom and Dad, sent the evening the TV interview was broadcast, *even before we went through the window with President Arnold and "saved the world,"* Kevin always reminded himself.

The fax read: "TV interview surprised us. Didn't know you had achieved prominence so quickly. We're proud of you, son, and like the looks of your Visitor friend. He's welcome in this family. Never doubt our love and support." The fax message was now framed and hung with other memorabilia on one wall of the office.

Alongside the fax hung three plaques. In the wisdom of the ages, now trite with repetition, but still powerfully true, they read respectively: "Know Thyself," "The Truth shall make you free," and, of course, "To thine own self be true, and it shall follow as the night the day, thou canst not then be false to any man."

Kevin had learned in college Shakespeare that Polonius was a pompous old fart and the Bard had meant those lines to be more funny than serious. The fact the non-scholarly world ignored the context and took them seriously suggested how really true they were.

His mother had sent the Socrates and Shakespeare. *She must have had a shopping attack in one of those cutesy boutiques.* The middle quotation from Jesus, embroidered on age-yellowed silk, had come from Sister Jennifer. She said she believed Margaret Mary Alacoque had stitched it herself years ago. Also framed on the wall were other faxes and telegrams, a congratulatory note from the President of Harvard, and a hand-written letter from Malcolm Arnold.

On the credenza against that wall with the framed sentiments, now sat a crystal vase containing a dozen long-stemmed lavender roses that were delivered this morning. The card, which Kevin now picked up from the desk and reread, said "Thanks, Kevin. You woke us up to some things. Sorry I fudged my agreement with you a little. It worked out okay. I made noon anchor today. Thanks to you and your great story. And John and I got hitched last week. Love, John and Joan Marshall. P.S., Say hi to my brother and tell him the good news. Okay?"

Kevin sat staring at the roses and at the wall of affection and congratulation in a kind of bedazzlement. *Is this all really real?* His reverie was interrupted by the ringtone of his dime.

"Hi, Kev," Tim Lewiston's voice was immediately recognizable, "Joel asked me to find out if you and 'Bel are going to be around for dinner."

"Well, we'll plan on it then. I haven't heard from 'Bel today. I know it's a workday for him. I stayed over on his side last night. I was in a rush to get to the office this morning and forgot to ask what we're doing."

"I know how it is," Tim answered so domestically.

"There ought to be some way to get a phone line or cell transmitter through the geometry window."

"You must have the longest commute of any couple, I know," Tim joked.

"Well, once the embassy's complete, it'll be easier."

"Did you see the morning paper?" Tim changed the subject.

"No. Something interesting?"

"Joel and I were thinking maybe we could start a franchise. But we'd need your help."

"Huh?" Kevin answered bewildered. "What are you talking about?"

"There's a Visitors fan club starting up. Joel said to tell you one of the organizers is Hazel Bunn. You know her?"

Kevin laughed. "Didn't Joel tell you? She's the lady that really saved the day."

"Oh," Tim answered, "Well, these women are volunteering to have babies with Visitor men in order to introduce the pigmentation genes to the human race. The article says they're pledging to keep exact records of their fertility times so they'll know exactly when they can conceive."

"I wonder what the Judges will think of that?"

"Ask 'Bel. Maybe we can start up an introduction service. Joel and I want to start a business together. You know, like a regular little couple. Maybe we can help assuage people's fears, like the Judge said."

"We can talk about it at dinner. Look, if we're late, it's cause I had to go over and get 'Bel and that means all the way out to the Golden Gate and back. That okay?"

"Don't be too late. We're gonna all listen to the radio tonight. There's a program at 8:00 we all want to hear."

Kevin knew exactly what he was talking about. Yes, he wanted to hear that too. Indeed, just yesterday with that broadcast in mind he'd bought a new state-of-the-art satcom receiver for his apartment. "Right. Bye, Tim."

Clicking off the dime he looked out the window. *It's a whole new world. Everything's going to be different. Because I told the truth.* He thought about 'Bel for a moment and his heart filled with pride and with love.

Then he remembered he had work to do and started back to his calculations. *I wonder how long it will be before we adopt the three day work week. Or before the Visitors adopt our six day week.*

*B*illy McMasterson was beaming as he started the evening broadcast from his booth overlooking the San Francisco Bay. He laughed happily to himself that he used to think he was changing not just the skyline, but San Francisco itself. Now it seemed San Francisco had changed him.

"Good evening, Listeners," he began. He ran through his regular spiel about his Church and his ministry for Jesus. Then he added, "I've got some fessin' up to do… to Jesus and to all of you out there who've been listening to these broadcasts.

"I totally misunderstood the sign God sent to me in the tremors of the Big Quake last year. It was not punishment that God was sending, but renewal. I have been shaken to my foundations. Believe me.

"Let me tell you what happened to me when I went through to the Visitor world." He noticed the call-in lines started to light up. But he wasn't going to take calls till he'd told his story. He hoped what he had to say would change the minds of all those callers, at least the ones who were phoning in to say they disapproved of his going through the geometry window into the queer world on the other side.

" I was quite surprised to see that the terrain looked so much like I was still in San Francisco.

"The Visitors were very friendly. No one seemed to object that I was there. I asked somebody where a church was. He pointed up the hillside from where we were standing, and indeed right there above us was a beautiful Gothic looking spire. The man offered to guide me.

"The Visitor—though I guess now *I* was the visitor and he was the native—told me I was just in time for the sunrise service and he walked me up to the entrance of the building. As he held the door open for me, I saw that his face was glowing golden in the morning sunlight. He smiled at me. For a moment, I thought he looked like, like a sunbeam…

McMasterson's voice broke for a moment. Then he continued.

"The room was filled with people. They were singing. I couldn't make out the words. The melody sounded like a familiar hymn, but I didn't recognize it. I stood at the back of the room watching.

"The man who'd acted as my guide urged me to go further up toward the front. But, you know, I'd heard that interview on CNN with Kevin Anderson, the young man who'd first gone through to that world. I had some idea of what the Visitors' religion was about, and I was apprehensive. I wasn't sure I wanted any of this.

"After the song ended, a very old woman came out to a podium in front and read from what I understood was their Scriptures. Her name was Mara Namara, Teacher of the Wisdom, and she read what she called the Story of the Origins of People.

"I have the text that she read. I will read it to you, Listeners, in just a minute. I think you'll be surprised.

"After she finished, a young man and a young woman came out and walked up to a raised platform where an altar would have been. They introduced themselves by name and thanked the congregation for coming to celebrate with them.

"I was naturally still apprehensive about what was happening, but it all seemed so innocent. Though, of course, you all know by now that in their world the Visitors do not wear much clothing. And these two young people were both completely naked. So this didn't exactly seem like a religious service. But when the congregation started singing again, I held my suspicions at bay. There was clearly nothing salacious or debauched here. And the music was so deeply religious.

"A gauzy curtain was lowered from the ceiling. It surrounded the platform and hid the couple, though through the fabric I could see them embrace and kiss. That's when something remarkable happened.

"A soft light began to glow through the gauze curtain. It seemed to be coming right out of the man and woman. And then the light began to spread through the whole room. I could see that all the people were beginning to glow and change color around me. Now I understand what that was, but I had never seen this up till then and was quite surprised.

"I tell you, I wasn't afraid at all. I could feel my own skin warming all over as the soft light seemed to engulf me as well. And then the singing became more and more beautiful and the light to grow golden.

"Behind that gauzy curtain, I knew, the man and woman were making love—and conceiving a child. I could hear their groaning in bodily pleasure. I could feel their pleasure and joy in my own body. I could hear and feel the groaning all around me. And I was sure all those other people in the room, many embracing one another, glowing in so many colors of gold and pink, were entering into the couple's joy even more intensely than I. And I understood that all of them loved one another and that they were naturally homosexual. And—it surprises me, of course, to say this—but I understood how natural, even admirable were those feelings in them.

"I saw, maybe for the first time in my life, that sexual joy and human love and affection are direct experiences of God, participation with the Divine Creator in bringing the cosmos into being.

"I am sure, Listeners, that you understand this has been hard for me to accept. But it was just so obviously true, true as nothing has ever seemed true to me before.

"Try to see with me, Listeners, how the love two men or two women feel for one another manifests the love God bears for Himself. God loves Himself, not as the union of opposites, as a complement—as in the holy procreative love of natural human couples, male and female, to conceive children—but as recognition of self, as His own reflection to express His pleasure with flesh as the mode of the universe's knowing itself.

"It shook me to the depths of my being to see these things, but I was truly transformed, and I came to understand that my mission on Earth now must be to change how religion has confused our understanding of human sexual nature and human mystical nature.

"Like so many of you, I think, I have always experienced sexual passion as shameful. In that holy moment, caught up in the ethereal light of that Visitor church, I saw how wrong—or at least how preliminary—that view is to real morality and real mystical perception of creation.

"I felt those feelings in my own flesh; I was aroused and excited and yet feeling deeply the presence of God. I saw that my feelings of bodily pleasure were my gift to God for showing me such a truth… and God's gift to me as reward for seeing it. It was God rejoicing in those passions in me.

"There was nothing exactly Christian, you understand, about this service. But I knew somehow that I was feeling the presence of their Jesus or whatever He is named in that world. It's hard to explain this to you, Listeners, but I tell you the singing and mystical lights in all shades of gold and pink and lavender felt clearly to me like I was in heaven, and meeting Jesus and his angels and saints for the first real time in my life."

"A week ago I would not have touched this. I would have called this an abomination and I would have called for all of you to rebuke the sinners and blasphemers who would proclaim a story like this. But, Listeners, I tell you, after my experience in that church, I cannot speak against them.

"I mean it literally when I say I have seen the Light.

- - -

"Let me read to you from the Book of Life, the Visitors' Bible:

"In the beginning God said, 'Let there be light.' And there was morning and evening the first day.

"Then God said, 'Let there be color so that the world might be filled with beauty.' And there were flowers and rainbows the second day.

"Then God said, 'Let living things swarm over the Earth and enjoy the waters of the oceans and the trees of the land.' And there were fishes and birds and animals the third day.

"On the evening of the third day, God walked upon the Earth and saw that everything She had made was beautiful and good. And She felt a longing to share Her enjoyment of Her creation. So at sunset of the third day of the week, God called to two young monkeys scampering in the trees. And immediately they came running to her feet..."

With a catch in his voice, McMasterson interrupted his reading to make a joke. "I don't think the Baptists are going to like what's coming," he said. "Be brave. We're all going to have to change how we've been thinking. Let us thank God."

He went back to the text. "God played with the monkeys, swinging them in the air and tossing them over her shoulder. 'Let us play for the rest of the week,' She said, 'to celebrate your new home.' And She continued asking of them, 'What do you think of your home?' But the monkeys could say nothing because they had not yet learned control of their tongues.

"And, finally, as the sun was setting, God put Her hand on the heads of the two monkeys and cast them into sleep. 'Dream,' She said, 'that you can be like Me, so that we can play together and so you can know My sorrows and My joys.' And then God lay down and slept in a bed of heather—for it was still spring and the heather was soft and comfortable where She lay Her head. And She clutched the sleeping monkeys to Her breast as She slept.

"At sunrise God awoke. She sang the Hymn to the Sun that all men and women now sing each morning in Her honor. And then she looked down and saw that in their dreams the monkeys had shed their fur and lost their tails and their sharp teeth had fallen out. And God was filled with compassion for their nakedness and defenselessness. And then She said, 'You will be People that you may talk to Me and tell Me of your sorrows and share with Me your joys.'

"And on the morning of the fourth day, Man and Woman awoke from their dreams. And God had disappeared. But the Man and Woman remembered that God had said to celebrate the rest of the week and to work only on the first three days. And they understood that celebration was more important than work.

"God created Man and Woman in the Garden and gave them everything they needed to live in peace. On the morning of the eighth day, when they knew the time of celebration was over, they searched through their dreams to recall what God might want them to do. The Man and Woman both remembered that God had spoken to them in sleep and instructed them in caring for the Garden and in gathering grain and vegetables and fruit to eat.

"In the dream She told them not to eat of the fruit of the Tree of the Knowledge of Truth and Falsehood. And for three days the Man and Woman joyfully tilled the soil and planted the seeds and learned to make flour and to bake bread with the fire that God sent from the sky at night when it rained.

"On the eleventh day of creation, when the Man and Woman rested to celebrate God's goodness to them, a jealous and competitive spirit, envious because God had chosen them for such blessing, came to them in the form of a beautiful plumed bird and tempted them, promising them mastery over the world if they ate the forbidden fruit, telling them they would not have to waste time celebrating when there was work they could be doing. But the Man and Woman loved God and knew that everything She had made was good. They decided this commandment too was good. And so they did not eat.

"God came the next day and banished the plumed bird from the Garden and congratulated the Man and the Woman. 'As a gift for your trust and obedience,' She declared, 'I will give you the fruit of the tree to eat from My own hand.'

"To the Woman She said, 'Because you have been trusting and obedient, to you I give the honor of bearing children in joy that you may share your trust in My goodness with progeny who will share My world with all the animals of the Garden.' And the woman felt her body change and Pleasure poured through her. 'And that you may always find joy in conceiving and giving birth I have given you the gift of Pleasure and Consciousness. Behold, like Me, you will always perceive the gestation of your children.'

"And after the Man had eaten of the fruit from God's hand, he looked on himself and saw that his body was changed also. And God said, 'Behold, the knowledge of truth and falsehood. No more can you deceive or be deceived, for the truth of your mind reveals itself in the color and loveliness of your natural body. And this beauty shall be to your children and your children's children that you may always reside in the Garden of Honesty.'

"Then God said, 'You and your children shall people the world I give you by loving one another, mothers with fathers, for the purpose of reproducing yourselves.

"'And you shall bless your lives by loving one another, sons with sons and daughters with daughters, for the purpose of sharing My joy in Myself. Never will you see the duality of good against evil. You shall not be pitted man against woman and woman against man. You shall see beyond the polarities. Your world and your loves shall all be reflections of My love for Myself and for you, My creation. For, behold, everything I have made is wonderful.'

"And so it was that People came to live side by side and to love one another in order to celebrate life and to thank God for the beauty of the Garden."

Again, with a catch in his voice, McMasterson said, "I think we all owe an apology…"

𝒥ollowing dinner at the apartment on Fair Oaks, Kevin , 'Bel, Tim, and Joel were enjoying the pear cobbler Joel had prepared to top off the fabulous meal he'd cooked. As the dessert was being served, Billy McMasterson's streaming audio broadcast came on over the new Phantazia satcom receiver Kevin had bought with his raise in salary.

As the program started, the three San Franciscans began making jokes about the preacher's smiling face displayed on the Phantazia's mini hi-def activity screen, his ministerial tone of voice, his choice of words, and whatever else one of them could find to make campy fun of. (With 'Bel looking bemused and confused, and a little bluish.)

But then they'd fallen silent as it became clear where McMasterson's speech was leading. They all listened carefully, especially to his reading from the Book of Life. (By now, 'Bel was smiling and glowing bright happy yellow!)

Kevin's head was spinning. Everything that had happened in the past few weeks all began to make sense.

What McMasterson read from their Book of Genesis said the pattern of homosexuality in the Visitors' society was a reward for their Adam and Eve's not eating the forbidden fruit.

Remembering the childhood catechism he'd been taught by sisters like Margaret Mary Alacoque, the last of the secrets of the Visitors finally dawned on Kevin. Their nudity made sense—their ability to move instantly from place to place, the absence in their world of the conflict between male and female, the non-existence of poisons, even things as banal as the absence of bad breath and hangovers.

Kevin realized that in the words of those old religious myths, *Their world is Earth as it would have been without original sin. The Visitors are Humankind still in innocence, before the Fall. Their world is the Garden of Eden.*

Kevin's emotions surged again and he burst out laughing just as the four of them began applauding Billy McMasterson's speech. Good for the Visitors. Thank God for the Visitors!

Then it occurred to him that they aren't Visitors anymore. Now they are Neighbors. And there aren't any more secrets.

Afterword
Mark D. Jordan

Picking up this new edition of *Secret Matter*, I recall how many thanks we owe to science fiction. For keeping our imaginations queer, I mean.

As a boy, I found in sci-fi novels (SF, s-f, fantasy…) a whole gallery of queer lives. I wouldn't have known to call them that, at least not at first, but I studied the portrayals as intently as if they held my secret. They did. During bleached Texas summers, sprawled on a thin rug in the coolest room of my grandmother's house, I read my way onto exotic worlds where people were allowed to be… unusual. Their lives had more colors and shapes than got mentioned around her formica dinette. Under wispy red suns or moons of ice, beside murmuring ruins of alien cities, men and women got to become what they could never have been earthside. Or in south Dallas. They unriddled strange religions. They endured demonic visions that transfigured them into gods. And often they ended by preferring life out there, beyond terrestrial certainties.

Then came the allure of sci-fi authors. I still remember the strange thrill I felt, over the thrum of the window unit, when I read that "André Norton" was the pen name of a woman. I knew from French class that "André" was "Andrew." How could a woman be an Andrew? And why had some of her novels been published originally under the cross-sex name "Andrew North"? Somewhat later, I was stopped at the local branch library when I tried to check out Brian Aldiss's *Starship*. The librarian looked at me sourly and explained that the book, now firmly in her hands, "talks about things that aren't for boys." My amused mother returned the next day to sign a form giving me permission to check out whatever I fancied. But the embarrassing episode taught me that some sci-fi writers, like dirty words and pictures of naked bodies, were restricted to adults. So I sought them out. My tastes veered from Isaac Azimov to gaudy, exotic, decadent writers. I came to idolize Alfred Bester's *The Demolished Man*. I raced to the drugstore for copies of *Analog*—despite my father's wondering why I was interested in computation. In the middle of uniform blocks of "ranch-style" houses, those private pages incited me to live otherwise.

Somewhere along the way, I got academic ambition and stopped turning those pages. Almost. During my senior year of college, I committed myself to *Gravity's Rainbow* by Thomas Pynchon. No one could accuse me of reading mere science fiction when I carted around that labyrinth of a text. A year later, in my first semester of graduate school, someone joked that if I could read Pynchon, I could probably also read a "massive" new novel, Samuel Delany's *Dhalgren*. I bought it that Saturday and added it to the stack beside my bed. A few weeks later, I sat up in bed when I reached the scene, not too many pages into the mass, when the Kid gets a blow job from Tak. Men with men: here was my desire right at a novel's surface, written onto its skin. Men with men were re-making themselves in the ruins of a city for the sake of a fierce beauty. I didn't understand that the fantastic landscape was an image of gay life in Manhattan. It was the seventies: rockets of desire lit up the moonless night of back rooms, warehouses, baths. *Dhalgren* was Delany's Village—and Dhalgren was my private dream of queerness. I was grateful for it.

I discovered Toby Johnson some years later and without knowing that he wrote science fiction. In a collection of first-person accounts by queer Catholics, Toby spoke incisively about that church's curious sexual tension, the endless pull of official homophobia against barely hidden homoeroticism. He talked too of his journey from authoritarian religion to a more life-giving practice of spirit. Since I was trying to write about queer Catholicism, and also struggling to imagine a gay Christianity for myself, Toby appeared as a helpful guide. I consulted the Library of Congress for a list of his books. There, between titles on the religious aspects of sex and the mythologies of Catholicism, I found a novel, *Secret Matter*. The only copies I could locate for purchase were from used and rare book dealers. I ordered one in. This time I didn't put it in the stack beside my bed. I started to read at once.

Secret Matter is: a double or triple love story; a radical social critique; a re-invention of religion. The love stories are about Ken and 'Bel (or, in comic register, Joel and Tim), but also about the city, San Francisco. Kevin meets 'Bel because he is wandering the city, half-searching for a consoling sunset and a rainbow community. The colors of the sunset over the Pacific are the colors of 'Bel's skin in joy and desire. (Re-reading Toby this time, I was reminded of the ravishing religion of light in another homoerotic fantasy, Jim Grimsley's *Kirith Kirin*.) On Kevin's first night west, Will had taken him up to Twin Peaks to show him what no earthquake could destroy—and what he would help rebuild: a city of improbable lights bordered by the black shore. In the parallel world, Kevin sees San Francisco as Eden—because it *is* Eden (more literally even than in Starhawk's *Fifth Sacred Thing*). To rebuild the damaged city is to protect a space for alternate human relations, which is the same as restoring the wholeness of creation.

The inhabitants of 'Bel's world cannot lie because they paint their emotions in vivid truth on their skins. Their bodies function as if before "the Fall," without the distortion and disruption of the turn away from God towards domination. Reproduction without domination is fully sacred. Homoerotic sex apart from both reproduction and domination can give pleasure while it grounds generous, lasting relationships. The homoerotic relations or recreations are expected to admit multiple partners and to avoid jealousy, as (fallen) Kevin concludes when he tries to understand the behavior of his (unfallen) boyfriend. "He was again aware of how strange it was to be with somebody who lived in openness and innocence." How strange—and how challenging both to our expectations of desire and to our bureaucracies for regulating it.

Secret Matter stands in a line of speculative novels that try to picture healthy queer lives beyond heterosexist institutions. Like lesbian-feminist dreams of utopia, or the myths told around Radical Faerie campfires, this novel proposes queer consciousness as an alternative to familiar prejudices and conventions. They tell us, "Sex can only be between one man and one woman bound in a monogamous marriage ordered to child-rearing and social stability." No. "Jealousy is an important safeguard on sexual purity." Not really. "Love needs lies." Imagine it otherwise.

In Toby's novel, the function of literary imagination is presented as a play within the play: people give meaning to their encounter with the visitors by appealing to sci-fi stories like *Childhood's End* by Arthur C. Clarke. The stories—Toby's too—help them to resist the bondage of familiar lies. In other places and times, the imagination of radically better and truer possibilities for human living has been a sacred task. Priests construe patterns for other lives in sacred texts. Prophets call them down. Oracles dream them in trance. Bards, seized by another sort of divine madness, sing them. I discovered *Secret Matter* while I was looking for queer religion, and I was not disappointed. It not only imagines queer lives, it proposes that they be religious through a combination of text, prophecy, trance, and song.

The book's conclusion describes a liturgy that rewrites the opening of the Jewish and Christian scriptures. In our world, in the radio programs that so alarmed the Visitors, Genesis is used to block the teaching of evolution or to underwrite discriminatory marriage laws. Toby knows that Genesis 1-2 is a grander form of religious truth. It is a cosmogony, a narrative of world-making that explains but also challenges the order we give to our lives. He knows as well that the passage is the first scripture read out at the center of old Christian liturgies, in the Easter Vigil that counts the dark hours before Jesus' resurrection, the transit from death to life. In the Visitors' world, the liturgy quotes a fuller (and truer) version of Genesis. Its creation myth vibrates with rainbow colors from the second day, and its explanation of human origins emphasizes diversity in continuity. Most importantly, in that Eden, woman and man reject temptation and the devil's deceitful praise of endless labor for labor's sake.

For the Visitors, religion is serious because it is truthful. No need for huffing and puffing and threatening to blow houses down—or to punish in a thousand more malicious ways. The Visitors do not encourage warlike fundamentalisms or imperialistic theocracies. Their religion is (as ours can sometimes be) the attentive celebration of reality. We hear the other version of Genesis in a liturgy that converts the dangerous evangelist Billy McMasterson. He is led reluctantly into a minimalist cathedral full of worshippers. After the reading from scripture, the congregation shares quite literally in the soft-gold light surrounding a human conception. It is light from the beginning of time. It is the signature of creation. There is no need to threaten anyone for dissenting, because there is no power besides a gentle divine reality.

Billy McMasterson's conversion may strike us as "utopian" in the negative sense. In our world, it is hard to imagine what miracle of divine intervention would be required to turn some "evangelists" away from their persecuting ideologies. But our trouble with McMasterson's conversion is no more than our cynicism about love without concealment or a God of celebration rather than of wrath. How to contend with our hopelessness? A sci-fi novel is not a guaranteed program for social reform or theological reformation, but it can be a boost to imagination. With more imagination, we might begin to see things otherwise.

A novel may also perform a little demonstration of change—if only in a few of its readers. I know that I will never look at the blush of desire across a lover's body in quite the same way. Or hear Genesis at Easter without wondering about a garden in which the temptation to identify God with abusive power falls away.

Mark Jordan teaches religion at Emory University. He writes about sexuality and religious rhetoric. He is author of *The Silence of Sodom: Homosexuality in Modern Catholicism*, *Telling Truths in Church: Scandal, Flesh and Christian Speech*, and numerous other titles. A discussion of science fiction as modern day myth appears in his book *Blessing Same-Sex Unions: The Perils of Queer Romance and the Confusions of Christian Marriage*.

Toby Johnson, PhD is past editor of White Crane Journal and author of eight books: three non-fiction books that apply the wisdom of Joseph Campbell, his teacher and the "wise old man" of his personal journey, to modern-day social and religious problems, three gay genre novels that dramatize spiritual issues at the heart of gay identity, and two books on gay men's spiritualities and the mystical experience of homosexuality.

Former Catholic monk turned comparative religion scholar, San Francisco hippie, gay psychotherapist, community organizer, writer, gay bookstore operator, B&B host, Johnson was one of the regular presenters at the Texas-based Shaman's Circles in the 1990s, and one of the organizers of the 2004 First Gay Spirituality Summit.

Since 1984, he and Kip Dollar have been partners in life and in business and champions of long-term gay relationships. They were the first male couple registered as Domestic Partners in the state of Texas.

There's more info about them both at **tobyjohnson.com**

Printed in the United States
104310LV00001B/99/A